THE GREATEST
BENGALI STORIES
EVER TOLD

Also translated by Arunava Sinha

Khauna-Mihir's Mound by Bani Basu
Seven Heavens by Samim Ahmed
A Mirrored Life by Rabisankar Bal
The Fifth Man by Bani Basu
The Love Letter & Other Stories by Buddhadeva Bose
Tagore for the 21st Century Reader
You are Neera by Sunil Gangopadhyay
The Magic Moonlight Flower and Other Enchanting Stories by Satyajit Ray
Black Rose by Buddhadeva Bose
Dozakhnama by Rabisankar Bal
Wonderworld and Other Stories by Sunil Gangopadhyay
The Rhythm of Riddles: Three Byomkesh Bakshi Mysteries by Saradindu
Bandyopadhyay
17 (short stories) by Anita Agnihotri
Fever (Mahakaler Rather Ghora) by Samaresh Basu
Harbart by Nabarun Bhattacharya
When the Time is Right (Tithidore) by Buddhadeva Bose
Three Women: Nashtaneer, Dui Bon, Malancha by Rabindranath Tagore
The Chieftain's Daughter (Durgeshnandini) by Bankimchandra
Chattopadhyay
What Really Happened & Other Stories by Banaphool
Striker, Stopper by Moti Nandy
The Middleman (Jana Aranya) by Sankar
My Kind of Girl by Buddhadeva Bose
Chowringhee by Sankar
The Merry Tales of Harshabardhan and Gobardhan by Shibram Chakraborty
Panty by Sangeeta Bandyopadhyay
The Master and I by Soumitra Chatterjee
Kalabati the Showstopper by Moti Nandy
Sabotage & Other Stories by Anita Agnihotri
Abandon (Ruho) by Sangeeta Bandyopadhyay
By the Tungabhadra by Saradindu Bandyopadhyay
There Was No One at the Bus-Stop by Sirshendu Mukhopadhyay
Illicit by Dibyendu Palit
The Director's Mind by Ujjal Chakraborty

The
GREATEST
BENGALI
STORIES
EVER TOLD

Selected and translated by

ARUNAVA SINHA

ALEPH

ALEPH BOOK COMPANY
An independent publishing firm
promoted by *Rupa Publications India*

First published in India in 2016
by Aleph Book Company
7/16 Ansari Road, Daryaganj
New Delhi 110 002

ISBN: 978-93-82277-74-3

3 5 7 9 10 8 6 4

Printed and bound in India by Replika Press Pvt. Ltd.

For
Sanghamitra and Srijon
(and Tingmo)

CONTENTS

My Love Affair with Bengali Stories ARUNAVA SINHA   ix

1. The Kabuliwallah RABINDRANATH TAGORE   1

2. The Offering PRAMATHA CHAUDHURI   10

3. Mahesh SARAT CHANDRA CHATTOPADHYAY   23

4. Einstein and Indubala BIBHUTIBHUSHAN BANDYOPADHYAY   35

5. The Music Room TARASHANKAR BANDYOPADHYAY   51

6. The Homecoming BANAPHOOL   74

7. The Discovery of Telenapota PREMENDRA MITRA   76

8. And How Are You? BUDDHADEVA BOSE   87

9 Thunder and Lightning ASHAPURNA DEBI   98

10. Ras NARENDRANATH MITRA   111

11. Two Magicians SATYAJIT RAY   131

12. India RAMAPADA CHOWDHURY   143

13. Raja RITWIK GHATAK   154

14. Urvashi and Johnny MAHASWETA DEVI   165

15. News of a Murder MOTI NANDY   189

16. Ten Days of the Strike SANDIPAN CHATTOPADHYAY   195

17. Swapan is Dead, Long Live Swapan UDAYAN GHOSH   209

18. Post-mortem SUNIL GANGOPADHYAY   224

19. The Marble Table SANJIB CHATTOPADHYAY   238

20. Flapperoos NABARUN BHATTACHARYA   254

21. Air and Water AMAR MITRA   265

Notes on the Authors   281

Acknowledgements   287

MY LOVE AFFAIR WITH BENGALI STORIES

ARUNAVA SINHA

One winter evening in Calcutta, when I was ten, we ran out of food in our third floor flat. It was a freak concatenation of circumstances, not poverty, that led to our predicament, but the fact remained that we had nothing to eat and no money to buy food. And so, to stave off my hunger pangs by distracting me, my mother decided to perform a heroic task. She read me a short story, one of her favourites. My mother loved reading, but not aloud. She did not care for the drama that it involved. A short story, to her, was almost like a guilty secret, something she hugged to herself. She would consume these delicacies at a single sitting, unlike novels that stretched out interminably. Naturally, these were Bengali short stories. It was the 1970s, Bengali literature was in its heyday—as it had been for some forty years—and who needed fiction in another tongue?

She began reading out loud a story of an ox and its miserable owner. As she read, her voice broke, though to my young ears the pathos seemed entirely unnecessary, for I was much more interested in the fate of the animal than of its human owner. But as she continued with the tale something extraordinary began to take place—I wasn't so much listening to the words as I was seeing and hearing all that was going on. I was right there in the very scene that was being described, not as an invisible observer, but as someone who was part of the story.

To this day, I cannot make a story my own unless it places me right in the middle of the action. And no novel can do this, for there is too much reflection, thought, shift of perspective, and other 'distractions'. But a short story, ah, now that's one breathless ride. And so it was that night, when I even forgot to be hungry. But when the fate of the beast was known, I felt the urge to repay my mother for her act of sacrifice. So I plundered the cache of coins I had saved up. All of them were foreign, except for two commemorative Indian coins, one for a rupee and the other for ten rupees. Those denominations were only available as paper currency at the time, which made the coins collectors' items. But no matter, it was money well spent. I wanted my mother to get her favourite Chinese meal from the restaurant next door—chicken asparagus soup and prawn chowmein.

From that night onwards, the Bengali short story has been my companion in grief and in joy. Take, for example, that glorious English summer day when I sat by a stream running through leaf and fern, almost certainly about to make a sudden sally. On that day, on a university campus in Norwich, in weather as magnificent as a human being can expect, I was in great humour and it was in that mood that I read one of the stories that feature in this collection: a story about a man who was quaking in fear at the prospect of an encounter with his son-in-law.

Or, to mention another time that a Bengali short story loomed large in my life, one evening, I was crouched beneath a desk to shut myself off from the world, loaded down with a despair whose origin I simply could not trace. In my hand was a copy of a tattered 'little magazine' from Calcutta in which there was a story about a mother who refused to acknowledge that her Naxal son had died. My own sorrow was forgotten as I plunged into hers. Only at the end of the story did I recollect an episode from my teenage years when I had gone to inspect a row of bodies gunned down by the police to check whether a relative was among them. (He wasn't.) So it is that I have my personal story to go with every story in this collection.

～

I am no scholar of Bengali literature, but I have had a passionate relationship with it for some forty years now. That passion has given me the courage, after all these years, to put together a selection of Bengali stories that are, in my opinion, among the greatest ever published. I must make clear though that this is not a selection based on literary eras, canons, trends, or any other form of critical sieving. Nor is it meant to be a representative cross section of the Bengali short story. These are, simply, stories I have loved and that have made a deep impression on me. Somewhat fortuitously—I wish I could claim that it is by design, but, frankly, it's not—the stories here collectively show the rich variety to be found in Bengali literature—whether in terms of form, voice, setting or subject. In all of them, though, I find one particular quality that haunts the characters, and me. It is the sense of something missing, and the search for it. In every story I have come to cherish, there is inevitably a seeking of what is not, what probably cannot be. But then again, isn't this what differentiates the meaninglessness of daily events from the world that comes from the imagination of an artist?

For all the stories in my mother tongue I've read ever since that day in my childhood when I was disabused of the notion that Buddhadeva Bose and the Buddha were the same person, I had only a fleeting notion of how the form came to be. It was not even emotionally wrenching when my uncle, something of an unsung poet, informed me that Rabindranath Tagore was not in fact the inventor of the short story.

He did, however, assure me that the Bengali short story did not evolve slowly from a primordial swamp, but sprang up, more or less fully formed, around the same time as its counterparts in other languages around the globe. The first short stories in the language—which were probably the first in India as well—were not gritty slice of life accounts, nor did they reflect the reality of Bengal or the world in any meaningful way.

It was, in fact, only with the arrival of Rabindranath Tagore—he wrote almost till his death in 1941—that the Bengali short story became a representation of real life. Redolent with the lyricism of his poetry, the Versatile One looked as much at the inner lives and psychology of his characters as at their circumstances, relationships, and positions within the complex matrix of class, caste, religion and gender.

With Tagore's shadow always looming large over his contemporaries, it needed Sarat Chandra Chattopadhyay's rare combination of sharp societal observation and high emotional quotient to give the short story a new form. He brought his readers much closer to the people and situations he wrote about than Tagore did, even as he attacked orthodoxy and hypocrisy.

Two strands joined the Bengali short story after this. From the Bandhyopadhyays—Bibhutibhushan and Tarashankar—came studies of ordinary people, from both villages and cities, though each of them wrote in his own distinctive style. And other Bengali writers, living and writing as they did in an environment of relatively enlightened education and ideas, responded not just to their home but also to the world. The anxieties of the World Wars, the freedom movement, and oppression of the downtrodden turned Bengali short stories into bundles of discontent, disillusion, anger and irony.

Gradually, short story writers turned their lens inward. They focused a merciless gaze on the flaws, inconsistencies and desires of individuals. As urban lives shrank into smaller physical, mental and emotional spaces, the short story became a powerful means of capturing the innate opposition between a degradation of circumstances and the potential for human greatness. From Satyajit Ray to Nabarun Bhattacharya, from Sunil Gangopadhyay to Sandipan Chattopadhyay, they narrowed the width of the canvas and dived deeper into the darkness of the mind and heart. But even as this was taking place, other writers continued to create on a larger canvas, constructing narratives laced with heightened political, social and gender consciousness and ideology. They adopted techniques like unreliable perspectives, authorial intervention, breathless monologues, narrators-as-characters, and other evolving forms of storytelling. In the hands of powerful writers and craftspersons like Buddhadeva Bose, Premendra Mitra, Ramapada Chowdhury, Mahasweta Devi, Ritwik Ghatak (the film director), and, always, Ashapurna Debi, the Bengali short story became something of a panoramic marvel, spanning worlds without number.

I would like to wrap up this introduction by repeating an earlier assertion—this is not a potted history of the Bengali short story. It is a selection that has been made from my close and devoted reading of the Bengali story throughout my life. You will find here authors you know and those you haven't heard about. Many of the writers you'd have expected to find here are included. It is because their reputations have not been lightly earned. I cannot claim I would have discovered these stories had they not been written by famous, even canonical, authors. But still, these stories spoke to me on the basis of what they are, not because of the aura of their writers. And, yes, all of these stories are from the Indian part of the Bengali-speaking world.

You will not find here some names whom you might have been expecting to feature because they are acknowledged as great short story writers—which they are. It is just that I have no romance to recall with their stories, though I have read, admired and marvelled at them. But somehow I haven't found myself in them—I have been compelled to read them with my mind and not with a combination of head and heart, that elusive thing that we Bengalis refer to as 'mon'.

And so, dear reader, welcome to an anthology of my personal love affairs. Like the one, for instance, from the day of my university convocation, when I was meant to be collecting my graduation degree. But I wasn't present at the ceremony. Instead, I was knocking—my heart hammering louder than the sound of knuckles on wood— on the door of the master moviemaker who also wrote the most unusual short stories. I had translated one of them, and this was the day he was going to pronounce judgement on the translation. What graduation degree could have been worth the thirteen minutes he spent with me, making three suggestions, offering his illustrations, and then showing me out?

Or, I could go back much further, to the day when I was perched in the crook of the friendly branches of the guava tree in my grand-uncle's yard, stealthily reading the short stories of the robed and bearded great-uncle of Bengali literature, not willing to give my officious elders the joy of knowing that I was enjoying them immensely. As I eavesdropped on a little girl and her peddler friend from Afghanistan, there was the crack of a gun being fired and the palpably hot whoosh of what turned out to be a bullet from an air rifle whizzing past my earlobe. My slightly shortsighted grand-uncle had mistaken me for a local urchin out to steal fruit, and let go with his weapon. This particular collection of short stories might not have come into being had his eyesight been better.

~

I was born and brought up in Bengal. My cultural, intellectual and emotional compasses were all set to their true north in Bengal. This collection is my personal statement of gratitude to the land which has given me a literature (of which the short story is the most important part) that has given me my life as a translator. Dhonnyobaad.

—Uroli, Uttarakhand,
December 2015

one

THE KABULIWALLAH

RABINDRANATH TAGORE

My five-year-old daughter talked all the time. It had taken her a year after her birth to master the language, and since then she has not wasted a second of her waking hours in silence. Although her mother often hushed her, this was beyond me. A silent Mini was so unnatural a being that I could not bear it for long. So I always encouraged her to prattle on.

I had barely started the seventeenth chapter of my novel that morning when Mini appeared by my side and began chattering at once, 'Ramdayal, the doorman, calls the crow kauwa instead of kaak, Baba, he just doesn't know anything, does he?'

Before I could talk about linguistic diversity, she had moved to another subject. 'Baba, Bhola says it rains because elephants spray water with their trunks from the sky. He talks such rubbish, my god. He keeps talking, talks all the time.'

Without pausing for my opinion, Mini suddenly asked, 'What relation is Ma to you, Baba?'

'Shaali,' I answered to myself. To Mini I said, 'Go play with Bhola, Mini. I'm busy.'

Flopping down by my feet, next to the desk, she began to play a game involving her knees and hands, accompanied by a rhyme uttered at express velocity. In the seventeenth chapter of my novel, Pratap Singh was about to leap with Kanchanmala in his arms from the high window of the prison into the river flowing below.

My room looked out on the street. Mini abruptly stopped her game to rush to the window and began to shout, 'Kabuliwallah, Kabuliwallah.'

A tall Kabuliwallah—one of those hawkers of dry fruits who

came all the way from Afghanistan to make a living in Calcutta—was walking slowly up the road, a turban on his head, a bag slung over his shoulder, holding two or three boxes of grapes. It was difficult to say what emotions he aroused in my daughter, but she continued to call out to him breathlessly. I was afraid that if the wily peddler, with a bag of things to sell, came into my room, I could bid goodbye to any prospect of finishing chapter seventeen that day.

The Kabuliwallah turned and smiled at Mini's shouts and began walking towards our house. Her courage gave way and she ran from the room at great speed, vanishing into the house. She was convinced that if the Kabuliwallah's bag was opened and examined it would reveal three or four children, just like her.

Meanwhile, the man himself appeared, offering me a smiling salute. Although Pratap Singh and Kanchanmala were in dire straits, I reflected that it would be discourteous to invite him into the house and buy nothing.

I bought a few things and we began chatting. We exchanged notes on frontier policies involving Abdur Rahman, the Russians and the English.

When he was about to leave, the Kabuliwallah finally asked, 'Where did your daughter go, Babu?'

I sent for Mini in order to dispel her fears. Pressing herself to me, Mini cast suspicious glances at the Kabuliwallah and his large bag. He offered her some raisins and dry fruit, but she simply wouldn't accept them, holding my knee tightly. And there the first meeting between them ended.

A few days later, about to leave the house on an errand, I discovered my daughter seated on the bench next to the front door, chattering away to the Kabuliwallah who sat at her feet, listening smilingly, and occasionally saying something in broken Bengali. Mini had never encountered such an attentive listener in the five years of her life besides her father. I even found nuts and raisins bundled into the aanchal of her tiny sari. 'Why have you given her all this?' I asked the Kabuliwallah. 'Don't do it again.' Taking an eight-anna coin out of my pocket, I handed it to him. He accepted it without demur, putting it in his bag.

I returned home to find the eight-anna coin at the heart of a hundred rupees worth of trouble.

Holding a circular, silvery object in her hand, Mini's mother was asking her daughter disapprovingly, 'Where did you get this?'

'The Kabuliwallah gave it to me,' Mini told her.

'Why did you have to take it from him?' Mini's mother inquired.

'I didn't want to, he gave it on his own,' Mini said, on the verge of tears.

I rescued Mini from imminent danger and took her outside.

There I learnt that it wasn't as though this was only Mini's second meeting with Rahmat, the Kabuliwallah. He had been coming to see her almost every day, bribing her with almonds and raisins to conquer her tiny, greedy five-year-old heart.

I observed that the two friends had established an easy familiarity between themselves, sharing private jokes and quips. For instance, on spotting Rahmat, my daughter would ask, laughing, 'What's in that bag of yours, Kabuliwallah?'

In an exaggeratedly nasal tone Rahmat would answer, also laughing, 'An elephant.'

The joke could not be termed particularly subtle, but nevertheless it kept both in splits—and the artless laughter of a middle-aged man and a child on an autumn morning brought me some joy too.

They had another ritual exchange. Rahmat would tell Mini, 'Khnokhi, tomi sasurbaari kakhanu jaabena. Little girl, you must never get married and go to your father-in-law's house.'

Most girls from traditional Bengali families would be familiar with the word shoshurbaari almost from the time they were born, but because we were somewhat modern, we hadn't taught our daughter the meaning of the term. So, she did not know what to make of Rahmat's request, but because it was against her nature to be silent and unresponsive, she would fire a counter-question. 'Will you go there?'

Rahmat would brandish his enormous fist against an imaginary father-in-law, and say, 'I will kill the sasur first.'

Imagining the terrible fate awaiting this unknown creature, Mini would laugh her head off.

It was the clear season of autumn. In ancient times, this was when kings set off to conquer other lands. I had never been anywhere outside Calcutta, but precisely for that reason my mind wandered all over the world. In the quiet corner of my room, I was like an eternal traveller, pining for places around the globe. My heart began to race as soon as another country was mentioned, the sight of a foreigner conjured up a vision of a cottage amidst rivers and mountains and forests, and thoughts of a joyful, free way of life captured my imagination.

But I was so retiring by nature that the very notion of abandoning my corner and stepping out into the world made me have visions of the sky crashing down on my head. That was why my conversations with this man from Kabul, this Kabuliwallah, every morning by the desk in my tiny room served the purpose of travel for me. Rugged and inaccessible, the scorched, red-hued mountain ranges rose high on either side of the road, a laden caravan of camels winding along the narrow trail between them; turbanned traders and travellers, some of them on the backs of camels, some on foot, some with spears, others with old-fashioned flint guns...with a voice like the rumbling of clouds, the Kabuliwallah would recount tales from his homeland in broken Bengali, and these images would float past my eyes.

Mini's mother was perpetually jumpy, her mind alive with imaginary fears. The slightest noise on the streets would lead her to believe that all the inebriated individuals in the world were rushing towards our house, bent on making mischief. Despite all the years (not too many actually) she had lived on earth, she had still not rid herself of the conviction that the universe was populated only by thieves and robbers and drunkards and snakes and tigers and malaria and earthworms and cockroaches and white men all intent on striking terror into her heart.

She was not entirely free of doubt about Rahmat, the Kabuliwallah, requesting me repeatedly to keep an eye on him. When I attempted to laugh away her suspicions, she would ask me probing questions. 'Aren't children ever kidnapped? Don't they have slaves in Afghanistan? Is it entirely impossible for a gigantic Kabuliwallah to kidnap a small child?'

I had to acknowledge that it was not entirely impossible but unlikely. The capacity for trust was not the same in everyone, which was why my wife remained suspicious of the Kabuliwallah. But I could not stop Rahmat from visiting our house for no fault of his.

Rahmat usually went home around the end of January every year. He would be very busy collecting his dues at this time. He had to go from house to house, but still he made it a point to visit Mini once a day. There did seem to be a conspiracy between them. If he could not visit in the morning, he made his way to our house in the evening. It was true that I experienced a sudden surge of fear at the sight of the large man in his loose shalwar and kurta, standing in a dark corner of the room with his bags. But when a laughing Mini ran up to him, saying, 'Kabuliwallah, Kabuliwallah,' and the simple banter of old was resumed between the two friends of unequal age, my heart was filled with delight once more.

I was correcting proofs one day in my tiny room. The cold had grown sharper; as winter was about to bid farewell, there was a severe chill. The morning sunshine filtering through the window warmed my feet; it was a most pleasant sensation. It was about eight o'clock—most of those who had ventured out for their morning constitutionals, their heads and throats wrapped in mufflers, were already back home. Suddenly, there was an uproar in the street.

Looking out of the window I saw two policemen frogmarching our Rahmat, bound with ropes, up the road, followed by a group of curious urchins. Rahmat's clothes were bloodstained, and one of the policemen held a dagger dripping with blood. Going out, I stopped the policemen to inquire what the matter was.

The story was related partly by a policeman and partly by Rahmat himself. One of our neighbours owed Rahmat some money for a shawl from Rampur. When he disclaimed the debt, an altercation broke out, in the course of which Rahmat had stabbed him with his dagger.

The Kabuliwallah was showering expletives on the liar when Mini emerged from the house, calling out, 'Kabuliwallah, Kabuliwallah.'

Rahmat's expression changed in an instant to a cheerful smile. Since there was no bag slung from his shoulder today, they could not have their usual discussion about its magical contents. Mini asked him directly, 'Will you go to your father-in-law's house?'

'That's exactly where I am going,' Rahmat smiled back at her. When he saw Mini wasn't amused, he showed her his arms bound with rope. 'I would have killed the sasur, but my hands are tied.'

Rahmat was in jail for several years for causing grievous bodily harm.

We forgot him, more or less. Going about our everyday routines it didn't even occur to us how difficult it must be for a man used to roaming free in the mountains to cope with years of imprisonment.

Even Mini's father had to accept that his fickle-hearted daughter's behaviour was truly shameful. She effortlessly forgot her old friend, and struck up a new friendship with Nabi, who groomed horses. Then, as she grew older, male friends were replaced by girls her age. Now, we seldom saw each other anymore.

Many years passed. Another autumn arrived. My Mini's wedding had been arranged. She would be married during the Durga Puja holidays. Along with the goddess from Kailash, the joy of my house would also depart for her husband's home, robbing her father's house of its light.

A beautiful morning had dawned. After the monsoon, the freshly-rinsed autumn sunlight had taken on the colour of pure, molten gold. Its glow washed over the crumbling houses of exposed brick in the neighbourhood, making them exquisitely beautiful.

The shehnai had begun playing in my house before the night had ended. Its notes were like the sound of my heart weeping. The plaintive melody of Bhairavi was spreading the imminent pain of parting all over the world. My Mini was to be married today.

There had been a great to-do since the morning, with crowds of people going in and out of the house. In the courtyard a marquee was being set up with bamboo posts; the clinking of chandeliers being hung up in the rooms and the veranda could be heard. It was very noisy.

I was going over the accounts in my room when Rahmat appeared and saluted me.

I did not recognize him at first. He had neither his bags nor his long hair—his body was not as strapping as it once used to be. It was his smile that eventually told me who he was.

'Why, it's Rahmat,' I said. 'When did you get back?'

'I was released from jail yesterday evening,' he answered.

His reply made me uncomfortable. Until now, I had never seen a murderer in the flesh, his presence here made me shrink back. On this auspicious day, I wished he would go away.

I told him, 'There's something important going on at home, I am busy. You'd better go today.'

At this he made ready to leave at once, but when he had reached the door, he said hesitantly, 'Can't I meet Khnokhi?'

He probably thought that Mini had not changed. Perhaps he expected her to come running up as before, chanting, 'Kabuliwallah, Kabuliwallah,' as she always had. To honour the old friendship he had even gone to the trouble of collecting a box of grapes and some nuts and raisins wrapped in paper from a fellow Afghan as he no longer had his own sack of goods to sell

'There are some ceremonies at home today,' I told him, 'meeting Mini is impossible.'

He looked very disappointed. He looked at me wordlessly for

a few moments, then said, 'Salaam, Babu,' and left.

No sooner had he left than I felt bad and was considering calling him back when I found him returning of his own accord.

Coming up to me, he said, 'I have some grapes and nuts and raisins for Khnokhi, please give them to her.'

As I was about to pay for them, he caught hold of my hand firmly and said, 'Please don't pay me. You have always been so kind, I will never forget your kindness...

'I have a daughter back home just like yours, Babu. It was thinking of her that I brought some fruit for Khnokhi, this isn't business.'

Putting his hand inside his long, loose shalwar, he pulled out a dirty piece of paper. Unfolding it carefully, he spread it out on my desk for me. It had the print of a tiny pair of hands. Not a photograph, not an oil painting, just some lampblack smeared on the palms to make a print on paper. Rahmat travelled to Calcutta's streets every year to sell his dry fruits, holding this remembrance of his daughter close to his breast—as though the touch of those tiny tender hands comforted the heart inside his broad chest, a heart wracked by the pain of separation.

Tears sprang to my eyes. I forgot that he was a seller of dry fruits from Kabul and I, a member of a Kulin Bengali family. I realized that he was a father, just as I was. The handprint of his little Parbati from his home in the mountains reminded me of Mini.

I sent for my daughter at once. They raised objections in the ladies' chambers, but I paid no attention. Mini appeared shyly in my room, dressed as a bride in her red wedding garb.

The Kabuliwallah was taken aback when he saw her. Unable to revive their old banter, he said nothing for a while. Finally, he said with a smile, 'Khnokhi, tomi sasurbaari jaabis?'

Mini knew now what the words meant, she could not respond as before. Blushing at Rahmat's question, she stood with her face averted. I remembered the day Mini and the Kabuliwallah had met for the first time, and felt a twinge of sadness.

After Mini left, Rahmat slumped to the floor with a sigh. He had suddenly realized that his own daughter must have grown up and that he would have to get to know her all over again—she would no longer be the way he remembered her. Who knew what might have happened to her over these past eight years? The shehnai kept playing in the calming sunlight of the autumn morning, but inside a house in a Calcutta lane all that Rahmat could see were the mountains and cold deserts of Afghanistan.

I gave him some money. 'Go back home to your daughter, Rahmat,' I told him. 'Let the happiness of your reunion with her be a blessing for my Mini.'

Giving Rahmat the money meant pruning one or two things from the celebrations. The electric lights display was not as lavish as I had wanted it to be, nor were the musical arrangements as elaborate as planned. The ladies as usual objected strongly but, for me, the festivities were brightened by the benediction of a father's love.

two

THE OFFERING

PRAMATHA CHAUDHURI

European civilization had not yet thrust its horns into our village; in other words, the railway line had bypassed us. So, to visit home from Calcutta, we still had to use traditional means of transport part of the way: the boat in the monsoon and the palanquin during summer and winter for the most part.

The road and the river ran in opposite directions. I always took the boat home, so for a long time I did not explore the land route. Then, in the year that I cleared my BA examinations, I had to go home in May to take care of some unfinished business. Today, I shall tell you of the strange incident that took place on that journey.

Getting off the train at six in the morning, I found the palanquin-bearers waiting for me. I cannot claim that the appearance of the litter was encouraging. I estimated it to be some three feet wide and less than five feet long. Then, I was transfixed by the appearance of the bearers. Cadavers such as these could probably be seen only in hospitals in other countries. Almost all of them had protruding ribs and withered flesh on their limbs.

To be carried by these fellow humans for twenty miles had at first seemed rather a unpalatable proposition. Inflicting my weight upon these spindly, half-dead unfortunates seemed exceedingly cruel. Observing my hesitation, the servant who had accompanied them from my ancestral home smiled and said, 'Get in, sir, you shall not find it uncomfortable. If you delay any more you will not arrive at your destination before four o'clock.'

Being told that travelling twenty miles would take ten hours did not boost my enthusiasm in the least. Still, I crawled into the palanquin after muttering a prayer, since there was no alternative.

At first, the glow and the breeze that filtered in from the east cheered me; the draught felt as wonderful to the skin as the radiance to the eye. My eyes as well as my heart were reborn along with the birth of the new day. I looked outside. There were fields stretching in every direction. No houses, no trees, only fields—endless fields—flat and identical, infinite and empty like the sky. Having escaped the concrete pigeonholes of Calcutta into this infinite expanse of nature, my soul experienced the bliss of deliverance. My mind shook off all worries and took on the clear, satisfied appearance of the sky with a faint red glow of joy.

But this happiness proved short-lived, for with the progress of the day the potency of the sun increased, as though nature was running a fever—the temperature rose to 105 degrees. By nine o'clock, one could no longer look out, for the sun was blinding. My eyes were thirsty for a shade of green—a search over the horizon only yielded an emaciated acacia or two. They barely quenched my thirst, for whatever other quality this tree might have possessed, it offered no green loveliness, no soothing shadow. Caught between this plain on which there was no green, no leaves, no shade, and the sunlight-stricken sky bereft of clouds, I felt a great fatigue growing. Unable to stand this dull appearance of nature any longer, I opened a book. I'd brought George Meredith's *The Egoist* with me—I had the last chapter to finish. Having read three or four pages, I realized I had paid no attention—not a word made sense. I shut the book and requested the bearers to speed up a little, promising them extra money.

This worked. We reached the halfway point at ten-thirty—half an hour early. I cannot claim this village amidst the desert was a lovely and pleasing example of an oasis. A shallow tank in the middle, eleven or twelve thatched huts on its bank, which was as high as a single-storeyed building, and a fig tree on one side. Setting the palanquin down under a tree, the bearers ran to the tank, took a dip in it and sat down to their meal in their wet clothes. We set off again half an hour later.

The palanquin moved rather slowly now, for lunch had made

the bearers slower than a pregnant woman. In the meantime, my body, mind and senses had become so weary that I shut my eyes and tried to sleep. The afternoon sun and the rocking of the palanquin brought on slumber, but that slumber was not sleep. Just as my body had adopted a posture midway between lying down and sitting up, my mind had also occupied a position somewhere between sleep and wakefulness. A couple of hours passed this way. I was suddenly awakened by a tremendous jolt, so powerful that it penetrated my body and struck at the very seat of the soul.

Looking out, I realized that the bearers had deposited their passenger with a thud beneath an enormous banyan tree and disappeared. When I asked why, the servant said, 'They've gone for a smoke.' I took the opportunity to escape painfully from the palanquin and stretch my limbs. A little further away I found the bearers huddled together, making a great noise. At first I was apprehensive, wondering whether they were conspiring to go on strike against me, for many excited speeches were being delivered. But almost at once I realized that there was a different reason for all the shouting. What they were smoking was not tobacco—it was 'king tobacco', as was evident from the smell. Their enthusiasm, their cheerfulness, their leaps and cries made it obvious why cannabis is universally referred to in Bengali as 'quickjoy'.

At first it was amusing to watch them smoke, but gradually I became irritated. The cannabis disappeared rapidly, but none of them showed the slightest inclination to get up. When I asked how much longer they would be, the servant said, 'They won't get up, sir, unless you force them to—there's danger ahead, so they're trying to smoke up some courage.'

I said, 'What danger?'

He answered, 'It must not be mentioned, sir. You'll see for yourself soon.' I became so curious that I decided to rouse the bearers myself. Their eyes had turned red under the influence of the drug. I had to pull each one physically to his feet, which forced me to inhale some of the smoke. Entering by way of my nostrils, it went straight to my head. I was overcome by nausea at once, my head spun, my eyes felt heavy—I took shelter hastily in the palanquin. It started moving again. This time I didn't feel in the least uncomfortable—for my body seemed to belong to someone else.

After some time—how long, I could not say—the bearers started shouting in unison, at the top of their voices. I had already found evidence that their vocal strength was more than their physical one, but for the first time I realized the extent of that strength. The one word that could be heard amidst the babble was 'Ram naam'—now the leader also added his voice to the chorus, chanting, 'Ram naam sat hai, Ram naam sat hai' continuously. It made me think I had died, and that spirits were taking me to their realm in their palanquin.

Whether the cannabis had anything to do with this impression, I cannot say. I felt a great curiosity about where they were taking me. Looking out, I saw that the sky looked as though the village were on fire, but the accompanying signs of a blaze—loud screams renting the air—were not to be heard. It was so desolate, so silent, that the unbreakable peace of death seemed to have enveloped the world.

A little further on, what lay before us was a wilderness—not of sand, but of scorched earth; this earth was like a fragment of brown pottery, without a single blade of grass. There was no human habitation now on this scorched land, but numerous signs remained to show that there once had been one. This was a kingdom of bricks, as far as the eye could see there were bricks and more bricks, some stacked together, some scattered on the ground, there were bricks in the thousands; and the bricks were so red that they seemed to be bleeding. What pushed upwards from this collapsed world were trees. But none of them was leafy, they were all barren, all dry, all dead. These skeletal trees stood in clumps at some places, and singly at others. And the bricks and the timber, the earth and the sky, all seemed to have gone up in blood-red flames.

It was hardly surprising that simple people like my bearers should be frightened at this sight, for I felt a bit shaken myself. A little later, the faint sound of sobs penetrated the silence and came to my ears. The tone was so soft, so pathetic, so distressed that generations of human agony appear to have been collected and distilled in it. It filled me with compassion. In an instant, I sensed the pain of all humankind.

Suddenly, a storm came up, the wind raged from all directions. The fire in the sky swirled madly, tormented by the wind. A typhoon seemed to rise above the sea of blood, flaming waves spreading in all directions. And in that fiery deluge I saw thousands of people flailing and writhing. At this sight the elements clapped their hands in glee and shouted aloud. Gradually all these sounds coalesced into one universal laugh—its merciless, grotesque noise dispatched waves of turbulence to the horizon. Then it diminished gradually, being transformed into the same soft, pathetic, distressed sobs I had heard earlier. The conflict between the grotesque laughter and the tragic sobs brought out in me old memories of this abandoned town—whether the memories were from this life or a previous one, I cannot tell.

Someone within me seemed to say, here is the history of this village… This brick-and-wood wilderness was the ruin of Rudrapur. The Roys of Rudrapur had once been the principal zamindars of the area. The founder of the clan, Rudranarayan, had received his title by virtue of working for the nawab, and along with it he had earned ownership rights to three divisions of land. People said the family had in its possession a deed, signed by the Emperor of Delhi himself, which gave them the power to execute anyone.

Whether they were empowered by the deed or not, there was no doubt that they did carry out executions. Legend had it that there had never been such indomitable zamindars in the land before. The strong and the weak alike bowed before them. Those who earned their wrath lost both their property and their lives. The number of people whose homes and lands they had captured was beyond count. There wasn't anyone within twenty miles who dared to disobey the Roys' commands. Under their iron rule there was not the faintest trace of crime in the area, for all who could use sticks, spears or swords were enlisted in the army.

Just like their boundless ruthlessness, their benevolence was limitless too. Providing food and clothes to the poor and medicines to the sick was an everyday affair. Countless people lived gratefully under their patronage. All the priests in the area had become rich landowners on the strength of the rights that the Roys had granted to Brahmins. And they spent unstintingly on festivals and rituals—Holi, Durga Puja and the like. In Rudrapur, the sky would turn crimson with abir during Holi—and the earth with blood during Durga Puja.

In the guesthouses, there were arrangements to feed a hundred guests daily. No Brahmin saddled with a dead father or mother, or a marriageable daughter, ever went back empty-handed from the Roys. They would say that the Brahmin's wealth is not for amassing but for spending on good causes. So, if money for such philanthropy ever ran short, the masters did not shrink from looting traders and moneylenders. In brief, they did good and evil according to their own fancies, for under the reign of the nawab, no one ruled over them. Consequently, common people respected them as much as they feared them, for they neither feared nor respected the people. As a result of such untrammelled tyranny, their estimation of their own excellence increased tremendously. Ingrained in them was the pride of race, of wealth, of power, of appearance. All the males in the Roy family were fair, tall and strong, and the fame of the beauty of their womenfolk had spread countrywide. Because of all this, it had become next to impossible for them to think of anyone else as a human being.

But, even before the advent of the English, the fortunes of the family had started falling apart, and later, in the era of the East India Company, they were ruined. Those factions which had become penniless, because of the division of property over successive generations, found their lines dying out, for in their eyes it was contemptible to earn a living by one's own toil. On top of that were the disputes over the sharing of property. The Roy family worshipped the goddess Shakti—so much so that in Rudrapur young boys and old men alike were regular drinkers. Not even the women objected, for they believed that drinking was masculine. When the lords assembled after paying their respects to the family goddess and got down to drinking, the prominent sandalwood-and-blood marks on their foreheads and their bloodshot eyes gave them the appearance of Shiva with his inflamed third eye.

During this phase no task was too daunting for them. They would order their stick-wielding soldiers to plunder grains from one subject and to rape the wife of another. Bloodshed followed. This family rivalry took them forward along the road to extinction. Whatever property and assets remained were transferred by virtue of the ten-year settlement (under which the government granted the Roys ownership of the land for ten years provided they fulfilled certain conditions). It never occurred to them that unless the last instalment was paid by the due date they would become permanently bankrupt. Because they were not used to doing it, they never managed to pay the revenue owed to the Company on time. As a result most of their property had to be auctioned off.

With time the clan of the Roys was almost obliterated. Where they had once occupied almost a hundred houses, only six branches remained about a hundred years ago. The property and assets of those six branches gradually passed into Dhananjay Sarkar's hands. This was because Dhananjay followed English law as carefully as he knew it. The various tricks of making money with the help of the law, while staying within it, were at his fingertips. He had earned a great deal of money from practising as an attorney at the district court. Channelled into moneylending, these funds had accumulated a massive amount of interest, swelling his fortune greatly.

Public opinion held that he had earned ten lakh rupees in about ten years. Even if it wasn't quite as much, there was no doubt that he had earned three or four lakh rupees easily. After making all this money, he wanted to be a zamindar, and so he started buying the Roys' property bit by bit—for he knew every acre of the estate like the back of his hand. His family had always worked for the Roys, and in his younger days, he too, had worked six or seven years for the head of the oldest branch, Triloknarayan. But, despite buying up the entire property and even the homes of every branch of the family, he had not dared to visit Rudrapur, for Ugranarayan, the son of his former master, was still alive. Ugranarayan had sworn by his sacred thread, placing his hand on the family idol, that if Dhananjay ever set foot within the borders of Rudrapur in Ugranarayan's lifetime, he would not return in one piece.

Dhananjay had no doubt in his mind that Ugranarayan would fulfil his oath to the letter. For he knew that no one as fearsome and courageous as Ugranarayan had ever been born into the Roy family. Some weeks after Ugranarayan's death, Dhananjay went to Rudrapur and occupied the Roys' ancestral home. Not a single male from the Roy family was present in the village, so he could have taken possession of every house had he so wanted; yet he made no attempt to turn Ugranarayan's only daughter Ratnamayee, who was a widow, out of her ancestral home.

For one thing, the subjects of Pathanpara, the village adjacent to Rudrapur, were determined to protect Ratnamayee's rights and ownership. The village comprised generations of people adept at fighting with sticks; Dhananjay knew that if he tried to evict Ratnamayee, injury or death was inevitable. He wasn't about to face such a fate, for there wasn't another person in Bengal as timid as he.

Second, Dhananjay harboured a modicum of fear and respect, arising from superstition, for the family that had provided sustenance to his own. Because of all this, Dhananjay left Ugranarayan's portion alone, occupying the rest of the Roys' family home—though only nominally. For Dhananjay's family consisted only of his daughter, Rangini, and her husband, Ratilal Dey.

After he had moved house, Dhananjay underwent a distinct change. While he had been making money, his desire for wealth had taken him over so completely that greed was all he harboured. In the grip of this desire, he had blindly gathered riches by any means whatsoever—it had never occurred to him to find out for whom or for what. But after he installed himself as the zamindar in Rudrapur, he woke up to the fact that he had made money simply for the sake of making money, not for anything else, not for anyone else.

He recalled that when his seven sons had died one after the other, he had not been perturbed even for a day, he had not neglected his business pursuits. The excessive love for money that he had harboured for a lifetime was now transformed into excessive possessiveness. He spent sleepless nights wondering how his amassed wealth could be preserved for posterity. Rudrapur itself was visible proof that even unlimited wealth could be lost over the ages. Gradually an idea took root in his mind—that man could accumulate riches by his own effort, but without the help of the gods those riches couldn't be preserved.

Although he knew the laws of the English by heart, Dhananjay was essentially uneducated. He had never outgrown his rustic orgins, the education he had received had had no effect in this regard. His mind was ruled by every superstition and blind belief that a lower caste person could be expected to subscribe to. He had heard in his childhood that if a Brahmin child were locked up with riches in a room and died of starvation, the child would be transformed into a spirit and guard the wealth forever. He was so obsessed with preserving his amassed wealth in this manner that he became convinced that doing this was his most important duty. In matters where Dhananjay had no doubts, he was used to getting his way in the face of every opposition. But in this case a great obstacle did arise. Hearing that Dhananjay meant to sacrifice a Brahmin child, Rangini gave up food and sleep. Consequently, it became impossible for Dhananjay to fulfil his heart's desire.

If Dhananjay loved anything in the world besides money, it was his daughter. Just as a tree might take root even amidst brick and mortar, this weakness for his daughter had taken root in a crevice somewhere in Dhananjay's hard heart. Though Dhananjay did not take the initiative himself, a certain turn of events fulfilled the last wish of his life.

Ratnamayee had a three-year-old son. His name was Kiritchandra.

She lived alone with her son, never meeting anyone. No one was allowed into her inner sanctum. The people of Rudrapur would actually have forgotten her existence had she not visited the family goddess's temple every day, after her bath, precisely at noon—guarded by two of Pathanpara's stick-wielding citizens. Ratnamayee was twenty or twenty-one at the time. Women as wondrously beautiful as she were extremely rare in the land. She resembled the family goddess. Her eyes slanted upwards like those of the idol's—and, just like those eyes, hers too were still, immobile. People said her lashes never closed. What burnt brightly in them was her total contempt for the men and women around her. Ratnamayee had inherited the ancestral arrogance accumulated over three centuries by her family. Needless to say, she also nurtured a fierce pride in her own beauty. To her, this beauty was clear proof of her nobility. In Ratnamayee's view, the purpose of beauty was not to attract people, but to slight them. When she went to the temple people on the road stepped aside, for her very posture told them, in the silent language of her complexion and figure, 'Go away. Even stepping on your shadow would mean having to cleanse myself.' She never glanced to the left or the right, with her eyes cast downwards she lit up the path on her way to and from the temple.

Behind closed shutters, Rangini watched Ratnamayee, and her mind and her body grew rigid with the poison of envy—for however much her possessions might be, beauty was not one of them. And this deficiency pained her a great deal, for her husband Ratilal was extremely handsome. Rangini loved her husband the way Dhananjay loved money—in other words, this love was nothing more than a terrible hunger, and this hunger, just like physical hunger, was blind and ruthless. What relationship it had with the heart was difficult to say, for the hearts of creatures like Dhananjay and Rangini are not external to the body, but included within it.

Like Dhananjay, Rangini treated the object of her love as her personal property. The very thought that someone might set hands on it made her ruthless, and there was no act in the world too cruel to preserve her property. A completely unfounded suspicion had risen in Rangini's mind—that Ratilal had been entranced by Ratnamayee's beauty; that suspicion was gradually transformed into certainty. Rangini suddenly discovered that Ratilal went to Ugranarayan's house secretly, loitering there for hours. The real attraction was drinking bhang with the Brahmin who lived under Ratnamayee's patronage. And then, the childless Ratilal had developed such a weakness for Ratnamayee's son that he couldn't pass a single day without setting eyes on Kiritchandra.

Needless to say, Ratnamayee and Ratilal had never even exchanged glances, for the inhabitants of Pathanpara guarded her inner sanctum. But Rangini became convinced that Ratnamayee had decided to steal her handsome husband from her. To take revenge for this, and to satisfy her innate enviousness, Rangini decided to use Ratnamayee's son to fulfil her father's wish. She let Dhananjay know that not only did she have no objection to his plan, but she would look for a suitable young boy.

This sort of thing had to be conducted with much stealth, however. So, after much discussion, father and daughter decided to use the room next to Rangini's bedroom to carry out their plot. In three or four days all the doors and windows of this room were sealed with bricks. Then, very furtively, all the gold and silver coins Dhananjay had amassed were put into large copper pitchers and arranged in rows inside the room. When all Dhananjay's wealth had been put in there, Rangini told Ratilal that Ratnamayee's son was so lovely she desperately wanted to hold him in her arms—and that he would somehow have to bring Kiritchandra to her. Ratilal answered that it was impossible, if Ratnamayee's bodyguards got to know they would smash his head. But Rangini became so insistent that Ratilal soon managed to wheedle Kiritchandra into accompanying him to meet Rangini.

As soon as Kiritchandra arrived, Rangini took him in her arms and smothered him with kisses. Then she dressed him in red, put a garland round his neck, a red sandalwood-and-vermilion mark on

his forehead and two gold bangles on his wrists. Seeing him dressed
up like this, Ratilal's face lit up with pleasure. Then Rangini took
Kiritchandra by the hand, pushed him into the sealed chamber
and locked the door. Pushing against the door, Ratilal realized that
Rangini had locked him in too, alone in his bedroom.

Although Ratilal tried to push, kick and hammer his way out
of the bedroom and into the sealed chamber, he realized his efforts
were futile. The door was so heavy and so solid that it would be
difficult to break it down even with an axe. Shut inside that pitch-
dark room, Kiritchandra started sobbing at first, and then called out
to Ratilal, 'Dada, Dada.' Two or three hours later, his sobs could no
longer be heard. Ratilal realized that he had cried himself to sleep.

Locked up in his room for three days and three nights, Ratilal
could hear Kiritchandra—now banging his head against the bedroom
door, now sobbing, now silent. At his wits' end, Ratilal attacked the
door a thousand times over those three days, but he couldn't budge
it even an inch. Every time he heard sobs he ran to the door to say,
'Don't weep so, Baba, don't be afraid, I'm here.' Hearing his voice
the boy would cry out even more loudly, bang his head against the
door of the sealed chamber even more often; Ratilal covered his
ears with his hands and ran away to the other end of the room,
screaming out to Rangini and Dhananjay at the top of his voice,
calling them whatever names came to his mind.

He had become so unhinged by this fiendish business that it never
occurred to him that there could be some other way of rescuing
Kiritchandra—his entire attention was drawn by those sobs from the
boy trapped inside that sealed chamber. After three days, the child's
sobs grew gradually weaker, fainter, and stopped altogether on the
fifth day. Ratilal realized that Kiritchandra's little heart had stopped
beating. He parted the iron rods on the window with his hands,
jumped out and ran directly to Ratnamayee's house.

That day there were no guards at the door, for all the people
of Pathanpara were out looking for the missing boy. Taking this
opportunity Ratilal appeared before Ratnamayee and narrated

everything to her. For three years no one had seen Ratnamayee smile. Hearing of the cruel murder of her son, her face and eyes lit up, she seemed to be smiling. Ratilal found this so peculiar that he fled from her presence and disappeared. Then, in the middle of the night, while everyone was asleep, Ratnamayee set fire to her room.

The houses adjoined one another. Within an hour the fire spread like the wrathful flames of the gods and attacked Dhananjay's house. Dhananjay and Rangini tried to escape, but at the front gate they saw Ratnamayee, surrounded by almost a hundred of Pathanpara's inhabitants armed with swords, spears and shields. At Ratnamayee's command they plunged their spears into the father and the daughter until they were covered with blood from head to foot, and threw them into the flames. Ratnamayee burst into laughter, and her attendants realized she had gone mad.

Then the people of Pathanpara went berserk. Dhananjay's servants, maids, employees, guards, doormen—whoever they found were skewered on their swords and spears, and the ancestral home of the Roy family was overrun by a river of fire above and of blood below. Then came a storm and an earthquake. When everything was burnt to smithereens, Ratnamayee jumped into the flames. Everything in Rudrapur stands in ruins today. Only Kiritchandra's sobs and Ratnamayee's insane laughter still rise up to the skies.

three

MAHESH

SARAT CHANDRA CHATTOPADHYAY

I

The village was named Kashipur. An insignificant village, with an even more insignificant zamindar, but such was his authority that his subjects went in awe of him.

It was the birthday of the zamindar's youngest son. Having performed the holy rituals, Tarkaratna, the priest, was on his way home in the afternoon. The month of Boishakh was drawing to a close, but there was not even a trace of clouds anywhere, the searing sky seemingly pouring fire on everything below. The field stretching to the horizon before him was parched and cracked, with the blood in the veins of the earth escaping constantly through the crevices in the form of vapour. Gazing at it coiling upwards like flames made the head reel with drunkenness.

Gafoor Jolha lived on the edge of this field. The earthen wall surrounding his house had collapsed, merging his yard with the road. The privacy of the inner chambers had all but surrendered itself to the mercy of the passer-by.

Pausing in the shade of a white teak tree, Tarkaratna called out loudly, 'Are you home, Gafra?'

Gafoor's ten-year-old daughter came to the door. 'What do you need Baba for? He's got a fever.'

'Fever! Call the swine! Monster! Godless creature!'

The screaming and shouting brought Gafoor Mian to the door, shivering with fever. An ancient acacia stood next to the broken wall, with a bull tethered to it. Pointing to it, Tarkaratna said, 'What's all this? Have you forgotten this is a Hindu village with a Brahmin zamindar?' Red with rage and the heat, his words were fiery, but Gafoor unable to understand the reason for the outburst could only stare at him.

'When I passed this way in the morning he was tethered there,' said Tarkaratna, 'and now on my way back he's still tethered the same way. Karta will bury you alive if you kill a bull. He's a devout Brahmin.'

'What can I do, Baba Thakur, I have no choice. I've had this fever for several days now. I collapse every time I try to take him to graze.'

'Then turn him loose, he'll find food on his own.'

'Where can I turn him loose, Baba Thakur? The winnowing isn't done, the grain is still lying in the fields. The hay hasn't been sorted, the earth is burning, there's not a blade of grass anywhere. What if he eats someone's grains or hay—how can I turn him loose, Baba Thakur?'

Softening, Tarkaratna said, 'If you can't let him loose at least give him some straw. Hasn't your daughter made any rice? Give him a bowl of starch and water.'

Gafoor did not answer, only looked at Tarkaratna helplessly and sighed.

Tarkaratna said, 'No rice either? What did you do with the hay? Did you sell your entire share without keeping anything for your beast? You butcher!'

Gafoor seemed to lose his power of speech at this cruel accusation. A little later he said haltingly, 'I did get some hay this year, but Karta Moshai took it away to pay for taxes left over from last year. I fell at his feet, I said, "Babu Moshai, you're the supreme authority, where will I go if I leave your kingdom, give me at least a little hay. There's no straw for the roof, we have just the one room for father and daughter, we can still manage with palm leaves this monsoon, but my Mahesh will die of starvation."'

With a mocking smile, Tarkaratna said, 'Really! What a loving name, Mahesh. I'll die laughing.'

Paying no attention to the taunt, Gafoor continued, 'But the lord had no mercy on me. He allowed me some rice to feed us for two months, but all my hay was confiscated and the poor thing got nothing at all.' His voice grew moist with tears. But this evoked no compassion in Tarkaratna, who said, 'What a man you are. You've eaten up everything but don't want to pay your dues. Do you expect the zamindar to feed you? You people live in a perfect kingdom, still you bad-mouth him, you're such wretches.'

An embarrassed Gafoor said, 'Why should we bad-mouth him, Baba Thakur, we don't do that. But how do I pay my taxes? I sharecrop four bighas, but there's been a famine two years in a row—the grains have all dried up. My daughter and I don't even get two meals a day. Look at the house, when it rains we spend the night in a corner, there's not even enough space to stretch our legs. Look at Mahesh, Thakur Moshai, you can count his ribs. Lend me a little hay, Thakur Moshai, let the creature feed to his heart's content for a few days.' Still speaking, he flung himself to the ground near the Brahmin's feet. Leaping backwards hastily, Tarkaratna exclaimed, 'My god, are you going to touch me?'

'No, Baba Thakur, I'm not going to touch you or anything. But give me some hay. I saw your four huge haystacks the other day, you won't even know if a little of it is gone. I don't care if we starve to death, but this poor creature cannot talk, he only stares and weeps.'

Tarkaratna said, 'And how do you propose to return the loan?'

A hopeful Gafoor said, 'I'll find a way to return it somehow, Baba Thakur, I won't cheat you.'

Snorting, Tarkaratna mimicked Gafoor, 'I won't cheat you! I'll find a way to return it somehow! What a comedian! Get out of my way. I should be getting home, it's late.' Chuckling, he took a step forward only to retreat several steps in fear. Angrily he said, 'Oh god, he's waving his horns, is he going to gore me now?'

Gafoor rose to his feet. Pointing to the bundle of fruit and moistened rice in the priest's hand, he said, 'He's smelt food, he wants to eat...'

'Wants to eat? Of course. Both master and bull are well-matched. Can't get hay to eat, and now you want fruits. Get him out of my way. Those horns, someone will be killed by them.' Tarkaratna hurried away.

Gafoor turned towards Mahesh, gazing at him in silence for a few moments. There was suffering and hunger in the bull's deep black eyes. Gafoor said, 'He wouldn't give you any, would he? They have so much, but still they won't. Never mind.' He choked, and tears began to roll down from his eyes. Going up to the animal, he stroked his back and neck, whispering, 'You are my son, Mahesh, you've grown old looking after us for eight years, I can't even give you enough to eat, but you know how much I love you.'

Mahesh responded by stretching his neck and closing his eyes in pleasure. Wiping his tears off the bull's back, Gafoor murmured, 'The zamindar took away your food, leased out the grazing ground near the crematorium just for money. How will I save your life in this year of starvation? If I turn you loose you'll eat other people's hay, you'll spoil their trees—what do I do with you! You have no strength left, people tell me to sell you off.' No sooner had Gafoor said this in his head than his tears began to roll down again. Wiping them with his hand, he looked around surreptitiously before fetching some discoloured straw from behind his dilapidated house and placing them near Mahesh's mouth, saying, 'Eat up quickly, if not there'll be...'

'Baba?'

'Yes, Ma?'

'Come and eat,' said Amina, appearing at the door. After a glance she said, 'You're giving Mahesh straw from the roof again, Baba?'

This was just what he was afraid of. Reddening, he said, 'Old rotten straw, Ma, it was falling off anyway...'

'I heard you pulling it out, Baba.'

'No, Ma, not exactly pulling it out...'

'But the wall will collapse, Baba...'

Gafoor was silent. The house was all they had left, and no one knew better than him that if he continued this way it wouldn't survive the next monsoon. But how long could they go on?

His daughter said, 'Wash your hands and come, Baba, I've served the food.'

Gafoor said, 'Bring the starch out, Ma, let me feed Mahesh first.'

'No starch left today, Baba, it dried in the pot.'

No starch? Gafoor stood in silence. His ten-year-old daughter knew that when the times were bad even this could not be wasted. He washed his hands and went in. His daughter served him rice and vegetables on a brass plate, taking some for herself on an earthen plate. Gafoor said softly, 'I'm feeling cold again, Amina, is it safe to eat with a fever?'

Amina asked anxiously, 'But didn't you say you were hungry?'

'Maybe I didn't have a fever then, Ma.'

'Then let me put it away, you can have it in the evening.'

Shaking his head, Gafoor said, 'Eating cold food will make things worse.'

'What should I do then?' asked Amina.

Gafoor pretended to think before solving the problem. He said, 'Why don't you give it to Mahesh, Ma? You can make me some fresh rice at night, can't you?'

Amina looked at him in silence for a few moments before lowering her eyes, nodding, and saying, 'Yes, Baba, I can.'

Gafoor reddened. Besides the two actors, only someone up there observed this little charade between father and daughter.

II

Five or six days later, Gafoor was seated outside his front door with an anxious expression on his face. Mahesh had not been home since yesterday morning. He himself was too weak to move, so his daughter Amina had searched high and low for the bull. Returning home in the late afternoon, she said, 'Have you heard, Baba, Manik Ghosh's family has taken our Mahesh to the police station?'

'What nonsense,' said Gafoor.

'It's true, Baba. Their servant said, "Tell your father to look for him in the Dariapur pen."'

'What did he do?'

'He got into their garden and destroyed their trees, Baba.'

Gafoor sat in silence. He had imagined all manner of mishaps that might have befallen Mahesh, but had not anticipated this. He was as harmless as he was poor, which was why he had no apprehensions of being punished so severely by any of his neighbours—Manik Ghosh, in particular, for his respect for cows was legendary.

His daughter said, 'It's getting late, Baba, aren't you going to bring Mahesh home?'

'No,' answered Gafoor.

'But they said the police will sell him in the cattle market after three days.'

'Let them sell him,' said Gafoor.

Amina did not know what exactly a cattle market was, but she had noticed her father becoming agitated whenever it was mentioned with reference to Mahesh. She left without another word.

Under cover of the night Gafoor went to Bansi's shop, and said, 'Khuro, I need a rupee,' and deposited his brass plate beneath the raised platform on which Bansi sat. Bansi was familiar with the exact weight and other details of this object. It had been pawned some five times in the past two years, for a rupee each time. So, he did not object this time either.

Mahesh was seen in his usual place the next day. Beneath the same tree, tethered to the same stake with the same rope, the same empty bowl with no food in front of him, the same questioning look in the moist, hungry, black eyes. An elderly Muslim man was examining him closely. Gafoor Mian sat nearby, his knees drawn up to his chin. When the examination was over, the man extracted a ten-rupee note from the knot in his dhoti and, smoothening it repeatedly, went up to Gafoor, saying, 'I don't need change, take the whole thing—here.'

Holding his hand out for the money, Gafoor remained sitting in silence. But just as the old Muslim's companions were about to untie the bull, he suddenly jumped to his feet, saying belligerently, 'Don't you dare touch that rope, I'm warning you.'

They were startled. The old man said in surprise, 'Why not?'

Still furious, Gafoor said, 'What do you mean, why not? It's mine to sell or not. And I'm not selling.' He threw the ten-rupee note on the ground.

They said, 'But you took an advance yesterday.'

'Here's your advance.' Retrieving two rupees from the knot in his dhoti, he flung the coins at them, and they fell with a clatter. Realizing that a quarrel was imminent, the old man said gently with a smile, 'You're putting pressure on us for two rupees more, aren't you? Go on, give his daughter two rupees more. That's what you wanted, isn't it?'

'No.'

'Are you aware that no one will give you a better price?'

'No,' said Gafoor, shaking his head vehemently.

The old man said in annoyance, 'What do you think? Only the skin is worth selling. There's nothing else in there.'

'Tauba! Tauba!' A terrible expletive suddenly escaped Gafoor's lips, and the very next moment he ran into his house threatening to have them thrashed within an inch of their lives by the zamindar's guards unless they left the village at once.

The possibility of trouble made them leave, but soon Gafoor received a summons from the zamindar's court. He realized that word had reached the landowner.

There were people both refined and unrefined in court. Glaring at Gafoor, Shibu Babu said, 'I don't know how to punish you, Gafra. Do you know where you live?'

Bowing, Gafoor said, 'I do. We're starving, or else I would have paid whatever fine you think fit.'

Everyone present was astonished. They had always considered him an obstinate and bad-tempered man. And here he was on the verge of tears, saying, 'I'll never do it again, Karta.' He proceeded to box his own ears, rubbed his nose into the ground from one end of the court to the other, and then stood up.

Shibu Babu said indulgently, 'All right, enough. Don't do all this again.'

Everyone was shocked when they heard the details. They were certain that only the grace of the zamindar and the fear of punishment had prevented the abject sinner from committing worse trangressions. Tarkaratna was present, and provided the scriptural analysis of the word 'go' for cow, enlightening everyone as to why it was forbidden to allow this godless race of heathens to live within village limits.

Gafoor did not respond to any of this, humbly accepting all the humiliation and vilification and returning home cheerfully. Borrowing the starch from the rice pots of neighbours, he gave it to Mahesh to eat, murmuring many endearments as he stroked the bull's back and horns.

III

The month of Joishtho was drawing to a close. The sun was still harsh and severe in the sky. There was no trace of mercy anywhere. People were afraid to even hope for change, hope that the skies could again be moist and pleasurable with the weight of rain-bearing clouds. It seemed that there would be no cessation to the flames burning constantly across the entire fiery earth—that they would not die down till they had consumed everything.

Gafoor returned home on such an afternoon. He was not used to working as a labourer on someone else's fields, and it had been only four or five days since the fever had subsided. He was as weak as he was exhausted. Still, he had gone out in search of work, but all he had got was the unforgiving heat and sun overhead. He could barely see for hunger and thirst. Standing at the door, he called out, 'Amina, is the food ready?'

His daughter emerged slowly and stood grasping the post without an answer.

Gafoor shouted, 'Not ready? Why not?'

'No rice at home, Baba.'

'No rice? Why didn't you tell me in the morning?'

'But I told you last night.'

Contorting his face and mocking her, Gafoor said, 'Told you last night! How can anyone remember if you tell them at night?' The harsh tone he was using stoked his anger. Contorting his face even further, he said, 'How will there be any rice? Whether the sick father gets any or not, the grown-up daughter will eat five times a day. I'm going to lock up the rice from now on. Give me some water, I'm dying of thirst. Now tell me we have no water either.'

Amina remained standing with her eyes downcast. When Gafoor realized after waiting a few moments that there was not even any water to drink at home, he could control himself no longer. Striding up to his daughter, he slapped her resoundingly, saying, 'Haramjaadi, what do you do all day? Why can't you die?'

Without a word his daughter picked up the empty pitcher and went out in the heat, wiping her eyes. Gafoor felt heartbroken as soon as she was out of sight. He alone knew how he had brought up his daughter after her mother's death. He remembered that it was not the dutiful and affectionate girl's fault. Ever since they had run out of the paltry amount of rice he had received for his work in the fields; they had not had two meals a day. On some days, just one—or not even that. His accusation that Amina was eating five times a day was as impossible as it was untrue. Nor was he unaware of the reasons for the lack of water to drink. The two or three tanks in the village were all dry. The little water there was in the pond behind Shibcharan Babu's house was not available to ordinary people. The water that could be collected by digging a hole or two in the middle of the tanks was fought over by a crowd of people.

Being a Muslim, the young girl was not even allowed near that water. She had to wait for hours, pleading for some water, and only if someone took pity on her, and poured her a little could she bring it home. He knew all this. Perhaps there had been no water that day, or no one had had the time to take pity on his daughter during the battle. Realizing that something like this must have taken place, Gafoor found his own eyes filling with tears. At that moment the zamindar's footman appeared like a messenger of death, screaming, 'Gafra, are you home?'

Gafoor answered bitterly, 'I am. Why?'

'Babu Moshai has sent for you. Come along.'

Gafoor said, 'I haven't eaten yet. I'll come later.'

Unable to tolerate such audacity, the footman swore and said, 'The Babu has ordered me to flog you and force you to come.'

Gafoor forgot himself a second time, uttering an unprintable word in retaliation and said, 'No one is a slave in the kingdom of the empress. I pay my taxes, I won't go.'

But for such a small man to give such a big reason was not just futile but also dangerous. Fortunately, such an insignificant voice would not reach the ears of the important man it was meant for—or else he would have lost both his home and his livelihood. There is no need for an elaborate account of what ensued, but when he returned from the zamindar's court an hour later and lay down in silence, his face and eyes were swollen. The primary cause of such severe punishment was Mahesh. After Gafoor had gone out, Mahesh had broken free from the post, entered the zamindar's yard, eaten his flowers, spoilt the paddy put out in the sun, and, when about to be caught, had made his escape after knocking the zamindar's youngest daughter to the ground. This was not the first time it had happened, but Gafoor had been pardoned earlier on the grounds of being poor. He might have been pardoned this time too had he begged and pleaded as in the past, but what he had said—that he paid his taxes and was no one's servant—was the kind of arrogance from a subject that Shibcharan Babu, being a zamindar, could never tolerate. Gafoor had not protested in the slightest against the thrashing and the humiliation, bearing it all in silence. Back home, too, he sat coiled up in silence. He had no awareness of hunger or thirst, but his heart was burning just like the noonday sky outside. However, when he heard his daughter's stricken cry from the yard, he leapt to his feet and ran outside to find Amina lying on the ground and Mahesh lapping up the water trickling out of the shattered pitcher. Gafoor lost his mind. Picking up the plough-head he had brought home yesterday to repair, he smashed Mahesh's head with it repeatedly.

Mahesh tried to lift his head just once, then his starving, skinny body slumped to the ground. A few tears rolled down his eyes, along with a few drops of blood from his ears. His entire body trembled once or twice, after which, stretching out his front and hind legs, Mahesh died.

Amina sobbed, 'What have you done, Baba, our Mahesh is dead.'

Gafoor had turned to stone, neither moving nor speaking, only staring at a pair of unblinking, bottomless dark eyes.

Within an hour or two, a group of cobblers from one end of the village arrived, and slinging Mahesh up on a pole took him to the dumping ground. Gafoor trembled when he saw their shining knives, but closing his eyes, he didn't say a word.

The neighbours said that the zamindar had sent someone to Tarkaratna to find out what should be done next, 'You may have to sell your house as penance.'

Gafoor did not reply to any of this, burying his face in his knees and not moving.

Late that night he woke his daughter up, saying, 'Amina, we must go.'

She had fallen asleep outside the front door. Rubbing her eyes and sitting up, she said, 'Where will we go, Baba?'

Gafoor said, 'To work at the jute mill in Phulbere.'

His daughter looked at him in astonishment. Despite all their troubles her father had never been willing to work at the jute mill. She had often heard him say that it was impossible to maintain one's faith there, that women had neither honour nor protection.

Gafoor said, 'Hurry up, Ma, we have to walk a long way.'

Amina was about to take the tumbler and the brass plate her

father ate from, but Gafoor stopped her. 'Leave them here, Ma, they will pay for my penance for Mahesh.'

He left in the dead of night, holding his daughter's hand. He had no family in this village, no one to inform. Crossing the yard, he stopped abruptly beneath the familiar tree and suddenly burst into tears. Raising his eyes to the star-studded black sky, he said, 'Allah! Punish me as you will, but my Mahesh died with a thirst. There was no land he could graze on. Do not forgive the sin of whoever it was who did not let him eat the grass you gave us, or quench his thirst with the water you gave us.'

four

EINSTEIN AND INDUBALA

BIBHUTIBHUSHAN BANDYOPADHYAY

I can't tell you why Einstein got off the train at Ranaghat on his way to Darjeeling, nor can I say why he wanted to deliver a lecture 'On…etc. etc.' at the municipal hall there. I was not present at that precise moment. Therefore, I am unable to provide you with an eyewitness account, but I can recount the story as I heard it from others.

The fact of the matter is that Einstein was possibly under some financial constraints following his exile from Nazi Germany. The objective behind his visit to India was to augment his income by delivering lectures. As everyone is aware, he had indeed embarked on a lecture tour in the country. I shall not repeat this.

Rai Bahadur Neelambar Chattopadhyay, professor of mathematics at Krishnagar College, was a worthy man. Einstein's extraordinary talk titled 'On the Unity and Universality of Forces' at the Senate Hall had overwhelmed him, as it had all the other intellectuals present. He was extremely keen that Einstein deliver a lecture at his college, but the principal appeared opposed to the idea.

'No, Rai Bahadur,' he declared, 'I have no other objection, but a German at the present juncture…'

Growing agitated (as he was wont to in the event of dissent from anyone present during the evening reading of the Bhagavad Gita at the lawyer Rammohan Babu's drawing room), the Rai Bahadur said, 'What do you mean, sir? German? What is German? Is Einstein German? Do supermen like him, sages and scientists like him, belong to particular countries? Are they to be limited by nationality? In my view—'

'I am not claiming that such is the case,' interjected the principal.

'But considering the situation today...' A bitter argument ensued between the two experienced teachers.

Proficient in philosophy, the principal cited the example of the most important preceptor of medieval scholastic philosophy, John Scotus. Despite being born in Ireland, he was so persecuted by the fundamentalists of the ninth century that he was compelled to seek sanctuary in France. He never returned to Ireland. No one cared about the real person, they only valued his viewpoint.

Eventually, as the principal refused to back down, the Rai Bahadur had no choice but to desist in his attempts. Meanwhile, he was informed that Einstein would travel to Darjeeling soon. Kept too busy by his lectures at different places in India to have set eyes on the Himalayas, Einstein was determined to visit Darjeeling, now that he was close to it.

'Why not have Einstein break his journey at Ranaghat en route to Darjeeling and deliver a lecture?' the Rai Bahadur asked himself.

He sought an audience with Einstein at the Grand Hotel in Calcutta.

'Enlighten me about Indian philosophy,' Einstein told him.

The Rai Bahadur was panic-stricken. A professor of mathematics, he knew nothing about philosophy, especially Indian philosophy. Fortunately, he had read the Gita occasionally, which enabled him to make one or two points. 'Vasamsi jirnani, etc.' Just as a person puts on new garments and so on.

Einstein said, 'Reading Max Mueller on the philosophy of the Vedanta had at one time inspired me to learn Sanskrit. In philosophy I am an intellectual disciple of Spinoza. His philosophical arguments are presented in mathematical form. Spinoza's mind is that of a mathematician's, which attracted me to him. But reading Max Mueller's essay on the Vedanta unveiled a new world to me. Spinoza's is a purely materialistic intellect, like Euclid's, where even sophistry follows predetermined paths. But at heart I am prone to imagination...'

The Rai Bahadur looked upon Einstein in wonder. 'You and

imagination!' he exclaimed.

Smiling, Einstein said, 'Do you not consider my unification of
space and time as having been cast in the mould of the imagination?'

The Rai Bahadur was even more astonished. 'You have brought
us intelligence of a new dimension,' he stammered. 'After Newton,
you are the discoverer of a new universe. To term you as someone
prone to imagination...'

But when the Rai Bahadur glanced at the scientist's long hair and
exquisitely dreamy eyes, his words did not escape his lips. Perhaps it
was impossible to be a great scientist without a powerful imagination.
He was about to speak when Einstein took a box of cigars from the
small table beside him and offered it to the Rai Bahadur. Taking a thick
cigar from the box and snipping the tip off with a penknife, he handed
it to the Rai Bahadur. The professor's Bengali sensibilities made him
shrink back. How could an insignificant mathematics teacher light
up a cigar in the presence of such a great scientist? Besides, he had
to consider the fact that Einstein was white-skinned. White-skinned
people were of the race of meat-eating gods. Accepting the cigar,
the Rai Bahadur said, 'What about you?'

'Thank you, I do not smoke.'

'I see.'

'I've been wondering...'

'What?'

'Do you think we will have an audience in Ranaghat? What
kind of place is it?'

'It is a splendid city. There will indeed be an audience.'

'I need some money at once. I left behind whatever I had in
Germany. They did not let me withdraw a single mark from my
bank. I am more or less destitute.'

'I am making special efforts in Ranaghat, sir.'

'Will a commodious theatre be available?'

'Not exactly. But there is a municipal hall which is not too
bad, it will do.'

The Rai Bahadur sought to leave soon afterwards, feeling that he had no right to make undue demands on the great man's time.

Einstein said, 'Take some pamphlets and handbills for my talks. I will inform you of the subject of my lecture in due course. How much should the tickets be?'

'Not very high—shall we say...'

'Three marks, which is ten shillings?'

'If you please, sir, no. That would be calamitous. We are a poor country. Ten shillings would amount to almost ten rupees. There is no one here who can afford tickets at that price, sir.'

'Five shillings, then?'

'Very well. One shilling for students.'

Einstein smiled. 'University students need not buy tickets. I am a schoolmaster myself. They have a claim on me. It was the same at Bombay University and at Benares Hindu University. Students won't have to pay. Here are the handbills and pamphlets...'

Trying to read the handbill he was holding, the Rai Bahadur said glumly, 'But, sir, this is in French.'

'But, of course, it is. I had them printed when giving my talks in Paris. Don't people here have any French? I was told they teach French at the university here.'

'No, sir, they don't. One or two people might have some French. It is not taught widely. English is the preferred language here. No one will understand this, sir.'

'That's true. Will you please have it translated into English and printed at a press here?'

'Er...um...all right...sir.'

The Rai Bahadur said to himself, 'I'd better take Binod's help. He knows French quite well. How many times am I going to say "I don't know" to such a great man?'

Binod Chowdhury was his eldest brother-in-law. A learned man who had several languages. Translating the handbills into English and Bengali with great enthusiasm, he said, 'Chatujjey Moshai, I'll go to Ranaghat that day. Of course, my acquaintance with the theory of relativity is only through that popular book of Lynder Bolton's.

Still, I consider Einstein a sage of our times. A genuine visionary sage who has been indoctrinated by those who discover truth. I may not be able to understand or solve equations the length of a train, but when it comes to understanding the worth of a person...'

The Rai Bahadur realized that his sly brother-in-law was mocking him. Laughing, he said, 'You must have determined my worth too, Binod Babu? Excellent.'

'God forbid! How can I say such a thing, Chatujjey Moshai?'

'You cannot?'

'Trapped in the illusion of the space-time continuum, can one swear as to what one has said, Chatujjey Moshai? Aren't you going to have lunch with us?'

'I can't. I have a great deal to do. I have to ensure that he can make some money. I shall try to prevail upon the chairman and vice-chairman of the municipality. Cunning foxes, all of them. If I can get the hall...'

'What are you saying, Chatujjey Moshai! How can anyone not let the hall be used by Einstein? It's tragic—imagine such a great scientist having to deliver lectures for money in his old age. The world does not know its greatest...'

'You are still a child, Binod. Your last statement is right, however. It will need a lot of lobbying. I'd better take the 5.40.'

The Rai Bahadur was kept extremely busy during the next few days. Meeting the chairman and the vice-chairman of the Ranaghat municipality, the headmaster of the school, barristers and attorneys, government employees and businessmen, he told everyone the entire story. To his joy, he discovered that all of them appeared pleased at the prospect of Einstein lecturing in their town. As though a god himself had come down to earth.

Abhay Babu, an attorney of advanced years, said, 'What did you say the Sahib's name is, Moshai? Aai...what?... Eenstain? I see. Yes, a famous person. These are renowned personalities—of course I have heard of him.'

Shaking with rage, the Rai Bahadur said to himself, 'My left foot, you have heard of him, you damned old idiot. Do you think this is cloth merchant Shamchand Pal? Famous indeed! Three new generations will have to be born before you will have heard of him. First, you ruin your chances of salvation by teaching people to give false witness, and now you think you can call Einstein famous! There must be limits to idiocy.'

On the appointed day, the Rai Bahadur, accompanied by several students from Krishnagar College, got off the morning train at Ranaghat. His brother-in-law, Binod Chowdhury, had written an anguished letter, stating that he had been detained by unforeseen circumstances, not everyone could have the good fortune of attending Einstein's lecture but, etc. The Rai Bahadur did feel a pang of regret, for the young man was indeed knowledgeable, and it was most unfortunate that he could not be present. Such was fate.

Emerging from the station, the Rai Bahadur came to an abrupt halt on catching sight of the wall of a house across the street. What was all this! A giant notice, in one-two-three colours, was stuck on the wall. It said:

Bani Cinema Hall (blue)
Coming! Coming!! (black)
Coming!!! (black)
Who is coming? (black)
When is she coming? (black)
Renowned filmstar Indubala Debi (red)
Today, Sunday, the 27th of Kartik, 5 p.m. (blue)
She will greet the audience!! (black)
Entrance Rs 5, 3, 2, and 1 (black)
Ladies Rs 5 and 2 (black)
Do not waste this opportunity! (red)

Disaster! Even on that winter morning, towards the end of Kartik, the Rai Bahadur had to wipe the perspiration off his forehead. He checked the date carefully once more. No doubt about it. Today, Sunday, the 27th.

Proceeding on his way distractedly, he noticed another handbill. Wherever he went, there were notices advertising the movie star's imminent arrival in three colours. He saw as many as thirty-six such advertisements at various places on the way to the house of the vice-chairman of the municipality.

Srigopal Babu, the vice-chairman, was seated on the little veranda that looked out on to his garden, dressed only in the dhoti he wore when he oiled his body. On seeing the Rai Bahadur, he adjusted his attire so he looked a bit more presentable. Smiling, he said, 'And to what do I owe this good fortune? Good morning.'

'Good morning. Were you about to go for a bath? So early, too, on a holiday.'

'Well, yes, I always bathe early.'

'At home?'

'No, I go down to the river. If I don't take a dip in the Churni... childhood habit, you see. But do sit down. Now that you are here, you must take your afternoon meal with...'

'Please do not trouble yourself. No formalities. My cousin Niren will be furious if I do not visit him. I could not call on him the last time I visited.'

'A cup of tea in that case?'

'I don't mind. All in good time. Now to get down to business— what is this new act I see? Indubala Debi at Bani Cinema today...'

'Yes, I noticed too.'

'Today of all days?'

'Indeed. That's what I was thinking too. There will be a clash.'

'Now we cannot change our date. All the arrangements have been made. Our handbills and notices have been distributed too. Einstein is coming on the Darjeeling Mail.'

'It occurred to me too. Yes, indeed... But you know what I think? Those who will go to the cinema for Indubala are not the ones who will come for the Sahib's lecture. Those who have decided to attend the Sahib's talk will certainly do so.'

The Rai Bahadur was enraged at Einstein's being referred to

as 'Sahib'. And this was the place to which he was bringing the world's greatest scientist! Was he a jute-mill manager or a railway inspector? Why refer to him as 'sahib' then? But he said none of this. All he said was, 'That is true.'

Srigopal Babu was renowned in Ranaghat for being a generous host. The tea arrived, accompanied by a plate of snacks. When he had finished his cup of tea, the Rai Bahadur left with a view to strolling around the town. He had to meet a number of people and make several arrangements.

As he was leaving, he said, 'The keys to the municipal hall...'

Srigopal Babu said, 'At once. I'm sending Rajnidhi, the servant at the hall. My servant here will go with him. They will unlock the hall and set everything up. There's a free reading room there, people will be coming to read the newspapers. It's Sunday. I'll take the help of the younger people to arrange the chairs and benches. Don't worry.'

As soon as Srigopal Babu returned after his bath, his eldest daughter (Srigopal Babu had been a widower for three years now, and his elder daughter had moved from her husband's house to run the household) said, 'Get us five tickets, Baba.'

'Tickets to what?'

'Don't you know, Indubala is coming to Bani Cinema this evening—she'll dance and sing. Everyone here is going.'

'Who's going?'

'Everyone. Ranu, Alaka, Tempi, Jatin Kaka's daughter, Dhyanrosh... They're getting a box—if you get a box for ladies it's two and a half rupees per ticket. Get a box for us.'

Srigopal Babu sounded irked. 'A box! Am I a rich man? I've been carrying this burden since 1903, I haven't been able to lay it down. All you want is money...'

Opening his drawer with an unhappy expression, he took out a ten-rupee note and some coins and handed them to his daughter.

A little later his neighbour, Radhacharan Nag, peeped into his drawing room. 'What's going on, Srigopal Babu?'

'Please come in, doctor. I hope you're going this evening.'

'Yes, that's what I came to ask. Are you?'

'Of course. Has Ranaghat ever been so fortunate? We must go.'

'That's what I was telling them at home. The expenditure... but no matter. An opportunity such as this...they were very keen at home, so I gave them ten rupees. I am nearly fifty-six, after all, who knows when I might die, at least once before that...'

'Of course. How many people have such a rare opportunity? We the citizens of Ranaghat are extremely fortunate that such a personality...'

'That's what I was telling them at home. I'm getting older, it's time to experience a few things, never mind if I have to spend some money.'

'And, besides, someone so famous...'

'Beyond a doubt. Everywhere you look, you see Indubala Debi. In advertisements, be it for soaps, perfumed oil or saris, it's all Indubala. How fortunate to see her in person, that too in a village like Ranaghat...most definitely we are fortunate.'

Srigopal Babu gaped at Radhacharan Babu unable to say a word at first. A full two minutes later he said hesitantly, 'But I wasn't talking about her. I was talking of the Sahib's lecture, at the municipal hall.'

'Which sahib?' asked Radhacharan Babu, frowning.

'You don't know? Einstein—Mr Einstein.'

'Oh, that German or is he Italian?' said Radhacharan Babu disinterestedly, as though he had only just remembered. 'Yes, my son-in-law did mention it. What is it that he's going to lecture on? But all this at our age... I haven't looked at a textbook in years. Let all those schoolboys and college students go... Hah!'

Srigopal Babu was about to protest when Radhacharan Babu continued, 'And what do you propose to do?'

'The girls are going to the cinema. But, I simply must go to the lecture. Rai Bahadur Nilambar Babu was pleading with us...'

'Who is this Rai Bahadur? Who might this Nilambar Babu be?'

'A professor at Krishnagar College. He has taken the initiative.

He specially asked me…'

Radhacharan Babu winked. 'Let me tell you something, my dear fellow. Let us go, just this once. There's a world of difference between Indubala on the screen and Indubala in the flesh. It will be the experience of a lifetime. We've seen enough of these sahibs. All you have to do is stand on the platform when the Darjeeling Mail passes twice a day. There'll be no dearth of sahibs to set your eyes on. But an opportunity like this…don't you see?'

Srigopal Babu said absently, 'Um…er…but I've given my word to the Rai Bahadur, what will he think…'

Contorting his face, Radhacharan Babu almost snarled, 'Hah! Given your word to the Rai Bahadur! Who is this Rai Bahadur! What obligation do you have, for heaven's sake! You can tell him that the girls insisted. What could you have done? And it isn't entirely untrue either.'

Srigopal Babu answered, still distracted, 'Er…yes…that is true. I must admit…'

Radhacharan Babu told him, 'That's what you can tell the Rai Bahadur when he comes. Why not request him to come along to Bani Cinema too?'

'Are you leaving?'

'I am. I'll be here on time in the evening.'

The Rai Bahadur was discussing the arrangements for the lecture at the house of the local zamindar, Niren Chatterjee.

Niren Babu was the Rai Bahadur's cousin and a lawyer. He may not have been formidable professionally, but the majority of the residents of Ranaghat could not match up to his earnings as a landlord and his inherited wealth. He was well-educated, too.

The Rai Bahadur had just finished a sumptuous lunch. The afternoon meal was taken very seriously in his wealthy cousin's household. He had all but succumbed to the attractions of sleep once or twice, but a sense of duty had kept him from giving in.

Niren Babu said, 'What will the lecture be about, Dada?'

'I'm not sure. On the unity of forces—that's the subject. Imagine the rest.'

'He has humiliated space, has he not?'

'What do you mean?'

'He says space is finite. Space is no longer endless and infinite as it once was.'

'Did you study mathematics for your MSc? Have you read *Geometry of Hyperspaces*?'

'Complex mathematics. I am aware of what you are referring to.'

'I am delighted to see that you are not just a zamindar, Niren, that you keep yourself informed of the important issues of the world. It may not be a great deal, but even the very little you know is unknown to many.'

'Is he leaving today, Dada?'

'Possibly. He said he was going to Darjeeling, and that he will get off on the way. We must pay special attention to ensure that he makes some money today.'

'Can't you bring him over to my house after the lecture, Dada? I can put him up for the night. There's no train to Darjeeling in the evening. Let him stay the night here. I'll ensure that he is comfortable.'

'Very well, I shall tell him.'

'Make sure that he stays. I'll have a report published in the newspapers tomorrow. *Free Press* and *Anandabazar* both have reporters here.'

The Rai Bahadur realized where his cousin's interest lay. But it was futile to talk of all this, for he had to ensure the success of the endeavour somehow. He would be relieved once the meeting ended.

Niren Babu's daughter Mina came into the room to say, 'Tell Baba to give us the money for the tickets, Jetha Moshai.'

'Go now, don't bother us,' scolded Niren Babu. 'We're busy.'

'Tickets for what, Minu?' asked the Rai Bahadur.

Mina said, 'Where has your mind wandered off to? Sabita next door studies in your college, she says you solve mathematics problems while walking on the road. Is that true, Jetha Moshai?'

Niren Babu rebuked her once more. 'Such a brash girl. Go now.

What a nuisance. Do you know what tickets she is talking about, Dada? Apparently, that Indubala is coming to our Bani Cinema tonight, there will be a performance, she will even deliver a lecture, the entire town is queuing up. The girls have been pestering me since morning.'

'Let them go then. They're not likely to attend Einstein's lecture in any case. But they would have had an experience to remember all their lives. Well, Minu, which one would you rather go to?'

'We'd better go to the cinema, Jetha Moshai. Ever since we saw Indubala in *Milon* we've been dying to see her in the flesh. Someone like her coming to Ranaghat...'

'...is beyond our wildest dreams.' The Rai Bahadur completed her sentence. 'Isn't that so, Minu? Give her the money for the ticket, Niren.'

Emboldened, Mina said, 'Baba and you must take us. We won't take no for an answer. Baba wants to, Jetha Moshai. It's only because he's afraid of you that...'

'What a naughty girl!' Niren Babu chided her.

Mina disappeared, laughing.

Before she left, she said, 'You have to take us, Baba. You can't get off so easily.'

⌒

It was time for the Darjeeling Mail to arrive. 5.30 p.m.

Along with several students, the Rai Bahadur, Niren Babu, and Srigopal Babu were at the station. But...what was all this? Why was there such a big crowd? All these young students, so many people, gathered on the platform. Had everyone here woken up to Einstein's presence, then? Had they all come here to welcome him as he stepped off the train? It was certainly a reception worthy of the great scientist. The platform was bursting with people. What a gathering! The Rai Bahadur was elated. The train arrived with a roar.

A long-haired, almond-eyed Einstein disembarked from a second-class compartment with a small suitcase. At the same time a lovely young lady, dressed in an expensive voile sari, her feet shod in embroidered sandals from Kashmir, a vanity bag slung over her arm, got off from the first-class carriage next to it. Two other young women accompanying her, both dark in complexion, and two menservants, busied themselves unloading her luggage.

Someone said, 'There she is. There's Indubala Debi!'

The crowd broke in her direction. The Rai Bahadur escorted Einstein through the multitude towards the exit with great difficulty.

Einstein had not realized the real reason for the turnout. He assumed the crowds were there to catch a glimpse of him. He asked the Rai Bahadur, 'Are all of them students at the local university? Are you not going to introduce me to them, Mr Mukherjee?'

The Rai Bahadur made no attempt to disabuse the simple-hearted missionary of science of his notion.

A university at Ranaghat! Alas, he had not identified this country for what it was. This was no Europe.

Niren Babu had requested the wealthy and well-known local businessman Gopal Pal for the use of his 1917 model automobile. As they got into the car, they could see large numbers of people still rushing towards the station. Someone was saying, 'The train's arrived already, there, it's standing at the platform. Run.' Another voice from the crowd said, 'She'll pass this way, no need to go in there. So crowded. We all know what she looks like, she'll be easy to spot. We've seen her so many times, just the other day in *Milon...*'

An amused Einstein said, 'These people are running to the station too? And they don't know that the person they want to see is getting into a car under their very noses. Most amusing. Which way is the university, Mr Mukherjee?'

Fortunately, a man from the crowd plunged into the path of the car and was about to be run over, whereupon the screeching of brakes and shouts from passers-by drowned the question. Once they had left the crowds behind, and reached the end of the road, Srigopal Babu and Niren Babu got out of the car. 'I hope you'll be there soon,' said the Rai Bahadur.

Srigopal Babu's response was inaudible. Niren Babu said, 'I'll be there as soon as I've taken them to the cinema. There's no one else at home to escort the ladies. With all that money spent on the tickets...'

The municipal hall was directly in front of them now. Not far from the station. But what was this? The scheduled time of the lecture was five-thirty, it was a quarter to six now, but no one had arrived. Not a soul. Only Jeebon Bhadhuri, the municipality clerk, sat behind a small table piled high with tickets, waiting for the audience.

The car drew up in front of the hall, and the Rai Bahadur helped Einstein out. Trying to summon a smile to his face, he said, 'Welcome, O Supreme Scientist. May the everlasting history of your setting foot on the soil of Ranaghat be written in letters of gold. We, the residents of Ranaghat are blessed today.'

Simultaneously, he cast a fleeting, worried glance at the empty hall. Where were the people? Where were the other representatives of Ranaghat society?

Staring in astonishment at the desolate hall, Einstein said, 'No one has arrived yet? They're all gathered at the station. I'll need a blackboard, Mr Mukherjee. I'll have to draw on it during the lecture.'

What use was a blackboard? The Rai Bahadur was a local. He had his finger on the pulse of the town. He looked around vacantly, without hope.

Coming up to him, Jeebon Bhadhuri whispered, 'Only sold three rupees worth of tickets. They've not even paid for them yet. What should I do, sir? Tell me how long I have to be here. I have to take the children to Bani Cinema. Indubala from Calcutta is here, they're badgering me at home. Just thirty-five rupees a month...but then what I say is, never mind, hardships will always be there. But people like them won't be coming from Calcutta every day. What harm will it do to spend five rupees? You'll have to let me go, sir. Who is this sahib? No one will come for his lecture, sir—who will come here today, after all!'

So saying, Jeebon Bhadhuri disappeared. Only two creatures could be seen in the unpopulated forest of chairs and benches—Einstein and the Rai Bahadur.

Einstein was busy arranging things from his bag on the table, he would need them during the lecture. The Rai Bahadur took the opportunity to go out on the pavement and cast worried glances up and down the street.

People were passing, well-dressed women went by in carriages, those on foot were running. All of them had the same destination— Bani Cinema.

A lawyer whom the Rai Bahadur knew was following the crowd swiftly, a cane in his hand. Spotting the Rai Bahadur, he said, 'Here you are. Is the Sahib here? Unfortunately, his lecture has clashed with the other thing. On any other day...no, I simply cannot... the ladies are all here, no one to escort them. I have no choice but to...you see...'

'Yes, with utmost reluctance,' the Rai Bahadur said to himself.

Half an hour passed. Six thirty. Quarter to seven. Seven.

Not a soul.

Bani Cinema was bursting with people. With the tickets sold out, hundreds were gathered outside. A group of people had tried in vain to force their way in. The balconies for ladies were so packed that there was a real fear of them collapsing. The curtains had gone up. Indubala, the filmstar, was singing—songs from her film *Milon*, renowned across the land, heard on the lips of the young and the old: 'The Swampy Wind is Startling', 'O Caged Bird from an Unknown Land', 'The King's Winged Horse', etc.

Pushing his way through the crowd, Rai Bahadur Neelambar Chattopadhyay entered the cinema hall, only to be astonished at the sight of Srigopal Babu. Niren Babu was sitting nearby. 'Oh, you here too?' he said.

Looking extremely guilty, Srigopal Babu said, 'I didn't really want to, what to do, the girls...had to bring them...er...how did the Sahib's lecture go? No crowd?'

'How could there be? All of you are here. Who's going to listen to him?'

'Where's the Sahib? Has he left?'

'Here he is.'

Einstein himself was standing behind the Rai Bahadur.

Jumping to his feet, Srigopal Babu took Einstein's hand and tenderly deposited him in his own seat.

I have saved a newspaper clipping on the events of the day. It is reproduced here.

> The price of potatoes is on the rise. Paddy is cheaper. Malaria has made an appearance. The attention of health department officials has been drawn to it, thanks to the efforts of the worthy subdivisional officer.
>
> The renowned film star Indubala Debi made an appearance at the Bani Cinema this past week. She conquered all hearts with her prowess at dancing and her heavenly singing talent. The display of high art visible in her performance of the Black Bat Dance shall never be forgotten by the residents of Ranaghat. There was an unprecedented gathering of people on the occasion at the aforementioned cinema house—a majestic spectacle in its own right. The large gathering damaged the beams beneath the ladies' balcony, the timely discovery of which saved everyone present from an accident.
>
> The famous German scientist Einstein had stopped at Ranaghat on his way to Darjeeling in order to deliver a lecture at the Municipal Hall. He too was among the audience at Bani Cinema House during Indubala's dance performance.

five

THE MUSIC ROOM

TARASHANKAR BANDYOPADHYAY

As was his habit, Bishwambhar Roy was pacing on the terrace after waking up at 3 a.m. Ananta, the aged retainer, laid out the carpet, cushion and bolster, and went downstairs to fetch the hookah and tobacco. Bishwambhar glanced at the arrangement, but did not sit down, continuing to walk to and fro as before, his head bent. Not very far away, beneath the Kali temple belonging to the Roys, the Ganga flowed by in a thin, clear stream.

Venus sparkled brightly in the southwestern sky. It seemed to be in competition with a particularly powerful electric light shining unblinkingly from the roof of the neighbouring Ganguly mansion—they were the noveau riche of the area. The clock on their roof struck three now. For two hundred years, the only clock in this area that had rung out the hours was in the Roy residence. But it had fallen silent. These days, habit and the murmuring of pigeons were what woke Bishwambhar Babu up. They began their cooing as soon as Venus was visible in the sky. A sweet fragrance wafted in with the breeze at dawn. Spring no longer arrived with pomp and ceremony at the Roys' home. Nor did the family have the means to lay out expensive gifts at its feet anymore. The flowers in the garden had shrivelled from lack of care. Only a few trees remained—muchkunda, bokul, nageshwar, champa. Like the family, they had no branches either, and were as withered as this palace with enormous cracks in its walls. Indeed, cavities had appeared within the trunks of some of the trees. Who knew whether it was Spring that tried to show itself on the edges of the worn-out branches, or whether it was the branches that tried to capture Spring?

A horse neighed in the stable.

Setting the bowl of tobacco on the hookah, Ananta said, 'Huzoor.'
Startled out of his reverie, Bishwambhar said, 'Hmm!'

As soon as he lowered himself on to the carpet, Ananta offered
him the pipe. The horse neighed again downstairs.

Drawing gently on the pipe, Bishwambhar Babu said, 'The
muchkunda flowers have begun to blossom, add them to my sharbot
from today.'

Ananta said diffidently, 'The petals aren't ripe yet.'

The horse was neighing impatiently in the stable. Sighing, Roy
said with a trace of pique, 'Is that blasted Netai sleeping like the
dead because he's getting older? Go call him. Tufan is restless. Can't
you hear him?'

Tufan was the name of the horse. The only survivor in the
nine stables in the Roy residence. The aged Tufan had been the
indomitable mount of Bishwambhar Roy in the prime of his life,
twenty-five years ago. In those days—not just in those days, even
two years ago—travellers on the imperial road would ask the locals
when they saw the large, fair-skinned man with a magnificent turban
on his head seated astride the gigantic white horse, 'Who is he?'

People would answer, 'He is our ruler, Bishwambhar Roy. A
famous hunter, he shoots tigers for sport.'

Raising his eyes reverentially, the stranger would watch as the
white horse disappeared into the distance with its rider. Only a spiral
of dust would be visible, a tornado hurtling towards the horizon
to merge with it.

The unconquerable Tufan would gallop off with Bishwambhar
Roy at dawn every day. Two years ago, when the Gangulys, traders by
profession, announced their new status of landowner in every village
with great fanfare, Roy had stopped riding Tufan. Since then, it had
been Netai, the stable-hand, who led him by the reins along the roads.

Taraprasanna, the manager of the estate, had said one day, 'Won't
your health suffer if you give up such a long-standing practice?'

The look in Bishwambhar's eyes stopped him from going any
further.

Roy had given just a two–word answer, 'Shame, Taraprasanna.'

Ananta was about to go downstairs. Bishwambhar called him back, 'Ananta.'

He turned.

Roy said, 'Netai was saying Tufan isn't getting his feed properly.'

Ananta said, 'It has not been a good season for chickpeas, so Nayeb Babu said…'

'Hmm.'

After a few drags on his hookah, he said, 'Has Tufan become very thin?'

Ananta said softy, 'No. Not really…'

'Hmm.'

A little later he said, 'Give him his entire feed, all right? Tell Nayeb I told him. Go now and send Netai to me…'

Ananta left. Leaning back on his bolster, Bishwambhar lifted his eyes to the sky. The pipe lay next to him. The stars were going out one by one. Bishwambhar began to rub his broad chest absently… one…two… These were the very ribs he had injured the first time he had tried to ride Tufan! What an animal Tufan had been that day! Such spirit! He would calm down only at the sound of music. When there was music he never set a foot out of rhythm. How he danced, arching his neck!

Bishwambhar Babu rose to his feet. Like constellations of stars that paled in the dazzling light of the sun, memories from the past were overshadowed by the glory of the Roy dynasty. The brightest star of these memories was Tufan, who dazzled in the sky tonight. It had been two years since Bishwambhar Babu had been downstairs. Today, he felt an urge to see Tufan. Slipping his feet into his wooden clogs, Roy descended to the first floor. The long and wide veranda of the pillared mansion resounded to the ringing sound of his footsteps. Startled from their little cubbyholes atop the arches in the veranda, several bats flew away, flapping their wings. More bats could be heard inside the locked rooms on the other side. The storage room for mattresses and pillows was next to the staircase leading to the roof. Bits of cotton were strewn on the floor. This was followed by the storage room for sheets, carpets and cushions, from which a stench emanated, as some of its contents must have rotted away. In the next room there was a ringing sound along with the beating of wings. Lamps were stacked in here. The Belgian glass chandeliers may have been swaying. The room after this one, in the corner, was also for the mattresses and bedding for different bedrooms. It was empty now.

Roy turned eastwards. This was the section for leaseholders. There were many rich and influential leaseholders in different districts under the Roys. The number of them who paid taxes ranging from five hundred to five thousand rupees was not insignificant. They stayed here during their visits to the estate. Large paintings hung on the veranda walls. Roy raised his face to look at them. The first one had no painting or glass, only a frame. The second had no glass. The space for the third was vacant. Sighing, Roy resumed walking, his head bowed. The pigeons murmured incessantly on the rafters overhead.

The staircase going down was at the end of the east veranda. Roy went downstairs. He was here for the first time in two years. The records rooms were piled high with documents. It was a history of the seven Roys. Bishwambhar Roy belonged to the seventh generation of zamindars. He smiled faintly in the darkness, recalling the founder of the family, who was believed to have said, 'You need the grace of Saraswati if you want to bind down Lakshmi. Ink scrawls on paper make for shackles very difficult to break. Make sure to keep the chains of your accounts in perfect shape, so that the fickle goddess has no opportunity to escape.' He used to be the nawab's land revenues officer.

Paper, pen and ink still remained, but Lakshmi had vanished.

A dog lying in the darkness of the veranda began to howl. Roy proceeded on his way without paying attention to it. The dog stopped barking and wagging its tail, it began to accompany Roy as he made his rounds. No one had taken it in as a pet. It must have been a descendant of one of the dogs that had once lived on leftovers here.

Beyond the entrance to the office lay a cowshed to the right and the stables to the left.

Further along the road was the shrine to the deities.

Roy called out, 'Netai!'

A voice answered reverentially, 'Huzoor!'

The response was buried beneath Tufan's loud neighing. An elephant was heard trumpeting from the other side.

Roy went up to the aged Tufan, who stamped his hoof impatiently, as excited as a child. Caressing his face, Roy murmured, 'My boy!'

Tufan rubbed his head against his master's hand. Meanwhile, the elephant had grown impatient too, calling constantly and trying to break free of the shackle around his leg. Aware of his master's arrival, Rahmat, the mahout, went up to the elephant, reproving Roy mildly, 'Chhoto Ginni will break her chains, Huzoor.'

The female elephant was named Chhoto Ginni, the younger wife. She had come as dowry for Bishwambhar's mother's wedding. Her name was Moti. But the head of the family, Dhaneshwar Roy, had become besotted with Moti after their hunts together. Moti had once lifted a leopard in her trunk and crushed it to death under her feet. The excessive care lavished on Moti had led Bishwambhar's mother to call the elephant her husband's second wife. 'Good idea, Roy Ginni,' her husband had said, 'let her name be Ginni too.'

Bishwambhar Babu's mother had said, 'Not just Ginni, but Chhoto Ginni, she's your second wife.'

At Rahmat's appeal Bishwambhar Babu left Tufan and went up to Chhoto Ginni. Tufan's angry neigh was heard. Roy said to Chhoto Ginni, 'Well, Ma Lakshmi?' Chhoto Ginni held up her coiled trunk in front of him. This was a request to him to mount her, for Roy used to place one foot in the crook of her trunk when climbing onto her back.

Caressing her trunk, Roy said, 'Not now, Ma.'

Chhoto Ginni understood. Placing her trunk on his shoulder,

she stood quietly like a docile little girl. Roy said, 'Take Tufan for a walk, Netai.'

With great hesitation Netai said, 'Tufan won't come with me today, Huzoor. Now that he has seen you, unless you ride him...'

Roy did not respond. Continuing to caress Chhoto Ginni's trunk, he said, 'You're a lovely girl.'

Suddenly the silence of the dawn was shattered by a band playing unfamiliar music. Startled, Roy pushed Chhoto Ginni's trunk away from his shoulder and asked, 'What's that?'

Netai answered softly, 'It's the Gangulys' son's mukhebhaat. His first meal.'

Out of habit, Roy said, 'Hmm.'

Tufan had started dancing in rhythm to the music, arching his neck. Roy went up to him with a smile. Behind him the chain around Chhoto Ginni's leg also began to ring in time like anklets.

Roy walked past the main entrance to enter the darkened palace. He remembered that once upon a time Tufan and Chhoto Ginni would dance the same way every morning to the music that was played here.

Climbing up to the first floor, he called out, 'Ananta!'

'Yes, sir.'

'Send for Nayeb.'

Roy went up to the roof and sat down. When Taraprasanna appeared, he said, 'It's Mahim Ganguly's son's annaprashon today?'

'Yes, sir.'

'I presume they have sent an invitation.'

Taraprasanna answered hesitantly, 'Yes.'

'Send a guinea and a plate—a bronze plate.'

Taraprasanna stood there in silence. He did not dare protest. But the idea did not meet with his approval.

Roy said, 'Take a guinea from me.'

The manager left. Roy sat in silence. Ananta replaced the tobacco bowl and held the pipe out to him, saying, 'Huzoor.'

Roy reached for it out of habit. Then he said, 'Bring out the seat and cover and bells for Chhoto Ginni. Nayeb will go to the Gangulys with the present.'

～

The Roys had amassed wealth over three generations. The fourth generation had ruled. The fifth and sixth squandered everything and accumulated debt. During the seventh generation, in Bishwambhar's era, the goddess of wealth was drowned in an ocean of debt. Like the king of the gods without his consort, Bishwambhar sat back and watched. That was not all. In its seventh generation, the dynasty ran out of descendants. Following the orders of the judges' court and the high court, the fortunes of the Roy family were wiped out. There was only the privy council's decision to wait for.

Almost in defiance, rousing celebrations began at the Roy residence. Luxurious feasts and meals for the poor flowed like the tide on a full moon night. And then came the ebbing, whose currents sucked out all the flow from the Roys. Within a week the gaiety turned to venom. There was an outbreak of cholera. In the space of just seven days, Roy's wife, both his sons, his daughter, and several relatives died. Only Bishwambhar Roy survived, like the Vindhya mountains waiting for Agastya to return, awaiting death, his head bowed forever.

No, that's not correct. No one knows whether he began his vigil for death that very day, but he did not bow his head. That came two years later, the day the privy council announced its judgement. For even after the death of his wife and children, the lights had come on in the music room, the strains of the sitar and the sarangi and the sound of anklets had been heard. The calm of the nights had been shattered by loud laughter. Chhoto Ginni had been dressed to go out on hunts. Tufan had torn free of the ropes in anger and despair.

Be that as it may, the judgement of the privy council meant that the Roys lost all their property. Only the house and the long-standing rent-free land remained. The forefathers had bound this land with ink on paper so firmly that no one could touch it. It paid for the rituals to the gods, for Chhoto Ginni's food, for Rahmat's salary. In short, whatever had remained was thanks to this. The larder was still replenished on the first of the month.

There was superb badshabhog rice every day, the lake on the rent-free land provided fish, and because birds flocked to the lake, they were available too. All this was in the past, but now beyond memory. Which was why this decrepit building with cracks everywhere was still called a palace, and why Bishwambhar Roy was still addressed as 'Huzoor'.

This was the fuel for the nouveau riche Gangulys' indignation. They had erected a temple of gold behind a barren mountain, but the world had eyes only for the barren mountain and not their temple of gold. The aged elephant was held in higher regard than their expensive car.

Mahim Ganguly said to himself one day, 'I must demolish the peak of that barren mountain.'

~

As soon as the ceremonial bells went up on Chhoto Ginni's back, she began to sway like a proud woman. The bells began to chime.

Taraprasanna appeared before Bishwambhar Babu, who was sitting in the hall. This was the only room he used now. Portraits of the men of the Roy family and their wives were hung on the walls. All of them had been painted during their advancing years. All of them were dressed in shawls bearing the goddess Kali's name with sacred rudraksha necklaces around their necks, and counting beads in their hands. Bishwambhar Babu was gazing at the portraits. When Nayeb entered, he turned towards Ananta slowly and said, 'Ananta, bring me my box.'

From it he extracted the key to the iron safe and unlocked it. A small chest of money was resplendent on the top shelf. Two or three boxes lay on the shelf below. Roy pulled out one of them, an exquisitely beautiful one. This was his dead wife's jewellery case. He opened it. It was all but empty. All that remained by way of ornaments was a chain used to adorn the parting in the hair. For seven generations it had been used to welcome the new bride home. Nothing else was left. A few gold coins lay in a compartment.

Some of these were from the ashirbaad ceremony before the marriage, the ritual before the actual wedding, while the rest were the first gifts from a young Bishwambhar to his wife. He had received them as tribute during his tours. Taking one of them, he handed it in silence to the manager. Taraprasanna left.

The sound of Chhoto Ginni's bells became louder a little later. Roy walked over to the window.

The elephant's head had been oiled, with a line of vermilion around the part of her brow smeared with oil. Chhoto Ginni ambled along.

In the afternoon, the Gangulys' gleaming car drew up at the dilapidated main gate of the Roy residence. Mahim Ganguly himself stepped out. Taraprasanna rushed out, welcoming him warmly, 'Do come in.'

Ananta had observed the arrival from the first floor. Going downstairs quickly, he opened the doors to the main drawing room.

Mahim said, 'Where's Thakur Da, I want to meet him.'

The Gangulys had always been traders in the Roys' realm. Even Mahim's father, Janardan, used to address the head of the Roy family as 'Huzoor'. Taraprasanna was displeased at Mahim's tone, but he kept his expression pleasant, saying, 'Huzoor isn't awake yet. He is taking a nap after his meal.'

Mahim said, 'Have him woken up.'

With a wan smile, Taraprasanna said, 'None of us dares do that. You'd better give your message, I will pass it on.'

Mahim said impatiently, 'No, I must meet him personally.'

Ananta appeared, and offered Ganguly sharbot in a silver tumbler. Accepting the glass, Mahim asked Ananta, 'Is Thakur Da up?'

'He is. I have informed him you are here. He is asking for you.'

Draining the glass, Mahim rose to his feet, saying, 'What a lovely flavour. What's this made from?'

Ananta lied, 'The flavouring is from Kashi, I don't exactly know.'

Entering the room on the first floor, Mahim said, 'We didn't see you at the afternoon feast, Thakur Da.'

Bishwambhar smiled and said, 'Come in, sit down.'

Mahim said, 'I was very upset, Thakur Da.'

Smiling again, Bishwambhar said, 'Think of me as an old man and forget my misdemeanour. My body won't take it if I break my routine at this age.'

Mahim replied, 'I won't be upset, but you have to come tonight.'

Bishwambhar was silent, pretending to draw on his hookah.

Mahim continued, 'I've got baijis from Lucknow coming to dance. Only you can appreciate their true worth, not any of us.'

Smoking in silence for a few minutes, Bishwambhar put his pipe aside. Then he said, 'I am not well at all, Mahim, I have chest pain these days which afflicts me badly at times.'

After a few minutes of silence, Mahim said, 'Very well, I shall go now, Thakur Da. I have to go into town to fetch the sahibs, they're coming, you see.'

Bishwambhar only said, 'Don't be upset, please.'

Mahim left. Stopping in the veranda, he said suddenly, 'What a state you've allowed the house to fall into, Thakur Da, it needs repairs.'

No one answered.

Ananta only said, 'Goodbye, Huzoor.'

～

The ground floor of the Ganguly residence was ablaze with light. There were multicoloured lights all around the marquee. A generator had been set up, and electric wires strung up for all the lights. The pillars were decorated with leaves and flowers. Colourful streamers hung everywhere. Thick sheets had been spread out on the lawn for the music session. There were rows of chairs on one side and mattresses and bolsters on the other for the audience. The women were seated at a distance.

The place filled up by 8 p.m. The tabla and the sarangi players were tuning their instruments. Two dancers from the northern provinces sat down, dressed in their peshwaj and urnis. The hubbub died down instantly. Now this was beauty.

The performance began. Mahim Ganguly was seated amongst the eminent guests on the chairs.

The older of the dancers was singing. Her long alaap seemed to send the gathering to sleep. The audience began to murmur. The eminent listeners were having a laugh about something. The chaprasis stood behind the hoi polloi, occasionally shouting to them to be quiet.

As the song was about to end Mahim said out of politeness, 'Wonderful.' The dancer seemed a little demoralized. Finishing her song, she sat down. Exchanging smiles with the younger dancer, she gestured to her to begin.

Soon everyone was absorbed in the performance. Her lively singing and dancing seemed to set a mountain stream flowing. Cries of admiration rose from the audience. The eminent listeners showered currency notes on the dancer in approval.

And then again, and again, and again. There was no lethargy anymore. When it ended, Mahim called the dancers and told them, 'Everyone's very happy.'

The older one said with a salaam, 'So generous of you.'

Indeed, there was no end to Mahim's generosity. Instead of the three days for which the dancers had been booked, the music sessions lasted for five.

On the day of their departure he displayed even more generosity. Sending them on their way, he said, 'Our raja lives here, pay him a visit. Bishwambhar Roy is a wealthy connoisseur. You may get an engagement to perform.'

The older one said respectfully, 'We have heard about him, Huzoor. We will certainly visit him. I had always planned to.'

Taraprasanna was furious. He had realized that this was a sly move on Mahim Ganguly's part. He was trying to humiliate Roy with a whore. Sternly he said, 'Babu is not well, there will be no performance.'

The older baiji said, 'If you could kindly...'

Interrupting, Taraprasanna said, 'Impossible.'

The dancer said regretfully, 'My ill fortune.'

They were preparing to leave when a voice rang out from the first floor.

'Taraprasanna!'

When he went upstairs, Bishwambhar Babu asked, 'Who are they?'

Taraprasanna answered with his eyes on the floor, 'They had come for the mujra at the Gangulys.'

'Hmm.' After a pause he said, 'You turned them away?'

'Salaam, Huzoor.' So saying the baiji bowed low before him.

From where they had been seated Bishwambhar Roy's veranda and room were partially visible. On hearing his voice, the dancer had come up to him.

Bishwambhar was annoyed that she had come into his presence without being announced, but his anger did not last. The beauty of the dancers melted his heart.

Bowing again, the baiji said, 'Forgive my transgression, meherbaan; we have come without warning.'

Bishwambhar was gazing at her beauty. A complexion like pomegranate seeds, kohl-lined eyes curving upwards, intoxicating glances, lips like rose petals, a tall figure, narrow waist, innate rhythms of dance in her body, waiting for a signal to come alive.

With a pleasant smile, Bishwambhar said, 'Take a seat.'

Sitting down on a nearby carpet deferentially, the baiji said, 'Your servant is here to sing for you at your court, Huzoor.'

Bishwambhar was about to say that he was unwell. But, he felt ashamed, the idea of lying to a tawaif seemed abhorrent.

The baiji said, 'I have heard everyone say Huzoor Bahadur is a connoisseur. Even Ganguly Babu said you are the king here.'

The sound from Roy's pipe ceased. With a smile he looked

at the baiji and said, 'We will have a majlis this evening.' Then he called for Ananta.

Ananta was waiting outside. When he came in Roy said, 'Make arrangements for them to stay. Unlock one of the talukdars' rooms.'

Ananta said, 'Follow me.'

Although the baiji could not speak Bangla, she could follow it perfectly. Rising to her feet and bowing low, she said, 'I am fortunate, Huzoor is most gracious.'

She followed Ananta out of the room.

Taraprasanna had been standing by in silence. A little later, he said, 'They took one hundred rupees a night from the Gangulys.'

'Hmm.'

Drawing on his pipe, Roy said, 'Do you have…'

He began to smoke again, the question unfinished. Taraprasanna said, 'The treasury has just about a hundred and fifty rupees.'

After some thought Roy brought the same box out of his iron safe. Taking the chain out, he handed it to Taraprasanna, saying, 'Write in the accounts book that this has been purchased for Anandamoyee, at a cost of one hundred and fifty rupees.'

Anandamoyee was the resident deity of the Roy family—the goddess Kali in stone.

—

After many years the Roy residence resounded with the clanging of doors being unlocked. The doors and windows of the music room were opened. The padlock was removed from the room where the chandeliers were stored. Light entered the premises.

Ananta was dusting the rooms. Netai and Rahmat were helping him. The long-standing housemaid was washing the big hookahs, the large trays, the ittar bowls. Taraprasanna was supervising everyone.

Ananta said, 'We have to send someone to the town, Nayeb Babu.'

The manager said, 'I've made a list. Here, see if I've missed out anything.'

Listening to his recital of the items to be procured, Ananta said,

'It's all there, but you've forgotten a couple of things. Two bottles of ittar and a few vilayti bottles.'

Taraprasanna said, 'There was one, wasn't there?'

'Only a little left in it. He has a drink now and then. But if you want some today, one bottle won't be enough, Nayeb Babu.'

Taraprasanna said, 'But whom should I send? Can someone walk there and be back by the evening?'

Ananta said hesitantly, 'Let Netai take Tufan then.'

Netai said, 'Without Huzoor's instructions…'

Taraprasanna said, 'Very well, I'll tell him.'

Bishwambhar Babu was lying on his bed. When Taraprasanna appeared, he said, 'I was about to send for you. Go over to the Gangulys and invite Mahim. We have to hand-pick guests from the village. You must go yourself to the Gangulys.'

Tarprasanna said, 'I shall.'

Roy said, 'Ask for Chhoto Ginni to be saddled.'

After a pause the administrator said, 'Netai needs to take Tufan to the town.'

'Hmm.'

A little later he said, 'Let him, then.'

Some time later he opened the window on hearing Tufan neigh outside. The back window offered a clear view of the path leading to the house, enveloped in the shadows of the deodar trees. The sound of hoofbeats rang along it. Roy saw Tufan galloping along, his neck arched, as spirited as always.

And then after some more time, the bells on Chhoto Ginni began to ring.

Bishwambhar Roy sat up. Through the window he saw the elephant walking along proudly. Leaving his bed, he began to pace up and down. His body and mind were both restless.

Celebrations. After a long time, there were celebrations in the Roy residence.

A tinkling sound emerged from the other side—probably from the music room. The sound of Belgian glass chandeliers. Roy went out into the veranda. Ananta was putting the chandeliers up on the hooks. On hearing footsteps, he turned towards the door and found Bishwambhar Roy standing there. He was gazing at the paintings on the walls. Portraits of various members of the Roy family in their youth were hung on the wall, running all around the enormous hall. From the founder Bhubaneshwar Roy to him—all the portraits were of people immersed in various poses of indulgence and sportsmanship. His great-grandfather, Ravaneshwar Roy, stood with his foot planted on a tiger he had hunted, with a spear in his hand and a shield strapped across his back. His father, Dhaneshwar, was seated on a cushion, with Chhoto Ginni by his side. A young Bishwambhar was astride Tufan.

The Roy family had lived out a storm in this room. Memories came flooding back to him. The indomitable Ravaneshwar was the first of the profligate sons in the family. It was he who had had this music room made, but had not dared to enjoy its pleasures. On the first day that he had organized a concert in this room, his wife and children had all died. The candles had been snuffed out in the candlestands when only half-used. He hadn't had the courage to unlock the door again.

Perhaps it would have been best for the Roys to have been wiped out forever that same day. But, with the approval of his family, Ravaneshwar had married his sister-in-law, claiming that such was the order of the deity Anandamoyee. It was his son, Tarakeshwar, who had again had the doors to the music room opened and the chandeliers lit. In a single night he had, in competition with a wealthy friend, showered five hundred gold coins on a baiji. Roy recalled Chandrabai. Away from his friends, the hours he had stolen with Chandra after the performance, were etched forever in his heart. She was like a bouquet of flowers.

Ananta had stopped working. As he gazed at his master, his hands refused to move. Roy's sombre face was red—as though a vein through which blood coursed upwards had burst, spraying its contents on his face.

Ananta brought sharbot in a silver tumbler on a tray and presented it in silence to Roy before sundown. Roy gazed at him, dressed in a zari-embossed uniform, with a cummerbund round his waist and a turban on his head, the family insignia resplendent on his breast. He took the tumbler in silence. Ananta left, returning a little later carrying a crinkled dhoti, a thin white kurta in the Muslim style, and a silk shawl. Roy recognized the outfit as the one made for him five years ago when he had visited a zamindar friend in Murshidabad.

He asked, 'Is everything all right?'

Ananta said softly, 'The lights are being turned on, Huzoor.'

'The guests?'

Ananta said, 'The Bhandaris, father and son, from Nakhrazda have arrived. Four of their sentries have come too, they are at the gate.'

The horn of a motor car was then heard.

Ananta rushed downstairs. Mahim Ganguly had arrived. Footsteps were heard on the stairs. Warm welcoming words to guests and polite conversations were audible downstairs. The music room was waking up to the soft strains of music. The tabla could be heard too. They were tuning up.

Ananta appeared at the door, saying, 'Huzoor.'

Bishwambhar had changed his clothes and was pacing around the room. He responded, 'Hmm.'

'The session cannot start...'

'Hmm.'

Moments later, Bishwambhar said, 'Bring me my shoes.'

Hesitating, Ananta opened the drawer of the corner table and took out a bottle of Scotch and a glass. Putting them on the table, he extracted the shoes and dusted them. Roy paused for a moment before resuming his pacing. Downstairs, the music grew louder.

Ananta said, 'Huzoor.'

Roy only murmured, 'Hmm.'

He walked around the room a few more times, a bit faster now. Ananta stood, waiting. Walking up to the table, Roy said, 'Soda.'

Mattresses, covered with sheets, had been laid out in long rows against three walls of the enormous hall. Bolsters were piled behind them. Three Belgian chandeliers dangling from the ceiling were lit up. The flames of the lamps placed in niches on the wall trembled occasionally in the breeze.

A few of the lights in the chandelier and some of the lamps had gone out. Short-lived but long shadows were being cast on the walls in places, like hidden sorrows.

The music had begun, but the pace was still slow. The resonance of the instruments was beginning to grow. Thirty or forty gentlemen were seated all around, conversing softly. Four or five hookahs were being used. The two tawaifs were seated in silence. Only Mahim Ganguly could be heard from time to time. Drawing on his cigarette, he pointed upwards, saying, 'Some of the lights have gone out.' No one answered. He said loudly, 'Nayeb Babu!' When Taraprasanna appeared at the door he continued, 'The lights are not bright enough. Tell my driver to fetch a couple of Petromax lanterns.'

Taraprasanna was silent. Only the older of the dancers said, almost to herself, 'Do those lights befit this room?'

At the sound of heavy footsteps outside, Taraprasanna looked over his shoulder and stepped away respectfully. Moments later Bishwambhar Roy appeared at the door. The two baijis rose to their feet reverentially. Everyone else at the majlis rose too. Mahim also half rose automatically before suddenly resuming his seat.

Smiling, Roy said, 'Pardon me for being late.' Then he took his seat. Mahim pushed away the bolster he was reclining against, dusting it with his handkerchief and muttering in irritation, 'How filthy it is!' Taraprasanna distributed the ittar. Changing the tobacco bowls on all the hookahs, Ananta placed Roy's personal hookah before him and handed him the pipe.

The older baiji rose and bowed. The music began. The same long and slow alaap. But there was a difference tonight. The gathering was silent. Roy sat there in a dignified manner, his eyes closed. His gigantic frame swayed in time to the slow rhythm of the music. After a while his left hand reached out and stroked the bolster by his side lightly. The tabla kept time with the singing. Roy opened his eyes to discover the dancer's anklets responding. The performance started. The dance of a peacock urgently fanning its tail upon seeing clouds in the sky. Her neck was bent slightly, her hands held the two ends of her peshwaj, she danced in step like the bird, her anklets ringing.

Roy exclaimed, 'Superb!'

At once the dancing feet stopped. The tabla sounded a finishing note.

Sidling up to Roy, Mahim said, 'Thakur Da, this is no good, my throat is parched. Krishnabai has turned us cold.'

Krishnabai smiled faintly. Possibly, she had understood. Ananta offered Mahim some sharbot. Mahim said, 'Never mind, staying up nights has given me a cold.'

Roy gestured to Ananta with a smile.

Ananta left and returned with whisky, soda and glasses on a large tray.

Preparing the drink, Ananta offered a glass to Mahim and then looked at the gathering with the second glass in his hand. Everyone looked at the floor. Deferentially, he approached Bishwambhar Babu, who accepted the glass. Mahim had been eyeing the younger baiji for a long time. Now, shifting a little, he said, 'Pearibai, can you light a fire now!'

Peari began to sing. A quick rhythm. Roy had his eyes closed, he only parted them slightly to say, 'Slower.'

But out of sheer habit, Peari used her lively dancing and vigorous singing to spread a wave of airy excitement across the music room.

Roy was frowning. Mahim's unbecoming excitement had disturbed him.

And, yet, his body was swaying like a cobra to the snake charmer's tune. The flow of blood in his veins, true to the blood of the Roys, had quickened. Peari was dancing like a multihued butterfly. Roy was reminded of Zohra of Lucknow. Krishnabai resembled Chandrabai of Delhi. Chandrabai, who had been a fond chapter. in his life.

Roy's memories came flooding back. His thoughts were interrupted by the ringing of coins. Mahim gave Peari some money. He had broken the rule. The host had the first right to offer an inaam. Roy looked around in a flash. Nothing—no silver salver before him, no receptacle of coins. He remained sitting, his eyes on the floor. Krishnabai had begun singing now. Like a wave her song swept from one end of the gathering to the other. Its quickened rhythms struck at the hearts of the listeners. She was singing—Keshava is playing his flute, an overflowing Yamuna is back in high tide, battering the banks with its waves, it is trying to draw Krishna to its breast. The exuberance of the dancing and the singing was exquisite. Roy had forgotten everything else. The music ended. Roy exclaimed, 'Beautiful, Chandra!'

With a salaam Krishnabai said, 'Your servant's name is Krishnabai.'

Mahim called out, 'Here's something for you, Krishnabai.'

Roy rose to his feet. He walked slowly out of the room. The sound of his footsteps disappeared along the length of the veranda.

Mahim said, 'One more from you, Pearibai.'

Krishnabai said, 'Let Huzoor Bahadur return.'

Mahim said, 'He'll be back soon, it doesn't matter. There, that's probably him.'

Not Roy—it was Taraprasanna who entered. He placed a silver bowl in the middle of the room. In it were two gold coins.

Taraprasanna said, 'Inaam from Babu.'

An impatient Mahim asked, 'Where is he?'

'He has a pain in his chest. He cannot return. Please carry on. He has asked me to apologize on his behalf.'

A quiet murmur rose amongst the gathering.

Rising to his feet, Mahim stretched disdainfully and said, 'It's time I left, Taraprasanna. The Sahib will be here tomorrow.'

Taraprasanna did not object. The rest of the guests got up too. The session ended.

Roy's wife's jewellery-box was open on the floor. It was empty. Roy was pacing about the room, paying no heed to anything, his head held high. The prestige of the Roys was intact. Pride and the effect of alcohol was making his blood tingle. Time and place had become confused in his mind. He left the room absently, attracted by the glow of lights in the music room. When he entered it he saw that it was empty. Only the descendants of the Roy family were awake on the walls. Bishwambhar looked out through the open window. The world was flooded with moonlight. The spring breeze was redolent with the fragrance of muchkunda flowers. Somewhere on a tree a brainfever bird repeated indefatigably, 'Piyu kahan, piyu kahan!' Music stirred in Roy's heart. Behag, sung by Chandra in a forgotten time. The moon rode high in the sky. He turned around at the sound of footsteps. Ananta was preparing to put out the lights.

Roy stopped him, saying, 'Not yet.'

Ananta made to leave. Roy said, 'Bring me my esraj.'

Ananta fetched the instrument. Sitting down with it at the window, Roy said, 'Pour.'

He pointed to the uncorked bottle on the tray. Ananta poured him a drink and left.

The bow ran across the strings. Melody arose in the silent palace. Roy was playing the esraj, rapt. Was the esraj speaking? The softly spoken words could be heard clearly.

The lyrics rang in Roy's ears. The hapless woman at midnight, the venomous guard at the door. 'I cannot sleep, in pretend slumber I think of you, why did you have to play the flute right now, my love?'

Pushing his esraj away, Roy rose to his feet.

Softly, he called, 'Chandra, Chandra.'

His Chandra! This song was Chandra's too. Someone called sweetly outside, 'Janab!'

Roy looked in that direction eagerly. 'Chandra, Chandra, come here. Everyone has left, Chandra.'

Appearing with a shy smile, Krishnabai bowed and tenderly completed the song that Roy was playing on his esraj. 'Why did you have to play the flute right now, my love?' Laughing, Roy lowered his baritone as much as he could and joined in, 'My love, on a night such as this, with the ecstasy of victory in my heart, how can I be alone?'

Roy picked up the whisky bottle. Stretching out her arm, Krishnabai said, 'If Janab so desires, his maid will serve him.' Roy relinquished the bottle with a smile. Krishnabai poured and handed the drink to him.

The esraj began to play again. Krishnabai began to sing along softly. And she danced. She sang, 'I do not make garlands of fallen flowers, my love. Give me the flowers from the highest branch. Hold me up, I will choose them myself for you.' She was dancing with her arms stretched out, her face upturned. Dropping his esraj, Roy lifted her in the air, clasping her legs, and made her move to the rhythm of her song. The song ended. Krishna shrieked, pretending to fall. The next moment she slid down to the floor. A drunken Roy called out adoringly, 'Chandra, Chandra, Peari.'

The songs flowed, as did the whisky. One bottle was empty. The second was about to be emptied too. A little later, the baiji's inert body slumped on the sheet. Bishwambhar still sat upright. He smiled at the baiji's condition. Placing her head with great care on a bolster, he helped her lie down comfortably. Then he began to play the esraj again. The Gangulys' clock rang thrice.

The pigeons began to murmur in the arches. Roy was shaken out of his spell. This was the sound he awoke to every day. He got to his feet. He caressed the sleeping Krishnabai just once, 'Chandra, Chandra, Peari.' Then he left the room and called, 'Ananta!'

Ananta was on the roof unrolling the carpet for his master. When he came downstairs, Roy said, 'Bring me my turban and my riding clothes. Tell Netai to saddle up Tufan at once.'

Ananta stared at his master in astonishment. Roy was stroking his moustache.

This figure was not unfamiliar to him, but he had not encountered it in a long time. Softly, he said, 'Wash your hands, Huzoor.'

A little later, Tufan's elated neighing resounded in the final hours of the night. Taraprasanna woke up. Through the window he saw Bishwambhar Roy astride Tufan, dressed in riding breeches and a long coat, with a white turban on his head. Although Taraprasanna couldn't see clearly in the darkness, he imagined the aristrocratic nagra shoes and the brushed whip. Tufan cantered away.

Crossing one field after another, Tufan galloped, raising a cloud of dust. The cool wind at the break of dawn fell on Roy's heated brow. His intoxication was leaving him. A village was situated at the far end of the expanse of land, its name was Kusumdihi. A cart piled high with vegetables was passing, with two occupants. Possibly on their way to the market. He overheard a snatch of conversation, 'Ever since Ganguly Babu has bought...'

Roy pulled on the reins sharply to stop Tufan.

The man on the cart was continuing, 'There's nothing left over after taxes. We were happy when the Roys ruled here...'

Looking around him, Roy was startled. Where was he? Gradually, he found his bearings, Kirtihat lay ahead of him. Straightening up, he loosened the reins and whipped Tufan. And again. Tufan galloped furiously onwards. Returning to his stable, Roy saw that the eastern sky had lightened. But the night was yet to depart.

Roy called out, 'Netai.'

He was panting. He felt Tufan trembling uncontrollably. Roy dismounted. Tufan's mouth was lacerated by the reins. His jaws were bloodied. Exhausted, he was shaking. Stroking his head, Roy said, 'My son.'

Tufan could not raise his head. The effects of alcohol had not left Roy entirely yet. He said, 'It's a mistake, my son, yours as well as mine. Don't be ashamed, Tufan. Straighten your head.'

Netai was standing behind him. He said, 'He's exhausted, he will look up as soon as he has cooled down.'

Roy handed the horse over to Netai and strode into the house. On the first floor he found the doors of the music room still open. Peeping in, he found it was empty, the women who had come for the tryst had left. Empty bottles of whisky were lying on the floor. The lights of the chandeliers and the wall-lamps had not gone out yet. Members of the Roy family were arrayed arrogantly on the wall, smiles of infatuation on their faces. Roy stepped back in fear. Suddenly, he felt he was looking at himself in the mirror—the same desire had manifested itself in him. Not just his own, but the desires of seven generations of Roys were gathered in this room.

He turned back from the door. Leaning on the railing, he cried out like a man struck by fear, 'Ananta, Ananta!'

Ananta ran up to him. He had never heard his master speak this way. Roy told him, 'Put out the lights, put out the lights, lock the music room, the music room...'

His voice could no longer be heard. Only the whip slipped out of his hand to strike the door of the music room with a sharp sound.

six

THE HOMECOMING

BANAPHOOL

You wanted a story, didn't you? Well, here you go, then.

I was on my way home from Shimla, a couple of days before Durga Puja. I am an insurance agent who has to travel on work. I had not succeeded in claiming the 'life' I had been chasing. Someone else had grabbed it before I could. I was feeling low.

The compartment I boarded turned out to have not one but three exquisitely beautiful women. My eyes were dazzled. A young man was accompanying them. He was extremely handsome too. Being dark and stout as I am, I felt embarrassed to take a seat next to them. Yet, I did. After a while, I asked the young man diffidently, 'Where to?' His eyes were glued to a film weekly—the photograph of a half-naked actress seemed to have mesmerized him.

'Where to?'

'I beg your pardon?' he asked, startled.

'I was asking where you're going.'

'Calcutta.'

'Me too. It'll be nice to travel together.'

He immersed himself in his magazine again.

The magazine had an advertisement for our company. In the hope of attracting his attention to it, I said, 'That's an ad for our company, the kind of bonus we offer…'

His eyes transfixed by the half-naked actress, the young man said, 'None of this stuff makes any sense to me.'

'Bonus payouts don't make sense to you! You *are* insured, aren't you?'

'Makes no sense to me. I'm looking at what does make sense.' He went back to the photograph. But I wasn't about to let go easily.

'I find it hard to believe that a man of such refined taste does not understand life insurance. If you'd just spend a nominal amount every month, your life would—'

'Don't bother me about money,' he interrupted. 'If you do want to discuss financial matters, do so with my mother.'

I greeted his mother cordially. 'It appears your son does not wish to discuss this,' I said. 'I'm sure you agree with me that life insurance is a must for everyone.'

The glow of a gentle smile spreading across her face, she said, 'I don't know much about it either. If you don't mind, would you care to explain a little more?'

'Certainly!' I began to spout our hypnotic catchwords—but, amazingly, they seemed to make no impression on her. The other two women listened to my sermon with close attention too, but remained unimpressed.

Pausing, I said, 'I hope I've been able to explain everything.'

'Oh yes, you haven't left anything unexplained,' said the first woman. 'It's just that I don't need life insurance.'

'Not you, perhaps. But your husband? Your son?'

'My husband has conquered death. Why would he need life insurance?'

At this point Ganesha poked his trunked head out of the top bunk and said in a stentorian voice, 'You people are talking too much. Do you suppose we'll get any sleep the next four days? Better get some sleep now while you can.'

My eyes popped out of my skull. I realized my error. Ma Durga was travelling to Calcutta, her children Lakshmi, Saraswati, Kartik and Ganesha with her. Prostrating myself, I said, 'I am an imbecile, forgive me.' Smiling, Durga said, 'You have done no wrong, son. Show me your form; let me get the Calcutta pujas insured. Your sermon has charmed me.'

seven

~

THE DISCOVERY OF TELENAPOTA

PREMENDRA MITRA

If Saturn and Mars—it must be Mars—are in conjunction, you too, can discover Telenapota some day.

In other words, if a day or two of leave can be obtained unexpectedly, just when you are gasping from work and multitudes of people, and if someone tempts you with the information that in a lake of miracles somewhere, the most simple-minded fish in the world are waiting eagerly to have their hearts impaled on a hook at the end of a rod for the first time in their lives, and if you have never had the good fortune of extracting anything but small fry from the water, then you too might unexpectedly discover Telenapota one day.

To discover Telenapota you must board a bus packed with people and their possessions in the waning sunlight one afternoon, suffer jabs from other passengers' elbows every time there is a bump on the road, and then, in the August heat, drag your sweaty, dust-caked body off the bus without warning, somewhere along the road. In front of you, you will see the road running over a low swamp like a bridge. After the bus passes along it with an eccentric rumble and disappears around a bend, you will notice that although the sun has not set yet, darkness has descended on the thick jungle all around you. You will not see a soul anywhere. The birds, too, will seem to have forsaken this place. You will become aware of the damp, sultry weather. A cruel, coiled source of venom will rise up slowly from the swamp, its invisible hood poised to strike.

You will have to step off the highway, walk down to the swamp, and wait next to it. It will seem as though someone has dug a muddy canal running through the dense jungle stretching out before

76

you. But even its line has petered out in the distance amidst the bamboo groves and tall, shaggy trees on both sides. You should have two companions for your discovery of Telenapota. They may not be drawn to fishing as you are, and yet they have come with you on this journey—no one knows why.

The three of you will gaze eagerly at the canal in front of you. From time to time you will stamp your feet to prevent the mosquitoes from getting too intimate, while you exchange questioning glances.

A little later, you will no longer be able to see one another's face in the gathering darkness. The chorus of the mosquitoes will grow sharper. Just as you are wondering whether to return to the highway and wait for a return bus, you will suddenly hear an exquisite sound, wondrous to your senses, from the point where the muddy canal has vanished into the jungle. Someone will seem to force even the silent forest to emit unworldly sobs.

The sound will make your wait restless. But be patient, and your patience will not be in vain. You will see, first, a pinpoint of light swaying in the darkness, and then a bullock cart will emerge slowly from the jungle, rolling from side to side as it moves along the canal.

The cart will match the bullocks—it will seem as though this minuscule version of the bullock cart has come from an underground land of the dwarves.

Without wasting words, the three of you will squeeze yourself beneath the hood on the cart, somehow solving the problem posed by three pairs of arms and legs and three heads—how to place the largest of objects in the smallest of spaces.

The bullock cart will then return the way it came, along the canal. In utter wonderment, you will see how the dense and dark jungle reveals the way forward little by little, like a narrow tunnel. At every moment, the wall of darkness will seem impenetrable, but the cart will move ahead slowly, unperturbed, as though clearing a path with its wheels.

For some time you will be uncomfortable and discomposed as you try to position your arms, legs and head suitably. At every moment, there will be inadvertent collisions with your friends, and then you will gradually realize that the last island of consciousness has been submerged in the dense darkness surrounding you. You will feel as though you have left the familiar world somewhere far behind. There is another one here, shrouded in fog, devoid of sensation, where the current of time is stilled, silent.

With time standing still, you will not know how long you have been sunk in this mist. Woken up suddenly by a cacophonous music, you will realize that the stars are visible from beneath the hood, and the driver is beating a tin canister at intervals with great enthusiasm.

Curious, you will ask why, whereupon the driver will inform you indifferently, 'To get rid of the damned wild animals.'

Once you have grasped this properly, the driver will reassure you before you can ask, your voice trembling, whether beating a canister is sufficient to keep tigers at bay, that he is referring to leopards, and unless the beast is famished, this sound will be enough to keep it at a distance.

While you wonder how a place infested by leopards can exist a mere thirty miles from the metropolis, the bullock cart will cross an enormous field. The delayed waning moon will have risen in the sky by then. Dimly, silently, a succession of giant men on guard will appear to pass slowly on either side of the cart. The ruins of ancient palaces—here a pillar, there the arch of a gate, elsewhere a fragment of a temple will be standing with the futile hope of offering their testimony to eternity.

Sitting as upright as you can in the circumstances, you will feel a shiver run down your body. Something will make you feel you have gone beyond the living world to enter a murky realm of memories from the past.

You won't know what time of night it is, but it will seem the night never ends here. Everything will be sunk in a deep silence without beginning or end, just like carcasses preserved in formaldehyde at the museum.

After two or three bends in the road, the bullock cart will finally stop. Reclaiming your limbs with great effort from the different places you have deposited them, you and your friends will disembark stiffly, one by one, like wooden marionettes. A foul stench will have been welcoming you for some time. You will realize it is the stink from rotting leaves in a pond. Just such a small lake will catch your eye by the light of the half-moon. Next to it there will be a decrepit palace, standing like the ramparts of a fort with a crumbling roof, collapsed walls and shutterless windows like empty eye sockets.

It is in a relatively habitable part of this ruin that all of you will have to make arrangements to stay. The driver of the cart will fetch a cracked lantern and set it in the room. With it, a pitcher of water. When you enter, you will realize that you are the first representatives of the human race to set foot in this room in a long, long time. Maybe someone has made a vain attempt to clear the cobwebs and the dust and the grime. A slightly musty smell will be evidence of the fact that the resident spirit of the room is unhappy. The slightest movement will cause the worn out plaster to flake off the walls and ceiling, falling on you like the curses of an angry soul. Two or three bats will fight with you all night for possession of the room.

To discover Telenapota, one of your two friends must be partial to the bottle, and the other, a soulmate of Rip Van Winkle. The moment you enter the room, no sooner will a sheet be laid out on the floor than one of them will stretch himself out on it and proceed to snore, while the other will immerse himself in a glass of whisky.

The hours will go by. The glass chimney of the cracked lantern will get progressively blacker with soot and eventually go blind. Having been informed by a mysterious wireless message, each and every adult mosquito in the neighbourhood will arrive to welcome the newcomers and establish a blood relationship with them. If you are wise, you will surmise from their manner of perching on the wall and on your body that they are the most aristocratic among mosquitoes—the one and only mount for Lady Malaria, the anopheles. Your companions will by then be unconscious to the world, each for his own specific reason. Therefore, you will abandon your bed slowly to rise to your feet, and then, in a bid to get some relief from the humidity, you will try to climb up the ruined stairs to the roof by the light of a torch.

The danger of plummeting to the ground at any moment, in case a brick or a tile loosens itself beneath your feet, will thwart you for a moment, but some irresistible attraction will make it impossible not to ascend to the terrace.

Up on the roof, you will discover that the railing has crumbled to dust in most places, and the fifth column of the forest has conspired to plant its roots in the cracks to make considerable progress on the task of demolishing this edifice. And, yet, everything will appear mesmerizing by the faint light of the waning moon. If you gaze at all this for a while, you will sense that, in a secret cell somewhere in this enchanted palace under the pall of the sleep of death, an imprisoned princess is sunk in the deepest and longest of slumbers with magic wands of gold and silver at her side. At that very moment, you may see a thin line of light through the window of what had originally appeared to be a ruin across the narrow street. An enigmatic, shadowy figure will appear between you and the light. You will wonder about the identity of this woman at the window at the dead of night, and why she is not asleep, but the answer will elude you. A little later you will think it was a mistake, for the figure will have disappeared, and the light will no longer be there. You will conclude that a dream had momentarily bubbled up to the surface from the depths of the sleep of this ruined palace, appearing fleetingly in the living world before exploding.

You will return downstairs gingerly. And you won't know when you will make space for yourself next to your two friends and fall asleep.

When you awake, you will be surprised to see that even in this land of the night morning does appear, and the call of birds can be heard everywhere.

Surely, you will not have forgotten the objective of your visit.

Some time later, having made complete arrangements for your act of worshipping the fish, you will settle down at one corner of the moss-covered, dilapidated flight of shallow stairs leading into the lake and lower your hook, complete with suitable divine offerings, into the green water.

The sun will climb higher in the sky. From the tip of a bamboo stalk leaning low over the water on the opposite bank, a kingfisher will repeatedly dive into the lake with an iridescent flash of colours, as though to mock you, and will return to its perch euphoric with its successful hunt to taunt you in an unintelligible tongue. To terrorize you, a long and plump snake will slither out of a crack in the flight of stairs to swim across the lake at a leisurely pace and climb up the bank on the other side. Beating their thin, glassy wings, a pair of dragonflies will compete to alight on the float of your fishing rod, while your mind wanders every now and then at the wistful cry of dove.

Then, a sound in the water will break your spell. There will be waves in the still water, and your float will bob up and down gently on them. Turning your head, you will see a young woman pushing aside the hyacinth to fill her shiny brass pitcher with clear water. There is curiosity in her eyes, but no bashfulness or stiffness in her movements. She will look at you directly, observe the float on your fishing rod, and then look away before balancing her pitcher against her hip.

You will be unable to gauge her age. The serenity and compassion in her expression will suggest that her journey through life has been long and cruel, but her lean, tall and undernourished frame will give the impression that her passage from adolescence to youth has been postponed.

As she leaves with her pitcher, she will suddenly turn back towards you to say—'What are you waiting for? Reel it in.'

Her voice will be so steady, sweet and composed that it will not seem remotely abnormal that she is spontaneously talking to a stranger. Only, your sudden surprise will make you forget to reel in the line. When the submerged float rises to the surface, you will discover that the bait is no longer on the hook. You will have no choice but to throw her a rueful glance. She will turn away and leave with measured footsteps, but it will seem to you that in that instant before she turned away, her serene, compassionate face had glowed briefly with the hint of a smile.

Your solitude will not be disturbed anymore. Unable to embarrass you, the kingfisher on the opposite bank will have abandoned its efforts and flown away. Probably full of contempt at your abilities, the fish will not be desirous of another round of competition. The recent incident will seem unreal to you. You will be unable to accept that there really can be a woman like her in this desolate place.

Eventually, you will have to pack up your equipment and leave. When you return you may discover that your prowess at fishing has somehow become known to your friends. Upset at their derision, when you ask who told them this story, your tippler friend may say—'Who do you think! Yamini, of course, who saw it for herself.'

You will have no choice but to ask in curiosity who Yamini is. Perhaps you will discover that the unreal woman with tragic eyes at the lake is a relation of sorts of your friend who loves his whisky. You will also learn that arrangements for lunch have been made at this woman's house.

Seen in daylight, the hideous decrepitude of the ruined building, where the fleeting appearance of a shadowy form had given you cause for wonderment last night, will pain you considerably. You would not have imagined that the retreat of the enchanted veil of night would make its bare, dilapidated form so very ugly.

You will be surprised when told that this is where Yamini and her family live. Arrangements for your meal have probably been made in one of the rooms in there. A frugal repast, perhaps Yamini herself will serve all of you. You have already observed that there is no superfluous reserve or awkwardness about her, but her tragic quietude will be even more conspicuous. The unarticulated anguish of this derelict, forgotten and abandoned locality will be reflected on her face. Even though she has seen everything, her eyes are submerged in the depths of exhaustion. As though she too will disappear within these ruins one day.

Still, you will see her looking uneasy and anxious once or twice while serving the three of you. Someone will be calling faintly from a room upstairs. Yamini will hurry out. Every time she returns, the agony on her face will seem a little deeper—and, with it, a helpless, distracted look in her eyes.

Perhaps, you will take a short rest after your meal. Hesitating near the door, Yamini will finally say in desperation, 'Just a minute, Mani Da.'

Mani Da is the tippler friend of yours. The conversation that will ensue when he goes up to the door will not be in voices low enough to prevent you from hearing.

You will hear Yamini say in a stricken, imperilled tone, 'Ma simply refuses to listen. I can't tell you how restless she has become since she heard you're here.'

'Still the same thing?' Mani will ask in irritation. 'She thinks Niranjan is here?'

'Yes, she keeps saying, I'm sure he's here. Just that he's too embarrassed to see me. I know. You must be hiding it from me. I don't know what to do. She's become so impatient since she went blind that she refuses to understand anything I tell her. She flies into a rage and creates such a scene that sometimes I think she'll die.'

'This really has become a problem. If she could at least see she would know for herself that neither of them is Niranjan.'

Now all of you will be able to hear the faint but sharp, angry call from upstairs. A distressed Yamini will plead, 'Come with me Mani Da, maybe you can explain things to her and calm her down.'

'Very well, you go along, I'll come in a while.' Re-entering the room, Mani will mutter to himself, 'Such an annoyance. She's blind and practically paralysed, but she's vowed not to die.'

Perhaps you will now ask, 'What's going on?' An irked Mani will reply, 'What do you suppose? When Yamini was still a child, her mother had arranged her marriage to a distant nephew of hers named Niranjan. Four years ago, the fellow had turned up to tell her that he would marry Yamini when he returned from his job abroad. Since then the old woman has been sitting here, in this godforsaken house, counting the days.'

You will not be able to stop yourself from asking, 'Has Niranjan not returned from his job abroad?'

'He would have had to go abroad first. He lied to her only because the old woman was so insistent. Why should he be interested in rescuing a pauper's daughter? He's long been married. But who's going to tell her? She won't believe it, and if she does, she'll die on the spot. Who wants to carry a burden of sin?'

'Does Yamini know about Niranjan?'

'Of course she does. But she can't tell her mother. Let me go pay for my sins.' Mani will proceed towards the staircase.

At that moment, you will also rise to your feet, not entirely of your own volition. Perhaps you will say, 'I'll come too.'

'You!' Mani will look at you in surprise.

'Yes, do you mind?'

'No, why should I?' A perplexed Mani will lead the way.

The room you will reach after climbing the narrow, dark and broken-down staircase will appear to be situated in an underground tunnel rather than on an upper floor. Just the one window, and closed, at that. Coming in from broad daylight, everything will appear blurred at first. Then you will become aware of an emaciated, skeletal figure lying on a dilapidated cot, wrapped in a torn quilt. Yamini will be standing by the bed, turned to stone.

Your footsteps will stir the cadaverous figure into showing signs of animation. 'Is that Niranjan? You've finally remembered your unfortunate aunt. My heart's been in my mouth waiting for you all this time. I couldn't even die in peace. You won't run away again, will you?'

Mani will be about to say something, but you will interrupt him to say, 'No, I won't run away again.'

Even without raising your eyes you will sense Mani's bewilderment and the shock and astonishment on the face of the young woman standing like a statue. You will be staring at the sightless eyes, holding your breath. Two black flames will appear to emerge from the empty eye sockets to lick at your body enquiringly. You will feel the stilled moments falling like dewdrops on the ocean of time. Then you will hear: 'I know you couldn't have stayed away. That's why I have been guarding this haunted house and counting my days.' The old woman will begin gasping for breath after this long speech. Flashing a glance at Yamini, you will wonder whether something is melting slowly behind her hard mask. It will not be long before the foundations of her stern vow against destiny and existence, fired by hopelessness, begin to crumble.

The old woman will continue, 'You will be happy with Yamini. It's not because she's my daughter, but there isn't another girl like her. My sorrows and suffering and illness and old age have made me a mad woman, I make her suffer endlessly with my constant nagging—I know only too well I do, but she doesn't say a word. This is a land of the dead, you'll have to scour a dozen homes to find a single man, only corpses like me live here, gasping for life and clinging to the ruins, and yet there's nothing she leaves undone, she's man and woman rolled into one.'

Despite an ardent desire, you will not have the courage to lift your eyes for a single glance. For then you will no longer be able to conceal the tears in your eyes.

With a small sigh, the old woman will say, 'You will take Yamini, won't you? Unless you give me your word I will have no peace even in death.'

All you will be able to say hoarsely is, 'I promise you. Nothing can shake my resolve.'

Then the bullock cart will draw up at the door again that afternoon. The three of you will get in, one by one. Yamini will come up to you as you are about to leave, raise her wistful eyes to your face and say, 'You forgot your fishing rod.'

Smiling, you will say, 'Let it remain here. I may not have been successful this time, but the fish of Telenapota cannot elude me forever.'

Yamini will not look away. Not from her lips, the grateful smile will come from her eyes, floating like white autumnal clouds across the horizon of your heart, gracing it with their beauty.

The cart will begin to roll. A hundred or a hundred and fifty years ago, the first malaria epidemic here had swept Telenapota away like an irresistible flood to this forgotten extremity of life, abandoning it there—perhaps this will be the subject of your friends' discussion. All this will not penetrate your hearing. The constricted space in the cart will no longer trouble you, the monotonous whining of its wheels will not sound harsh to your ears any more. Only a single phrase will resonate in time with your heartbeat—'I shall return, I shall return.'

When you reach the crowded, brightly-lit avenues of the metropolis, the memory of Telenapota will still be burning bright in your heart. The days will pass, punctuated by minor obstacles. You will not be aware of whether a fog is gathering in your head or not. Then, the day that you will have overcome all hindrances to prepare to return to Telenapota, you will have to burrow under a quilt because of a sudden headache, shivers and chills. The thermometer will signal one hundred and five degrees, the doctor will ask, 'Where did you get malaria?' You will sink into a feverish haze.

Much later, when you drag your weakened body into the sunlight on tottering steps, you will find a good deal of your mind and body wiped clean, unknown to yourself. Like a star that has set, the memory of Telenapota will appear to you as a blurred dream. It will seem as though there isn't really a place named Telenapota anywhere in the world. With her stern, serious expression and her distant, pensive eyes, the young woman, just like the derelict building, will feel like nothing but a misty figment of your imagination, conjured up in an idle moment of vulnerability.

Having been discovered for a fleeting moment, Telenapota will once again become submerged in the depths of eternal night.

eight

AND HOW ARE YOU?

BUDDHADEVA BOSE

Sometimes I want to know how you are. When I go to sleep, when I wake up, when I drive at ninety miles an hour, when the weight of time suddenly drops after a few quick vodkas and brandies.

Dawn breaks, night falls; dawn again, night again. The same way, day after day. Sometimes it feels as though something will happen. Nothing does. Day after day.

Believe it or not, I look at myself in the mirror at times. When I shave? No, I think of other things then. But sometimes, alone in the room, after a bath, or before going to bed eventually, I stand face-to-face with myself, eyeball-to-eyeball. Just me, without adornment; a lump of flesh, flab and filth. Completely bald, blunt nose, bags under the eyes, a broad hairy chest, the spitting image of a powerful, aged baboon after removing the glittering false teeth. I enjoy taking off my dentures and making faces, balling up my fists—like two wild beasts poised for battle—when I open my mouth wide the darkness seems to be the road to hell.

How are you? But I don't even know where you are.

Come, let me introduce the characters. This aged baboon before you is called Abanish Ghoshal, with degrees in engineering from Glasgow and Berlin, who learnt the ropes at the Ford factory in Detroit, and is now engaged in making steel at Pippalgarh. His monthly income is five thousand rupees, more or less; he has been around the world thrice at his company's expense; he has to visit Japan or Germany or Sweden or Russia or America once a year. In other words, this aged baboon is a very important person.

But, actually, I am someone else.

＿＿

Alas, there's so much ugliness a tailor can hide, so much pus that formidable degrees can conceal. Fame, honour, riches, influence— all of it may have been achieved, but after that? What lies behind, covered, within?

Was there really a ritual in Athens where young women would emerge naked after bathing in the sea for the ancients to select the most beautiful among them that year? But how else can beauty be judged? All we consider are the adornments. Degrees, learning, 'qualifications'. Everyone wants to know what I can do, no one knows what I am.

You know. Do you?

The population of Pippalgarh is fifty thousand. Everyone's livelihood, their lives too, in fact, is this steel factory. We are building the new India; creating wealth for the people, earning foreign exchange for the country, with four hundred million by our side, we are marching ahead, marching ahead. Can we ever say that the people involved in such a gigantic endeavour are not successful?

But I remember you from time to time.

Pippalgarh has a reputation around the country of being progressive. We have delivered radios to the homes of the workers; we have swept out cholera and smallpox; our huge cooperative store is a veritable showpiece. We have a school, a library, clubs at different levels and of different kinds, doctors, nurses, a free hospital, even a contraception clinic adjacent to the maternity home. Everyone here is happy; they work with healthy bodies, with resolve in their minds and with hope in their hearts—work goes on round the clock, smoothly; our productivity is the highest in India. We value life here.

Do you remember that morning—those dewdrops on the grass, and the soft, tender, pink sunshine?

＿＿

There are hills in the distance here, a sea of earth lies grey beyond the town. There is only emptiness in the vast expanse stretching to the horizon, and nothing but emptiness in the enormous sky above. Nothing at all happens—the sun rises, the sun sets, nothing happens at all.

Everyone says Mr Ghoshal works like a demon. They don't lie; I feel no fatigue when it comes to work, I do not have the skill to rest awhile. My routine stretches from eight to eight; I fell the day with a single blow. Yet, the victory does not seem to be complete; sometimes I go back late at night—where huge fires burn furiously, I walk around supervising things, when I come out I find the darkness thinning. There's no need, of course, there are people specifically meant for this task—but this is what I enjoy. I like to think that something is happening. This pit of fire, this fierce sound, the mechanical movements of the factory workers, all these help me forget that I am actually someone else. And I can be seen at almost every one of the innumerable parties that are thrown here in Pippalgarh—I always make an appearance, even if only for ten minutes—and if I ever feel like 'letting myself go' I can put away one-and-a-half bottles of Scotch and still continue with my measured smiles, my conversation, my flirtations with women, without breaking my stride. I am on cordial terms with everyone, but none of them means anything to me. That's the way I like it.

Like it? That's incorrect. There's no question of liking or disliking anything. I work—since I have nothing else. I go to parties—since I have nothing else. Nothing else. I do not have the one thing that would have meant having everything. So I have nothing.

But, is it even possible that I am the only one who has come to know this, but no one else has? Is it even possible that I am the only one among this fifty thousand who wonders how you are?

～～

Everyone is happy at Pippalgarh, but the happiest are the women; meaning, the wives of those 'sahibs' who earn more than two thousand rupees a month. There's a separate club for them, meaning, the 'memsahibs'. There they can attempt self-improvement without

the company of men—swimming, sports, hair-dressing, manicure—
nothing's absent from the arrangements. Coffee party at ten-thirty,
gimlets around one, back home for lunch, a nap in an air-conditioned
room, tea after the nap, after the evening cocktail—if there's nothing
else to do—dinner at the Cosmopolitan Club, and perhaps an hour of
dancing after dinner. At least three days a week can easily be passed
this way. They're safe for the other four days too: there are different
kinds of invitations and events to attend, so there they are, adorning
their bodies, adorning their homes, taking on the responsibility of
being graceful hostesses at their own parties, the responsibility of
being eye-catching embellishments in this land of coarse soil and
steel. Their children? They spend their infancy in their nurses' laps,
attend public school as soon as they turn five, missionary schools—in
Darjeeling, in Dehradun, in Ernakulam. The mothers have no time;
their lives are busy, happy, fulfilled.

Ah time, cruel time, how ferocious the battle between you and
man! Escaping you, avoiding you, defeating you is his objective, his
only objective, his only concern. He continuously creates so many
unusual, extraordinary, extreme ways to do it, but still no one wins
in the final round. Year, month, weekday, hour, minute; morning,
noon, afternoon, evening, night, morning. And again the dawn, and
again the night. Endless. Such torment!

Beasts don't worry about all this. Nor do the gods. What if there
really is a god somewhere? Is it entirely impossible?

Don't look at me doubtfully; I have not forgotten I am a very
important person, an aged baboon, a beastly lump of flab, flesh and
filth. But actually I am someone else.

～

You were in the garden that morning. The dew, the grass, the soft,
innocent pink sunlight, the fresh green tender scent in the air. You
were brimming over at sixteen, slim, fair—the goddess Saraswati
to my adolescent mind. Your blouse was a deep red, wrapped in a
white sari with a red border; you were like light, you were light,

you lit up the world.

How did it turn out that I don't know where you are now?

My wife's style is different; she has become a social worker. Adult education among the workers, teaching hygiene to their wives, that there are no such things as ghosts and the milk of cows is more beneficial than liquor—imparting such wisdom, along with her disciples, is how she spends her days. Not just that, she also runs two or three—what's the right word?—cultural societies for those housewives whose husbands earn only between five hundred and fifteen hundred a month. The membership of the women's society in Pippalgarh numbers five thousand, it has its own office, built at company expense; its calendar is packed with the events it organizes; playback-singing stars, award-winning writers, fiery orators are invited to its annual festivals; the subjects of the monthly lectures it organizes range from the Upanishads to Sputnik. The director of all these activities is my wife—Milu—Urmila. Everyone says it is a worthy match; they are not wrong. Milu has the same capacity for work that I do, she is as indefatigable as I am; but if someone were to force the issue, at least I have the excuse that I need an income, but hers is pure unpaid labour. Noble Milu.

But does Milu know who her enemy is?

Milu is not callous about anything; she writes two letters a week to our son in Chicago, who is a doctor, spends a few days every year with our daughter and son-in-law in Rome, and she does go to all the parties with me. She has to; it is the rule in Pippalgarh for 'high-valued sahibs' to appear at parties as a couple. This gives me an opportunity to meet Milu sometimes. We meet, but we don't talk much—what is there to talk about? And things have come to a point where we are either dining at someone else's house or entertaining guests at our own almost every evening; if we have to unexpectedly dine together at home by ourselves, both of us try our utmost to suppress our unease. No, I don't see much of Milu anymore.

It is we who are Pippalgarh's 'ideal couple', both of us are profusely honoured. Alas, our achievements conceal so many failures; people's respect is a shroud for ruthless emptiness.

On my way to and from parties, when I drive with Milu by my side, sometimes I think of you.

And how are you?

When did I see you last? Was it forty years ago? Ten? Three or four? Yesterday? I don't quite remember. After visiting so many different countries over and over again, I am confused by places, I am confused by time. Was it in Manila or in Capri that I had seen the sunset from the balcony of the bungalow on the hilltop? Where was that inn with the blazing log fire, the sparse old-fashioned furniture, the plain but delicious food, the pleasing wine, and the snowy night outside, the frosty breath of the forest? Was it in Tyrol? In Denmark? Or in Big Sur? And that other time when I saw you when travelling by car—was it on the road to Ootacamund from Mysore, or in Canada, or in Scotland? It must have been some such place, or perhaps somewhere else altogether. I was in a car, there was another one alongside. It was a bright day, there were tall trees on either side, the play of light and shade on the road. A blue Italian Fiat, with you in it. A handsome young man next to you, his luxuriant moustache made him appear like an airline pilot, or perhaps a famous sportsman. You were brimming over at sixteen, the red blouse was like light on your body, you lit up the day. I looked at you for a long time, then the blue Fiat took a turn into another road.

Just look at the mistakes I make. Could you possibly be sixteen still? By now you must be…wait…let me calculate… But, is it even possible that you too have grown old? You, too, who is charm herself?

Milu had been sitting next to me that day. When I could no longer see you I looked at her. A sudden suspicion sprang to my mind. Milu was not you, was she? Or was it possible that Milu—Urmila, the famous Mrs Ghoshal of Pippalgarh—was in fact you?

Is it possible?

Sometimes my mind cries for rest. No work to be done—

nothing—I'm sitting on a rattan chair in a veranda somewhere, the blue sea before me. The blue-green-indigo turbulent water, wave after wave, white birds, white sunshine, the hazy distance. I'm in a cane chair, gazing at all this. Holiday, rest; forgetting all the things that make up life. Why don't I? Let me tell all of you the truth, do not laugh, do not look at me suspiciously. How long the day will be when it holds no work to be done. How enormous the weight of that lightness that holds nothing but holidays?

Will I be able to bear it? I don't know, I am afraid. We are allowed a month's leave every year; I don't take it. I could take continuous leave for a year-and-a-half right now if I wanted to; I don't. I am afraid.

My health? Don't worry about it. In our hospital in Pippalgarh we have doctors with degrees from Vienna, modern equipment; everything except the soul is examined there at regular intervals; are we eating, or not eating, scientifically; walking, exercising, or giving up exercising; 'feeling poorly' is a term unfamiliar to us. Besides, remember, Milu and I make the ideal couple; although we do not meet very frequently we look after each other flawlessly; although we converse very little we never quarrel. We are beyond annoyances like unhappiness, surliness, differences of opinion, arguments. I remind Milu that she should visit the dentist; in her desire to save me from death, Milu encourages me to give up smoking. Apart from such things, each of us is in our own world, engrossed in our own work. We are not dependent on each other, life goes on the same way even without each other; but we are mercilessly imprisoned by the announcement that we are husband and wife. This is the ideal arrangement in Pippalgarh for the 'sahibs'.

I like the discipline of Pippalgarh, its conflictless class differences, and its unwritten laws which dispel worries. The people here are divided into three classes—'workers', 'officers' and 'sahibs'. The workers drink hooch, the sahibs Scotch, and the officers down their deconstipating potions and go to bed with their wives. The workers are allowed to get drunk at times, there's no objection to their raising a ruckus and getting into fights; but the sahibs are forbidden from losing their poise. The officers are permitted to be devoted to their wives and children (they are 'domesticated creatures', after all); but the sahibs' offspring must be either invisible or non-existent, and what their conjugal life must have is not intimacy but faithfulness beyond doubt. They shall make their appearances, as far as possible, as a couple—even if they are merely taking a stroll in front of their house, it is unseemly to abandon each other. But, if it ever comes out that they enjoy each other's company, that is completely unworthy of approval. If there is attraction, forming an attachment is very easy; but what is expected of the sahibs is that they will adhere to the rules, beyond likes and dislikes, in other words. That does not mean they have to be deprived of tasty morsels of their choice; laughing and joking at parties with women or men of equal rank is their duty—it is a failing not to be capable of this; but you must know where to draw the line. You must not go too far with anything, things just need to be touched upon, you have to float briefly in the shallows, deep diving is illegal. You must be able to express an opinion on any subject at once, but too much attention to a subject is not in good taste. The existence of the sahibs is in these two worlds of 'social life'—that is what we call it—and, of course, of work, and those who are equally adept at both enjoy the benefit of unimpeded ascent. I, too, am one of those chosen ones.

And yet, I am actually someone else.

Did I say something to you when there was dew on the grass, fragrance in the air, and a pink sunshine spread over the face of dawn? Did you say something to me? Do you remember? You don't? You came and stood on the stairs, the morning-sun-coloured dawn was face-to-face with you—and there I was gazing at you, the touch of dew on my feet, the euphoria of daybreak in my body. You were slim, fair, your hair blue and indigo in the tender sunlight. Your blouse was a deep red, wrapped in a white sari with a red border. Like light you lit up the universe, it was your fragrance that pervaded the fresh green air. My light, my life, my soul, how did it come to pass that I lost you?

That one time I saw you suddenly in the lift in a hotel in Amsterdam. You were dressed in slacks, a bright-red woollen cardigan, joy in your face as sixteen brimmed over. Lighting up the grey of the cloudy day spread out outside, you came and stood there. You recognized me, you smiled; you responded at once in German to some trivial observation of mine. You got off the lift before I did; I didn't see you again.

Was I mistaken? Perhaps—yes, definitely mistaken. You cannot have remained sixteen so many years later. And, if it was indeed you, why was your hair golden? Why would you talk to me in German even after recognizing me? But, if that woman was not you, then where are you? Tell me, answer me.

Where? I don't even know whether you still live.

But, is it even possible that you have died? You too, celestial beauty?

Yet, Pippalgarh runs smoothly. How strange, how terrible, how unbelievable that not one of these fifty thousand people except me wonders whether you are still alive or not. But this is the only thing that is real, important. Yet everyone is happy living by the rules.

Everyone? Who knows whether it is everyone.

To tell the truth, following the rules without demur is quite difficult. Some of the sahibs do have a fall, sometimes literally on the floor of the club, sometimes in the form of some other weakness. Some people actually get friendly at a party—instead of mingling with everyone they spend the entire evening in the company of a single person—that is a big mistake. Others earn infamy by bringing up serious subjects for discussion. Someone may display signs of excessive attention towards someone else's wife, taking an axe to the root of their prospects in the company. I've even seen one or two people who do not go to parties, reading books of their choice instead when they go back home in the evening—their behaviour is considered scandalous too. This may not harm anyone, but we term them undependable; the wise principle of Pippalgarh is that those who are moved easily by things or want to nurture a part of themselves in private, are—even though they are morally innocent—not worthy of being given important responsibilities. But, I wonder, why do these people fall? Did they ever see you and were not able to forget you since then? Like me, do they also wonder where you are?

Perhaps.

However, things that are difficult for many people come easily to me. I am very clever—I do not allow anyone to even guess that I am actually someone else; even though they see me round the year they never suspect that I have known you for ten thousand years. Everyone knows, thinks, believes, that I am only a very important person—an aged baboon. And, indeed, that is what I am. Once you are an aged baboon, there's nothing more comfortable; I am fortunate to have reached that stage.

Milu? Does Milu suspect anything? No, not even Milu. But what if the truth is that Milu is indeed you? Is that not possible? I do vaguely remember a time when Milu was—who knows if she was almost like you. But if that is so, then it must be accepted that Milu does not exist anymore. And if Milu does not, nor do I. Is that possible? Certainly. Definitely possible.

But Milu, I—we are nothing. We may exist, or we may not. It does not matter. But the real, important, critical question is—do you exist or not?

Tell me, answer me. Say something.

To please Milu I had once been to one of her women's society events. The speaker was a renowned professor from Calcutta. Happiness does not make man happy, pleasures do not bring joy, what man needs is ambrosia—he stated this eternal truth in different ways, taking a long time over it. He spouted a great deal of Sanskrit; words like 'love', 'beauty', 'infinite' and 'immortal' were heard over and over again. Why was he saying all this—it suddenly struck me—these were just words, just shells, just envelopes, had he ever wondered whether they held anything within them? Had he not heard of you yet, if he had, then why all this noise? All those words of his—if they did hold any meaning, any substance, an abstract, an essence, then it is you! You—you are everything—but if you are indeed everything then how can there be a question mark over whether you are alive or not?

One day I will take that holiday—I will have to. I will go away from this place—I will have to. I will sit in a rattan chair on a veranda somewhere, the sea before me. The blue-green-indigo turbulent water, wave after wave, the hazy distance. No work, I am idle; no worries, I am idle; no thoughts, I am idle; and yet, I do not fear the morning, the afternoon, the evening. I want to go somewhere where there is no work, and because there is no work, there is no fatigue either. I want to go somewhere where there is always time, but where I do not have to wage a war against time.

Where is that land, that sea, that blueness? It is where you are. You are brimming over at sixteen, your body smells of the dew, your face glows in the pink sunlight, like light, you light up this universe. You just sat down by my side.

But what if it turns out that you do not exist?

nine

THUNDER AND LIGHTNING

ASHAPURNA DEBI

It did take place eventually. The horrifying, shameful incident. The one which the family had been living in terror of, like waiting for a knife to be plunged into its side.

The terror had ended.

The knife had pierced the ribs, leaving the family soaked in blood.

Bula had run away.

The youngest of the daughters-in-law, Bula, whose full name was Bulbul.

Strictly speaking, I'm not part of their family, for ostensibly I'm the landlord's daughter. But I've been told that they've been tenants on our ground floor since the time before my birth, which meant that the first place I visited, after learning to walk, was downstairs, their home.

Ever so many winters and summers, ever so many years have passed since then, but their home remains my primary destination when I go out. I'm practically part of the family, and I know all there is to know about them.

I knew there was a conflict of imagination raging within each of them—would the embedded knife actually wreak such terrible violence, or would it lose its sharpness and slip out?

And yet, no one had ever discussed the possibility explicitly. They hadn't because they couldn't. I knew why they couldn't.

No one wanted to annoy Bula. She looked after all of them, took care of all their needs, none of them could do without her.

Bula's father-in-law, Rajen Babu, would call out to her twice a day at specific times, 'Chhoto Bouma!' 'Coming, Baba,' Bula would answer at once. I knew that she would massage her father-in-law's knees with Ayurvedic oil for a long time. At night Bula would go up to his door to ask, 'Are you asleep, Baba?' Clearing his throat in his unique way, Rajen Babu would respond, 'Not yet, but I was about to go to sleep.'

Bula would go in with a piece of flannel and a charcoal flame. Rajen Babu would sleep after a hot compress was applied to his knee, which was then wrapped in warm flannel.

Bula's mother-in-law would summon Bula three hundred and fifty-six times a day. 'Chhoto Bouma!'

I may not be able to account for each of the summons, but I knew that most of Sushilabala's calls were for unnecessary tasks. For instance, 'A little less supari in my paan from tomorrow please, Chhoto Bouma, can you air my sheets, Chhoto Bouma, have the wet clothes been hung up to dry, Chhoto Bouma, who was it knocking at the front door, Chhoto Bouma?' If there was no task to ask about, she would inquire, 'Have you any idea why are there so many ants in the room these days, Chhoto Bouma?'

Bula's widowed sister-in-law would seek her out at least nine hundred and ninety times a day. 'Bula, light the stove now, have you put the kettle on, Bula? Bula, not done slicing the vegetables yet? Hurry up, Bula.'

Bula's husband's spinster sister, Usha, who was much older and had been bedridden even before Bula's wedding, would croak every now and then, 'Are you done, Chhoto Boudi?'

Bula would rush up to her. 'What is it, Usha?' 'Nothing,' Usha would snarl back. 'I didn't say anything.'

The widowed sister-in-law had several children of different ages, each of whom called Bula several times a day, 'Chhoto Kaki!'

'My blue notebook was right here, Chhoto Kaki, where did it go?'

'Where have you put my belt, Chhoto Kaki?' 'I'm getting late for school, Chhoto Kaki.' 'She's beating me up, Chhoto Kaki.' 'Can you tie my ribbon, Chhoto Kaki?'

Chhoto Bouma, Chhoto Boudi, Chhoto Kaki.

Variations on the same theme. What they said was the same thing too, on the same note, differing only in the actual words.

Still, I never saw Bula get angry. She was always smiling, always working, always scolding the children, doing up their buttons, washing clothes, humouring Usha as though she were the older one.

She had often volunteered to do things for me too. 'What's this, why are you using a safety pin? Let me sew on a button.' When I protested, she said, 'How bashful this girl is.'

That was Bula for you.

She couldn't be avoided easily. So the eagerness with which she scanned the next door window elicited only a covert comment or two, accompanied by meaningful glances being exchanged between the members of the family. Glances that said, 'She's not going to be tied down at home much longer.'

The eldest sister-in-law's daughter, who had just got into the ninth standard, joined the exchange of glances, whispering, 'Chhoto Kaki just got a letter in an envelope.' She added, 'That Biju Kaka next door seems to have no other work but to gaze at Chhoto Kaki's window all day long.'

'Her window is open, isn't it?' Sushilabala hissed.

'It's open all the time,' answered her grandmother, curling her lips.

And at once anxiety welled up within the family. 'Heaven knows what calamity she'll bring upon us.'

Not just up there in heaven, everyone knew now.

Bula had brought a real calamity upon everyone, severing all the thousands of bonds she had with the family and running away.

'I knew all along,' said the eldest sister-in-law. 'I saw Biju with my own eyes tossing letters through the window.'

Beating her forehead, Sushilabala said, 'I knew even earlier. I knew her tricks. Why else would my Sukhen have renounced everything and left?'

No one protested Mashima's statement. Who knew whether it was because Mashima would be furious if they did, or because it would lighten the gravity of Bula's crimes?

Well, someone could easily have easily pointed out, 'But your

Sukhen was always consorting with monks, he'd been half a monk himself from the age of eighteen. You had to force him out of the Ramakrishna Mission to get him married.'

I suffered from the bad habit of protesting but I could make no headway either. Ever since I had left college and taken up a job, neither Mashima nor Mesho Moshai spoke to me.

That apart, there was nothing about this family I didn't know.

To tell the truth, the young man in question, Sukhen, was extraordinarily handsome. In my childhood I was more or less mesmerized by his good looks. Had he been a real man, there would definitely have been a love affair within this house.

But at seventeen, or was it sixteen, he developed this precocious obsession. This business of spending time with monks. Going off to monasteries on holidays, getting hold of scriptures and great men's lives and reading them, not looking at women—all sorts of ominous signs. I had tried to laugh it off at first, but then I realized Sukhen was serious.

Giving up, I concentrated on studies instead.

Meanwhile, Sukhen grew even more recklessly involved with his strange obsession, which made a worried Mashima resolve to get him married. One day before his wedding, Sukhen ran away.

How the world had to be turned upside down to find and bring him back makes for its own story.

But Sukhen had surprised everyone in the first few days after his wedding. Dressed in a dhoti with embroidered borders, freshly-shaven and his hair doused in fragrant oil, he had abandoned his sacred practice of reading the scriptures until midnight to hover around the bedroom from the evening onwards.

How everyone had laughed. The laughter had even turned bitter at times. 'Chhi-chhi, shame on him.' 'Talk about frauds.' 'Really, what a joke.' And Bula began to be criticized. 'What a temptress. Anyone who can sway a devotee from his path can't be entirely innocent.'

Mashima had even said that Bula had apparently committed a grave sin in making her pious son get interested in lowly things. It seemed the shastras referred to such females as transgressors. One's wife was supposed to be a spiritual fellow-traveller and help her husband progress along his chosen path. 'Haven't you read the lives of Ramakrishna and his wife, Saradamani?'

But then Bula didn't have to hear all this for very long. Sukhen came to his senses quite soon. This was discovered one morning.

Sukhen had apparently left as soon as he had woken up.

Gone. But where?

It soon became obvious where. Sukhen had been to the Ganga to bathe. Back from his ablutions, he announced that he would fast all day, maintain three days' silence from tomorrow, and formally renounce the world on the fourth day. And if they tried to stop him? He would disappear.

That was the only time I saw tears in Bula's eyes. Her cheeks looked as hard and dark as planks of wood, and a single line of tears flowed along it, drying instantly.

Later, she told me, 'Those were not tears of rage, but of humiliation.'

But it was just that one day.

No one had ever seen Bula look unhappy since then.

But that wasn't good, was it?

Surely that was wrong too, condemnable, in fact.

How could a wife whose husband had abandoned her for the path of renunciation actually have the desire to laugh, to chat, to play with children? The young ones doted on her. And why not? Who would indulge them as much? Where had Bula learnt all these rhymes and poems and stories and skits? There were three other women in the family, but none of them could chatter like her, or sing as many songs.

The others barely managed to pay the daily instalment of their cosmic debt. But Bula, who should not have been having a sparkling life, who should have been shrinking back in shame all the time, seemed to be overflowing with a passion for life.

And no one was in the dark about the fact that those passionate waves were lapping at the shores of the window next door.

'You couldn't tie down your husband, and now you're trying to tie down another man?' No one may have actually said this, but the bile was directed at Bula all the time.

But, of course, Bula might have been an unmitigated sinner had she turned her husband's attention to a lowly life, but then at least the family would have benefited, wouldn't it? Through insinuations and signs of one kind or the other, Bula had to hear things to this effect constantly.

The pain of losing Sukhen was fading, but the difficulties that ensue when the only earning member of the family repairs to a monastery were far from fading. On the contrary, they worsened.

The objects of everyday use broke, tore, and wore out, but they could not be replaced. Daily necessities had to be curtailed. Many practices had to be discontinued. There had never been a cook, now even the solitary servant was told to leave.

And...

And, at the beginning of every month, Baro Boudi's second daughter would appear upstairs with an ashen face, saying, 'Dida says we can't pay the rent this month either...'

Perhaps she had been taught to say more, to be a little more humble, to plead some more, but the poor thing couldn't say anything else, pausing after an ellipsis.

No matter how close the two families appeared to be, my mother began to frown at this, while my father grew grim, but the girl was spared all this because she never raised her eyes from the floor.

Rajen Babu and Sushilabala, their widowed daughter-in-law and sick daughter—all of them held Bula responsible for plunging the family into this crisis. It signalled her gross incompetence, for which Bula should have been feeling guilty all the time.

But Bula did no such thing.

Bula was completely different.

Bula seemed to have forgotten that she was a daughter-in-law. She wanted to live like the eldest, unmarried daughter.

But who could tolerate such a thing?

So everyone said behind her back, 'This woman won't remain here much longer.' They said, 'Who knows what ruin she'll bring upon the family.' And Usha sighed, 'Chhoto Boudi has usurped my place entirely.'

But when Bula left, vacating a great deal more space, Usha sighed even louder. 'Everybody in the world can do as they please,' she said.

But what pleasure had it offered?

Why had Bula felt the need for the satisfaction that comes from sending the household up in flames, from breaking its ribs?

Even I felt that such pleasure was not a part of Bula's nature.

In the olden days, no one made a fuss if the daughter or the daughter-in-law ran away.

'She died of cholera at night, we cremated her the same night'... 'She was bitten by a snake after midnight, the corpse was cast off on a raft before dawn'... People floated misinformation to save themselves from social censure.

Behind the scenes, of course, the conspirators joined hands. 'Celebrate, but make no noise.'

There was no social aggression now, no fear of being ostracized. Lies were not necessary either. If a daughter or a daughter-in-law went missing, it was all right to create an uproar, all right to advertise in the papers, all right to plead, 'Come back!'

Rajen Babu didn't advertise in the papers, of course, but he conveyed his anger and indignation to everyone in the neighbourhood. At home he delivered his verdict as loudly as possible, 'If anyone so much as mentions the name of the haramjaadi I'll bury them alive.' He added, 'I don't want to see a single sign of her in this house, burn everything to ashes.'

Bula possessed four books, which Sushilabala tore into shreds and dumped into the basket where material to light the oven was kept. Hauling Bula's wedding photograph down from the wall, she stamped on it until the glass broke, and then told her eldest granddaughter, 'Cut Sukhen's picture out of this and burn the rest.'

Bula's elder sister-in-law asked, her expression softening, 'Was her jewellery with you, Ma, or with her?'

'What do you mean, with me?' Sushilabala said angrily. 'When did the shameless hussy ever give it to me?'

'Then she's taken them,' declared Bula's sister-in-law, her expression still soft. Was it because the neighbours' attitude towards Bula might also soften if they learnt that she had taken nothing except the clothes she was wearing?

I looked at her in surprise, wondering if she had forgotten. Can anyone forget something like this?

Bula did not possess much jewellery. Her mother's brothers had financed her wedding. Still, they had been reasonably generous. But Bula had sold all those ornaments, one by one, to her sister-in-law's family jeweller. And it was the sister-in-law who had arranged the sale.

Somehow, I always managed to find out everything. I knew that Bula's sister-in-law had made subdued protests at first, and I also knew that Bula had presented an unusual argument to overcome her objections.

Apparently Bula did not care for jewellery. And since she didn't, what was the point of keeping it? It would do nothing but rot in its case.

I was astonished to think that Baro Boudi had forgotten such a momentous decision. I wonder why I couldn't remind her of it at once?

Usha was my age, she would address Bula as Chhoto Boudi, but not I. I used to call her by her name. 'How can you work so hard?' I used to ask her. 'Hard-up people can do nothing but work hard,' Bula would reply, smiling. 'What else will they live with besides hard work?'

'Should I write Sukhen Da a letter, Bula?'

'Don't make people laugh now.'

'But what sort of dharma is it to shrug off the responsibility of looking after your wife and family and aged parents and become a monk instead?'

'When did I say it's dharma?'

'Shouldn't he be made to wake up?'

Bula would laugh. 'Will hurling a single letter wake up someone who only wants to sleep?'

I no longer liked to go there after Bula had left, but I had to visit them even more often. As the unpaid rent mounted, Mashima sent me loving invitations to listen to her tearful accusations and litanies of neglect.

Like a block of wood I had to hear how all her clothes were torn, how she couldn't afford new ones, how Mesho Moshai's medicines couldn't be bought anymore, how there was no option but to stop sending Baro Boudi's three children to school, how Usha was inching towards death simply because of a lack of nutrition.

No, Sushilabala wasn't making any of it up. Ever since they had run out of the money from Rajen Babu's provident fund, I could see their poverty turning increasingly hideous. These complaints were not imaginary, but the last one was.

'I don't know what venomous snake I let into the family, all of us have been bitten.'

In other words, Bula was responsible for all this.

I felt a terrible rage, but what could I say. There was no opportunity to speak up for Bula.

Leave alone speak up for her, was it even possible to speak *of* her? I didn't dare tell even Usha that Bula had secretly met me in my office, that Bula had run away from home to join the movies.

But such stories couldn't be suppressed.

A fire never goes out until it has announced its presence. The flames reached Rajen Babu's family in the form of news brought by Baro Boudi's eldest daughter.

Bula had joined the movies.

She had seen Bula's photograph in a cinema magazine. Newcomer Bula Banerjee, sparkling with laughter, brimming with emotion.

Bula's life as an actress had begun with a story written by author Bijoy Bose.

Bijoy Bose.

That is to say, Biju next door. In other words, a puzzle had now been solved, an unfinished arithmetic problem resolved. Which had sharpened, like a question mark, ever since Bula's departure.

Had Biju also disappeared along with Bula, there could have been a sigh of relief over two plus two turning out to be four, but this had not happened. Biju was still ensconced at home, just as before, unmoving.

What could they do in that case?

They couldn't go to Biju's house and abuse his parents, nor could they tell everyone in the neighbourhood. All they could do was stop everyone from visiting them.

Biju was a writer, his house was strewn with magazines, which was why both of Baro Boudi's daughters spent all their time there, while the bedridden Usha treated his house as her library.

'I'll break your legs if you visit that scoundrel's home again,' Rajen Babu had warned his granddaughters. This was not to their liking. But then had anyone succeeded in passing a law anywhere in the world to seal the openings for playing hide-and-seek?

This was the route that the fire-breathing news took into the family. In their excitement the girls forgot that they would have to answer the question, 'How did you find out?'

'Go get the magazine,' said Baro Boudi. Her daughters had got it already. Now they took it out from beneath their bed to show her.

The eldest daughter-in-law took a look, as did her other children, as did Usha. Everyone wanted to see the photograph, and it couldn't be kept away from the karta and his ginni.

'What's that you said, Bouma?' Sushilabala exploded like a bomb. 'You people can still discuss that evil, fallen woman?' She said, 'Let her go to hell, how dare you bring her photograph into the house?' She said, 'Throw it away. Kick it into the rubbish outside.'

'How did you find out? Answer me!' Rajen Babu flailed his limbs like a lunatic. Not that they had a chance to answer. Rajen Babu kept screaming. 'I'll chop all of you to bits, let there be a river of blood, I'll hang but I'll murder all of you. Is there nothing else to talk about? No mangy dogs in the world? No rotting vermin? No worms or insects in the drains? Can't you discuss them?'

After this, the hide-and-seek did have to stop, they did have to stop discussing Bula. But the walls outside were plastered with her face. A 'newcomer', yes, but of such striking appearance.

'I'll have to leave the country,' said Rajen Babu.

'I'll have to hang myself,' said Sushilabala.

'If only Baba's desire to leave the country was more violent,' Usha said to herself in her bed.

If her father left, surely her mother wouldn't leave him, and would Usha's parents abandon her?

But what if Sushilabala's will was stronger than Rajen Babu's?

Usha told me with a sigh after a lot of thought, 'You know what I think, Ranu, at least there would be some variety in my life. It would mean some change at home at the very least.'

'Bula leaving meant such a big change…' I said.

'Shh, don't even mention her name,' said Usha. 'Your throat will be slit.'

But Bula was beyond their reach. Perhaps she had no fear of having her throat slit, so she sent an actual letter, which she had signed herself.

Bula wanted to visit them once, to meet everyone.

'What? Visit us? Meet us? Written for permission? How can a woman be so bold? What a nerve!'

Rajen Babu said so, Sushilabala said so, the eldest daughter-in-law said so. Everyone was stunned by her brashness.

The letter was torn into as many tiny bits as possible and burnt.

Bula came to my office once again.

In a large car.

The director's car. Sitting across the table from me, she toyed with a pin for some time, her eyes lowered, before asking, 'How are things over there?'

'What does it have to do with you, Bula?' I asked in disappointment.

Bula's eyes brimmed with tears. Bula, who was always cheerful.

'They don't even mention you, Bula, they tore up your letter,' I told her.

Raising her eyes to look at me, she said, 'What else could they do? I brought shame upon them.'

She sat for a while, lowered her eyes, and raised them again. 'I realize they can't bear to set eyes on me. Will you do something for me, Ranu? Will you take something for them?'

'Anything you send will end up in the dustbin, Bula, or in the flames,' I told her.

Sighing, Bula stood up. 'Then what was all this for, Ranu? Why did I...' Without finishing, she looked away, and then left.

But still Bula didn't accept defeat, still she didn't stop trying. When Sushilabala said, 'She's dangerous, a schemer,' she wasn't wrong. Even I was astounded at Bula's audacity. I saw it for myself. When the peon came and said, 'I'm looking for Sushilabala Debi,' it was I who showed him the way.

A peon asking for Sushilabala!

Yes, there was some money, sent by insured registered post, she had to sign for it. Bula had sent money.

Bula had sent Sushilabala money! Incredible! How could Bula have been so reckless, so foolhardy? I was terrified, waiting with goose pimples on my skin, for a cataclysmic thunderstorm to ensue. What was going to happen now!

I was worried for the peon. The poor fellow had better not be beaten up. Everyone had gathered.

But there was no storm, no thunder, no lightning. All of nature seemed to turn sullen.

There was silence for a minute.

Then Sushilabala was heard asking grimly, 'Who did you say had sent the money?'

'I told you already, Bula Banerjee. Please sign this quickly.'

'H...how much?'

'Two thousand!'

'Two thousand!'

I felt as though the words were hanging in the air, waiting to be echoed by everyone present.

'No need, send it back.'

Passing his verdict hoarsely, Rajen Babu went into his room. His pronouncement sounded unconvincing, and his departure listless.

'What should I do, Ranu?' asked Sushilabala.

'What can I say,' I said indistinctly. What could I tell her, really? The only saving grace was that I wouldn't have to see Bula's expression when the money was given back to her.

I didn't respond, I couldn't. Baro Boudi seemed to reply on my behalf. 'She'll be very hurt if we send it back. She's sent it with so much hope, after all...'

'That's what I was thinking. But your father-in-law is so angry that...'

'Sign quickly, please,' said the peon impatiently. 'Or else write down that you don't want the money.'

'Really, what's the hurry, can't a person have a moment to think? Where do I have to sign?'

All the rage of nature had been neutralized. The imminent storm was quiet now, without any force. There was just a solitary flash of lightning in the cloudless sky. 'Now you know, Baro Bouma, that I don't lie. Have you seen how bold your sister-in-law is?'

I was relieved to see the peon escape unscathed, but it took a long time for my goose pimples to settle down.

ten

RAS

NARENDRANATH MITRA

Motalef began to tap the palm trees in the Chowdhurys' orchard around the middle of Kartik. And before a fortnight had passed, he married his neighbour Razek Mridha's widow, Majukhatun, and brought her home. Not that this was the first time for Motalef. His previous wife had died two years ago. But, Motalef was twenty-five or twenty-six, in the prime of life. As for Majukhatun, she was nearly, if not actually, thirty. She didn't have any children to worry about, though, having married off her only daughter to the Shaikh family at Kathikhali. But while she had no anxieties, she didn't have much of her own either by way of property or riches. It wasn't as though Razek Mian had left behind chests full of gold and fields full of crops for her to get a share of. All she got was the 700 square feet or so of the family land, and a dilapidated hut. So much for her riches. And then she wasn't exactly a paragon of beauty. Majukhatun had nothing but the firm body of a fiery woman with which to attract men and win their hearts.

The wives of the Sikdars and Qazis nudged and winked at one another. 'The bitch knows black magic, she's cast a spell over his eyes.'

'Good for her,' declared Sakina, the youngest of the Munshi wives. 'Why shouldn't she? It's best to cast a spell over the eyes of a man like that. The lord hasn't taught him how to look away. Have you seen that peculiar stare of his? Good for her if she's managed to snare his attention.'

She was right. Motalef did have a peculiar stare. He used it on beautiful women in particular; his eyes were always roving, looking for a pretty face. He had been trying all this time to find a young, beautiful woman to marry. But he couldn't afford the asking rate. Anyone who had a grown-up, pretty daughter set a high price. Motalef had been bowled over most of all by Phulbanu. The daughter of Elem Shaikh from Charkhanda, she was about eighteen or thereabouts. Her body oozed promise, her heart was eager. Phulbanu was second-hand material, however. She had obtained a talaq from Gafoor Sikdar of Kaidoobi on the pretext that he did not take care of her and that he beat her frequently. Actually, Phulbanu had been put off by Gafoor because he was much older than her and not handsome either. That was why she had deliberately picked fights with him. But being second-hand had not harmed Phulbanu's looks in any way. If anything, her body had grown ever more alluring and attractive with the passage of time, and a torrent of sensuality coursed through her heart. Motalef had seen her on the banks of the river at Charkhanda. He knew at a glance that he had caught her eye too. Motalef was no laggard himself when it came to appearance. Slim and fair, he cut a fine figure of a man in his blue lungi; and besides, how many others hereabouts could boast such stylish and abundant flowing hair? Motalef was in no doubt that Phulbanu approved of him. He made his way to Elem Shaikh's house. But Elem paid no attention to him, saying he had learnt his lesson the last time around. He wouldn't hand his daughter over to anyone without making enquiries and weighing his options. In truth, all he wanted was money. He wanted to recoup his expenses on securing a talaq for his daughter, with interest added on. Motalef had estimated that the compensation would come to not twenty or forty, but a full hundred rupees. Elem would never agree to anything less. But how was he to get so much money?

Motalef had to come away unhappily. He ran into Phulbanu again amidst the wild bushes near the river. She was on her way to the river with a pitcher. Motalef realized that her need for water was well timed.

Looking around furtively, Phulbanu chuckled. 'Well, Mian, angry?'

'Why wouldn't I be? Didn't you hear the price your father quoted?'

'I heard,' said Phulbanu. 'And what's wrong with that? You want to get what you like without paying my father for it?'

'It's not the father but the daughter who's set the price,' said Motalef. 'Put yourself into a basket and go on sale at the market.'

Phulbanu laughed at Motalef's rage. 'Not just a basket, I'll go in a carriage. With fistfuls of gold and jewellery. Show me what kind of man you are, what kind of fists you have.' Motalef was about to stomp off.

Phulbanu called him back. 'Don't be angry, handsome. Listen to me.'

'Listen to what?' asked Motalef, turning back.

Looking around again, Phulbanu went a little closer to Motalef. 'Listen to my heart, that's what. Listen, my father's daughter doesn't want either money or jewellery, all she wants is that her man doesn't sacrifice his honour. She wants to see his spirit. Understand?'

Motalef nodded to say he had understood.

'But don't do anything stupid, Mian,' warned Phulbanu. 'Don't go selling your land or anything.'

Not that Motalef had enough land to sell—but his pride would not allow him to reveal this to Phulbanu. 'All right, just let winter go by,' he said. 'I'll show you my honour and my spirit. But will Bibijaan have the patience to wait?'

'Of course she will,' smiled Phulbanu. 'Don't mistake me for an impatient woman.'

Back in his village, Motalef attempted once more to borrow some money. He tried with the Mullicks, the Mukherjees, the Sikdars, and the Munshis, but without any luck. When he borrowed money, Motalef was not in the habit of paying it back quickly. As getting him to return a loan was very difficult no one was going to give him one willingly.

But although he didn't get a loan, Motalef did get a commission to tap nearly a hundred palm trees towards the beginning of winter. The number of trees in the Chowdhurys' garden had been growing since last year; there were more than one hundred and fifty now. The trees would have to be tapped and the palm juice collected in pots. Half the juice would go to the owner, and half to him for all his efforts. It was no small enterprise. The dead branches would first have to be trimmed off each tree. The blade would have to be honed, and then the bark scraped off the trunks to insert thin pipes made from reeds. Earthen pots would have to be attached properly at the ends of these pipes. Only then could the juice, dripping all night, be collected in the pot. It involved a lot of work, a great deal of attention. It needed sweat to extract the juice from the dry, unyielding palm trees. It wasn't like your mother's milk, or a cow's, that you could just suck from the nipples.

Of course, it wasn't enough to work hard. You had to know how to climb up and down trees. You needed skilful hands to get the tapping exactly right. It was this skill that made the sharp blade—the slightest touch of which could break the skin—extract the sweet syrup from the palm trees. This wasn't like harvesting paddy or jute, where you could simply cut the entire plant along with the root at one stroke. This was tapping a palm tree, which meant both slicing and squeezing. The tree must not be hurt or damaged. The slightest slip of the fingers and the tree would die before the year was out, with only its stump left. The wood from the trunk might be used to make flights of stairs for the river ghat or your home, but the tree would no longer ooze its juice one drop at a time all night.

Razek Mridha had trained Motalef to tap palm trees. It was he who had set all these rules and dos and don'ts about tapping. There wasn't a tapper as famous as Razek. His fingers could even coax syrup out of trees three-fourths dead. A tree that yielded half a pot of juice to others filled Razek's pot to the brim. Householders would be confident that when they gave him the commission, their trees would not be harmed, and the pots would be full. Motalef had spent several years as Razek's pupil, following him everywhere and helping him. Razek had a couple of other pupils too—Maqbool from the Sikdar family, and Ismail from the Qazis. But none of them became as expert as Motalef did. Only Motalef could have replaced Razek.

But it wasn't enough to tap the trees by the score, nor to bring the juice home in pots balanced at either end of a long stick placed on the shoulder—you needed someone to make gur out of the juice. A man could only tap the trees and fetch the juice, but it was up to a woman to make the unoon, the clay oven, get hold of kindling, and bring the sweet syrup to a boil over and over again, till it was converted into a thick paatali gur. Only when the raw juice had ripened into gur would there be fulfilment, only then would all the toil and effort yield results. But for some time now, there had been no such person in Motalef's home. His mother had died when he was a child. When his wife died two years earlier, there was absolutely no one left to carry out the task.

That evening, Motalef arrived at Majukhatun's hut. The door was locked. 'Are you awake, Maju Bibi?'

'Who is it?' Majukhatun responded from inside.

'It's me, Motalef. Have you gone to bed? If you'd go to the trouble of opening the door... I want to talk to you.'

Opening the door, Majukhatun said, 'I know what you have to say. Since it's the season for gur it's time to come to Majukhatun. The syrup has to be boiled and thickened. But you have to pay four annas a seer, Mian. I can't do it cheaper. I don't feel strong in the body this year.'

'Why blame your body, Bibi?' Motalef said sweetly. 'The body follows the heart. If the heart is happy, so's the body.'

'Whatever you may say, Mian, I can't do it for less than four annas,' said Majukhatun.

Motalef flashed his winning smile. 'Never mind four annas, will you agree to take the full rupee if I offer it, Bibi?'

Majukhatun's heart fluttered a little at his smile, but her response was brisk. 'Never mind the sweet talk, Mian. If you want to talk business, I'll listen, or else I'm going to bed.'

'Of course, you'll go to bed,' answered Motalef. 'That's what the night is for. But going to bed doesn't mean sleep, does it, Maju Bibi? How do you endure the long winter nights?'

Abandoning his hints and innuendoes, Motalef now made himself clear. He did not wish to take unfair advantage of her. He wanted to summon a priest to read the scripture so that he could marry her and take her home. He wanted to give her complete responsibility for his home and household.

Majukhatun was astonished at the proposal. 'Can't you find someone else to joke with?' she chided him. 'Is there a dearth of young girls? Why are you knocking at my door?'

'Why should there be a dearth, Maju Bibi?' said Motalef. 'There are plenty of young women. But despite everything they are nothing but pots of raw juice.'

'Really?' Majukhatun was amused. 'And me?'

'You're different. You're toddy for a drink and gur for a meal. How can I compare you to them?'

Although Majukhatun sent Motalef on his way that evening, she couldn't quite forget what he told her. His words played havoc with her mind as she lay on her lonely bed in the dark. She had known him a long time. Motalef used to visit this house from the time he worked with Razek, when Razek was still alive. They had known each other since then. But there was no intimacy in that acquaintance. They would laugh and joke with each other sometimes, but that was as far as it had gone. Motalef was married, and Majukhatun had her husband. Razek was a stern, unromantic man. He spoke harshly and sharply. In winter he would fetch scores of pots brimming with syrup, which Majukhatun would boil repeatedly to make gur out of. Her touch was magic. The gur she made sold at a higher price than anyone else's in the market. After Razek's death, most of the palm trees nearby were handed over to Motalef to tap. He offered her a couple of pots of juice out of courtesy now and then, but her yard was no longer filled with pots. Last year, Motalef had engaged her for a month or so to make gur from his syrup. He was supposed to pay her two annas a seer, but about a month later Motalef began to suspect her of stealing gur and getting someone else to sell it in secret. In other words, Motalef wasn't getting the full share. This dispute made their arrangement fall through. But this time Motalef had not proposed giving her the juice to make gur from; he had proposed taking Majukhatun home as his wife. One or two of the middle-aged men in the neighbourhood had made similar propositions earlier, but Majukhatun had paid no attention to them. She had threatened to cut off the ears of the younger men who had approached her with less honourable intentions. But Motalef's proposal was entirely different in nature. She couldn't dismiss him the same way. Even if she could, what he had said kept coming back to her. No one hereabouts had such a honeyed tongue; no one, come to think about it, was as handsome either.

Motalef had to visit her one or two more evenings before Majukhatun followed him to his house, dressed in a glittering blue sari and multicoloured glass bangles.

Motalef's house was completely devoid of grace; things were strewn all over the place and there was dirt and grime everywhere. Wrapping the end of her sari round her waist, Majukhatun got down to work. She swept the yard clean, and scrubbed and swabbed the floors until the entire place shone.

But Motalef had no time for his home and his wife; his time was spent on trees. He had taken commissions for the trees owned by several others in the neighbourhood—the Boses and the Banerjees. He was busy tapping the trees, lowering the brimming pots and dividing the syrup. He had made a canopy and makeshift walls with jute-stalks for Majukhatun in the western half of the yard. In this covered space, Majukhatun built a row of ovens, on which she placed large earthen vessels and brought the syrup to a boil from morning till afternoon. Motalef brought sheaves of straw from the fields as kindling, dried palm tree branches too. But it was never enough. Majukhatun swept up dry leaves from people's gardens and the jungle, bringing them home in baskets. In the late afternoon, she chopped the branches with an axe to make kindling. Without rest and without a break, with no feeling of fatigue. Majukhatun had once again discovered work after her heart, as well as a man after her heart.

Motalef took the gur to nearby markets in baskets, selling it at high prices. His was the best gur in the marketplace. At dusk he went back to the trees to fix fresh pots. Funnels of bamboo hung from the trees for the juice to drip through. When he unfastened the pots in the morning, he left the funnels tied to the trees. Dirty juice accumulated in the funnels. At dusk he changed the funnels, made fresh cuts in the bark and left empty pots to collect the juice. The dirty juice gathered in the funnel did not go to waste. It was boiled to make a different kind of gur, which was mixed with tobacco for hookahs. Even this sold in the market at five or six annas a seer.

All this climbing up and down trees twice a day made Motalef pant heavily; even in the cold of December and January he perspired all over. Beads of sweat glistened on his hairy chest in the morning. Motalef's neighbours were astonished when they saw him. He had always been hardworking, but no one had ever seen him toil morning to night with such enthusiasm, almost like a machine. What was going on? Tapping trees was indeed work that Motalef loved, but had he finally found a match for his heart too?

Motalef arrived at Elem Shaikh's house in Charkhanda with two pots of the sweetest syrup from the best trees and about three seers of paatali gur. Greeting him, Motalef placed the offerings at Elem's feet, and then pulled five ten-rupee notes from a knot in his lungi, saying, 'Half in advance, Mian Sahib.'

'Advance for what?' asked Elem.

'For your daughter's...' answered Motalef.

He had picked crisp notes for his offering. They weren't even slightly frayed at the edges, and didn't have a speck of dirt from his fingers on them. Fifty rupees in cash. Running his fingers over the notes, Elem said, 'But what will I do with this advance now, Mian? I believe you have already married Razek Mridha's widow. Why should my daughter share a husband with someone else? Do you want them to quarrel and fight, and then kill each other one night?'

Motalef chuckled. 'Don't worry about that, Mian Sahib. Majukhatun will be in my home only as long as the sap lasts in the trees and winter lasts in our land. Everything will be cleared out as soon as the spring breeze starts blowing.'

Elem Shaikh offered Motalef a stool to sit on, and handed him his own hookah. 'You are clear-headed, Mian,' he said approvingly. 'It's a pleasure to work with you.'

Motalef received permission to meet Phulbanu. Not that Phulbanu hadn't already eavesdropped on the entire conversation. But still she pouted when she saw Motalef. 'Now who was being impatient, Mian? Here I was waiting for you and you brought someone else home.'

'What else could I have done?' Motalef said.

He had been forced to resort to this trick to maintain his honour, even to survive. How was he to live without someone at home to look after him? How was the gur to be made from the syrup without someone at home to do it? And how was his honour to be preserved if he couldn't sell this gur and make some money?

'That's all very well,' said Phulbanu. 'Your honour is intact and you have survived. But how will you get rid of the scent of the other woman from your body?'

Although the thought occurred to Motalef, he did not actually say that the scent of a man or a woman did not remain on another's body after they were gone; for, if that were the case, Phulbanu would have had such a scent on her body too. But suppressing this retort, Motalef answered evasively, 'Don't worry about the scent, Phul Bibi. I'll get soap from the market and wait at the ghat for you. You can rub the scent off my body.'

'Oh really?' said Phulbanu, covering her mouth with the end of her sari.

'Do you think I'm lying?' said Motalef. 'Smell me after that, you will only find the scent of my new woman. Just wait a couple of months more.'

'Don't think I'm impatient,' Phulbanu assured him again.

Motalef was as good as his word. Phulbanu did not have to wait more than two months. As soon as Motalef had made another fifty rupees from selling gur, he gave a talaq to Majukhatun. He even informed his neighbours of the reason openly. Maju Bibi was not faithful to him. Her behaviour with Razek's brother Waheed Mridha was objectionable.

'Shame,' said Majukhatun, biting her lips. 'You are only handsome, Moti Mian, but you aren't good. So this is what you were plotting? You stuck to me like an ant for the gur, but now that the season is over, you're kicking me out.'

But Motalef had neither the time nor the patience for all this.

The mango trees filled with buds, and the gaub trees, with tender copper-coloured leaves. Winter was followed by spring, and Majukhatun by Phulbanu. She lived up to her name. Her face was like a flower; her breath carried the fragrance of flowers. 'This time they are made for each other,' said the neighbours. 'Now there truly is spring in his house.'

Motalef couldn't have been happier. He worked as a hired hand on the farms all day. And then, even before the sun had set, he had the end of Phulbanu's sari in his hand. 'Throw away all those pots and pans. Come sit by my side.'

'Patience,' giggled Phulbanu. 'How did you get through all those months, Mian?'

'With the trees,' answered Motalef.

Phulbanu almost choked in his strong arms. Catching her breath, she laughed. 'Go back to the trees then. Only the trees can make love to you.'

'But the trees run out of juice in three months or four, Phuljaan,' answered Motalef. 'You, on the other hand, keep oozing your juice year after year.'

～

Majukhatun took shelter again in Razek's dilapidated hut. She had planned to go back to her old routine. But even if she managed to pass the day, the nights simply would not pass. Motalef had ruined her life. Neighbours described Motalef and Phulbanu's home in great detail, adding their embellishments, and taking Motalef to task with what seemed to be amused indulgence, 'The man is mad about his wife. He cannot talk of anyone else.'

Majukhatun felt her heart churn. She thought she would go mad with jealousy. That she would die of heartbreak.

A few days later, Razek's elder brother Waheed carried a proposal to her. He had taken pity on her condition. Waheed was friends with Nadir Shaikh from Talkanda, across the river. Nadir was a boatman. His wife had died of cholera a month or so ago, leaving behind numerous children. The poor fellow was in trouble with them. He didn't want a young wife. Someone like that might be a beautiful bride, but she wouldn't be able to look after the children. He preferred a mature, serious woman, like Majukhatun. He would be able to depend on her.

'How old is he?' asked Majukhatun.

'About my age,' answered Waheed. 'Fifty, maybe fifty-one.'

Majukhatun nodded happily—yes, this was what she wanted. She didn't trust young men. She had no faith in youth anymore.

'He isn't a tree-tapper, is he?' Majukhatun asked. 'He doesn't go off to collect palm juice in winter, does he?'

'Why should he tap trees?' asked Waheed in surprise. 'He doesn't know how to do all that. He rows a boat in the monsoon, works as a farmhand in winter, thatches roofs too. Why, don't you want to marry anyone besides a tree-tapper?'

'Just the opposite,' said Majukhatun. If she were to get married, it would only be to someone who had nothing to do with palm juice, someone who didn't go anywhere near date palms in winter. She despised the whole business of palm syrup.

'Then shall I talk to Nadir?' asked Waheed. 'He doesn't want to wait.'

'No need to wait,' said Majukhatun.

It didn't take very long. Everything was finalized within a week. Majukhatun climbed into a ferryboat with Nadir and crossed the river.

'Good riddance,' Motalef told his wife. 'Her breathing sounded like a witch's, she would heap curses on me all the time. We are free of her now, aren't we Phuljaan?'

'Are you afraid of witches, Mian?' Phulbanu laughed.

'Not anymore,' answered Motalef. 'The witch is gone. Now all I see is a fairy. It's the fairy I fear now.'

'Why, what are you afraid of the fairy for?'

'Shouldn't I be afraid? What if the fairy spreads her wings and flies away?'

'No, Mian, the fairy has no wish to fly anymore,' answered Phulbanu. 'She's got what she wants. So long as the man of the house doesn't change his taste or the way he looks at her.'

'So long as he has eyes, the way he looks at her won't change,' said Motalef.

Motalef treated his wife with great love and care. Before he went to the market he checked what kind of fish she wanted; if he couldn't afford it, he borrowed money to buy the fish. Eggs, vegetables, spices—he bought whatever he could for her. Also, paan and everything else that went into it.

'Why do you bring so much paan?' Phulbanu asked. 'You don't care for it much, do you? All you do is smoke all the time.'

'The paan's for you,' Motalef answered. 'Have all the paan you can, I want your lips red.'

'Why, aren't my lips red enough?' pouted Phulbanu. 'You think I have to chew paan to redden them? I'm going to make some for you, you'd better start. Your lips have turned black from smoking, you can redden them too.'

'Men's lips don't turn red from paan, Phuljaan,' smiled Motalef, 'but from someone else's reddened lips.'

Motalef did not own any land of his own. He sharecropped on some of the land owned by the Mullicks and Mukherjees. But he had no reputation as a skilful tiller, for his plots did not yield as much of a harvest as the others. He worked as a hired hand on the land owned by the Sikdars and Munshis, cutting, washing and spreading the jute out to dry. Hard labour. Motalef's fair skin turned brown under the sun. Not much of the jute from sharecropping came home. The Sikdars and Munshis paid cash. Motalef only brought home some of the jute from the small plots owned by the Mullicks and Mukherjees which he sharecropped, piling a boat with it and arriving at the ghat on the canal. Phulbanu was very keen on sorting the jute. But Motalef didn't let her touch it at first. 'It's hard work,' he said, 'the smell will rub off on you.'

'What if it does?' Phulbanu said. 'Here you are burning under the sun, and you think I cannot sort the jute because it will be hard on me. The things you say, Mian.'

It wasn't a large amount of jute that they could call their own—it didn't yield many stalks to be used as fuel. Phulbanu wanted to sort the jute that other families got as their share of the crops, so that she could claim the stalks. But Motalef refused, for he wasn't going to have his wife work so hard.

The paddy ripened around the middle of October. Motalef took a ride on someone else's boat to work as a farmhand during the harvest. Standing in water up to his waist, he cut the paddy, loading the boat with bales of it. But his blade didn't run as quickly as those of Momin or Karim or Hamid or Aziz. Motalef's fingers were too slow, he was troubled by the water. One day he found a leech lodged in his armpit. 'Can't you even get rid of the leech yourself, Mian,' said Phulbanu as she prised it away. 'You have hands, haven't you?'

'The hands to cut the paddy with were with me,' answered Motalef, 'but I forgot the one to get rid of the leech with.'

With great care, Phulbanu dabbed lime on the spots that the leech had sucked. Motalef worked on the paddy with four other farmhands, and got a fifth of the labourers' share. He brought it home in a basket. Phulbanu cleaned it and put it out to dry. 'Hard work, isn't it, Bou?' said Motalef.

'Yes, the hard work is killing me,' said Phulbanu. 'Who do you think you're talking to, Mian? Was I not born in an ordinary family? Or do you think I dropped from the sky?'

Spring passed, so did monsoon and autumn, and winter returned. The season of gur was the time for Motalef's real business. But this time winter seemed to have arrived a little late. Never mind, Motalef would take on additional trees to compensate. The number of palm trees increased every year. Motalef was renowned in this line of work; he was the best in the village. This time, too, the Banerjees had thirty or so new trees.

Soon the tree-tapping was in full swing. Motalef had no time for a break or for rest; he didn't even have the time for his love-games with Phulbanu. The loans had to be returned, and he had to put away enough money for the year from the sale of syrup and gur. Motalef worked like a demon all day, falling asleep the moment he hit the bed. Phulbanu nudged and poked him, wrapped her arms around him, but it was like embracing a tree rather than a man. Motalef slept like the dead. Only his nose emitted a sound, but no other part of him responded. Phulbanu shivered even under a thick quilt. How could a quilt keep the cold out without a man's warmth?

It wasn't enough to get the juice home, kindling was also needed to bring it to boil for the gur. Motalef brought dry leaves and twigs home from wherever he could find them. 'Boil the juice over and over,' he told Phulbanu. 'The gur must be as sweet as you are. I want the best and tastiest gur to sell in the market.'

But Phulbanu turned pale when she saw the sheer quantity of syrup. She had made gur from a pot or two of juice at her father's house, but she had never seen so much of it in one place, leave alone boil it to make gur.

Laughing at her apprehension, Motalef said, 'Don't worry, I'm here too—ask me if in doubt, I'll tell you. The pot must bubble the way your heart does.'

But all the juice in Phulbanu's heart evaporated as she sat by the ovens from morning till afternoon. The flames ran low, her beautiful face was scorched, but still the gur did not meet Motalef's high standards. The paatali remained soft; sometimes it was burnt and turned bitter.

'What kind of woman are you,' Motalef said roughly. 'I explained everything to you, but you just don't understand. Do you expect customers to spend their money on gur like this?'

'Why won't they?' Phulbanu tried to smile. 'They'll buy if you know how to sell.'

The smile did not please Motalef. 'Then go sell it yourself in the market. They might buy it if they see a pretty face, because they certainly won't buy the gur when they see it.'

Phulbanu was not a fool, nor was she absolutely incompetent. With all the instructions and guidance, she learnt how to make passable gur in a few days. The gur was no longer unfit for selling. But the price couldn't match last year's, and buyers weren't happy.

The regular customers stared at the gur and at Motalef alternately. 'What kind of gur is this, Mian? I bought some last market-day but it wasn't as tasty as last year. I remember your gur then, the taste is still on my lips. But not this time. Chandan Shaikh and Madan Sikdar have better gur than yours this year.'

Motalef's heart burned; he seethed with anger. His gur was not as tasty this year. Why? He wasn't working any less hard. Why was his gur still not tasty, why couldn't he charge a higher price for it, why weren't people happy at its sight and after they had tried it, why was his gur not being praised? Why was he being made to listen to such criticism, for what?

In bed that night Motalef repeatedly explained the technique for bringing the syrup to a boil to Phulbanu. 'You have to check the ladle continuously to see if it's time to take it off the fire, if it's time to pour it out of the vessel to set.'

'Yes, I know,' said Phulbanu glumly. 'Stop chattering now, let me sleep.'

Motalef was suddenly reminded of Majukhatun. He had discussed the whole thing with her many times in bed. She had never snapped back, never complained about her sleep being disturbed. She had listened to him eagerly, joined the discussion happily.

The next day, Motalef appeared in the afternoon with a huge load of kindling. Putting it down near the makeshift room for the ovens, he asked, 'What's the gur like today, Phuljaan?'

But there was no answer from Phulbanu. Calling her again and still getting no response, Motalef poked his head in through the door. But Phulbanu was nowhere to be seen. There was a strange smell—was the gur burnt? The syrup was boiling and bubbling in five large pots all in a row. Motalef looked closely. Just as he had thought. The furthest pot had boiled over, and the gur had burnt a little—the smell came from there. Motalef felt a red hot flash of rage in his chest. A scream tore out of his throat—'Where are you, bitch?'

Phulbanu emerged from the house hurriedly. She hadn't been able to bathe for two days because she was working late into the afternoon. Her skin had felt dry and bristly so she had used some soda and soap and taken an early dip in the river. She had dressed in a blue sari after her bath. Drying her hair on the towel, Phulbanu was running a comb through it when she heard Motalef's cry. She ran out to meet him still holding the comb. Her wet hair clung to her back. Motalef stared at her for a moment with his eyes blazing, and then grabbed a fistful of wet hair. 'Bitch, the gur is burning and you have no idea, you're busy dressing up, you think you're a goddess stepped out of a painting, this is why my gur is bad, this is why I'm humiliated. I've earned a bad name everywhere because of you.'

'Don't you dare touch my hair because of that,' Phulbanu kept saying. 'Don't you lay a hand on me.'

'I see, you're too good to be beaten by hand, are you?' Picking up a thin strip of bamboo lying on the floor, Motalef began to whip her. 'Being beaten with a cane won't rob the Shaikh's daughter of her honour, will it? It's wrong to slap you, but not to whip you.'

Motalef had a foul temper. His anger was as terrible as his love was impatient and unreasonable.

Elem Shaikh heard about the beating when he arrived from Charkhanda. He threatened, scolded and shouted at his son-in-law, but did not spare his daughter either.

'Take me home with you, Abbajaan,' Phulbanu told him. 'I'm not going to live with a hot-tempered man like him.'

But Elem Shaikh persuaded his daughter to stay. If he gave in to her, Phulbanu would demand a talaq again. And that just wouldn't do—how could a girl from a family like theirs keep switching husbands and homes? How would that preserve her honour? If she could only be a little patient, Motalef would calm down on his own. They would make up soon. Domestic quarrels. Started by day, ended by night. Nothing to worry about.

It did end. Motalef made the first move to make up. He pleaded with Phulbanu to relent. She began making the gur again the next day. In the afternoon, Motalef took the gur to the market in his basket. Before leaving, he said, 'Your troubles will be over once these two months have passed somehow, Phuljaan.'

'What trouble?' said Phulbanu.

But this wasn't sincere, just politeness. Neither of them seemed able to speak their hearts anymore. Their exchanges were different now, in form and in sound; and neither had any problem recognizing this. The speaker knew it, and so did the listener.

The market days came and went, the season neared its end; the fame of Motalef's gur did not spread, and its price did not rise. Motalef no longer took Phulbanu to task over this when he came home; he only smoked in silence. The sap oozed out of the tree through the pipes into the pots. Motalef awoke at dawn to unfasten the pots brimming with syrup and bring them home, but he was neither as happy, nor as eager, as last year. His body was still soaked in perspiration, but his heart was as dry as jute stalks, as desolate as the roads in the afternoon sun. Pots of syrup lined the yard, a voluptuous woman moved about the home, but still Motalef felt no fulfilment, still the world seemed empty.

One day he ran into Nadir Shaikh at the market.

'Salaam, Mian Sahib.'

'Walaikum salaam.'

'All well, I hope?' said Motalef. 'The children…'

About to ask after Majukhatun too, Motalef held back. 'Yes, Mian, they're all well,' Nadir smiled. 'We're surviving by god's grace.'

After a little hesitation, Motalef said, 'Why don't you take a little gur for the children, Mian? It's good gur.'

'Of course it is,' Nadir smiled again. 'Your gur has never been bad.'

'No, Mian, it's not the same anymore,' Motalef blurted out suddenly.

Nadir looked at Motalef in surprise. What kind of a trader was he? Imagine criticizing the very gur you're trying to sell!

'How much?' asked Nadir.

'Never mind the price. I'm giving you two seers for the children. Tell them their uncle sent it for them.'

'No, Mian,' said Nadir anxiously. 'You're selling your gur, how can I take it without paying for it?'

'Why don't you just take it and try it...you can always pay me next time,' Motalef told him.

The words seemed to stick in Motalef's throat. He had to say such things to ensure sales, he had to sing praises to his own gur; but in his heart he knew he was lying. Customers would not buy his gur under any circumstances next season; they would not crowd around his baskets anymore.

After much coaxing, Nadir agreed to take one seer of gur free, but insisted on paying for the other two seers.

Majukhatun was furious when she heard. 'Give the gur to your children if you wish, but if I am my father's daughter I won't touch it with my hands.'

Another market-day came, but Nadir did not go anywhere near Motalef. Majukhatun had forbidden him to. 'If you dare be nice to that man, I will leave your house. You won't see me again in the morning.'

Nadir was terrified of Majukhatun. Her housework was very good and her conversation was pleasant, but when his wife lost her temper, she took leave of her senses.

A few days later, Motalef climbed into a ferryboat with two pots of the best syrup from his two finest trees. He took the road past the shaggy jujube tree to enter Nadir's front yard. 'Are you home, Mian?'

Nadir emerged from his room, holding his hookah. 'Who is it? Oh, it's you, Mian. Please come in. Why did you bring all this, Mian Sahib?'

Nadir may have welcomed Motalef formally, but he grew apprehensive because of Majukhatun. The man his wife couldn't stand was here in person. Who knew what awful things would happen now?

Just as Nadir had feared, when she spotted Motalef through the fence, Majukhatun summoned her husband inside. Then she said, making sure that Motalef heard, 'Tell him to leave this house, tell him to leave at once. Does he have no shame? How dare he show up here?'

'Softly, Bibi, speak softly,' Nadir whispered. 'He'll hear you. You can't say such things about a visitor. We don't even drive a dog out this way.'

'You don't understand, Mian, some people are worse than dogs, more dangerous than the devil,' said Majukhatun. 'Ask him, does he have no fear, no shame, bringing syrup for me?'

Majukhatun didn't say any of this softly—Motalef heard every word. But strangely, though the statements were harsh and rude they did not hurt him. On the contrary, he felt there was something loving in all the condemnation and abuses heaped on him. Behind Majukhatun's sharp, distorted tone was the voice of a hurt and deprived—and consequently unhappy—woman. Syrup was oozing out, drop by drop, at the touch of a sharp tool on the bark of the tree.

Climbing the steps outside the front door, Motalef put the pots down on the floor and called out to Nadir, 'Just a minute, Mian.'

Nadir emerged, looking embarrassed. 'Sit down, Mian. Here, have a smoke.'

Motalef accepted the hookah from Nadir, but didn't draw on it immediately. Still holding it, he told Nadir, 'Will you tell your wife something on my behalf?'

'Why not tell her yourself?' said Nadir. 'Nothing wrong with that.'

'No, you tell her,' said Motalef. 'I dare not. Tell her that Motalef

Mian knows better than to bring syrup for her.'

'Then what has he brought it for?' Majukhatun exclaimed inside the house before Nadir could reply.

Still looking at Nadir, Motalef answered, 'Tell her that he has brought it for her to make a couple of seers of gur. Motalef Mian will take the gur to the market. He will sell it to new customers. He has not been able to sell any good gur this year. He has tapped all the trees in vain.' Motalef's voice sounded hoarse. Controlling himself, he was about to continue, when he suddenly spotted a pair of large black eyes on the other side of the fence, brimming with tears. He looked on in silence, unable to say anything more.

Nadir Shaikh seemed to wake up suddenly. 'What's wrong, Mian, you're just holding your hookah. Don't you want to smoke? Has it gone out?'

Bringing the hookah up to his mouth, Motalef said, 'No, Mian Bhai, it hasn't gone out.'

eleven

TWO MAGICIANS

SATYAJIT RAY

'Five, six, seven, eight, nine, ten, eleven.'

Having counted all the trunks, Surapati turned to his assistant, Anil. 'All right. Send them off to the brake van. Just twenty-five minutes to go.'

'Your compartment is ready too, sir,' Anil said. 'It's a coupé. Both berths are reserved for you. No one will disturb you.' Chuckling, he added, 'The guard's a fan too. He's been to your show at the New Empire. Ah, here he is—this way, sir.'

Biren Bakshi, the guard on the train, extended his right hand towards Surapati with a wide smile.

'If I may, sir, allow me to be honoured by shaking the hand whose tricks have given me so much pleasure.'

A single glance at any of Surapati Mondol's eleven trunks would reveal his identity. The words 'Mondol's Miracles' were stencilled in bold letters on the lids and sides of every trunk. No other explanation was necessary—for, just two months earlier, at the New Empire theatre in Calcutta, the audience had conveyed its appreciation through prolonged applause. The newspapers had been full of praise too. Mondol had been forced to promise the theatre authorities that he would perform again during the Christmas holidays.

'Please do let me know if you need anything, sir.'

The guard escorted Surapati to his compartment. Looking around, Surapati breathed a sigh of relief. It looked comfortable.

'Now if I may take leave, sir…'

'Thanks very much.'

When the guard had left, Surapati leaned back against the window and took a packet of cigarettes out of his pocket. This was probably the start of a triumphal journey. Delhi, Agra, Allahabad, Benares, Lucknow. That was all this time around, but there were so many states yet to be covered, numerous cities and towns. And why think of India alone? There was a world beyond—a huge expanse. Being a Bengali didn't mean being unambitious. Surapati would show everyone. His fame would reach as far as America, home of the magician Houdini, reading about whom used to give him goose pimples once. He would prove to the world how far a boy from Bengal could go. Just let a few years pass. This was just the beginning.

Anil came running. 'All okay, sir. Everything.'

'Have you checked the locks?'

'Yes, sir.'

'Good.'

'I'm just two carriages away.'

'Have they cleared the line?'

'Any moment now. Will you have a cup of tea at Burdwan?'

'Not a bad idea.'

'I'll get you some.'

Anil left. Surapati lit a cigarette and looked out the window. A constant and noisy stream of porters, passengers and vendors streamed past in both directions. As he gazed at them his mind wandered. His eyes clouded over. The hubbub on the platform died down. He went back a long way in time, to a place far away. He was thirty-three now, but then he was only seven or eight years old. A tiny village in Dinajpur district—Panchpukur. It was a quiet autumn afternoon. An old woman was seated in front of Moti the grocer's shop with a gunny bag. People old and young were thronging around her. How old was she? Could be sixty, could be ninety. Her sunken cheeks were criss-crossed with hundreds of creases, which doubled whenever she smiled. She kept up a torrent of words through her missing teeth.

'Bhanumatir khel. Magic!'

The old woman had put on a magic show. For the first and last time. But Surapati never forgot what he saw, and never would. His own grandmother was sixty-five—her entire body shook uncontrollably when she tried to thread a needle. And this old woman had so much magic in her wrinkled hands. She was making things disappear under everyone's noses, and then conjuring them from thin air the next moment—money, marbles, spinning tops, nuts, fruits. Taking a rupee from Kalu Kaka, she made it vanish, sending him into a rage. When she made it materialize again, going off into peals of laughter, Kalu Kaka's eyes turned into saucers.

Surapati had been unable to sleep for several days after this magic show. And even when he eventually did, apparently he would often cry out, 'Magic! magic!' in his sleep.

After this, whenever there was a fair in the village, Surapati would visit it in the hope of watching some more magic. But he hadn't come across anything remarkable.

At sixteen, Surapati moved to his uncle's house on Bipradas Street in Calcutta to study for his intermediate degree. Alongside college textbooks, he read books on magic. Surapati had bought them within a month or two of arriving in the city, and had taught himself all the tricks in the books soon afterwards. He had had to buy several packs of cards. He would stand in front of the mirror for hours on end, practising. Surapati would sometimes perform his magic tricks on Saraswati Puja celebrations in his college or at friends' birthday parties.

He was invited to his friend Gautam's sister's wedding during his second year in college. It was a memorable day in the history of Surapati's magic training, for this was where he met Tripura Babu for the first time. A marquee had been erected in the field behind the enormous house on Swinhoe Street, and Tripura Babu was sitting in one corner, surrounded by guests. He had appeared nondescript at first glance. He was about forty-eight years old, with wavy, parted hair, a jovial expression, and traces of paan juice at the corners of his mouth. You saw countless such people on the streets. But what was happening on the sheet in front of him forced you to change your mind. Surapati couldn't believe his own eyes at first. A silver fifty-paisa coin rolled along to a gold ring placed three feet away, and then escorted the ring back to Tripura Babu. Surapati had been so stupefied that he hadn't even been able to summon up enough strength to clap. And then, the very next moment, another extraordinary piece of magic. Absorbed in the performance, Gautam's uncle had spilled all his matchsticks from the box while trying to light his cigar. As he was about to bend over, Tripura Babu had said, 'Why put yourself to trouble, sir? Allow me.'

Piling the matchsticks in a heap on the floor, Tripura Babu had held out the matchbox in his left hand, calling, 'Come, boys, come along now…' And, just like pet dogs or cats, the matchsticks had trooped into the box, one by one.

After the wedding dinner, Surapati had gone up to Tripura Babu who was standing by himself in a corner. Tripura Babu had been astonished by Surapati's interest in magic. 'Bengalis are happy enough just to watch,' he had said, 'I don't find too many people interested in performing. I am genuinely surprised that you're interested.'

Surapati had visited Tripura Babu at home within two days. He lived in a tiny, ramshackle room in a boarding house on Mirzapur Street. Surapati had never seen anyone live in so much poverty and deprivation. Tripura Babu had told Surapati how he made a living. He charged a fee of fifty rupees for a magic show. He barely got two commissions a month. Making more of an effort might have helped, but Surapati had realized that Tripura Babu was not that kind of a man. He couldn't have imagined that such a talented person would be so lacking in ambition. When he said as much, Tripura Babu had answered, 'What's the use? Who's going to value good things in this accursed country? How many people really understand art? How many can tell the original from the counterfeit? You praised my magic so effusively at the wedding the other evening, but no one else did. As soon as they were told dinner was served, they abandoned the magic to line up to worship their bellies.'

Surapati arranged for Tripura Babu to perform on special occasions at a few friends' and relatives' houses. Partly out of gratitude, and mostly out of affection, Tripura Babu had agreed to pass on his magic skills to Surapati. He had objected vehemently when Surapati had mentioned paying him. 'Don't even bring it up,' he had said. 'What is important is that I will have an inheritor. Since you are so interested and so enthusiastic, I will teach you. But don't be in a hurry. You have to dedicate yourself. Haste will achieve nothing. If you learn properly, you will experience the joy of creation. Do not expect too much money or fame. But then you will never share my plight, because you have ambition, which I don't...'

'You'll teach me all your tricks, won't you?' Surapati had asked hesitantly. 'Even the one with the coin and the ring?'

Tripura Babu had laughed. 'One step at a time. Don't be impatient. You have to keep at it. It needs dedication. These are ancient arts. This form of magic came about at a time when man had genuine willpower and concentration. Modern man cannot take his mind to that level easily. Have you any idea what an effort I had to make?'

Something happened after about six months of training with Tripura Babu.

On his way to college one day, Surapati noticed colourful posters on every wall in Chowringhee for Chefalo the Great. Going up to a poster to read the details, Surapati learnt that Chefalo was a famous Italian magician who was coming to Calcutta to perform. He would be accompanied by his fellow magician Madame Palermo.

At the New Empire Surapati had watched Chefalo's magic from the one-rupee seats. Incredibly eye-popping and mind-blowing acts, all of them. Surapati had only read about such magic in books. Entire humans disappeared in smoke in front of everyone's eyes, emerging again like Aladdin's genie from coils of smoke. Putting a girl inside a wooden crate, Chefalo sawed the box in half; the girl appeared from a different box within minutes, laughing, without a scratch on her. Surapati's palms had turned red with clapping.

And Chefalo himself was a source of continuous amazement for Surapati. The man was as good an actor as he was a magician. He was dressed in a shiny black suit and a top hat, with a magic wand in his hand. Was there anything Chefalo couldn't conjure out of that hat with his magic skills? On one occasion, he reached into a hat and pulled out a rabbit by its ears. The poor thing had barely finished shaking its ears when pigeons flew out—one, two, three, four. The magic pigeons flew around the hall, their wings rustling. Meanwhile, Chefalo was pulling chocolate bars out of the same hat and tossing them into the audience.

And throughout, Chefalo kept talking. Verbal fireworks. Surapati had read that this was referred to as patter. This patter was the magician's mainstay—while the audience drowned in its currents, the magician performed his sleight of hand unnoticed.

But Madame Palermo was a strange exception. She didn't utter a single word, performing her tricks like a silent robot. When did she perform her sleight of hand, then? Surapati had later found out the answer to this as well. It was possible to perform certain magic tricks on stage that required no sleight of hand. These tricks depended on machines, which were run by people behind the black curtain at the back of the stage. Cutting people into two halves and rejoining them, or making them disappear in smoke, was all a matter of machinery. If you had enough money you could buy these machines—or have them made—to put on these magic tricks. Of course, there was a certain flair and art involved in performing them with showmanship and panache, making them more attractive with glittering clothes and shiny props. Not everyone had mastered this art, which was why wealth was not enough to be a magician. After all, not everyone could...

Surapati's web of memories snapped suddenly.

The train had just left the platform with a bone-rattling jerk when the door to the compartment was flung open and the man who entered was...what! About to shout in indignation, Surapati held his tongue.

It was Tripura Babu! Tripuracharan Mullick!

Surapati had had similar experiences earlier. Someone he knew well, but hadn't met in a long time, suddenly cropped up in his thoughts or in a discussion and, the next thing you knew, the person was actually in their midst.

But still Surapati felt that Tripura Babu's sudden appearance put all those incidents in the shade. For a few moments he could not even speak. Wiping the perspiration off his forehead with the edge of his dhoti, Tripura Babu set his bundle down on the floor and sat down on the opposite end of the bench. Smiling at Surapati, he said, 'Surprised?'

Gulping, Surapati said, 'Surprised in the sense that—first, I didn't know you were alive.'

'What do you mean?'

'I visited your boarding house shortly after my BA exams. I found the door locked. The manager—I forget his name—said that you'd been run over...'

Tripura Babu burst into laughter. 'Something like that would have been wonderful. I'd have been relieved of all my worries.'

'And the second thing is,' added Surapati, 'I was thinking of you just the other day.'

'What's that?' A pall of gloom seemed to settle on Tripura Babu's expression. 'Thinking of me? You still think of me? I'm surprised to hear that.'

Surapati looked contrite. 'What are you saying, Tripura Babu! You think I can forget so easily? You introduced me to magic. I was especially reminded of the old days today. I am travelling for a show. Outside of Bengal for the first time. Did you know I'm a professional magician now?'

Tripura Babu nodded.

'I do. I know everything. And I came here to meet you today because I know everything. Everything that you have done over the past twelve years, how you have established yourself and achieved the fame you have today, is known to me. I was present at New Empire that evening, the first day. In the very last row. I saw how everyone appreciated your craft. I admit to feeling some pride. But...'

Tripura Babu paused. Surapati was silent. What could he possibly say? Tripura Babu could not be blamed for feeling disappointed. It was true that Surapati wouldn't be what he was today if Tripura Babu hadn't taught him the fundamentals. And what had Surapati done for him in return? On the contrary, his memory of Tripura Babu had faded over the past twelve years. Even his sense of gratitude had diminished.

Tripura Babu continued, 'I was proud of your success that day. But it was mixed with regret. Do you know why? The path you have chosen is not one of pure magic. A lot of what you're doing is fooling people with smoke and mirrors, tricks using machinery. It's not your own magic. Do you remember mine?'

Surapati had not forgotten. But at the same time he had felt that Tripura Babu had been hesitant about teaching Surapati his best tricks. 'Not yet,' he used to say. The time never came. Chefalo came before that. Surapati began to weave dreams, putting himself in Chefalo's place. He imagined himself travelling around the world performing shows, making a name for himself, giving pleasure to people, earning their approval and applause.

Tripura Babu was gazing out the window absently. Surapati observed him closely. He seemed to be in a bad way. His hair was almost entirely grey, the skin on his face was slack, his eyes were sunken. But had his eyes dimmed at all? It didn't seem so. He had a strangely piercing gaze.

With a sigh, Tripura Babu said, 'Mind you, I understand why you chose this path. I know you believe—and perhaps I am partly responsible for this—that purity is worthless. To perform magic on stage you need a little glitter and showmanship. Isn't that so?'

Surapati didn't deny it. He had concluded as much after watching Chefalo. But was glitter necessarily bad? Times had changed. How much could you earn performing your magic tricks at a wedding, and how many people would come to know of you? He had seen Tripura Babu's plight with his own eyes. What use was magic if performing it in all its purity couldn't even bring you two square meals a day?

Surapati told Tripura Babu about Chefalo. Was something which gave pleasure to thousands, earning their praise, not to be appreciated?

Surapati was not disparaging pure magic. But there was no future down that route. So he had chosen this one.

Tripura Babu seemed to become agitated suddenly. Hoisting his feet on to the bench they were sitting on, he leaned towards Surapati.

'Look, Surapati, if you had really understood what genuine magic is, you wouldn't have chased the fake kind. Sleight of hand is just one aspect, although there are countless kinds. Like yogic acts, you have to practise them for months and years. But there's so much more. Hypnotism. Bringing people under your control with just a look, turning them into putty in your hands. Then there's clairvoyance, telepathy, thought-reading. You will have unrestricted access to people's thoughts. You can check someone's pulse and tell them what they're thinking. Once you've really mastered the art you won't even have to touch them. Just looking at them for a minute will tell you their innermost secrets, what's in their heart. Is all this magic? These things lie at the root of the finest magic in the world. There are no levers and pulleys here. There is only dedication, devotion, concentration.'

Tripura Babu paused for breath. He had had to talk above the sound of the train, which had probably exhausted him. Now he moved closer to Surapati, saying, 'I wanted to teach you all this, but you didn't care. You couldn't wait. You were taken in by a flashy, foreign charlatan. You abandoned the real path for the one that leads to quick wealth.'

Surapati was silent. He really could not deny any of these allegations.

Placing his hand on Surapati's shoulder, Tripura Babu softened his tone. 'I have come to you with a request, Surapati. I don't know if you can tell from my appearance—but I have really fallen on hard days. I know so much magic, but the magic of making money has eluded me. The lack of ambition has been my undoing—I would hardly have had to worry about how to make a living otherwise. I have come to you out of desperation, Surapati. I have neither the strength nor the youth to establish myself now. But I do have the faith that you will help me during this difficult time, even if it means a little sacrifice. I shan't bother you after that.'

Surapati was perplexed. What did the man want?

Tripura Babu continued, 'The plan may appear somewhat drastic to you, but there is no other way. The trouble is that it isn't just money that I need. I've developed a new desire in my old age, you know. I want to demonstrate my best acts to a large audience. Perhaps, for the first and last time, but I simply cannot suppress this wish.'

Surapati's heart quaked with an unknown fear.

Tripura Babu finally got to the point.

'You're going to Lucknow for a performance. Suppose you were to fall ill at the last moment. And instead of turning back a disappointed audience, what if someone else...'

Surapati was flabbergasted. What was Tripura Babu saying! He really must be quite desperate to make such a proposal.

When he didn't speak, Tripura Babu said, 'Because of unavoidable reasons, your guru will perform instead of you—this is what you will inform them. Will people be very disappointed? I don't think so. I am certain that they will enjoy my magic. Still, I propose that you will get half of what you would have been paid for the performance. Whatever's left over will be enough for me. After which you can continue as you are doing now. I won't bother you anymore. But you must give me this one opportunity, Surapati.'

Surapati was furious.

'Impossible! You don't know what you're saying, Tripura Babu. This is my first show outside Bengal. Don't you understand how much depends on the Lucknow performance? Should I begin my career with a lie? How could you even imagine such a thing?'

Tripura Babu looked steadily at Surapati for some time. Then his measured, restrained voice was heard above the clatter of the wheels.

'Are you still interested in the coin-and-ring trick?'

Surapati was startled. But there was no change in Tripura Babu's gaze.

'Why do you ask?'

Smiling, Tripura Babu said, 'I shall teach you the trick if you agree to my proposal. Right now, if you give me your word. And if not...'

A train bound for Howrah passed theirs with a grotesque shriek of its whistle. Tripura Babu's eyes glowed repeatedly in the light from the compartments of the other train. When the lights and sound had died down, Surapati said, 'And what if I don't agree?'

'The outcome will not be pleasant, Surapati. There's something you must know. If I'm in the audience, I can disrupt and humiliate any magician—I can even make them completely incapable of performing any magic.'

Taking a pair of cards from his pocket, Tripura Babu extended them to Surapati.

'Show me your sleight of hand. Nothing very difficult. Basic tricks. Bring the jack of clubs from the back to the front with a shake of your wrist.'

It had taken Surapati a mere seven days to perfect this trick in front of the mirror at the age of sixteen.

But today?

Picking up the cards, Surapati discovered his fingers turning numb. Not just his fingers, but also his wrist and elbow. All numb. His vision blurring, Surapati could only see a strange smile on Tripura Babu's lips; he was looking into Surapati's eyes in an almost inhumanly penetrating way. Surapati's forehead was covered in perspiration, and he felt himself shaking.

'You realize my power now?'

The cards slipped out of Surapati's hand. Gathering them, Tripura Babu said grimly, 'Are you willing?'

Surapati was no longer feeling incapacitated.

In a weak, exhausted voice, he asked, 'You'll teach me the trick, won't you?'

Holding the index finger of his right hand in front of Surapati's nose, Tripura Babu said, 'Because of your indisposition, your guru Tripuracharan Mullick will perform his magic skills instead of you at the first show in Lucknow. Correct?'

'Correct.'

'You will give me half the payment due to you. Correct?'

'Correct.'

'Come, then.'

Fishing a coin out of his pocket, Surapati handed it over, along with the ruby ring on his finger.

Anil arrived at his boss's compartment with some tea when the train stopped at Burdwan, only to find him fast asleep. Surapati sprang up when Anil called out to him softly after some hesitation.

'What…what is it?'

'I got you some tea. I disturbed you, please don't mind.'

'But…?' Surapati looked around frenziedly.

'What is it, sir?'

'Tripura Babu?'

'Tripura Babu?' Anil was bewildered.

'No, of course…he was killed by a bus…in 1951…but my ring?'

'Which ring, sir? The ruby's on your finger.'

'Oh yes, of course. And…'

Surapati took a coin out of his pocket. Anil noticed that his hand was shaking uncontrollably.

'Come in for a minute, Anil. Quickly. Shut the windows. Yes, watch now.'

Surapati placed the coin at one end of the bench and the ring at the other. Then, praying for all he was worth, he applied the technique acquired in his dream to cast a concentrated gaze on the ring.

Like a dutiful child the coin rolled up to the ring and escorted it back to Surapati.

The cup of tea would have slipped from Anil's hands had Surapati not taken it into his own with a miraculous sleight of hand.

When the curtain rose on the first day of the magic show in Lucknow, Surapati started by expressing his respect for his departed magic teacher Tripuracharan Mullick.

The last trick of the evening—which Surapati termed Pure Indian Magic—was the one with the coin and the ring.

twelve

INDIA

RAMAPADA CHOWDHURY

The army code referred to it as BF 332. It was not strictly a station at all, having neither a platform nor a ticket counter to call its own. One morning, we just found the railway line fenced in by shiny new barbed wire. That was all. None of the trains stopped there, either up or down, except one. This special train would only arrive on some mornings, not every day. We were the only ones who knew when, and at what time. The five of us, including the Bihari cook, Bhagwatilal.

There was no station, trains wouldn't stop here, and yet the railway workers had given it a name. We used it too: Andaahalt.

Andaa, meaning eggs. There was a village of the Mahatos at the feet of two squat hillocks near the Andaahalt, where chickens would wander in and out of homes. The Mahatos would travel all the way to the Saturday market at distant Bhurkunda to sell chickens and eggs. Sometimes they would tuck their favourite roosters under their arms to take part in cockfights. But this was not the reason for BF 332 being named Andaahalt.

As a matter of fact we had no interest in the eggs of Mahatogaon.

Our contractor had an arrangement with the railways. He had a trolley that could be pushed along the tracks. Flying its red flag, it would trundle along the railway lines and deliver our things. Among these were heaps of eggs. Bhagwatilal would boil the lot.

But this was not the reason for the name either. The name came from the rising heaps of shells from the boiled eggs beyond the barbed wire. The shells were growing into mounds.

We were under the impression that the first two letters of BF 332 did not stand for any kind of code, but for breakfast.

There was a POW camp in Ramgarh then, with Italian prisoners surrounded by bayonets and barbed wire. Sometimes they would be loaded on the train and despatched somewhere unknown. We, of course, had no idea where, or why.

All we knew was that a train would stop at dawn.

Checking the contractor's letter, we would point to the baskets of eggs and tell Bhagwatilal, 'Three hundred and thirty breakfasts.'

Bhagwatilal would count out 660 eggs, and 25 extra ones. In case a few turned out to be rotten. Then, when they had become hard as bricks after being boiled, he would join hands with three of the server porters to shell them.

Those were the shells that would pile up beyond the barbed wire.

The train would come to a stop early in the morning, and at once the military police would jump off on both sides to stand guard, their bayonets pointed skywards.

The foreign prisoners in their striped garments would disembark one by one, holding large mugs and enamel plates.

The three server porters would turn two large drums upside down and use them as tables, standing behind them. The prisoners would line up for breakfast. One of the servers would pour coffee into their mugs, one of them would put two slices of bread on the plate, and the third, two eggs. After which the prisoners would get back on the train. The guard in his khaki bush-shirt and identity tag on the shoulder would blow his whistle and wave his flag, and the train would leave.

None of the Mahatos ever ventured near the train. Pausing in the sowing of maize seeds in their fields in the distance, they would straighten up and stare uncomprehendingly.

After the train had left we would leave the tent in Bhagwatilal's care and go off sometimes towards the Mahatos' village in search of vegetables. They grew mustard, eggplant and gourd on rocky slopes.

Overnight, Andaahalt turned into a full-fledged halt. Gravel was spread next to the tracks to raise the ground and make a platform out of the area enclosed in barbed wire.

Now it wasn't just the POW trains but also military specials that halted at times, carrying American soldiers in gaberdine trousers, their hip pockets stuffed with money bags. The military police would get off the train, walk up and down the platform, tossing off a joke or two, while the soldiers would line up the same way for their coffee, bread and eggs. Then they would go back into their compartments, the guard in the khaki bush-shirt would blow his whistle and wave his flag, and I would run to get the supply form approved by the major.

The train would leave, none of us would know to what destination.

That day, too, the American soldiers' train came to a halt the same way. The three porters were serving coffee, bread and eggs. Bhagwatilal was keeping a watch on whether anyone was tossing away his eggs on account of their being rotten, or his bread because he had got the hard slices from the very end of the loaf.

Suddenly, my gaze fell on a scene on the other side of the barbed wire fence.

One of the Mahato children was staring wide-eyed at us from a spot behind the fence. I had seen this little boy once, with a piece of iron tied to his loincloth, sitting on the back of a young bullock.

The boy gazed in wonder. Either at the train or at the red-faced American soldiers.

Spotting him, one of the soldiers shouted, 'Hey!' and at once the boy in the loincloth raced away towards his village. Some of the American soldiers were laughing at the top of their voices.

I thought the boy would never come back.

That day, none of the Mahatos came. They only paused during their work in the fields to straighten up and stare at the train.

But then, the next time the train came to a halt at the station I saw the boy with the iron piece knotted into his loincloth standing near the barbed wire once again. There was another boy with him, this one slightly older. He had a zinc amulet hanging round his neck by a red thread. I'd been to the market at Bhurkunda once, they sell piles of them there, heaps of vermilion, amulets of brass and bronze and zinc, coloured threads hanging from poles, bead necklaces. I had seen a vendor, his legs caked with dust, walking towards the Mahatos' village in the distance carrying piles of beads on his shoulders.

The boys were looking with amazement at the American soldiers through the barbed wire. The boy from the first day had a fearful expression, and his knees were ready to turn him into a speeding fawn the moment anyone's gaze held a touch of admonition.

I was walking around with the form, smiling at the Major whenever I had the chance, to keep him happy. Standing at his compartment door sipping his coffee, one of the soldiers commented on the sight of the boys to the GI next to him, 'Awful!'

This had not occurred to me all these days. The Mahatos worked on their fields happily, hunted civets with their arrows or catapults, listened to their own songs, drank, and sometimes stood up in protest, as taut as highly-strung bows. Slim bodies in loincloths, dark and rough. But that damned GI's 'awful' stung me. I was furious with the two boys.

One of the soldiers sang a snatch of a song loudly, one or two soldiers were laughing, another one drained his mug of coffee and winked at the server with a request to refill it. The guard walked up to find out how much longer it would take. He was a Punjabi, but he added a nasal twang to his voice to sound American when speaking to the Major.

Then the whistle blew, the flag waved, everyone piled into the train quickly, including the military policemen with the broad red armbands.

After the train had left it was back to the desolate emptiness, and only the barbed wire remained, like cactus in a desert.

Another train arrived a few days later. This time it was full of POWs, Italian prisoners of war being transferred somewhere from Ramgarh. We neither knew where, nor asked.

They were dressed in different striped garments, unsmiling soldiers constantly guarded by military policemen with upraised rifles. We were a little scared. In Bhurkunda we had heard stories about how one of them had tried to dress in a Bengali style dhoti-and-kurta and escape. He had failed. Being a Bengali, I felt a little more afraid.

After the train had left I noticed that the two boys across the barbed wire had been joined by a fifteen-year-old girl in a short sari and two men who had abandoned their work in the fields. They had a conversation amongst themselves, laughed, and then moved away towards the Mahatos' village like a gurgling stream.

One, two, five, and then I found about ten of the people from Mahatogaon running from the fields towards the station as soon as the next train arrived. Maybe they knew from the khaki in the windows. Two passenger trains would flash past like mail trains every day, and two goods trains would trundle along. But no, the people of Mahatogaon never crowded around the station waiting for them to stop.

Earlier I had asked the oldest of the Mahatos to send people to our tent at Andaahalt with vegetables, prawn, and fish for us to buy.

'We won't stop our work on the farm,' the old man had replied with a smile.

Which was why I looked at them now with astonishment. At the dark-skinned men in their loincloths, and the women in their short saris. Only the bare-bodied old Mahato had a pair of shoes on, made for him by Mridha from the village. They lined up along the barbed wire.

The train had halted by then. The American soldiers had leapt off and were moving forward in a queue with their mugs and plates.

Two hundred and eighteen breakfasts were ready at BF 332. BF 332, meaning Andaahalt.

There was a nip in the air. The hills in the distance were wrapped in mufflers of fog. The trees were washed green by the dew.

One of the soldiers expressed his appreciation in a Yankee accent.

Another of them was standing outside the carriage, staring intently at the destitution across the barbed wire. Suddenly, setting his coffee mug down on the steps leading into the train, he put his hand into his hip pocket, took out a shining eight-anna coin, and tossed it towards the Mahatos.

They looked at the soldier in surprise, exchanged glances with one another, and continued to gaze in wonder.

As they were about to return to their village after the train had left, I said, 'The Sahib left some baksheesh for you. Take it.'

They exchanged glances again, but none of them came forward.

Picking the coin up, I handed it to the old man. He stared at me blankly, and then left in silence with the rest. None of them spoke.

I hated our servility towards the contractor. Not a soul anywhere, not a single passenger train halted, just Bhagwatilal and three porters occupied the tent. Deserted, completely deserted. The earth was unfriendly, the afternoon sky looked ominous. I was spoiling for a fight.

The people from Mahatogaon didn't come anywhere near us. Sometimes I would go to their village to buy vegetables and small fish. They wouldn't come to our camp to sell, although they walked six miles to the Bhurkunda market.

There was no news of a train for a few days. Quiet, so quiet.

One day, the boy with the piece of iron knotted into his loincloth appeared and asked, 'No tiren, Babu?'

'It'll come,' I chuckled.

Why blame the boy—here in this land of low hillocks and rough terrain, you had to walk four miles through bushes and shrubs just for a glimpse of a bus filled with locals. In the morning, a passenger train whistled past without slowing down even slightly. The down train in the evening didn't stop either. But still we rushed out of our tent for a look at the indistinct faces in the window. We were choking without the company of people, of fresh faces.

Which was why we were both perturbed and happy when we heard that a special train carrying American soldiers was on its way.

A few days later, the Military Special steamed in. The GIs jumped out, lining up to collect their bread, eggs and mugs of coffee.

Suddenly, I discovered that all of Mahatogaon seemed to have gathered outside the barbed wire fence. Twenty, maybe thirty of them, who knew how many, if you counted the children. Even the women in their short saris stared with befuddled eyes. I felt apprehensive at the sight. This was not the first time I had felt that way. I used to feel afraid whenever Bhagwatilal or the three server porters wanted to go to the Mahatos' village.

There was no platform. As I have said, only a bed of gravel had been laid to make it easier to get in and out of the train. The American soldiers were strolling up and down with their coffee mugs. Some of them had fixed their eyes on the dark-skinned people of Mahatogaon.

Without warning, one of them went up to Bhagwatilal, took his wallet out of his hip pocket, extracted a two-rupee note, and asked, 'Do you have coins?' Soldiers didn't like carrying coins—they would always tell the shopkeeper or vendor or taxi driver to keep the change. I'd seen this often in Ranchi.

Bhagwatilal was giving the soldier change in the form of one-anna, two-anna and four-anna coins, when I suddenly saw the boy with the iron piece in his loincloth stretching out his arm through the barbed wire, smiling and asking for something.

At once the soldier took the coins from Bhagwatilal and tossed them at the crowd.

By then, I had got the approval on the supply form, and the guard had blown the whistle.

When the train had begun to move, I turned towards the Mahatos.

They were still standing in silence, looking on. Then the boy with the iron piece in his loincloth and the boy with the amulet around his neck slipped through the barbed wire and threw themselves on the coins scattered on the bed of red gravel.

At that moment the old Mahato in shoes shouted, 'Khabardar.' He screamed his admonition so loudly that even I was startled.

But the boys paid no heed. They had already gathered as many of the one-anna, two-anna and four-anna coins as possible. The smiles on their faces were like tender grains of corn. The entire crowd of men and women were smiling.

Furious at this, the old man launched into a tirade in his native tongue. The crowd laughed.

Glowering with rage, the village elder stalked off homewards all by himself. The people of Mahatogaon left too, gurgling and laughing like a mountain stream.

As soon as they left, Andaahalt turned silent and desolate again. Sometimes I would feel desperately unhappy. In the distance were the hills, mahua groves, a tiny stream, and, beyond the shrubs and bushes, the green farmland of the Mahato village. Beautiful to look at, utterly beautiful. Dark-skinned people in loincloths dotted the landscape.

Meanwhile, the American trains arrived frequently, the soldiers leaving after their regular breakfast of bread and eggs and coffee. On one such occasion, the inhabitants of Mahatogaon crowded around the barbed wire. 'Baksheesh, Saab, baksheesh, Saab.' A number of rustic voices cried out in unison.

I stopped suddenly as I was going up to the Major to get his approval on the form.

Not just the children, several of the grown-up men had stretched out their arms as well. Even a woman with an alluring body in a short sari.

When I had been buying vegetables earlier, the same woman had asked me with a smile, 'When is the train coming?'

~

These days they would appear in a group even when there was no train; after waiting for a while they would leave. When the train did arrive three or four American soldiers with stripes on their shoulders would toss fistfuls of coins in their direction. Without waiting for the train to leave, they would throw themselves at the money. In the stampede, some of them would scratch their arms and legs on the barbed wire, while others would have their loincloths ripped.

I would observe them closely after the train had left. It would seem as though half of Mahatogaon had gathered here. All of them would be smiling, each of them seemed to have got some money. But I would not find the village elder anywhere among them. The boys had not thrown away the coins despite his objections. He was probably too angry to come back.

I savoured the thought of the old man ploughing the earth all alone on the farm.

We passed our days somehow, the five of us, including the cook, Bhagwatilal. Every now and then, a train packed with soldiers would arrive, stop, and leave. The people of Mahatogaon would cluster around the barbed wire, stretching out their arms and screaming, 'Baksheesh, Saab, baksheesh, Saab.'

The Mahato village elder also began to make an occasional appearance. Abandoning the fields, he would stride furiously towards the crowd, brushing the dirt off his hands and scolding them agitatedly. When they paid no attention, he would stare at them in helpless protest.

But no one would spare him a glance. Laughing uproariously, the soldiers would toss coins from their pockets towards the crowds. The inhabitants of Mahatogaon would fling themselves at the money, bickering with one another. The soldiers would be even more amused.

Eventually, I noticed that the old man in shoes no longer turned up. I used to feel a certain pride in the fact that he was furious with the other Mahatos, which was why he was not coming to Andaahalt anymore. Because their behaviour had begun annoy us—Bhagwatilal and me. We were ashamed. The soldiers probably mistook them for beggars because of their tattered, filthy clothes. And I was very upset that they did.

That particular day the Mahatos were screaming 'Baksheesh, baksheesh' as usual, from the other side of the barbed wire, while I was chatting with khaki bush-shirt-clad Janakinath, the guard of the train. An officer marching past us briskly spat out, 'Bloody beggars,' when he heard them screaming.

Janakinath and I exchanged glances. Red with humiliation, we could barely lift our eyes, burning with impotent rage.

Bloody beggars, bloody beggars.

All my anger was channelled towards the Mahatos. As soon as the train left, I charged towards them with Bhagwatilal. Tucking away the coins they had picked up, they left, laughing.

All this while I had swept away my embarrassment for them with a pride which stood as tall as a mountain before my eyes in the form of the village elder of the Mahatos.

All my agony abated soon afterwards. I got the news on my way to meet the contractor at Bhurkunda. Two of the server porters were kicking away the drums we used as tables to the other side of the barbed wire. Another was dismantling the tent. Delivering a mighty kick to one of the drums, Bhagwatilal said, 'Khel khatam, the game is over.' Wheeling around at a sudden uproar, I saw the people of Mahatogaon running towards us. We looked at them in surprise. Bhagwatilal laughed loudly for some reason. By then they had gathered along the barbed wire. At once, we heard a whistle, followed by the sound of an approaching train. The train had rounded the curve and was coming up to Andaahalt, the windows lined with khaki uniforms. We felt disturbed and perplexed. Had the Bhurkunda office forgotten to inform us? Or was the news we had heard wrong? The closer the train came, the more a strange sound seemed to echo. Not a sound, singing. Soon we discovered that the entire train, each and every soldier on it, was singing in chorus.

Bewildered, I looked alternately at the train and the barbed wire. And that was when my eye fell on the Mahato village elder. Merging with the crowd, he too had extended his arm through the fence and was screaming, 'Baksheesh, Saab, baksheesh, Saab.'

They were yelling like lunatics, like beggars. They, and the old Mahato.

But, unlike other days, the train filled with American soldiers did not stop at Andaahalt. Just like the passenger trains, it ignored us and whistled past. We knew the train wouldn't stop anymore.

The train left. But everyone at Mahatogaon turned into beggars. All those people who lived off the soil—all of them had been turned into beggars.

thirteen

RAJA

RITWIK GHATAK

Suddenly, it began to rain impossibly hard.

Bad timing. Raja was about to go out looking for business, now he was held up. And it wasn't just plain old rain, it was a deluge. Lines of rain as thick as rope, blurring everything in an instant. The water flowed in a torrent out of the drainpipe, splashing on the road. Raja moved away from the doorframe, gesticulating obscenely and muttering beneath his breath.

Raja was a poet. Raja was a pickpocket. In other words, both a poet and a pickpocket. A little unusual perhaps, but not impossible. He wasn't just a poet, but also a reader of poetry. And he wrote, too, of unusual things. And he was not just a pickpocket, but also a drunkard. It wasn't clear whether he picked pockets to pay for his drinking, or whether he drank to squander the money he made by picking pockets.

Everyone has a past. When it's extraordinary, it turns into history. Raja was poor in that respect. He had a very ordinary past. Born into a decent family, he dropped out of college while studying for his BA. For, he discovered one day, education amounted to nothing. Making money was everything. So he had his name taken off the college rolls. His parents were dead already. He had no family responsibilities. There was a house, which he sold and set off with some cash in his pocket to find his place in the wide world. For now, Calcutta had become that wide world.

What followed was quite simple. Being a poet, he had to experience life, and he acquired the firm conviction that life was contained in the wine glass and the whore's chambers. In no time he had gathered an entourage of suitable companions. Our Raja proceeded to experience life. Gradually foreign liquor was replaced by pints of hooch, and the simplest way to live also revealed itself. After this the old Raja, the Raja of the college days, receded into history, and the Raja of slim and nimble hands began to rule.

All this was nearly five years ago.

Like the jostling of the sun and the moon in the same sky, the dispute between the two Rajas over the right to a single body had been resolved long ago. All that had remained was his love for poetry—when he drank, he began to read, and quote, Auden and Spender, Lawrence and Pound and Eliot. This, more or less, was our Raja.

The torrential downpour early in the morning soured his mood. It was eight thirty. He would have to walk to the main road to take a tram, the office crowds would thin down only after ten. He wouldn't be able to move about in the business district soaked to the bones. It was impossible. 'Damned rain,' he muttered to himself again.

No, there were no signs of it abating. It was still raining ceaselessly. The water was already knee-high in the streets. Solitary cars passed through it noisily. The dirty water from the drains gathered in pools by the side of the main road at the end of the lane. Its feathers sopping wet, a crow was perched on the second floor parapet of the Mullick house, fluttering its wings and making noises. It was also suffering from depression.

Half-lying on his rush mat, Raja shut his eyes. Last night's celebrations had gone on till one in the morning, his body felt tender now. He was enjoying himself, if only he could just stay here like a piece of rock, listening to the monotonous sounds of the rain. Raja yawned...

...Raja shot up into a sitting position. How long had it been? He looked at his watch—a few minutes past ten. His mood worsened. He hated everything...

...The rain had relented. The streets were no longer waterlogged, people were out and about. There was mud everywhere, his eyes smarted. Raja splashed water on his face and combed his hair.

There was a rattle at the door. Raja opened the door, a peon thrust a letter into his hand and departed.

A letter? How extraordinary! A thick envelope with his name written on it in a pleasing, cultivated hand. What was going on?

He couldn't go out. Raja went back into his room. He was a little afraid, this was not one of those things that happened every day. A letter? Indeed. But who would write him a letter?

He tore open the envelope. An invitation card—golden letters printed on blue paper. The annual reunion of their group Banhi Chakra, Circle of Fire. With tomorrow's date. On the back of the card was a short handwritten note:

'I don't know whether this letter will reach you. You must come if it does. I'll be expecting you—Sunil.'

Circle of Fire. Raja along with eight of his classmates in college had formed this group. So many memories. So many hopes and aspirations were linked to the name. Raja had chosen it. Buddhadeb, his friend Buddha, had painted the sign. They would gather at Sunil's house. So many meetings and celebrations. Persuading singers and well-known writers from Calcutta to attend. Collecting subscriptions under the merciless afternoon sun. Carrying ladders around town at midnight to put up posters on walls.

Circle of Fire. The name seemed to bring his entire college life back to him. Those glorious days—the first flush of youth, the cricket field, the debating society, socials, literary clubs…Gouri, Snighdha, Maya…and what was her name now, roll number 67, he couldn't quite recollect, all the girls in his class standing in a row. Buddha, Sunil, Ananda, Bimal—all the boys.

These boys and girls would never die, never age, they would always remain fresh and young to him. The wheel with the crimson flame whirling, a smiling, half-concealed sun god at its centre, holding the reins to the seven horses drawing his chariot towards the horizon.

The inert memories of the past were coming alive.

But how had they got his address? No one knew his whereabouts. He read the signature at the bottom once more. Sunil. So Sunil was still the editor. None of them had left the group yet. But how had they got their hands on Raja's address?

And yet, was that the most important thing? No matter how they had got his address, they had invited him, they had invited him to a session of Circle of Fire. He would go, yes, he would definitely go. Sunil was calling, Buddha was calling, his friends from his student days were calling; his discarded past, complete with its love and quarrels and laughter and tears, was calling. He would go.

He'd go? Raja looked at himself in the mirror. The past five years of his life had pushed his eyes back into their sockets, lined with dark circles. Possibly out of rage at this, they glittered from their holes like the eyes of a carnivorous beast. Two ugly lines ran down his face, one on each side. When he smiled, blackened gums and rotting teeth became visible behind the charred lips lined with white spots. His long, unkempt hair had not had a touch of oil in years. Would it be proper to visit?

And one more thing. Were they still as they used to be once? Had their lively dispositions survived the pressures of life? Perhaps Raja would find them transformed, their spirit of innocence gone altogether. The form in which he pictured them in his mind was immortal, he had preserved them in that mould even today.

In the middle of the afternoon, Raja opened a bottle of liquor in despair. Perhaps there was no better cure for his uncertainties and doubts. There was a strange sensation in his chest, his agitated head was throbbing, his jaws shook uncontrollably, something was rising in his throat. Raja was weeping, drunk.

But he had made up his mind. His train would leave at dawn the next day, arriving in the late afternoon. He would set off again the following morning. A matter of a few hours.

Raja got off the train at the mofussil station late in the afternoon. The sky was covered in low, scudding clouds. It was drizzling. His old haunts seemed to welcome him the moment he arrived at the stairs leading out of the station. There was a familiar scent in the wind. Freshly bathed green trees, tall blades of grass, and the mud on the road had combined to create the smell. It resonated deep in his heart. How long it had been since he had experienced it! How odd that the mud was not an annoyance here.

Pleased, Raja began walking. He had spent most of the afternoon by the window of the train, largely awake. A wave of sleep had come over him at first, bringing with it a dream that electrified him. His old life had appeared before his eyes, it was as though he was back in his second year in college.

He could clearly see his mother calling him, having served his food. 'Khoka, O Khoka. Come along now. How long must I wait?'

He strode in. 'What is it, you old woman? Oh yes, of course. What's that fish, is it ilish? Good, Mother, bring it on quick, I'm late.'

She sat down with a hand-held fan, using it to cool the hot rice. 'Come back quickly today, Baba.'

He grew suspicious. He was more used to abuse. All these endearments did not seem propitious. Softly, he said, 'What's the matter?'

'It's Shoshthi tomorrow. You'll bring me some fruits, that's all.' his mother answered, averting her eyes.

Setting his glass down with a clatter, Raja jumped to his feet. 'I knew it. No chance. Someone else has to get you fruits, I have a game to attend.'

He wanted to get away quickly.

'You haven't touched the ambol, you monkey,' his mother said.

'Give me some,' said Raja, cupping his hand.

The next moment his mother's smiling face vanished like a puff of smoke. He had woken up. Sweat on his skin, tears in his eyes. He hadn't gone back to sleep.

His mother had died of asthma shortly afterwards. She hadn't been treated properly. She was the one who had kept the household going as long as she was alive, doing the work of ten people single-handedly. A very ordinary mother, just like all others. Raja used to imagine that someone like his mother couldn't possibly die. In his head she was eternally loving, someone who would tolerate all his waywardness, who would console him in his grief.

Not just his mother, but all his relatives from those days were still alive in his head—they would never die. Nor would his friends from that time ever grow older, always remaining vibrant, young students. 'As long as...as long as I live,' he muttered to himself.

The familiar surroundings, the little things he used to see every day, all made him exuberantly happy. The sun appeared suddenly from behind the clouds, its glare strong. The drops of water on the grass began to glisten...

He recalled how much he loved the monsoon. The sight of clouds used to make him unaccountably joyous. The rain poems of Kalidasa and Rabindranath Tagore would madden him. How strange—where had he been all this time, with all this forgotten? This was his favourite place, the one that suited him best. There was Kaviraj Banamali's front room, and then all the houses of their neighbourhood in a row. Gouri used to live with her family high up on the second floor there, was she still around?

Gouri was his classmate. Demure and quiet, fair of skin, light-eyed. Most definitely not pretty. But he had discovered an allure in her. Small and slim, whenever she spoke shyly, it was like music to his ears. It was true that nothing had happened between them, but word of their friendship had spread with the support of the illustrious wall poets of their college. Perhaps this happy bond had no real value, but even today it was Gouri he thought of whenever he encountered innocence and purity. How was she, where was she? Let her be well, he made an uncharacteristically emotional wish, let her be happy, virginal and innocent Gouri, let things go well for her.

The next turn in the road brought him to his neighbourhood. He passed the old house he used to live in, which he had sold before leaving. A little boy was playing in the yard; a young girl was encouraging another boy of thirteen to pluck some guavas from the tree in the corner. Their old guava tree. Raja's family had been obliterated from this house now. New inhabitants, new faces.

The evening lights came on in the streets. Sunil lived in the house at the head of the main street. Bright beams of light fell diagonally on the road. Frequent bursts of laughter shook the earth like jabs of lightning.

Raja had wandered around on the muddy roads all afternoon, taking in the familiar sights of his city all over again, conversing with many people. Now he climbed the steps and went in. The same rug on the floor, the same old signboard. The paint had faded, but it still glittered. Above the door was the poem he had written when Circle of Fire had been established. There was Sunil, there was Ananda, there was Buddha in a corner. Bimal was sitting on the rug, along with Chhoto Khoka, Amar, Prabir, Jiten. Raja ran his eyes over all of them in turn. None of them had changed much.

The next moment there was a shout. A welcoming roar emanated from eight powerful lungs. Their owners were elated by the sight of their long-lost dear friend, whom they had not really expected tonight.

'And who's that? Is that you, Raja?'

'Aju mohu gehen Shyam awal. Shyam has joined us today.'

'Hurrah! Cast the boat off, Raja is here.'

'Incredible! Colin Clout's come home again. Sit here with me. O Mary, go and put the kettle on. A little tea is indicated.'

'So you got the letter, Raja?'

'I've written a new poem today, Raja. You must hear it.'

Buddhadeb was the first to realize that they were overwhelming him.

'Quiet now, all of you. He's just got off the train, give him a chance to catch his breath.'

He got his rest. Then Raja listened to Amar's poetry. Ananda was a glutton. But he suffered from chronic dyspepsia, forever stroking his belly as he ate. Raja had to hear all about his illness. He asked after everyone. Jiten had just been promoted to collector, and Chhoto Khoka to professor. Ananda's business was flourishing, while Amar had set up his legal practice here. Sunil was the secretary of a students' unity movement, and quite famous. Buddha was a rising star as a commercial artist, doing excellent work. He was told about other fellow-students, who were spread far and wide, earning a living. He found about Gouri too—she was married now.

Raja leaned back against a bolster, his eyes closed. Here he was, not in his dreams, but in reality, seated contentedly among his friends in a familiar world. Meanwhile, Buddha and Amar were quarrelling. He found it funny. He was used to their bickering, which was almost a daily affair. Buddha was teasing Amar about his poetry. None of them had changed.

Sunil was talking about how all of them gathered here on this day every year, no matter where in the world they might be. Just the eight of them, no one else. They had had no idea of Raja's whereabouts all this time...

'But how did you get my address?' Raja opened his eyes to ask.

'Didn't you meet Borda a few days ago somewhere?'

Raja remembered. He had indeed met Sunil's elder brother, Saroj, fleetingly in a tram a couple of months ago. Saroj had probably asked for his address too. He had no idea why he had told the truth. So Saroj hadn't forgotten the address.

'Never mind all that,' said Sunil. 'What are you doing these days? You were the brightest of us all...'

Raja told them. A string of lies. He concocted the story so beautifully that he began to enjoy it himself. He was a mining officer in Madhya Pradesh. Salary? Not too bad. Free quarters, and some perks. Yes, but he had got married suddenly, there had been no time to inform anyone. They had a son. He hadn't been given a formal name yet, but Raja called him Munna, and his wife, Khokon. Yes, she was pretty. They were well, a hilly area, delicious food. He was on holiday for two months, living in Calcutta now. Yes, he would bring his wife to meet them, but a few days later. They had to visit his in-laws. There was a wedding. Raja was speaking. Raja. Raja of Circle of Fire. Student leader, apple of his friends' eyes, object of their pride. They were seeing him after such a long time.

And then there was laughter and music and the tabla and the

harmonium were brought out. The night advanced. They were called to dinner. They ate. Nine young men in a row, a raucous meal. Raja ate with joy after ages.

Much later at night, the others left. Ananda and Buddha stayed back. The three of them stretched out on the rug in the front room. Sunil switched off the light and went inside.

Sweet. Life was sweet. Sorrows were sweet, and so were happy memories. Sighing alone for no reason was sweet. Reading travelogues written by other people about parts of the world he had not seen was sweet too.

Let his new journey begin today. He would not drink anymore, he would give up the company of criminals. He wouldn't even return to Calcutta. Couldn't he get himself a job here? Here, this was where he would live. His mother, Gouri, Buddha, the shy new professor of English...his mother, Gouri, Sunil, Ananda, the college, the pot-bellied principal, Gouri, his mother...they were all getting mixed up. A fog...a fragrance rising from the grass. The irresistible movement of the yellow moon through water-laden clouds... The Ramgiri Range, a skeletal figure wrapped in a shawl standing with his arms raised, his hair flying in the wind, a circle of gold around his wrist...

Kaschit kanta viraha-guruna svadhikarat pramattah
shapenastangamita-mahima varshha-bhogyena bhartuh

The Yaksha's year of cursed existence had ended...he was now flying towards the fulfilment of his desire...he would be reinstated in all his glory in the abode of eternal beauty...

Raja turned over on his side. Buddha was snoring.

His train was leaving at 5 a.m. Sunil shook him awake at four-thirty.

It was the calm, contemplative hour before dawn. Raja took deep breaths. The air was cool and clean. Clouds had gathered in the sky. The rain was yet to start. Raja went to brush his teeth.

Sunil's mother had woken up before dawn to make him breakfast.

A mother's blood ran in her veins. Raja chatted with her for a few minutes, his heart filling with joy. Just a few hours. But the sweetest. He realized that he had no choice but to come back.

It was time. Going into the front room, he changed back into his travelling clothes. Buddha and Ananda were fast asleep. He wouldn't wake them up. They were so tired, poor fellows. Slipping his vest on, he told himself that he would be back to meet them. He would return. As though to convince himself, he kept muttering, 'I'll be back. I'll be back again.'

Raja couldn't find his shirt. Maybe it was buried beneath the other clothes on the rack. Raja began to look for it.

Sunil appeared to tell him to wait a minute or two. His mother wanted to give Raja some aamshotto, Sunil would bring it. They would go to the station together.

There it was, his shirt, beneath the blue one. When he lifted the blue shirt, something fell out of the pocket.

A wallet. A fat, stuffed wallet. Raja's slim, skilful fingers tingled. Before he knew what he was doing, he grabbed the wallet. His heart thudded. Hurling a quick glance at his sleeping friends, he opened the wallet. A wad of notes. It must be Ananda's, filled with cash from the shop. He put the wallet back in the pocket of the blue shirt before putting on his own.

He felt a buzzing in his head. His tongue felt thick. This would mean wiping out his past, his beautiful past.

The fog was coiling upwards. The sun-charioteer of the Wheel of Fire held the reins in one hand, a half-raised whip in the other. His eyes were dancing with joy, a smile lit up his face, the hateful fog was snaking past the window panes… it was rising, obliterating the sun god's face. His mother, Gouri, his mother…the cloud-messenger, Ananda…all of them were swallowed by the fog. Raja raised his arms to disperse the mist.

Sunil had gone out already, he was calling him insistently. It was almost time for the train. Sunil held a small packet, the aamshotto wrapped in cloth.

'Come on, Raja, if you're planning to leave, better not be late. It's nearly time.'

'Coming.' The spell was broken. Raja gulped. Before leaving, he threw a wary look at Ananda and then dispassionately lifted the wallet out of the pocket of the blue shirt with his slender, artistic, adroit fingers.

fourteen

URVASHI AND JOHNNY
MAHASWETA DEVI

Johnny was sitting with Urvashi in his lap, for she wouldn't sit anywhere else. If she was asked to sit elsewhere, she would just flop dramatically on the floor. What sort of coquetry was this? Was Urvashi going to sit in Johnny's lap in full view of the doctor? The doctor wasn't pleased at all. Eventually, he said, 'Get up, come this way.'

Settling Urvashi in the chair carefully, Johnny got up. The doctor talked to him while keeping an eye on Urvashi. As usual, Urvashi didn't answer the doctor's question. The only person she spoke to was Johnny.

'What was the problem with the throat at first?'

'Sore throat, hoarseness.'

'And then?'

'Coughing.'

Johnny's eyes turned yellow with jealousy whenever the doctor looked at Urvashi. The doctor ignored this and said to Urvashi, 'Didn't you realize earlier? Didn't you see a doctor?'

Johnny said with a smile, 'This woman, you see, Doctor, is eating me up. You know what a bitch is like, she won't tell you when something's wrong. Look at that face, she still makes your head spin. I did go to a doctor.'

'Which doctor?'

'Kaviraj, hakim, the lot.'

'Have you brought a letter from Dr Husain? Did he check?'

'He was the one who sent me. I don't like what I'm seeing, Johnny, he said. This Urvashi is killing you. Your life will be hell because of her.'

'Did he say what's wrong?'

Johnny's face fell. As though a familiar figure—a doll or an ancient statue—had suddenly cracked and faded from constant exposure to rain and storms. Johnny said, 'You know very well, Doctor, that without Urvashi all the shows will flop. She will sing, chat, dance, sway her hips, laugh. The public will say, how are you, Urvashi? She will say, I'm so happy. I'm the queen of happiness. Johnny keeps me in such comfort.'

'Get to the point.'

Johnny whispered, 'What Dr Husain told me has scared the shit out of me, Doctor.'

'What did he say?'

'He said, it'll all come to an end, Johnny. Your Urvashi will no longer laugh or sing or speak.'

'Do you know why he said that?'

'Something wrong with the throat.'

'What's wrong?'

'Something.' Johnny twisted his neck from side to side, like a sacrificial lamb who knows the blade is about to fall.

'It's throat cancer, Johnny.'

'Give us medicines, injections.'

'It's too late, Johnny. You went to the cancer hospital too, didn't you? Didn't they tell you?'

'They did.'

Johnny's voice broke, sobs welled up. 'That's what they said, saar,' he said. 'I beg of you. If Urvashi can't sing or dance we'll starve to death.'

Johnny wept. Urvashi kept sitting without turning a hair. Suddenly the doctor felt a stab of fear. Of what, he couldn't say. He was delivering a death sentence. There were so many different kinds of death. *End of life. Being killed. Ceasing to be. That object which has ceased to be is dead.* Urvashi is dead, deceased, rejected. For everywhere in the throat from which Urvashi spoke and sang and laughed, the windpipe, the food pipe, the membrane, the vocal cords—cancer has claimed all of them as its kingdom. The throat was the cancer's throne.

When its term ended, the cancer would take its throne and depart.

But Urvashi was detached, alluring, exquisite, her breasts arrogant, her lips reddened, her eyes still. Only Johnny wept. His despair and Urvashi's indifference chilled the young doctor to the bone. As though it was he who had died and frozen. But why the fear? After death there could be neither fear nor courage.

'Say something, Doctor.'

'Johnny, at the hospital, the cancer hospital...'

'They know nothing at the cancer hospital, Doctor, you can have stomach cancer, lung cancer, have you ever heard of throat cancer?'

'Getting admitted there might...'

'Urvashi can't be left alone.'

'This is madness, Johnny. What harm can Urvashi come to?'

'You won't understand.'

Johnny got to his feet with a sigh. Wiping his eyes, he said, 'Let's go home, Urvashi.'

'Johnny, I've known you a long time, I'm giving you good advice. You can't do at home what can be done at the hospital.'

'Will going to the hospital make Urvashi dance again, sing again, talk again?'

'No, Johnny.'

'The voice with which she sings Kar le muhabbat Lolita...will it be repaired?'

'No, Johnny.'

'Then why?'

Johnny lost his composure. 'All the 'bastards' have signed up with that one-eyed Kani Moti,' he said. 'You want to separate me from Urvashi. Shut up, you swine, say the word hospital again and I'll stick a dagger up your arse.'

Johnny began to shout. A flood of invective, starting with bastard. The nurses and orderlies and hospital staff came running. All of them scared stiff.

'Get away, all you bastards—yes, fuck off. I'll kill the lot of you. All you motherfuckers have joined hands with Kani Moti. You think

I don't know. Come on, Urvashi, I'm not letting you go. Shaala thinks he's a doctor. Wants to separate you and me.'

The doctor said, 'Let him go, he's gone mad.'

'YOU have gone mad. Weren't you staring at her all this time? If you're talking about illness, motherfucker, why were you looking at her tits? You think I don't understand?'

The doctor rose to his feet. Placing his hand on Johnny's shoulder, he said, 'Don't shout, Johnny. Not another word. Speak softly, then leave.'

'You're telling me Urvashi won't talk or sing anymore, and you expect I won't shout?'

'No, you won't.'

Johnny lowered his voice fearfully. 'I won't shout?'

'No.'

Johnny began to cry. In his patched and floppy trousers, bright T-shirt, the bandanna round his neck, the oversized shoes, and the feathered cap, the old man looked like a weeping monkey. Like a sobbing clown on a poster stuck on a wall. Still weeping, he gathered up Urvashi tenderly in his arms and left.

Outside the hospital, where bottles of medicine were sold, Ramanna, the cripple, was selling tea. Johnny squatted in front of him, helping Urvashi take a seat on a packing box.

'Well, meri jaan?' said Ramanna. 'A cup of tea? A red skirt today, I notice.'

'Shut up, you cripple,' said Johnny.

'You have some then.'

'Give me a cup.'

'Ginger?'

'Yes.'

'What did the doctor say?'

'Cancer.'

'Where?'

'Throat.'

'Huh!'

Pouring scorn into his voice, Ramanna said, 'Who gets throat cancer? Don't show me cancer, Johnny. I've grown up with death. If it's cancer there's a rotten smell even when alive. Don't you remember that fellow? When they were lowering him from the ambulance the stench was everywhere. When he died, you know, Johnny, they doused him in perfume, still the fucker didn't stop smelling.'

'I remember.'

'When he died everyone scattered coins, the bastards.'

'You slipped when you tried to pick them up.'

'And you ran away with my money, you fucker. Two rupees sixty paise.'

'Who paid for the drinks the next day?'

'Did I say you didn't?'

Johnny drank his tea. Then he said, 'What do you think I should do?'

'Go to Lengri.'

'Why?'

'Because Kani Moti can't handle this. Lengri will tell you.'

'Why do you say that?'

Scratching his belly with his amputated arm, Ramanna said, 'I went to Lengri. She's greedy. Says, get me good cigarettes, some fries. She wanted a pillow from a dead body. The corpse of a married woman. I told her I'd get her one. So I brought her cigarettes and fries...'

'With your own money?'

'Who owns money? Whom do you belong to, money? Whoever I'm with. No, not my own money. Do you know what happened that day?'

'What?'

'Bhagirath had sold the medicines. Meant for the patient. When the patient died the family went to fetch a cot. Bhagirath disappeared with the medicines and Horlicks, everything. He paid.'

'What did Lengri say?'

Ramanna looked grave. 'You're blaming Kani for nothing, Johnny,' he said. 'She loves you.'

'Fuck off! Kani, that hag. Who wants her love?'

'No, Johnny. True love is a very good thing. She gives you food, doesn't even take rent every month. Just the other day she was sitting with me in tears. She said, 'Johnny just has to ask once, I'll support him for life. But, yes, he has to leave Urvashi.'

'What did you say?'

'I said, forget it, Kani. Johnny won't leave Urvashi, talk about other things.'

'What did Lengri say?'

'She said, someone else wants Urvashi. So he's done some black magic. You can't get throat cancer otherwise. So I said, Johnny is my closest friend. I know everything about him, Lengri. Tell me.'

'What did she say?'

'She said, "Tell him to come to me tonight."'

'Should I go to her today?'

'No, it's that man's chautha today. Lengri is a boss at gathering leftovers. She'll be there with her people. So much fucking trouble everywhere. There are rules. Lengri and her people will get the leftovers from all the feasts on the left of the Lakka field, and Magandas on the right. But now these fucking beggars have abandoned all principles, you know? Lengri never goes to the right, but Magandas and his gang have begun targeting the left and creating trouble. They don't know Lengri. She's taking Badri and Hamiza with her today. If Magandas creates trouble they will fuck him all the way to hell and back.'

'Badri and Hamiza are going?'

'Bloody right, they will! They manage their own areas, no problem. Who allotted the Lake Market pavement to Badri and the Kamlavilas pavement to Hamza? Lengri, of course. Do you know how much Badri collects from the market? Meat and fish entrails, vegetables, Badri has a lot of clout. So he said, Mashi, as long as Badri is around Magandas will not be able to collect food from your dustbins.'

'Big feast tonight, then.'

'Fuck off. It's not Bengalis doing their last rites, there's no meat or fish or anything. But then Lengri said this is a battle for our rights. I'll lose face if I give in. Lengri knows what it is to fight.

Even after she's gone her reputation as a fighter will remain. We'll fucking name a pavement for her.'

'Then I shouldn't go today?'

'Go tomorrow. Full moon, a good time.'

'Will she give medicines?'

'Of course! Lengri never goes back on her word. But don't go in the morning. She cleans taxis in the morning, in shorts. Making lots of money. Go at night. Take a bottle.'

'Kani Moti is innocent?'

'Yes, Johnny.'

'Call for a rickshaw.'

'You'll go home?'

'Yes. If I take Urvashi out in the sun she...'

'Johnny.'

'Yes?'

'Do you consider me a close friend?'

'Of course.'

'From naked butt days.'

'Of course.'

'Leave Urvashi.'

Johnny's heart froze in fear. Ramanna, Ramanna! Such an old friend of his. And here he was, saying the same thing. The icy coldness of a morgue settled in Johnny's heart. Was he to die of fear? What if he did? But what was all this fear, this terror, even after death? Surely, man went beyond fear and courage when he died? At least, he was supposed to.

'Why are you saying this, Ramanna?'

'She will eat you up.'

'I know.'

Johnny looked mournful. As though the clown on the posters stuck on the walls had decided not to show a smiling face to the city anymore. Like a melancholy, aged ape he said, 'I know, Ramanna. But you know how I've spent so much of my life in joy and in sorrow with my love. I'll die if I cannot see her eyes, her face, her smile.'

'I know.'

'Would anyone survive, you tell me. You know how beautiful life is, everyone wants happiness. People ask her, how are you, Urvashi? She says, I'm very happy. People say, and how are we? She says, you're very happy too. People say, then sing a song of happiness. She laughs and sings: O jeenewale. Jeena. Living.'

'I know.'

Ramanna grew sorrowful too. He said, 'Urvashi is a witch, a prisoner of the devil, a djinn. She has finished everyone she's been with. She will finish you too. And no one knows who'll be next.'

Johnny said, 'I'll kill her before that.'

'You!'

'Yes, me.'

Ramanna sighed. He said, 'Go to Lengri at night. Take her something to eat and drink. She won't talk otherwise.'

'Of course, I will. Urvashi will dance, she'll sing Bareilly ke bazaar mein jhumka gira re. Lengri will give medicines. Or else I will plunge a dagger into my heart and in hers too.'

Ramanna clucked. 'A knife through those breasts? Fuck off then, I won't organize your chherad.'

Winking with one clouded eye, Johnny chuckled. 'That comes later, first you have to decide whether to burn me or to bury me. Do you have any idea?'

'To hell with you, as if you have any religion.'

'Bury me and burn me too.'

'Will be there two corpses, you fucker?'

'Me and Urvashi, got it? Get a band with bagpipes, get acetylene lamps, cover us with flowers, buy all the flowers in the city. Then light the pyre. And then bury the ashes. Have a grand chherad. Lengri's gang, Magandas's gang, Badri's gang, Hamiza's gang…give all of them a feast on the pavement. Get uniformed bearers from the canteen.'

'Who'll pay for all this?'

'Oh, everyone will do everything for free. Johnny's dead, Urvashi's dead, everything's free. Fuck it, Laila and Majnu are leaving us. Who will ask for money? When we're dead, you'll see, no one will fly pigeons, no one will sing. They will die too, beating their breasts and chanting, hamein gam dil, hamein gam dil. We'll take all the joys with us when we die, fuck everything.'

Ramanna, the cripple, and Johnny began to laugh. Still laughing, Johnny helped Urvashi into a rickshaw. He lit a bidi, taking care not to burn Urvashi's silky tresses. Winking at Ramanna, he blew out a mouthful of smoke.

The miraculous light of the moon bathed Calcutta in love. As though the moonlight was Laila herself, and the city, her lover Majnu, filthy because he was mad with passion for the moonlight, which was why the amorous Laila had to bathe him.

It was very late at night. Hours made no difference to the night anymore. No one but a few street dogs, maddened by the moon, were taking advantage of the flood of passion. Everyone else was either asleep, or wandering around in the hope of getting drunk, or searching for flesh without love after closing the windows through which the moonlight could have entered.

Under such a moon, drenched in this deluge of love, Johnny leant against a pillar, crying. He was very sad. Now he was both Laili and Majnu. Asmaanwaale teri dunia hamein ghabra diya, saare dunia men chandni kyun mere liye badal ho gaya?'

He was plunged in despair. Even Lengri had clucked sympathetically. When Lengri realized at the age of seventy that she would have to become a warrior goddess to retain control over the footpaths, she gave up her sari and began to dress in shorts and T-shirts, swapping her flowing white hair for a bob. She kept a cloth bag tied at her waist and a mirror hanging from a black wire around her neck.

Mirror in hand, she pulled out and examined the patterns made by the nail of a new-born baby, the beak of a hornbill, the hair of one pregnant corpse, and the vermilion of another. Then she said, 'No hope, my darling. Someone has done some black magic, a demon. I no longer have the power to do any counter magic. My heart is breaking at your misfortune. If you did have to come, why couldn't it have been when the trouble had begun with Urvashi's voice?'

Johnny was crying brokenly. He was dressed in his floppy trousers, bright T-shirt, and bandanna. Oversized shoes and feathered cap. He didn't look like a man, but like a clown who had walked out of a poster stuck on a wall. Determined not to smile, or to make others smile. Rebelling, because his heart was broken.

The pain of a cracked, damaged heart is unbearable. A burning in the breast. The flames of anxiety blaze stronger than the funeral pyre. Johnny was weeping, transformed into the clown on the poster. What did he have to laugh at, after all? The flood of love in the moonlight could not heal him. Where was he to go now with his broken heart? Yeh dil kahan le jaaun?

The voice with which Urvashi—seductive like a swaying skirt, unpredictable like lightning, beautiful like dawn, always alluring, woman of the forest—sang dukhia ziara rote naina, sang love me darling, sang tomar golay gaan chhilo, amaar golay shur, sang banska khirki banska duara aao banaye gharwa pyaara, would now be stilled. The glorious moon would set—mujhe bhi le chalo sapno ke paar. And so Johnny was weeping.

The moonlight laughed at his tears, the dogs copulated. Lengri gazed at the full moon with her clouded eyes, weeping. 'You're Ramanna's closest friend, darling. I don't have the power to stop the black magic, my son. I can't even see clearly anymore. That is why I cannot see his reflection in the mirror.'

'It's not Kani Moti then?'

'No, my son. She loves you very much.'

'I'm afraid of her love.'

'Afraid of what? Leave Urvashi. Set up home with her. She will cook for you, feed you, don't forget you're getting old.'

'But how can I leave Urvashi? What will happen to her?'

'Someone will buy her.'

'Who?'

'That I couldn't see, darling. Someone who wants her has done black magic.'

'That's what I suspect. Everyone is jealous.'

'You've gone mad, my boy.'

'I wasn't mad, Mashi, she made me mad. I was young then. I travelled all over in a coach with her on my lap. Dholpur, Banda, Khani, Lalthapur, Hasirpur. What performances those were, Mashi. When she sang ankhia milake jia bharmake chale nahin jaana, I would say, kabhi nahi pyare. She would sing jaanse na jaane doongi, jaake raasta tokh loongi, saiyan ke paiya par par jaoongi, roke kahoongi, aankhiya milake.'

'I know everything, darling.'

'But all dead, Mashi. The throat from which her songs come—it's got cancer.'

'Not cancer, sweet, someone has done black magic.'

'Do you know anyone?'

'Know whom?'

'Someone who can stop the black magic.'

'No, my boy. There was Ansari at Tiretti Bazaar...'

'Dead.'

'Now ask for the lord's mercy.'

'Lord!'

Johnny walked off with a glance at the moon, his head bowed. Kani Moti loved him? Pyaar? Mohabbat? Pyaar se phir kyun darta hai dil? Because of Urvashi, because of Urvashi. Suddenly, he felt that Urvashi was alone. Kani Moti leered at Johnny and despatched Urvashi to the crematorium twice a day. Johnny began to run. And as he ran, he changed into little Johnny fleeing the orphanage.

Who had left him at the orphanage door? He didn't remember anything. The orphanage belonged to Puranchandji. Along with all the other boys, Johnny too would sing deene daya karo on the train to Bandel and back. It was his singing that made Dalip Singh lure him away.

'I'll show you the world,' Dalip would say.

Johnny had not realized that Dalip was another Puranchandji, who used to take away all the alms they would get, and had the children's limbs amputated. It was he who had turned Ramanna into a cripple. Johnny was spared because he could sing well.

Ramanna and Johnny had run away together. Dalip had given Ramanna a clay pot. He would use his amputated arm to hold the pot against his body and drum on it with the other hand. Johnny would sing. In train compartments.

Johnny had learnt in childhood that people loved pleasure. He could see the sheer effort made to give people pleasure. Horse-drawn coaches would pass, distributing handbills about royal astrologers, non-surgical cures to injuries, and films. Musicians played on the roof. Happy songs, all of them.

The coaches would race along, happy tunes wafting from them, and young boys would run behind them, collecting the confetti that Johnny scattered in the breeze. Johnny knew that everyone loved big pleasures. Puranchandji from the orphanage used to love them too. He would distribute sweets on his parents' birthdays. Those whom he had crippled were not left out. Puranchandji would climb on to a large table and sit cross-legged. He wouldn't even drink a glass of water till he had performed his puja to Shiva; he had a permanent trident drawn on his forehead with sandalwood paste. From a huge basket he would toss the sweets to the boys, and order them, 'There! Pick them up! Eat! Laugh, sing, dance.'

Johnny and his companions would laugh and sing and dance uninhibitedly. The cripples and the one-eyed among them would laugh the loudest. Johnny had discovered that people loved pleasure. Pink handbills would turn the air of the city pink. Some of them would say that the astrologer was the storehouse of happiness. Some would say, the most terrible wounds could be cured without pain. Abdalla would sit with his parrot on the pavement, distributing happiness. The movies offered 200 per cent happiness. The heroes would always get the heroines at the end.

Even when Dalip turned into another Puranchandji and took away the money that Johnny and Ramanna made from singing in trains, Johnny used to sing songs of happiness. He knew people went to the movies in search of pleasure. All these Bengali clerks, salesmen, peddlers, middlemen, shopkeepers, hawkers, all of them went to the movies for happiness. They tolerated the sad scenes and sad songs because all sorrows would ultimately be converted to joy.

So Johnny would sing a sad song, yeh dil kahan le jaoon, first, followed by, main ban ki chidiya, to make everyone happy. People could become happy quite easily. Those who did not watch films because they had no money got their pleasure from the queues at the cinema halls. The penniless people who could not afford sweets got their pleasure from licking the pots thrown into the street. Legless and armless beggars who rolled on the melting tar of Chowringhee to collect money for Puranchandji got their pleasure by staring at the apple-like foreign women.

He had realized right then that he would have to escape from Dalip's reach. He would peddle happiness all by himself, all over the country.

Ramanna did not leave, staying on in Calcutta instead. Kani Moti had not become blind in one eye yet. She was the landlady's niece at the time. Ramanna and Johnny had pimped for Chandni and Reshmi and Bedana and other women for some time.

Johnny would also sell film tickets on the black market. He slept on the pavement. When he came into some money, he ate seekh kabeb at Habib's. Johnny was one of those beggars who felt Calcutta was in their pocket when they had twenty-five paise to call their own. Eternally happy, independent. Which was why he ignored the landlady. Marry Moti, start a family—he didn't care for such advice. Who was going to marry Moti? Who wanted to become another Puranchandji, another Dalip, and become rich on the money earned by Chandni and Reshmi with physical labour?

Pleasure was to be found in the air in Calcutta. Johnny had said, 'You can stay here.'

'What will you do?'

'I'll pick up pleasure from the world, phir sab ko de dega—it'll be the biggest charity, motherfucker. I'll give everyone all the pleasure they want. I'll tell them, you bastards, sleep on the pavement, eat on the pavement, dress up and leer at women. Sing, laugh. Happiness is the greatest jewel of life. I'll put the jewel in everyone's hand.'

'And am I just going to die here, you fucker?'

'Not at all. Let me find my pleasure first, then I'll take you along.'

'So you won't marry Moti?'

'Never, motherfucker.'

'She won't marry me.'

'You're a cripple.'

'My heart will break if you leave.'

'But you're my closest friend. Even if I leave I'll send for you.'

'You must go.'

'You're sure?'

'My word.'

'You remember everything we decided?'

'Ev...erything.'

'You'll take care of my chherad if I die. If you die, I'll take care of yours.'

'Sign in blood.'

'Okay then, bastard. Here.'

They had sliced their skin open with the same knife. Laughed in unison. Watched a film with their arms round each other's shoulders. Had seekh kabab at Habib's. Then Johnny had gone off to Howrah Station, climbing into the first train he could see. He hadn't bought a ticket—he had just curled up on the floor.

He was in Ranchi before dawn.

That was when Johnny had planned his life. Master Johnny's One Man Show.

Ranchi, Daltanganj, and then, going further north, westward through Benares, Allahabad, Lucknow.

Different lives, different performances. Like the patterns of performances, the patterns of life also varied. When the film ran, Johnny could see the pattern.

At the market, on the street, at the crossroads. As Majnu he would sing, chalti hai karvan. As Laili he would sing, aasmanwale teri dunia mujhe ghabra diya. As the villain he would say, bachho, mere chakku se tere kalije nikal dunga. As the joker he would stuff a pillow into his pants and dance.

The coins would rain into his bowl. Those who were in the greatest need of pleasure had no money. All of them would crowd around to watch Johnny's performance. Johnny would say, 'People of the world! Pleasure is a bird in this world. It flies around. I've captured it to give it to you.' As Tansen he would sing like Saigal, bina pankhe panchhi hoon main. As Akbar he would say, Tansen! Tumne yeh gaana kyun gaaye, Tansen?' As Tansen he would say, 'Yeh gaana nahi, Shahenshah! Yeh tute huye dil ka pukara hai.' Still as Tansen, he would lie down and say, 'Mera pyaas bujhao!' Back on his feet, he was the singer again, raising his arms to the sky and singing, Barso re! Kaale badaria, piya par barso.

Johnny would return to the station platform after vending pleasure to the public, and lie down by himself on a bench. Every life had its own pattern. The sahibs and memsahibs went to Shimla with their dogs. He was very keen to have a street dog as a pet in this lonely life of his. He would name it Rover. Rover would walk around with him on a leash. He would tell people it was an *alchechhian*. Stunted because I can't afford meat.

He had many other desires. Of travelling in a coach with Phulkalia from the Nautanki troupe. Of putting up dance shows with Anar from the bazaar. Of spending the night with Panna from the tea shop.

But the pattern of life was strange. Phulkalia and Anar and Panna had heard richer people than Johnny talk of the same dreams, and spent themselves trying to fulfil them. All that the women would say was, will you marry me, make a home with me?

Johnny would say, 'Never. Free men don't become slaves. Only donkeys get married. I'm saying I'll bring you happiness from all over the world.'

The women would roll with laughter. 'You can't get happiness free, Johnny.'

'What do you mean free? I'll give you bangles, clothes, meat for dinner every day.'

'Everyone makes the same promises. Who keeps them?'

Phulkalia's aunt was a fortune-teller. She said, 'You're wasting your time trying to bind him down. There's just the one Laili for him who will find him and make him her Majnu.'

The arrogance of youth made Johnny eternally free. He would laugh with joy. 'The girls aren't willing, Mausi. You come with me. Will you be my Laili?'

'Die like a dog.'

'You'll be the one to die.'

'You'll die first.'

'If I do my best friend will organize my chherad. We've sworn in blood. There will be gas lanterns all around my corpse, a band will play, all the people I've given pleasure too will beat their breasts and lament, hai! gam-e-dil! hai! dunia ke khushi ki roshni bujh gailo. They will weep all the way. When you die the cleaners will take your body away.'

The old woman would try to slap him. Johnny would run away, laughing. But one day Phulkalia threw herself at his feet. 'I've fallen in love with you, Johnny. I can't think of anyone but you. I don't want you to marry me or give me a home, just take me with you.'

'Take you where?'

'Wherever you go.'

Phulkalia was a voluptuous woman. She had pockmarks on her face, her complexion was shiny, she sported a tattoo on her forehead. Her body was like a pitcher brimming over with milk, spilling as she walked.

When Johnny looked into Phulkalia's eyes he realized that a dagger had been plunged into her heart. Imagine a woman who wasn't willing even to take a coach ride with Johnny unless they were married now saying she was ready to go wherever he wanted to take her.

Was Johnny afraid? What was the woman saying? He was a vagabond, a nomad, wandering from place to place. Johnny did not dream of freedom. He had been free since birth. He knew that happiness was a bird. Its iridescent feathers flashed in the sunlight. Johnny kept capturing the bird to offer it to penniless, naked men. How was he to take responsibility for Phulkalia's full and desirable body, of her bleeding, passionate heart?

Johnny had run away. Phulkalia's aunt's curse may have followed him. Why else would he have ended up in Mumbai? Why would Hamid have told him at Bhuleshwar Chowk, 'What is this one man show of Master Johnny's? Have you seen my Urvashi's performance?'

'I will if you show me.'

'Put on an amulet with the pir's blessings before you do, Johnny. Or Urvashi will make you mad for her.'

'Hmmph, I've seen hundreds of Urvashis.'

'Not like her.'

'What does she have?'

'Name the one thing she doesn't have.'

'Hah! Everyone says the same thing.'

That evening Urvashi had dressed in a peshwaz and blouse with a churni. Hair-ornaments, necklace, earrings. Urvashi was singing on Hamid's lap. Talking. Her complexion was like an apple's, her breasts were like ripe pears, her eyes like lotus petals, her eyebrows flying hawks, her lips a blooming rose...

Johnny was thunderstruck. Why did people flock to his performance when there was Urvashi? She was singing huskily, speaking, telling the audience jokes.

After the show Hamid told Johnny, 'Come with me.'

'Why?'

'Urvashi will sing so sweetly.'

'Will she sit on my lap?'

'On my lap and on yours.'

It was Johnny who had added new acts to the show. He had been educated a little at the orphanage. Then, in his quest to capture the bird of pleasure, he had picked up a working knowledge of Hindi, English, Marathi and Gujarati during his travels. He used to buy film magazines all the time. 'You bloody Hamid, there's no *bichhnechh* unless your *invess*.'

He would say, 'The show must finish with *comedy*. Happy ending. Look, start with the happiness of the hero and the heroine in the rain. Second part, *tajidy*. But if it ends in *tajidy* people feel sad. A *comedy* ending puts the bird of happiness within their reach. *Comedy* endings are best.'

Now, half asleep next to Urvashi, Johnny could still see Hamid. Hamid was crying. 'I sold her to you when I was drunk, Johnny. Don't take her. I'll die if I don't see her. I'll sell my tent and pay you. Don't take her.'

'Fuck off, who wants money?'

'I'll stick a dagger in your chest, Johnny. She's an enchantress, a djinn. I got her from a Lahori. Now you're taking her from me? The witch will finish me and then punish you.'

If only Johnny had known. Oh god, how beautiful she was. Tere gore badan mein gori kaale kaale ankhiyan.

Johnny fled Mumbai the same day with Urvashi.

Kanpur, Jhansi, Agra, Delhi, Peshawar, Lahore, Karachi, Bhopal— so many different cities. Everywhere at the crossroads and markets and on the pavements penniless, naked people wanted the bird of happiness in their hands. All of them traders in a currency of no value. When they got money they drank, they smoked hash after Johnny's performance. If they didn't have money they died on the streets without taking the world to court.

But times change. Back then, at the height of his youth, Johnny had asked Ramanna to join him. Ramanna would play his music with one hand, gripping the instrument with his amputated arm. Johnny and Urvashi would ride around the city in a coach. Johnny would throw pieces of pink paper up in the air, colouring it with the pink feathers of the bird of pleasure. By then everyone had come to know that Johnny was madly in love with Urvashi. Urvashi was the rose, and Johnny her nightingale. The penniless, pleasure-hungry boys would run behind the coach to grab the coloured sheets.

Johnny began to grow old racing along the desolate streets under the passionate moonlight. Like a gooseberry branch which had lost all its leaves in winter. Just as the leafless branch is all that's left behind when all the green has been shed, so too had the good days fallen away from Johnny's life, leaving him bereft.

The good times hadn't disappeared overnight. Gradually, Johnny's shows stopped drawing people. He had to leave the glittering big cities and start touring Bardhaman, Krishnagar, Suri, Bolpur, Baharampur, Rampurhat and other small towns. Tattered tents, out of tune music. Johnny's floppy pants, bright T-shirt, oversized shoes, and feathered cap saw him through.

But this was a performance of love. Johnny had loved Urvashi for thirty years and become her Majnu, mad for her. The things that Laili wanted were imitation-pearl necklaces, glass bangles, satin skirts. Then to Calcutta. Come into the tent, pay nineteen paisa, watch the performance. At every fair and festival in the city, wherever they were held.

Moti had sacrificed one of her eyes to the goddess, Sheetala, to become Kani Moti, one-eyed. She had fallen on bad days. Reshmi and Chandni and Bedana had all been carted off the crematorium, one by one.

It was Kani Moti who settled them into a slum behind Beckbagan. 'You too?' asked Johnny sympathetically.

'Naturally.'

'Did it have to happen?'

'It did.'

With Kani Moti's help Ramanna set up a tea shop on the pavement outside the hospital. The shop was a packing crate, the bench for customers to sit on was a plank raised on bricks. Hot tea and country biscuits. Drink from your little cup, throw it away.

Kani Moti gave Johnny and Urvashi a home. Three rooms, partitioned with pieces of cardboard and rotting wooden crates.

'Pay me ten rupees as rent, Johnny,' Kani Moti told him.

A slum. Putrid living. A single hole in the ground masquerading as a toilet for twenty-two families. There were many other landladies like Moti in this slum. Little children and old men and women sat in the doorways. The air was heavy with the stench of garbage.

Johnny's heart grew heavy. Would Urvashi have to live in a room like this? There was no reaction from Urvashi. Kani Moti had made things worse.

After the performance Johnny began to cough till he almost died.

Kani Moti brought him a concoction to drink. Medicines from a hakim, an amulet from a pir.

'Why do you do all this for me, Moti?'

Kani Moti said, 'That Urvashi's going to eat you up, Johnny. Leave her.'

'Why? What's your plan?'

'Live with me.'

'Get away from me, you witch.'

Kani Moti left, weeping. But she hadn't asked Johnny to pay his rent for the past seven years, taking it only when he offered. She brought him tea and biscuits and bread and sweets. Johnny called her a witch. Moti said, 'I'm going to set that witch on fire one day.'

Johnny wasn't afraid when Kani Moti spoke in anger. But sometimes her heart broke so much that her tears were converted to song. On those nights she sat with her legs splayed out, giving people medicines and singing. Just as Johnny's songs were old, Kani Moti's songs were ancient, primal. The heartfelt lament of all fallen men and women. She croaked, out of tune:

I was as beautiful
As the moonlight
Just like all of you
At home I wore the best clothes
Coaches lined up at my door
The men came
To love me so
And to call me

Darling moon

Johnny's heart broke too at such songs. Kani had lived in Calcutta all her life. Had she not realized the need for pleasure?

Johnny came home.

A foul odour. Sunlight and moonbeams were forbidden from entering the slum. Johnny lit a lamp. Urvashi was sitting on the bed, looking at him, leaning against a pillow. Johnny alone could tell her eyes were heavy with sadness from being neglected.

'I'm back, my love.' Johnny kissed Urvashi loudly. Urvashi did not respond. Absolutely quiet.

Johnny interpreted the question in her eyes correctly.

'Lengri knows nothing. Says someone's doing black magic on you. To hell with all this nonsense. We have a show tomorrow. We'll make love tonight.'

Uncorking the bottle that Lengri had returned, Johnny raised it in Urvashi's direction. 'Cheers! Only love tonight. Love with you.'

He lit a bunch of incense sticks, and then put on his red trousers and green coat. He was emptying the bottle down his throat. The universe was spinning inside his head. Putting his cap on, Johnny winked. 'What does Lengri know? What does the doctor know? My coat and pants are old, it's been so long since I bought you a skirt to replace the torn one. How do I buy new clothes?'

Caressing Urvashi's breasts, Johnny said, 'Everything will change from tomorrow. The show you'll put up, the songs you'll sing will have everyone asking for more.'

Urvashi did not reply.

'Let's rehearse today. The whole city will be in our pocket again tomorrow, Urvashi, promise me you won't leave me.'

Urvashi was silent.

'We'll do that song tomorrow. I'll start with Urvashi ka khel. She's my Laila, I'm her Majnu. All of you are her Lakshmi. She will answer any question you ask. She will sing any song you want. She will do whatever anyone asks her.

Urvashi was expressionless.

Everything had turned misty. The universe was whirling inside Johnny's head. Puranchandji, Dalip, Ramanna, Hamid, Phulkalia, Moti, Lengri, the doctor—they were all laughing. Pointing at him and saying, 'You lost, Johnny.'

'Never,' Johnny roared. Dressed in his bright coat and trousers, his oversized shoes, and his feathered cap, Johnny said, 'Who dares defeat me. Show me. Main Johnny hoon. Bastards, swine. Did I or did I not bring you the bird of pleasure?'

Everyone was laughing, the laughter of cynics.

Johnny said, 'Who am I anyway? Urvashi is my mistress, I'm her servant. Urvashi sings aayega aanewala. Don't you people know? Don't you ask her at the end of the show, how are you, Urvashi? Doesn't she answer, I'm happy? Johnny keeps me like a queen. Don't you ask, how are we, Urvashi? Doesn't she say, you're well, all of you are happy?'

They left. Suddenly Johnny found himself alone in the room with Urvashi. He put his arms around her. He said, 'Promise me that you won't leave me? Promise me, I'll die if I don't see you.'

Urvashi was silent.

'Should I turn out the light? You can talk to me in the dark. I can hear everything. Shall I turn out the lamp?' Urvashi did not reply.

Johnny began to cry. A putrid room, filled with smoke from the lamp and the incense. Urvashi was smiling, the smile she enchanted the world with.

Johnny sobbed.

Urvashi's show. Johnny and Urvashi's show. The last show of the season. Nineteen paise for a ticket. Buy and enter.

The curtain parted. Johnny entered and sat in a chair, with Urvashi on his lap.

Johnny had made up his face today, put fresh feathers in his cap.

Today Urvashi was dressed in a shiny silk sari, with a crown of imitation pearls on her head and wearing costume jewellery.

Johnny said, 'You've never seen the kind of show that Urvashi has for you today. Urvashi, say hello to the people.'

'Hello hello hello people. I am Urvashi. Aami Urvashi. Main Urvashi hoon.'

'What can you do?' asked the people.

'I sing, I dance, I talk.'

'Why do you sound hoarse?'

'Because you came as my lover and got me ice cream.'

A wave of laughter.

'Will you sing a song, Urvashi?'

'Kya gaana? Ki gaan? Which song?'

'One Hindi, one Bangla, one English.'

Urvashi smiled and bowed her head. Then she tilted her neck and said something to Johnny. Johnny nodded in agreement.

Urvashi said, 'One lover got me ice cream, another got me thandai. My voice doesn't feel right. Can I sing soft and warm?'

'No, sing hard and hot.'

Urvashi sang in three languages: Chalte chalte alvida mat bolo, Jhilimili kancher churi shohag rani go, Do re mi.'

'Listen to her. Her voice has cracked.'

'Lovers' torture.'

'Then talk instead.'

'Ask me questions.'

'Oye Urvashi! What will you do if you get a thousand rupees?'

'Johnny and I will have fun.'

'If you get a lakh?'

'Johnny and I will have fun along with all of you.'

'Ten lakh?'

Urvashi whispered, 'I'll catch all the birds of pleasure and put them in your hands.'

'What is it, why don't you answer?'

'Why don't all of you tell me instead?'

'Why so soft today? Are you shy?'

'I'm shy.'

'Why is Johnny crying?'

'Stupid, randy old man.'

'How are you, Urvashi? How are we? Tum kaise ho? Hum kaise hai? Speak up, like you used to. We've paid, do you realize we can't hear you speak?'

Urvashi was silent. Johnny had a terrified look in his eyes. Why wasn't Urvashi speaking?

'What's happened, Urvashi?'

Urvashi didn't answer.

'What is it? Is the show over?'

Urvashi forgot her usual soft and sweet tone. Suddenly, she screamed. Urvashi screamed in a discordant, harsh, tearful, desperate voice.

'I'm not well. My voice has been silenced. I won't laugh any more, I won't sing any more. I won't talk to you any more, people. The Urvashi who used to catch the birds of happiness for all of you, that Urvashi is no longer happy. Do you know why? My voice has fallen silent, there will be no sound any more. Everything has ended, people. I'm not well, I'm not happy, how will any of you be well? Your happiness has taken away my voice.'

The audience was dumbstruck.

Urvashi grated, 'My voice is gone, I am not well any more. Not well any more. Not well any more.'

'Not happy any more.' Urvashi shouted at the top of her voice. But suddenly her sobs, her screams, stopped. The curtain fell. The frightened, terrorized audience began to shove and yell. Everyone shouted, 'What is it, what's happened?'

Something behind the curtain was breaking, falling apart, loud sounds. The bewildered, curious public rushed onto the stage, tearing away the curtain. And then all of them fell silent.

Silence, silence, silence.

In fear, the audience watched Johnny tearing his talking doll apart, sobbing loudly.

Johnny's eyes and face and chest were soaked in tears. His lips kept moving. They said, 'I'm not well, because my voice has been silenced.'

But not a sound came from his throat.

fifteen

~

NEWS OF A MURDER

MOTI NANDY

Even though Bibha and Nirmal subscribed to an English newspaper, Bibha hardly looked beyond the photographs and headlines. So she had no idea about this particular piece of news. In the afternoon, Manashi, the housewife next door, had a big laugh as she said from her balcony, 'Oh my god, you haven't read it yet? Never mind, I'll give you our newspaper. Someone with the same name as yours has been murdered. And such a coincidence! A housewife in north Calcutta, aged under forty, under the jurisdiction of Shyampukur Police Station, one son. I was shocked. Actually, it was my husband who read it first, then he made me read it too. "Go check next door whether she's alive or has been murdered," he told me. I ran to the window to find your husband coming out of the toilet while you were in the yard, scolding Balai about something. Oh, how we laughed!'

Bibha felt a stab of curiosity. 'Let me see the newspaper,' she said.

Manashi offered her the newspaper, saying, 'My husband isn't done with it yet.'

'I'll give it back in a minute.'

A triple-decker heading in fairly large letters announced: 'Housewife Bibha Das murdered. Assailant leaves money, jewellery untouched. Servant absconding.'

It was minor news at best. But it had been stretched to provide a thrill to readers. In fact, Bibha did feel her skin prickle and her heart skip a beat.

Her seventeen-year-old son, who was studying for his final examinations, was in school. Bibha Das was alone at home in the afternoon. Somebody—or some people—strangled her to death, leaving her body in the kitchen. The dead woman's body bore no injuries. The keys to the wardrobe were beneath her pillow, but the wardrobe hadn't been opened. Neither the money nor the jewellery had been touched. Her son came home from school to discover the front door wide open. Entering, he called out for the servant. Going upstairs, he found his mother lying face down in the kitchen. Her blouse was missing. Her sari was raised above her knees. The police could not be certain whether she had been murdered after being raped. The servant was twenty-four years old and he had been employed there for two years. He was absconding.

'They didn't mention where it took place,' Bibha said, when she returned the newspaper. 'Must be somewhere close by.'

'Shyampukur is our police station too. It should be easy enough to find out.' Manashi even informed Bibha that she would inquire.

Bibha's husband, Nirmal, telephoned a little later. 'There's news of a murder in the papers today.'

'Manashi from next door showed it to me a minute ago.'

'Where's Balai?'

'Downstairs, must be asleep.'

'Lock the door at the top of the stairs.'

'I was thinking of doing that.'

'Some of the people in the office know your name. Sukumar came by to check. Apparently, he was worried sick after reading the news this morning. No one was at home in the afternoon besides a full-bodied male servant, he said, and Mrs Das is pretty, too.'

'Oh no, Balai is a decent boy. He's been with us three years, after all.'

'There was something in the papers today...' Soumitra said as soon as he came home from school.

'I read it.'

'What horrible things they write. Apparently, her blouse had been removed. I had an argument with a couple of friends. Many women take their blouses off on these sultry afternoons. They wouldn't believe me... Forget it.'

'Why do you have to argue over such things?'

'Why do they write about them in the papers, then? Some of my classmates have seen you. They're the ones who claim to be concerned.'

'About what?'

'About your being alone at home all afternoon... I'm hungry.'

When he returned from office in the evening, Nirmal said without any preamble, 'You'd better lock the house and go next door or something every afternoon. Staying all alone at home does not seem wise. This kind of murder is becoming commonplace in Calcutta these days. Apparently the majority of the victims are beautiful women.'

'The way you're talking is scaring me.' Bibha tried to sound coy, but could not. She really was afraid.

'Boudi, Boudi,' Balai was calling Bibha from downstairs. As she turned towards the stairs, Nirmal said, 'Do we have Balai's village address?'

'I certainly don't.'

'Get it, get it right now.'

The next day Manashi came up to Bibha on her own to hand her the newspaper, saying, 'Just imagine! How terrible, at this age, and with a son too, to have an affair with the servant!'

The headline was just as large as the previous day: Bibha Das had had an illicit relationship with the servant.

'Those who know you will think of you straightaway when they read this...so many resemblances, after all. The girl in the house behind ours, she's a schoolteacher, she was telling me.'

'What was she telling you?' Bibha's limbs grew numb. What horrible things people were saying!

'Nothing awful. She was just saying the headline made her think of you at once. The two Bibha Dases have a lot more in common than just their names.'

'A lot more? What do you mean?'

'She was probably referring to the similarities in age, in your homes, one son, a young servant—things like that. My husband said the same thing too. The news gives you a nasty and dirty feeling, doesn't it?'

'Naturally.'

'I'll take the newspaper back from you later after you've read the whole thing.'

What have I got myself into? Bibha sat down heavily on her bed, newspaper in hand. This witch of a Bibha Das had made a mess of her life. Manashi and the house at the back effectively meant the entire neighbourhood. They must be gossiping about her in every house right now. If only she had had two or three or four children instead of just the one. It was all thanks to Nirmal's poor advice— one's enough, that way we can bring him up properly.

Bibha paced up and down impatiently. Everyone who knew her would immediately think of her when they saw the name. And how strange, she was in fact home alone every afternoon, and Balai was young too. The very term illicit relationship was terrifying!

The telephone rang. Bibha ran to answer it. You didn't feel lonely when you were talking to someone.

'Is that Bibha? This is your pishi, how are you? How's Nimu?'

'I'm very well, Pishi. We're all very well.'

'I read something in the papers that scared the life out of me. Have you read it?'

'Something about a murder?'

'Yes, not just a murder though, there's much more to it.'

'There's nothing like that going on here, Pishi, you mustn't think…'

'Didn't I see a servant at your house? Is he still there?'

'Oh no. Balai was sacked long ago. Nearly six months…no, almost a year. We have a maid now.'

'Very wise of you. You can never trust these young servants. Doesn't Soumitra take his higher secondary exam this year?'

'Yes.'

'I haven't seen you in a long time, I must visit soon.'

'Please do.'

Bibha shuddered as she replaced the receiver. The aunt was bound to see Balai if she came over. Bibha sat down on the bed, holding her head in her hands. She felt sick all over.

The phone rang again. Bibha ran to answer it.

'Nirmal here. Have you locked the door?'

'Yes.'

'I'd asked you to get Balai's address in the village.'

'I'll get it now.'

'Not now, not now. He's alone downstairs now... I wish you wouldn't forget these important things!' Nirmal's voice was bristling with annoyance.

Bibha lost her temper suddenly. 'What kind of horrible fate will befall me if I go downstairs?' she shot back testily. 'Balai is a very nice young man.'

'Bibha Das also used to think that her murderer was a very nice young man.'

The slamming of the receiver rang in Bibha's ears. She stood with her eyes closed, swaying. Taking a step or two to grab the side of the bed, she stared helplessly at the headline in the newspaper.

When he came back from school, Soumitra said as usual, 'I'm hungry,' without coming up to his mother. Looking out blankly through the window, Bibha said, 'Tell Balai downstairs to give you your food...never mind, I'll get it myself.'

'No,' Soumitra practically screamed. 'You don't have to go downstairs, I'll go.'

Bibha's lips began to tremble. She went out into the balcony to stare at the road. Let the neighbours and the people on the street see her. She had not been murdered, she was not having an affair either. 'You can see, I'm here all by myself,' she muttered.

Back from office, instead of coming upstairs as he did every day, Nirmal began to talk to Balai. About to go downstairs, Bibha paused on the staircase when she heard their voices.

'What have I done, Dada, for you to ask me to leave? How will I get a job now? Give me the rest of the month at least.'

'Absolutely not, you have to leave the house tomorrow. Didn't I tell you I have a problem with you? Why should you be in trouble, I said I'd give you the full month's salary, didn't I?'

As soon as she heard Nirmal's footsteps approach the stairs Bibha retreated.

Bibha was sitting on the balcony. Two maids were passing on their way to work. It was that time of the day when municipal water would flow through the taps. 'Wait a minute,' Bibha cried out to them from the first floor.

After a brief pause, they continued on their way.

'Don't go away. Do you want to work for us? Don't run away.'

The maids didn't stop. But one of them said to the other, 'They've had five maids in six months, no one's lasted more than a fortnight. She's gone mad, that woman.'

~

sixteen

TEN DAYS OF THE STRIKE

SANDIPAN CHATTOPADHYAY

It was 27 September, Thursday. The month, October. The toilet of Shubhobroto's flat had now been blocked for ten days in a row. From the morning of Tuesday before last. Before going to the market, Shubho normally checked, to the accompaniment of a cup of tea and two biscuits, how the week would go. That day, too, he had just fixed his eyes on Aries when his seven-year-old daughter, Pinky, came out of the bathroom and said, 'Bapi, the pan filled with water when I pulled the chain.' 'Hmm,' said Shubho, hoarsely.

'Yes, it's still full. Take a look.'

Shubho had never heard of such a thing. They had eventually twisted the arms of the company sufficiently to extract an 8 per cent bonus. Screaming 'We want' and 'Meet our demands' for the past one- and- a- half months had almost deprived him of his vocal cords. And, at last, since the sky really was looking blue now, as there were no clouds obscuring it, he had assumed that, as before, this time too the Durga Puja holidays would go well. What strange mockery of the gods this was at such a juncture.

⌐

Shubho's ancestral house was in Ahiritola, on Joy Mitra Street. Five years ago, when the company had moved to Joka from Behala, he had also been forced to move home with his wife and daughter. After all, a three-shift job couldn't be held down from Ahiritola. The house was over sixty years old, and he had spent thirty years of his life there at a stretch. But even in that house he had never heard of anything like this. Naturally, it didn't seem plausible.

Shubho rushed to the bathroom, still holding the newspaper.

There he saw, what rubbish, there wasn't a drop of water in the pan. Some stool was still stuck to the side. There had been water in the pan once, certainly, but there was no more water now, all of it had disappeared. So, without going in for any more chain-pulling, he filled a ten-litre bucket with water and dumped all of it into the pan.

Oh god! Look, not only had water and stool come rushing up, racing each other to fill the pan, but they had also overflowed onto the bathroom floor. He swooped down on the sweeper's broom to at least clean the floor before Kuntala turned up. Her mania for cleanliness had reached a stage where, except for sex, everything at home had been classified as 'yours' or 'mine'. So much so that their toothbrushes on the glass tray above the basin didn't dare knock against one another. In fact, even the plastic clothesline on which Kuntala's and Pinky's clothes were hung up to dry was different from his—theirs was the shade of deep anger. Although he had had this explained to him repeatedly, in his mild rush after his bath to get to work, he had hung his towel on that line one day and then—good god—what a row! All the way through getting dressed and eating, the bickering had continued up to the moment he had shut the door behind him. He had even suspected that she would throw the rest of her invective at him from the veranda. So Shubho quickly tried to at least... Just as he'd thought. The girl had told her mother. Or perhaps the racket made by those ten litres of water had made Kuntala rush out of the kitchen and turn up in person to investigate, the end of her sari tucked into her waist. Although the bathroom floor was more or less clean, the toilet was still a grotesque mess of shit and piss. His pyjamas were wet up to the knees.

'Oh god!' said Kuntala. Untwisting the end of her sari from her waist, she clamped it on her nose with a force which suggested that she wouldn't stop until she had unwrapped the entire thing.

The first thing Shubho did was to run to Gopal Babu, the ancient tenant on the ground floor. He dealt in milk products in Notun Bazaar, quite a solvent business. Spreading out ten odd saris on the bed, his wife was explaining her Puja gift purchases to him, while he was saying, 'Oh no no no, this one suits you, don't give it away.' He wasn't particularly pleased when Shubho entered suddenly through the back door and appeared in the bedroom without so much as a by your leave. 'What is it?' he asked.

On hearing the whole story, be said, 'Come now. You realized it today? We're ground floor. Our stuff hasn't been passing since last week.'

'What! But you never told me! How did you manage?'

'Come now. We're refugees. Came over and settled on a platform in Sealdah Station. Never mind us. Me and my son go shit in that field there.'

'What!' Shubho gulped. 'And the ladies?'

'They take a rickshaw to my wife's sister's place over in Unique Colony. Why don't you tell the landlord?' Changing the colour of his eyes like a cat, Gopal Babu smirked and said slyly, 'You're very thick with him.'

He had been living there for fifteen years. His rent hadn't been raised by a paisa. After five years, Shubho had voluntarily increased the rent he paid by twenty-five rupees, in the hope of a few dribs and drabs of favours. A bolt on the door had broken, the landlord hadn't bothered to have it repaired. To rub salt into the homeless Gopal Babu's wound, the landlord had put up a tin-roofed room under his very nose and taken in a Muslim tailor named Liaqat Ali as tenant. The new tenant had no toilet. Apparently he raised the iron lid of the septic tank at dawn every day and, along with his offspring, defecated inside directly. And today Gopal Babu was being snide with him about the landlord! Shubho really had been mistaken. When merely letting out a two-room flat brought in an advance of ten thousand rupees that wouldn't have to be returned, twenty-five rupees a month was nothing but a pinch of snuff. His lips had assumed the shape of the letter 'O' for a long time now. Seeing him in a fix, Gopal Babu probably felt sorry for him. Changing his tune, he said he and his family could cope, but Shubho and his family were cultured people, their case was different. There was something

Shubho could do—he could go to Kalikeshto Babu, the conservancy block officer of the ward. Nutu's tea shop near Pushposree Cinema Hall—that was where the gentleman was to be found every morning. If Shubho went right away, he'd find him there. Kalikeshto Babu would come up with a solution.

At that moment Gopal Babu got a phone call from Notun Bazaar. Grabbing the receiver, he said 'Hello-who-yes-no-yes-no-yes-yes-no...' into it. When he found Shubho still standing there, he arranged his fingers and the upturned palm of his left hand into a Bharatnatyam pose, telling Shubho to go quickly.

The gentleman was middle-aged, with the aggressive appearance of one who has to deal with shit and bad food. Two-day stubble on his cheek, without a single white hair. Shubho found him exactly where he was supposed to be. And yes, Shubho was definitely efficient, for he managed to get the gentleman into a rickshaw and straight home within fifteen minutes. Sitting on the sofa, Kalikeshto Babu took a luxuriant pinch of snuff between his fingertips, some of it spilling onto his half-dirty kurta. Gesturing towards the TV set, he asked, 'Watching the Olympics?'

'Yes.'

'Not as good as the Russian one.'

'No. But...'

'Saw the P. T. Usha thing? Choo-choo.'

'Oooh, just a hair's breadth.'

'Yes. Juuuust a little more...'

'The Bengali newspaper had the best headline—Usha Touches Gold and Returns.'

At that moment, quite a lot of fried rice, with two—yes, two—entire sweets arrived on a quarter-plate, carried by—not Panchidi—but Kuntala herself. 'Tea or coffee?' she asked.

'En-no-no. Tea...'

Shubho saw Kuntala standing by the curtain. He didn't hesitate anymore and said, 'Well, Kalikeshto Babu, about our toilet...'

'That's being taken care of. I've told Tulsidas. He'll be here any moment.'

The bell rang downstairs almost immediately. Pinky ran to the balcony. 'Is that Tulsidas?' bellowed Kalikeshto Babu.

Before removing the lid of the first tank downstairs, Kalikeshto Babu asked Shubho to step away. Even Gopal Babu drew the curtains of his windows. Standing astride the opening to the septic tank, Tulsidas rotated a long, curved pole inside. Because of the horrible, fearsome stench, the windows of the first floor closed one by one. Only Kalikeshto Babu stood tapping his nose with his index finger, while Shubho held his handkerchief over his nose.

Putting the lid back, Tulsidas jumped down from the cement tank. Shubho noticed his splendid physique for the first time. He was completely naked except for the short dhoti wrapped around his waist, at least six feet tall, with thick hair on his chest, and an aluminium disc hanging from a chain around his neck. Shubho suddenly recalled that their print of Nandalal Basu's painting *Kiratarjan*, which used to hang over the dining table, had fallen to the floor during a storm, breaking the glass. It would have to be framed again. Tulsidas said, 'The tank isn't completely blocked yet. It'll work for a few days more. But vanishing is a must.'

Vanish? What was that? To make something vanish was to hide it. Like making a corpse vanish. Or stolen goods. What was it that was to be made to vanish here?

Kalikeshto Babu said, 'Do you know how long it's been since the tank was cleaned?'

'I know,' said Gopal Babu, drawing the curtain. 'Eighteen years.' He drew the curtain back. Kalikeshto Babu said to the man behind the purdah, 'That does it. Do all of you use acid to clean your pan?'

No reply. Shubho said, 'We do.'

'Then don't,' said Kalikeshto Babu. 'The insects that breed in the tank eat up the stool, that's why the water flows easily between the tanks. Four tanks in all. What happens is that if the acid kills off the insects, the outlet of the first tank gets jammed with stool and dead insects.'

Shubho said something that had occurred to him right at the beginning. 'Kalikeshto Babu. The sanitary privy in our Ahiritola house is at least forty years old. But it never...'

'Look. That is in Calcutta. It is connected to the central sewerage. Goes straight to the dumping ground in Dhapa through the underground system. And this is Behala. It's a personal system here.'

'I see.' The basics of socialism and capitalism became somewhat clearer to Shubho.

The meaning of 'vanish' also became obvious. It was nothing but the use of a bundle of rags tied to the end of a long bamboo pole. Since there weren't enough rags, Kuntala had to hand over a frilled petticoat. The drawstring was removed to tie everything together, but it didn't work. So Kuntala eventually had to offer her scarlet, for-her-majesty-only, plastic clothesline. Then, fill the pan with water and apply vacuum-pressure on its mouth with the rag-covered battering ram. This, in short, was vanish.

But, worse luck, not even half an hour of vacuum pressuring could clear more than an arm's length of the stuff. As soon as it had been used once or twice more, the pan filled with stool again.

That's how matters stood on the sixth successive day. All this time, a yard or so of shit had been clearing up on its own every night, while Shubho managed to make another arm's length worth disappear with fifteen minutes of effort every morning. The three of them somehow managed to do their business once a day, their faces covered. But, for the last three days, the stool had accumulated in the pan without budging an inch.

Shubho had been urinating outdoors since the beginning. The bathroom was a completely forbidden zone to him for this particular activity. Kuntala had made it clear on the very first day. 'You can do that wherever the hell you can. Don't you set foot in the bathroom.' But two days ago, seeing that the stuff in the pan hadn't cleared at all, she dealt a heartrending blow. 'You can shit outside the house too. I don't know where.'

As a result, for the past two days, Shubho had been unloading where Monica—a former student of Kuntala's—lived, across the road. He went over only after the men folk had left for work. He had had to take casual half-day leave at his office all those days. Never mind that, but not only was it embarrassing for a thirty-five-year-old man to use the toilet in someone else's house, it was also, oh god, no little trouble. First, which of the mugs to use? Then, there were pieces of red-blue-yellow-differently-coloured soap on the window sill. Obviously, one was Monica's, one her parents', one her aunt's or brother's. Alas, couldn't there have been one colour from the VIBGYOR exclusively for Shubho? Crossing the road every day with a mug from his own bathroom was unthinkable. He had completely forgotten to pull the chain the day before yesterday. Of course, it wasn't as though there had been any stool left in the pan. It had all disappeared while cleaning himself afterwards. But Kuntala sent him back all the same. Glaring, she practically shouted at him, 'Go pull the chain. Someone else's toilet, after all—shame on you.'

So, for the last two days the stuff in the pan had remained in the pan. Covering their face, shutting their eyes, mother and daughter had been unloading on the existing heap. There was no question of pouring water in either. The pan would immediately fill with water and, now, it wouldn't even flow. Instead, it would splatter on them. Kuntala's foresight had consequently forbidden Pinky to spit into the pan. Indeed, Kuntala was more dedicated than the Anand Marg people in her quest for cleanliness. One felt not sorry but like weeping for her.

There was no option now but to clean the four tanks. If the municipality were informed it might be done, but that would cost four thousand rupees and neither the landlord nor Gopal Babu would pay a paisa. Kuntala had still been willing to pawn her jewellery. But Kalikeshto Babu said the municipality wouldn't send its vehicle before six months. So it had been decided that he would employ a dozen sweepers overnight to clear 80 to 90 per cent of the stuff in the first tank, on payment of three hundred rupees for the moment. Six months of relief, at any rate! 'Where?' Kalikeshto Babu answered with a half wink, 'What business is it of yours? Here and there,' swinging his arm in an arc that included India as well as the rest of the world. Shubho's earlier notion of the word vanish would be given this new interpretation in the early hours of Sunday—even before the birds had risen. Or so things had been fixed. Which meant four more days in hell.

Actually, four more days in hell wasn't the right way of putting it. It was quite wrong, in fact. As in all small flats, the toilet was separated from the rest of the bathroom by a six-foot-high partition. Which meant that it was exposed at the top. The unbearable stench flowed out, filling the flat at all times. Not even incense could keep the stench at bay. So Kuntala had hung up a packet of Odonil in each room—including the kitchen. And—this was a lack of foresight on her part—the constant scent of five packets of Odonil had turned the entire flat into a unique two-room toilet, complete with kitchen, storeroom and dining space. So, instead of four more days in hell, four more days in the shit house would be a better way of putting it.

It was about three in the morning. Cring-cring, cring-cring. The phone was ringing downstairs in Gopal Babu's flat. Even a sound as soft as this could wake Shubho up. But he went back to sleep with its sounds in his ears.

Kuntala woke him up about fifteen minutes later. His mother had died a little earlier.

She had been quite old. This time her cold had taken a detour towards pneumonia. A couple of weeks ago, she had appeared to have turned the corner. He hadn't been able to check on her during the toilet crisis. Did she have to take the opportunity to escape this way?

'What went wrong so suddenly?' he asked absently.

'They didn't say. Come on, hurry up. Go to Madhu Da. Ask him to get the taxi out.'

'Y-yes, I'm going.' Holding up his pyjamas with his hands, he was running to the bathroom to urinate. Kuntala objected mildly,

'Where do you think you're going? The pan's full. Nothing's gone down all night. You're going out, aren't you?' Meaning, do it outside.

'O yes, O yes,' he said and, unbolting the door, was about to totter out bare-bodied, trapped between semi-somnolence and grief for his mother. Kuntala handed him a singlet. The first thing he did outside was to squat by the open drain.

Sunrise was some time away. One of his brothers was standing by the small iron gate of the house where his mother had died. Reaching in through the window of Shubho's taxi, he unlocked the door and said, 'Ah, you're here. Come in. Couldn't let you know earlier. My god!'

The Ahiritola house was dilapidated. Nearly all of it was now under the control of Shubho's brothers. There weren't enough rooms for everyone, so only when someone died did one of the young men get married. The eldest brother had died quite young of cancer, and his wife had moved with their children to the room on the roof. Shubho had got married. Their mother, of course, had delayed things considerably, and Shubho's brother had no choice but to move her downstairs from the first floor. He had set a bed in a corner of the dining room and settled her on it for her final repose, so that his nephew Boltu had a room to himself and his wife after his wedding last month. The room that Shubho had shared with his eldest brother a decade ago was now in the joint possession of the family deity and his brother's youngest son, Punpun.

Ignoring the formal gestures of deference for her brother-in-law, Kuntala led Pinky directly into the dining room. Shubho sat with his brother in the front room. His brother switched on the table lamp and the fan. Some plaster flaked off the wall, falling on the floor. They were both quiet. When the cook came and asked, 'Tea or Viva?' Shubho's brother said, 'Tea? Mmm…um…'

'Viva then?'

'Viva gives me wind. Okay, Viva.'

'Tea for Chhoto Babu?'

Shubho nodded. His brother's chest heaved as he sighed. 'She

drank all the holy water in my hand and then passed away. Before
that she threw away all the medicine Gouri had given her.'

Shubho was silent.

He was thinking of the last time he was here. His mother had
obviously known she didn't have much time left. Taking his hands,
she had said, 'Come back soon. I want water from your hands before
I die.' Since her illness began, Shubho had been visiting twice a week
anyway. Suddenly, out of the blue, while all the toilets in the world
were in working order, theirs had to be the one to be knocked out.

Shubho was her favourite child. Before he got married, he had
taken her on all the pilgrimages she had wanted to go on—Kashi-
Vindhyachal, Haridwar, Kedar-Badri. At Vindhyachal he had been a bit
short with her about something. That had done it—the old woman
had disappeared from the dharamshala. A terrible loo was blowing
in the middle of the afternoon. Searching for her everywhere, he
had finally found her under a banyan tree. The way she had turned
away her face in a rage on seeing him was not to be forgotten. Only
after much pleading had he succeeded in getting her into a tonga.

That last day he was here, his mother's meal had just been served.
When Shubho's sister-in-law saw a couple of rats scurrying about,
she exploded. 'Oh, Ma, can't you even shoo them off?'

What a moonglow had spread over her face! Between the rise
and set of a faint smile, she had said, 'What can I do? I used to
shoo them off. They'd run away. Now they don't pay any attention.
So I call out to god now.'

That night Shubho had told Kuntala. 'I'm bringing Ma over
tomorrow.'

'Your brother won't let you. Ma still wears that necklace. Besides,'
Kuntala had said, 'Ma won't leave her home either.'

'Of course she will, of course she will,' Shubho had said, thumping
the bed. 'Does she have to die in a damp room amongst rats and
cockroaches? Must Gouri talk to her that way? Can you imagine
how she must be treating Ma?'

'Yes, bring her over if you can.' Kuntala had sounded keen.

It hadn't been possible. The toilet had become blocked immediately afterwards.

It was getting light outside. A taxi drew up. Shubho's sister Kamala and her husband Jagadish got out amidst the ear-shattering din of street dogs barking. Switching off the table lamp and draining his cup of Viva, a final sip, Shubho's brother rose to welcome them. As he walked off, he said, 'I believe your toilet's choked?'

Drinking his tea, Shubho felt his bowels stir. He hadn't yet been to the room of the dead. His entire being was telling him not to go in there, not to witness the one completely believable thing in life that could not be disbelieved at all.

He went to the toilet instead. A toilet that needed the light to be switched on even in the daytime. The light revealed an uneven wall and hundreds of cockroaches. A cracked, scarred pan. The sweeper came just once a week. No cistern. And yet, because it was connected to the central sewerage system, look, just two mugs of water made the shit dance away.

As Shubho's brother's wife touched his mother's forehead with the bangle and vermilion of a married woman before she was placed on the cot that would take her to the crematorium, all the other married women, including Kuntala, lined up behind her—while Shubho's brother told the photographer, S. Kumar, 'For the rituals I want a photograph of my beautiful mother, absolutely young,'— Shubho entered, threw a single glance at his mother and averted his eyes. Her final expression, when she was still alive, hadn't yet been wiped off her face. 'Thank god!' it seemed to say.

His brother was still saying loudly, 'Oho, is there anything I haven't done for my mother? When she had cholera... Shubho was a little boy and she was pregnant with Kamala...' Shubho took the opportunity, put his head on his mother's feet and said, softly, twice, 'Forgive me, Ma.'

There was a long line of corpses in front of the electric furnace at Nimtala Crematorium. It was evening before Shubho's mother's turn came. Before bathing her and dressing her in fresh clothes, during the rite of 'severance of earthly ties', the priest at the crematorium said, 'All this is mine,' and started taking everything away, from the old clothes to the amulet tied around the corpse's arm. There was a tight knot in the sari, which simply couldn't be loosened. All of them bent down for a closer look—Shubho, his brother, his nephew, his brother's brother-in-law. What could it possibly be? Gouri had already removed all the jewellery. Shubho's mother had displayed her last remaining possession—the necklace at her throat—just a few days ago, telling everyone, 'This is for Pinky.' Gouri would never hand it over.

After a great deal of tugging and clawing, the knot was loosened and a twenty-rupee-note was found. No one knew how long it had been there. It had undoubtedly been washed several times. Holding the pulpy currency note gingerly, Shubho observed a distinctly displeased expression on the priest's face. Taking his hands, he said, 'Look, Purut Moshai, you can still read the serial number, you just have to go to the Reserve Bank office, they'll exchange the notes for you outside on the pavement, they'll keep a rupee at most.' Shubho apologized repeatedly for his mother's inconsiderate behaviour.

Dressed in her new clothes, his mother entered the furnace on a trolley. Just like a slice of bread into a toaster. At a switch the flames leapt up. The enormous gates of the furnace came crashing down.

The next day, Friday, they went back to Behala. Shubho had phoned his office the day before, getting verbal sanction for a fortnight's leave. Maulik would come by with the application form. In the taxi, Shubho recalled the thought that had occurred to him the evening before while standing chest-deep in the Ganga. How would he go to Monica's place the next day in this outfit—in the traditional garb of a son who had lost his mother? Of course, it was a matter of one day only. He was already done for today. And, early on Sunday, 80 to 90 per cent of the stuff would be made to vanish. Which would mean six months of relief. Really. The death of Shubho's mother had changed Kuntala overnight. She hadn't mentioned the toilet even once. She would definitely cope with it one more day. And, oh, Sunday was the first day of the Durga Puja fortnight. The morning programme on the radio would return like the childhood poem, 'It's dawn, night's gone,' waving its blue flag.

Back home, spreading sand between fresh bricks, Shubho and Kuntala were huffing and puffing for all they were worth over a nearly extinguished fire of sticks and wood—fanning was forbidden—with a boiling pot upon it, when, suddenly...whoosh whoosh!

What was that? They looked at each other with reddened, streaming eyes. Because of the smoke, the heartache of one of them was now rolling down as the tears of the other. But the language of their eyes was the same. Wasn't that sound from the bathroom? Their eyes expressed the same hope. Pinky had run to the bathroom before anyone else. Opening the doors of the toilet, she screamed, 'Bapi! Ma!'

Kuntala raced to the bathroom behind Shubho. What could this be but divine intervention? Despite a little stool still stuck to the sides, the pan, my goodness, was absolutely empty. There was no doubt that the pipe had opened up miraculously, and all the stuff had rushed out and sunk somewhere!

Shubho poured in an experimental mug of water. Did you see that, it just slid away like a gleeful rat. He couldn't hold his impatience any longer. The muscles in his arm hardened in expectation of the ten-litre bucket filled with water. He poured in all ten litres at one go.

With bulging eyes he stared for a few seconds at the unblemished and clean white of the pan. Just like the inside of his thick head, which also felt uncluttered. His head had never felt so weightless! Swivelling, he did something very strange. He held his daughter up to the sky, piercing the roof of the bathroom with his screams. 'Ma! Ma!'

Putting his daughter down, he shook Kuntala, his face lighting up as he told her, 'Yes, yes, Ma! My mother, Kunti! Ma couldn't stand our trouble any more. She's cleaned the jammed outlet in the tank with her own hands, believe me, look, my hair's standing on end.'

'You loved me so much, Ma,' wailed Shubho, rolling and writhing on the ritual bedding of a rush mat and a blanket laid out on the floor. He sobbed noisily. Neither Pinky nor Kuntala could calm him down. In the kitchen, the food of mourning boiled in two earthen pots placed side by side on the brick stove, hardening like bricks themselves.

seventeen

SWAPAN IS DEAD, LONG LIVE SWAPAN

UDAYAN GHOSH

Dharitri Debi no longer looks at herself in the mirror. She cannot comb her own hair, either. She stopped oiling it long ago, now she has virtually given up washing it too. Her whims, obstinacy, and laconic nature have always led her to being treated deferentially by everyone, including her sister Bhubanmayee. And it's been a different story over these past eleven days. She is either hard of hearing or completely deaf. She forgets to eat, or asks, even after eating, 'Where's my food?' Despite the eleven days of ritual mourning for the dead with strong restrictions on food and clothing, despite her changed situation now, she follows no rituals. That she is not in her own home but in her sister's has caused no sense of temporary displacement. No one gives her instructions. No one can do anything about the fact that she's sleeping alone at night, though she should not be doing so during this period. When she was brought to this house after the calamity that befell her, she entered the room alone the very first night and bolted the door, although Bhubanmayee's second daughter, Khuku, had followed her with the intention of sleeping in the same room. You could say she slammed the door in Khuku's face. Still, no one is saying anything to her about all this. All of them have accepted everything. For everything pales in comparison to the calamity that has befallen Dharitri Debi.

Of course, it would have been simpler if it was only a matter of the calamity, but it isn't that exactly; actually, Dharitri Debi refuses to believe that the calamity has occurred. The facts are as follows: It's been a year now since her youngest son, Swapan, has been missing. Just as she was almost reconciled to his not coming back, she was told that Swapan had died in jail. Apparently, he had been killed in a skirmish with the guards while trying to escape. His corpse was handed over to his family. The family, which basically meant Bhubanmayee's eldest son, Khokon, second daughter, Khuku, and even Bhubanmayee herself, accepted the corpse as Swapan's. The autopsy report was not given to them, but they drew their conclusions after viewing the corpse. But Dharitri Debi did not believe as they did. She would not acknowledge the corpse as her son's. She even did what is considered impossible for her or for any mother of a dead child. She had the undertaker turn the bruised, contorted body over for a closer look. After which she refused to identify it as Swapan.

The corpse had no skin in places. No eyes. Even its ribs were mostly missing. Not even the blue birthmark on the buttocks, which would have confirmed the body as Swapan's, was present. Either because of the autopsy or because of the beating he had received, the body had been sliced and then stitched up with coarse guts which did not close all the wounds. It was possible to see the innards. Dharitri Debi actually saw them. There should have been twelve pairs of ribs in the chest. There were only remnants of the last three pairs, and nothing at all of the remaining nine. So, from start to finish, Dharitri Debi considered this body wrongly attributed to Swapan and refused to identify it as his.

Standing in the dirty yard outside the morgue, she screamed, 'This isn't a human corpse,' driving everyone present insane. Eventually, inserting her finger into the body, she said, 'See, this is pulp, this is mud, could pulp and mud be a human being?' The word 'body' did not appear on her lips. Nor did the word 'rose', though the corpse appeared to be a rose to her rather than a body. Someone, possibly Bhubanmayee's daughter, Khuku, whispered in her ear, 'They've beaten him to a pulp, Phool Mashi.' Only then did Dharitri Debi, who was also known as Phool, cry. Her wild, unrestrained sobbing made the rifles slung from the shoulders of the armed forces lose their potency. The hands clutching the barrels drooped. No, her tears were not remotely heart-rending. For she couldn't find the eyes. Where were this body's eyes? Why was the blood so cold, so congealed, so dark in colour? All these factors existed. By then it was proved that Dharitri Debi was deranged.

Of course, the body had already been handed over to the legal heirs, subject to certain conditions.

Condition 1: Only 'close family' would be involved in the cremation. In view of the special circumstances, the Home Ministry had included Bhubanmayee and her children under the category of 'close family'. This status was temporary, applicable only until such time as the cremation was completed. The mother, Dharitri Debi, would be permitted to be present at the cremation only on obtaining a 'fitness certificate' from the jail doctor.

Condition 2: Besides those who had been included in the category of 'close family' under special orders, no one who was not legally related—in other words, those who had no permissible claim on the corpse, such as neighbours and fellow-Indians—was allowed to shed tears or place flowers or wreaths on the body.

Condition 3: The cremation would be performed in complete accordance with Hindu rituals.

Condition 4: Any manner of procession or processions and/ or shouting of slogans related to the corpse was banned. Writing, printing, or publishing graffiti, posters, bulletins or handbills was punishable by law.

Condition 5: Section 144, banning the gathering of an unlawful assembly with deadly weapons, would be operative during the cremation.

Accepting these conditions, Bhubanmayee and the rest of them took charge of the body. As mentioned before, however, Dharitri Debi did not. She was not taken to the crematorium, either. She was moved to her sister Bhubanmayee's house here in Jadavpur. It has also been mentioned that she has been here for eleven days now.

What also needs to be said is this: It isn't just Swapan's death that Dharitri Debi is unwilling to accept; she does not believe Bhubanmayee and her family either. For they had always been aware of Swapan's activities. Perhaps it is wrong to say all of them knew, but at least Khuku did. And yet, Dharitri Debi was not informed. Not even her two eldest sons, who are defence department officers, were told. Only the third son, Tapan, was informed. However, it has only been a month since Tapan was made aware of the events. He was instructed to explain the situation at his discretion to his brothers. The news of Swapan's arrest, that is. Apparently it was explained to them. But no one knows what action they took when they got to know. But it is known that Swapan was taken from one jail (Alipur) to another (Behrampur); he was even placed in isolation. But it is not known what role his brothers had to play in this, nor whether this was a serious punishment or a lighter interim sentence. But it has come to light that he had been interrogated and that the skin disease which had erupted was also being treated. Apparently, Bhubanmayee received permission to meet Swapan at this time. No one knows who had arranged this, or whether she had actually met him. No one is saying anything clearly, at least not to Dharitri Debi. From the bits and pieces that are being revealed, it appears that Swapan was, well, he was comfortable, he would have been released eventually, but because he had asked to be freed earlier, this situation had ensued, that is to say, he was beaten till he died, just like a prisoner attempting a jailbreak. Of course, if 'a prisoner attempting a jailbreak' is only a description of a thief or dacoit, it must be said that no one has heard of such criminals being beaten to death. And far from being a thief or a dacoit, Swapan was a jewel. Unbelievable, it's unbelievable, there was no question of beating him to death. In fact, if what people heard was correct, his sentence was about to be reduced. No one is stating clearly that his brothers had a hand in his. Even if they did, there is no way for anyone to know. It is difficult to say whether the brothers, who are defence officers, have any connections with the Calcutta Police, the Central Reserve Police or the Intelligence Bureau. But they might have some contact with the Home Department or the Governor, considering that the military is literally patrolling the streets in this state; perhaps it isn't impossible, but who can say for sure?

The even bigger question for Dharitri Debi is why her sons have not told her anything yet. In fact, despite being informed of Swapan's death eleven days ago, they haven't taken any steps. They could at least get in touch, but why haven't they even done that? Why weren't they present at their younger brother's cremation? It's impossible to believe that the need to stay in the good books of the military or to avoid censure would have forced them into silence, Swapan was their brother, after all. This clearly suggests that Swapan's death is fictitious. They must have investigated the rumour of this death within the relevant circles. And discovered that nothing had happened to Swapan. The person who was being assumed to be Swapan was someone else.

That is why Dharitri Debi is not performing Swapan's last rites. For one who is alive, she is determined to perform only the rites of the living, which is what she's doing. She won't tell anyone what she's doing. It's all in her head. That's why she is in Jadavpur. Not because people have told her to be there, but simply for her own reasons. Of course, Bhubanmayee and the rest of them feel Dharitri Debi should not be alone at home at this time. For they think Swapan is dead. That's why, on the third day of the rumour, Bhubanmayee had performed some rites of her own. At least, Dharitri Debi had sensed without an iota of doubt that a priest was in the house, accompanied by the smell of moistened rice grains, a new gamchha, a fresh dhoti and brass utensils—all the ingredients of a ritual, in other words. Today, on the eleventh day, Bhubanmayee started talking about Swapan; had she been allowed to complete what she was saying, she would inevitably have brought up the question of the eleventh day rituals for the dead, realizing which Dharitri Debi didn't let her continue.

This is how it started. Swapan wasn't the type to attempt a jailbreak. Nor was it possible for him to have tried it as part of a group, because he had been kept in isolation. Besides, the Swapan they had seen the other day behind the iron bars did not have the ability even to walk, never mind making a run for it. Even from a distance of five yards there had been no mistaking the circular ringworm scars on his face. And the way his arms and legs were shackled, the slightest movement would have made the chains clang. Swapan had even said there was no point visiting him. Their meals weren't served on time. Only after the first batch of prisoners had finished their meals and washed their dishes themselves did the second batch get to eat. The afternoon slid by this way. They no longer allowed anyone to eat food brought in from outside the jail. Even if they did, they tested it thoroughly, a process that made the food rot. Bread or bananas were mashed so completely to check whether anything had been hidden inside that they were no longer edible. This system had been put in place after discovering pencil sticks of dynamite in a loaf of bread, and a file within a banana. Any delicacies were stolen by the authorities. Besides, they didn't provide clothes. There wasn't enough water to bathe. They had to wear the same set of clothes for days on end. Every week, they could bathe once and wash their clothes once. Why blame skin diseases? Dinner was foul-smelling chapattis and a curry of potato peel, with a dal made of the officially banned pigeon peas. Every meal was followed by acidic burping. The rice for lunch was full of grit. Swapan's prison cell was so small that he could neither stretch both his arms out without touching the walls, nor sleep at night without having to curl up. Still his head brushed against the wall. Swapan had to sleep on the floor. He pissed and shat inside the same cell. He had told them many more things in the same vein. He had wanted to know whether the newspapers wrote about these things. Whether people discussed them. And immediately afterwards, he had said, 'Not in this country. People think this is the world's largest democracy. People also think the ruling party in India is not very cruel. Certainly not as much as Hitler. In fact, they are even more cruel, for their faces are effeminate. They invoke Indian tradition at the drop of a hat. But there's no such thing as Indian tradition anymore. All of it has been usurped by British imperialism. With Vande Mataram on their lips, they handed the country over to imperialists. There's nothing we can do. Because, unless there is a people's army, the public can do nothing. It cannot even protest. It cannot even revolt...' When he said these things, it was impossible to tell from Swapan's lips or eyes that they might tremble or run dry. The eyes and lips of the Swapans of the world are never destroyed. Even in death, Swapan's eyes and lips are just like those of people who don't lose hope easily, who are always spirited or alive. That was as far as it went... Dharitri Debi did not want to hear anymore, for she had heard a great deal of all this.

On her very first day in this house, Khuku said many more things.

What Khuku said was something like this: He could be seen approaching exactly at two in the morning. Only because the window above her head had been open did the ball of paper hit her precisely in the middle of the forehead. Thank goodness Khuku had been alone in the room, and precisely because there was moonlight, she had seen him through the open window, as startled as though she was seeing a ghost, no she hadn't been scared, but in a sense she had, she hadn't known what to do. This was apparently how she had given Swapan shelter the first time, six months ago. That first night, no one had told her to open the front door carefully, without making a noise, but still she had felt that she should let him enter without waking anyone, without telling anyone. And when he had come up to her, although she wasn't supposed to hug him, on the contrary, she should have retreated, but still she had had no choice but to hug him at once. The heat from his body had not remotely felt like that from a male, but it had felt terrible. Leading him into the room without switching on the light, she had locked the door and shut the window carefully. The pleasure or regret of seeing her after such a long time had made him put his hand on her shoulder. He said, 'Give me something to eat, I haven't eaten anything for four days.' This had made her wonder whether this country was a starving Biafra, whether we were the guinea pigs of rich nations who burnt their harvest for fear of prices crashing. The first day she hadn't been prepared, after all, so her clandestine foraging hadn't yielded anything but a tin of biscuits. The way he had wolfed down fistfuls of biscuits from the tin would ensure that the crunching sounds would stay with her even after she died. He had wanted to leave immediately, but after a request for a second glass of water, the way he had sat down on the bed, and the way his eyes had begun to close, as suggested by his voice in the darkness, made it clear that he had gone even longer without sleep than food. He had not said how long it had been since he had slept, he had not said it even once. But as soon as she had said, 'Then get some sleep now, I'll wake you up at dawn, I'll stay awake and keep watch,' he had slumped on the bed and fallen asleep without a pillow, in a way that clearly showed how long it had been since he had slept. No, what use was it counting the days, actually it was the eyes that needed to be counted, for even though the pair of eyes they used to sleep with and the pair of eyes they used to look around with, or the pair of lips they kept closed in order to rest and the pair of lips they used in order to speak when necessary were beyond counting, but still she felt like counting them, especially when she was told, 'It's just a dog' as soon as she made to open the window on hearing a sound. Or when she asked, 'Is that a car?' even before actually hearing one. And yet, deep sleep. No, there had been no danger that night. There had been no danger on any of the nights. He used to turn up this way frequently, exactly at two in the morning. But she had never found out where he spent the rest of the day, what all of them did, who the others were, she had never got to know any of this. So many times she had asked the same questions in a roundabout fashion, so many times she had said contemptuously, 'Working for the country, my foot.' Still, she had not found out anything. Only once had she felt horrifying doubt. Aren't they human, she had wondered. Were they different? Did they feel no fatigue? Did they have no time for peace? Would they never sleep? Would they never taste the pleasure of lying back awake? Would they never feel the joy of setting eyes on women? Did they have no hunger in their bellies? No thirst in their hearts? Or tenderness? I hear they have compassion, but where is the trust to take someone's hand? Am I not worthy of trust? Still, at least once, when suffering from a stomach ache, he had been looking for something, when even after lying awake by his side and asking him, 'Why don't you say something?' I had not been able to put my hand on his shoulder when the words 'Where does it hurt?' had escaped my lips nevertheless, when he had clutched my hand and gritted his teeth against something—only on that one occasion had he said, 'I'll tell you everything one day. For now, just listen to this. I have an ulcer, but that's not what I suffer from.' He did not reveal what he did suffer from. Apparently, they were forbidden to talk of personal suffering. They could only talk of social suffering. They merely mentioned their personal suffering in the context of social suffering. They could only say that wherever there was oppression, there was resistance. They loved nothing but blood. Their flags were spattered with blood too. They wanted to bleed as well. As long as there was oppression, there would be resistance, and they would have to bleed. But still he couldn't make me bleed. I came to know him, I touched his bleeding body, but my blood did not sing. I had nothing more to do besides giving him shelter, but he never took me along. He never understood that my blood curdled. Is all the blood in the world gathered only in their flags, can it not curdle anywhere else, in someone's body? There was no blood in his lips that day. They were like raisins in winter, but not moist. I saw it on those same lips after his death… His friends informed us. I couldn't recognize any of them. They said the police had apparently arrested Swapan.

Dharitri Debi hears Khuku say all this. She only hears, she doesn't want to listen. But she ends up listening. And she draws the conclusions she has to. They don't know Swapan, she concludes. Some of them know his lips, some his hunger, some the eyes, some a promise, some the belly, some his sacrifice, some assume he has ended up as pulp, a lump of mud. But still no one wants to rake through this mud. They think Swapan is a heap of ashes under the flames, but no one wants to rummage beneath the ash for the precious stone. How can they imagine that a man can be beaten to a pulp? Is a human being only a lump of clay? A human body is supposed to have bones, supposed to have a spine and ribs, hands and feet, at least it should have eyeballs, hair and teeth The dead body had none of these. How can they assume it's Swapan? Dharitri Debi is astonished at the thought. She even feels a stab of sadness. They seem determined to declare the body as Swapan's. Did they know Swapan's body? Had they nurtured him in their wombs? Were they aware of every moment during those ten months and ten days? Had he kicked inside anyone else's womb besides Dharitri Debi's? How then would they know what he sought when he was in pain, or what he looked like when someone hurt him? It was true that he slept like the dead, but that was only sleep, this was pulp. And why would the police beat him to a pulp anyway? He didn't even have the strength to escape. Apparently, he had ringworm on his face, his cheeks, his body—apparently his arms and legs were in iron chains—but where were the ringworm marks on the corpse, where were the marks left by the chains? Where, for that matter, was his birthmark, a large blue mark covering much of his fair right buttock? Which had prompted his father to say, 'He's got the blue blood of the Chakraborty family in his veins.' Can a birthmark be wiped out? Birthmarks cannot be removed. Dharitri Debi has never heard of a birthmark being obliterated unless a body is skinned. She cannot understand how they benefited from acknowledging the body or the pulp as Swapan's. The thorn keeps pricking their hearts, isn't that all? There's no more hope, isn't that what it all boils down to? They had been saying from the outset—they'll die, these boys will die. They had been saying—this deadly politics will kill them first. Was this road to hell meant for students? The path for students had been fixed for an eternity. Walking into danger can only lead to death. To them Swapan is dead, he has long been dead. They are bound to wish for his death, for Khokon here used to criticize him openly. He would say, 'Swapan and his types are anti-social elements, robbers, murderers, deluded, insane, suicidal.' This same Khokon had apparently been the first to identify the body as Swapan's. That Khuku is no better. An overnight convert who spouts jargon. She was the one who said, 'They're nihilists, they may work in the villages, but eventually it's the city that they return to when they have to go into hiding.' How will Swapan trust you? All you know are his eyes and lips. How can you put your hand on his shoulder? There's nothing to be said about Bhubanmayee, she can be persuaded to believe anything anyone wants her to believe.

It's nothing but fiction that at two in the morning a young man will not go to his mother for a meal, but to that overnight convert. Someone who simply sleeps. Does she stay up all night the way Dharitri Debi does? Does she keep the door open? Does she keep a plate of food ready all the time? Does she always keep one side of the bed unoccupied? Or keep an extra pillow at hand? It's nothing but fiction that at two in the morning they sawed through the bars of their cells and broke the iron railings and used them to attack the cruel, heartless policemen. Were they babies or angels or gods who could jump across the twenty-three-foot-high walls despite the bruises from the chains on their arms and legs, despite their starvation diet and wasted bodies? And besides, they could barely walk, a single blow would have been enough to stop them. Why would they have to be injured so badly so that their eyes were ripped out, their hands and feet blown away, their ribs pulverized, their lips smashed, their hair removed? This is nothing but fiction.

Dharitri Debi has seen jails, you see. She has heard the jail clock strike 2 a.m. She has even heard the alarm bells go off. She was pregnant with Swapan then. Four months pregnant. They lived in Raniganj at the time. Returning home from Asansol Club at two in the morning. Past the high walls of the Central Jail, just after the courthouse, she remembers the walls being red, it was exactly 2 a.m., the jail clock was striking two, the alarm bells had rung too. They had been very scared. They learnt afterwards that robbers were let out of jail at that hour. And then let in again at dawn, when they had finished whatever they had to. The alarm bells were for show. Needless to add, the loot was shared. But this proved that the alarms were false, the credit of recapturing the robbers in the morning was also shared. They belonged to that breed which spent their life capturing—or not—criminals. They were those demons who oppressed people without shedding blood. How could they ever beat tender young students, the shining lights of their schools and colleges, into a pulp? Those who spread such rumours believe that this is a central government conspiracy to kill all the brilliant young men and women in this state. The rumours even went so far as to claim that all the young men in this state would be killed in the course of this decade. Can young men ever be killed and annihilated? They are born every second, every nanosecond. What do those people know of giving birth or being born? Does any of them have a womb? Do they possess the patience of ten months and ten days?

This is what Dharitri Debi thinks—one can say, this is what she has concluded. Especially since all that she has been witness to, do not negate these conclusions. On the contrary, they become even more true with every passing day. For Dharitri Debi can see every night, precisely at 2 a.m. on a slice of green by the pond here in Jadavpur, a handful of young men who, despite knowing that many births on this earth have been wasted, journey to the source of fresh currents and return to the purity of the sun to claim the water, grain, light, land, etc. whose dust and grass and flower buds felt like nectar.

Dharitri Debi has seen them on each of the eleven days that she has been here. Precisely at two in the morning, when the clock at some jail strikes two, on the road just below her first floor room which runs a long way in both directions, at the spot where the road forks at the large tree towards the station on the right and the colony of houses on the left, where there is a wall on the left and a canal on the right. A police van appears silently at this very spot. There is a blackout across Jadavpur instantly. The wind dies down. The leaves on the trees and the water in the canal do not quiver. The police van seems to appear without its engine running, and seems to stop without its brakes being applied. For the van makes no sound. Its headlights sweep over the area just once. And then they go out. Nothing but darkness remains. Still Dharitri Debi can see four policemen taking a corpse out of the van. But the clouds in the sky part at that very moment. The moon becomes visible. Mistaking this moonlight for dawn, the birds in the large tree flutter their wings. The leaves tremble at this. Terrified, the four policemen drop the corpse and rush into the van. The van disappears along the fork to the right, which leads to the station. A real breeze springs up. The leaves tremble even more. The water in the canal trembles too. Then the rain comes. Meanwhile, Dharitri Debi does what she has to. The door is open already, she only has to walk across the long veranda to climb downstairs and open the front door. The rain turns torrential as soon as she steps on to the road. Torrential enough to obliterate the earth. The corpse lying on the roadside is obliterated too. By the time she gets close to it, it has turned to pulp. To mud. She rakes the mud but finds no corpse. Even if her hand does meet something she cannot find its buttocks. Everything has turned to a pulpy mud.

It is very surprising that, despite making all arrangements to arrive on time, she has not found the birthmark over these eleven days. She is relieved at not finding it. But her doubt is not entirely dispelled. Her heart turns cold at the thought of what she might see if she does find the birthmark. That's why this search is her persistence, her mission. Still, she has appeared at the same time on each of these eleven days, when the corpse has no skin, no flesh and blood, not even bones, when there's no question of its having eyes or lips or buttocks. At that moment she really does lose her head. Her dishevelled hair billows in the wind. Only a single noble wish remains alive on the way back. Which is to perform the rites for the living for Swapan. When the lights come on in the streets they arrive. They inevitably do. Seven of them with guns. Three of them take positions beneath the large tree. And three more near the front door. Firing with perfect aim, the remaining one puts out the three streetlights one by one. There are three successive sounds like balloons being burst. Then one of them comes up to the wall and writes rapidly: 'The revolution cannot be halted by killing us.' Dharitri Debi takes up her position too by then so that she can catch him. But as soon as he finishes, the same thing happens on each of the eleven days. He stands up straight and croaks like a frog. At once three others approach from each side. The barrels of their guns point in seven different directions. Poised this way, they rush wildly towards another piece of graffiti on the wall. Where it says 'Workers of the world, unite.' Over these words they write again, 'Workers of the world, unite.' All seven take turns to write. They don't exactly write, they run their hands over the letters. But by then several other young men jump off the wall, landing with thumps. Silently they surround these seven young men. Each of the newly arrived young men holds a curved sword. They pierce the breasts of the seven young men with their swords. And laugh loudly. And as they laugh they don't hold back from saying, 'Do you dare to touch our words again with your dirty hands?' They threaten them. But the seven are not thwarted. Dharitri Debi realizes that the battle will now start. And so it does. She runs towards them. By then what had to begin has begun. How inhuman and cruelly they behave! Such blind rage! None of them can even see Dharitri Debi. But no one can stand up to the guns. The seven are triumphant. They disappear, pursuing the sword-wielding group. One of the gun-wielders remains. He's a little injured. But he's still on his feet, upright. Picking some things up from the road, he tries to run off towards the colony of houses. Dharitri Debi pursues him. She catches him before he has covered the length of the canal. Because his feet are trapped in the mud. When he pitches headlong into the mud, Dharitri Debi doesn't hesitate anymore. She pounces on him. And searches for his waist in the mud. She places an unerring hand on the spot. It descends like a paw. She tears his trousers off. His buttocks are revealed in the light from her eyes. She takes in the sight. She cannot stop taking it in. She sees that the blue birthmark on one of his buttocks is as clear as she has been hoping it will be. No other sound except 'Swapan' emerges from her throat. Before she can put his arms around him, he runs away.

In this way, she finds the blue birthmark on the buttocks of eleven young men on eleven successive days. She has no difficulty in surmising that Swapan is alive. And that he will remain alive for a long time.

eighteen

POST-MORTEM

SUNIL GANGOPADHYAY

'May I know your name?'

'Samita Majumdar.'

'At 5.25 the other evening did you…'

'Yes, I leave my office at exactly ten past five, although we close at five I choose to leave a little later… It doesn't take more than five minutes to cover the short distance…'

'How far away do you live?'

'I live near the Jagubajar bus stop…'

'And you? Were you there that evening?'

'Yes… You remember?'

'Yes, why shouldn't I remember? Although I didn't see it with my own eyes, I was seated near the front…'

'What's your name?'

'Ratna Dasgupta…'

'And you?'

'I was standing next to the door…'

'Just a minute, let me get your name.'

'Sarbari Mukhopadhyay?'

'You've got the spelling wrong, there should be an 'h'… Sharbari?'

'I'm sorry…Yes, so you were standing by the door, weren't you? Where do you work, by the way?'

'Central Bank…'

'The one that caught fire?'

'No, I work at a different branch…'

'I see, how long does it take you from there?…'

'Five or six minutes… Sometimes I work late—I miss the tram those evenings…'

'Where do you live?'

'I live near Tollygunge Bridge, here's Reshmi, we live together...'

'Is your name Reshmi...Reshmi Sengupta...'

'What! Why should I be a Sengupta...'

'No, I mean I used to know someone with that name, that's why I was mistaken... She looked a lot like you... So your name is...'

'Reshmi Chowdhury...'

'And before you were married?...'

'I was a Chowdhury then too... Why does that surprise you?'

'Oh no, I'm not surprised...'

'So, Reshmi Debi, were you standing by the door next to your friend, Sharbari Mukhopadhyay?'

'No, I wasn't near the door.'

'Then the two of you didn't board the tram together? Or maybe one of you got a seat, but not the other.'

'I took the tram from the terminus, Sharbari got on two stops later... We live in the same neighbourhood.'

'Do you live in adjoining houses?'

'We live next to each other, but not exactly in adjoining houses.'

'I don't quite understand.'

'I live at home. The building next door is a hostel, where Sharbari lives.'

'A hostel? Are you a student?'

'No, it's a working girls' hostel... Haven't you heard of such hostels before?'

'I've read about them in English novels.'

'I myself know of at least five such hostels in Calcutta.'

'Does that mean you've come from some other town to work in Calcutta? Please don't mind my asking, you're married, aren't you, judging from the vermilion... But then this is becoming a little too personal.'

'You're asking why I live in a hostel even though I'm married, aren't you? We used to live in a flat on Anwar Shah Road earlier... My husband and I... He has to travel a lot on work. At least twenty days a month... Most of the time I had to live by myself... Managing a flat on your own... It's a lot of trouble.' (laughter)

'I'll tell you... Sharbari had to live by herself most of the time... A couple of louts in the neighbourhood began to make a nuisance of themselves, kept turning up on flimsy pretexts... You men think a woman has no right to live by herself... And if she does, she must be romanced.'

'So, now you're clubbing all men together.'

'Certainly! You lot are all the same.'

'But... Let's take your husband and those neighbourhood louts, surely they're not the same though they're all men? Local ruffians are a distinct breed, and husbands, another... Or take familiar and unfamiliar people... Surely, they're different breeds too, even if they're male as well...'

'If a man puts his hand on the shoulder of a woman he knows, while another does the same to one he doesn't know... These are quite different matters. Or take a young man and an old man, they're different from each other too.'

'Why this unwarranted conversation?'

'If you have objections I can go away at once...'

'Why should we object? One moment, Samita, let's see what he has to say...'

'I only want to get one or two pieces of information. Now, Sharbari Debi, there'd been some trouble in your previous neighbourhood...'

'That's why I gave up the flat. I live in peace at the hostel now.'

'But when your husband returns to Calcutta from time to time, I'm told he's in town at least ten days a month...'

'We have our own house in Ranaghat. When he's not on tour, that's where he stays and goes to work from. I join him on Saturday evenings, and go directly to the office on Monday mornings.'

'Wonderful, such a modern arrangement.... Did your husband come to know of the trouble in your previous neighbourhood? Did he think you... No, never mind, you needn't answer this question, I can see you're getting angry... Then I take it that both of you are living contentedly now, there's no trouble anymore in your lives... But why shouldn't there be trouble? There's always some trouble when you're married (laughter)... Never mind, we're digressing, you were standing near the door the other day... You remember the entire incident... Did you talk to him?'

'No. I think Anjali Di may have exchanged a word or two.'

'Here, Anjali Di... What's your full name?'

'Anjali Roy.'

'Did you talk to the man?'

'No, I didn't.'

'Were you also standing near the door...'

'Anjali Di, didn't you say you spoke...'

'No, I didn't talk to him.'

'Were you standing near the door too?'

'I don't remember.'

'It was only two months ago. Don't you remember?'

'I've already told you I don't.'

'All right, do YOU remember? Excuse me, I'm asking YOU.'

'I wasn't even on the tram that day.'

'Do you alternate between the tram and the bus on your way back? Depending on whichever is easier?'

'No, I normally take the same tram. But I was on leave at the time you're referring to.'

'It was Tuesday. Can you recollect the date, Reshmi Debi?'

'No idea, I don't know.'

'Do YOU remember, Sharbari Debi?'

'That's easy enough. It was the first of the month. Many of us were paid that day.'

'Sharbari is right. I remember, too, it was the first, it had been overcast since the afternoon. It had probably begun to rain by then.'

'No, it wasn't raining, but it was overcast.'

'What are you saying, Samita! It started pouring in the afternoon... I was soaked by the time I got on the tram.'

'Do all of you know one another's names?'

'Many of us do. We return together every day, naturally we get to know one another... We can always tell when someone new gets on.'

'People who commute every day by local trains also get to know one another this way. Some of them even form clubs... Card clubs, or singing clubs... Many of them even rehearse for plays inside the compartment... Do you have anything like this?'

'No, we don't have a club or anything.'

'You just chat with one another?'

'Yes, we chat.'

'Did you discuss that evening's incident afterwards?'

'Are you a reporter? Why are you asking so many questions?'

'No, I'm not a reporter. Reporters only gather fresh news. But this incident is two months old.'

'Then why are you asking so many questions?'

'No particular reason. If you have objections to answering...'

'It's 5.25. Why isn't she here yet?'

'There's a meeting at Brigade Parade Ground. There must be a traffic jam. She's certain to be late.'

'She may be late, but she'll come.'

'The man was blind.'

'And you are...?'

'My name is Shiuli Dasgupta. I saw the whole thing. I'll tell you, take it down.'

'You're saying the man was...'

'Yes, he was blind. I was startled. The sockets of his eyes were absolutely empty, there was nothing inside.'

'No, not at all, he wasn't blind at all, I saw him. He wore glasses... No, not even glasses, he was staring at everyone... He was flustered when he saw us laughing... How can you say he was blind, Shiuli..? He wasn't blind at all, if he had been blind we would...'

'Well then, Shiuli Debi, many people are protesting. All of them are saying the man wasn't blind.'

'Maybe both his eyes were shut, then.'

'By the way, men often sleep on a bus or a tram, but women don't, do they?'

(laughter)

'There was no question of his sleeping, because he wasn't seated, he was standing... No one sleeps on their feet.'

'Some people do sleepwalk.'

(laughter)

'Do any of you remember whether the man said anything?'

'Yes, he did. Anjali Di was talking to him.'

'No, I wasn't.'

'Then someone else was. He had even replied...'

'Then we can safely assume he wasn't asleep.'

'I even remember what he was told. Someone asked, "Don't you have eyes?"'

'A person without eyes can certainly be termed blind. Is that why Shiuli Debi said he was blind?'

'Whatever Shiuli Di may have said, he was definitely staring.'

'At first I thought he was mad.'

'Rubbish, he wasn't mad, he looked quite decent.'

'Can't decent people be mad?'

'What I mean is, his clothes were quite... He didn't look mad... He was dressed in a clean dhoti and kurta.'

'Dhoti and full-sleeved shirt. A grey shirt. Keds on his feet.'

'Wonderful, you remember quite a lot. Your name, please?'

'Chandra Basu. I've dreamt of him thrice since.'

'Why?'

'No idea.'

'How old was he?'

'About fifty-one or fifty-two.'

'Seventy.'

'Not more than sixty-five.'

'Below sixty, I think.'

'Nonsense! Not a day below seventy.'

'Let's hear Chandra Basu's opinion. Since she's dreamt of him thrice, what she says is more credible.'

'People see strange things in dreams.'

'I did see him in my dreams. Looking at me sort of surprised.'

'Did you dream the same scene all three times?'

'Yes.'

'Have you ever dreamt thrice of a stranger before?'

'No.'

'How do you dream so much, Chandra? I never have dreams.'

'I do dream frequently, but I can never remember anything the next day.'

'I remember everything. I have a lot of dreams.'

'In your dreams, how old was the man, Chandra Debi?'

'About seventy, I think.'

'Your estimate is correct. The doctor thinks so too.'

'Do you know him?'

'I'll tell you later. First, I have a few more questions.'

'Your tram has a male conductor. Have you ever demanded a female conductor?'

'Yes.'

'No.'

'Makes no difference.'

'The poor man suffers all the while. Has a hangdog expression.'

'Why do you take this one in particular on your way back instead of other buses or trams? You don't like travelling with men?'

'It's not that, it's just that there's room in this one.'

'Surely, not everyone gets a seat. Some people have to stand by the time it leaves, it must get even more crowded, right? People must be jostling one another.'

'That's true. But no one does anything indecent. I feel suffocated in a bus.'

'You're saying people act indecently in crowded buses and trams? Is it only men who do it, never women?'

'Never.'

'Then the question can be phrased this way, men act indecently, they brush against women, this annoys women at times, but don't they enjoy it ever?'

'Enjoy it? How awful!'

'I don't know about young girls but it's intolerable to us.'

'Do you think they merely brush against you? They do a lot worse...'

'That's true. Some people take advantage of the crowds to do horrible things, some pick pockets, some snatch necklaces, and some also give up their seats deferentially, don't they?'

'Why shouldn't they? Everyone's not the same, there are some gentlemen too.'

'Most gentlemen take the minibus these days.'

'Does a young woman ever give up her seat for an old man?'

'Certainly.'

'If a woman gives up her seat for an old man she'll have to suffer indecent advances from some other man pressing up against her.'

'Still, many women do give up their seats for very old men.'

'Have you ever done it yourself?'

'Yes, I mean, why shouldn't I?'

'Have you?'

'Who are you to ask all this?'

'No one really. Don't answer if you'd rather not.'

'No such occasion has yet arisen. If it had, I would certainly have.'

'Don't louts get into your tram sometimes?'

'Some do by mistake, others to create mischief.'

'How often has this happened?'

'Frequently.'

'What do you do in those cases?'

'What can we do?'

'Don't you tell them to get off?'

'Why should we? That's the conductor's job, he'll tell them.'

'Do they get off when the conductor tells them to?'

'They do, actually.'

'What do you do until they get off? Do all of you stare at

them together?'

'What nonsense.'

'What if Uttam Kumar or Soumitra Chatterjee were to board your tram by mistake one day? Would you ask them to get off?'

'Of course not!'

(laughter)

(laughter)

(laughter)

'It was Tuesday. The first of the month. The sky was full of threatening clouds, it had started drizzling. Did the man in the grey shirt get into the tram by mistake, or to create mischief?'

'How should we know that?'

'He leapt into the tram suddenly just as it started moving after the Lindsay Street stop.'

'Yes.'

'Some of you were near the door too. For instance, you, Sharbari Debi. Weren't there some other people near you?'

'Two or three, yes.'

'I don't remember who they were.'

'I was there.'

'You are, um, Chandra Debi. Did the man try to shove you aside when he got in?'

'No. He was probably flustered because all of us laughed.'

'After which someone pushed him off.'

'That's a lie. A complete lie.'

'Who told you he was pushed off?'

'Can anyone possibly push an old man of seventy off a tram?'

'Let me talk, be quiet for a minute, Sharbari, I saw it all clearly, I remember very well. He was flustered, he muttered something, whereupon everyone laughed some more. Then the man...'

'You said he was blind, Shiuli Debi.'

'He may not have been blind but he behaved as though he was...'

'And still he was pushed off.'

'Certainly not.'

'That's a lie. How strange...'

'Many of you use the feminine versions of your surnames... You do not object when women brush against each another. But you dislike it when there are men in a crowded tram.'

'What are you trying to say?'

'Nothing. Only information.'

'We really can't stand the indecent behaviour of men in crowded transport after a hard day's work at the office.'

'It was the first of the month, salary day. All your handbags were full of cash.'

'Handbags full of cash? Do you suppose we earn thousands every month?'

'We have to bring larger handbags on salary day, Anjali Di.'

(laughter)

'At any rate, many of you were carrying your salaries. When he leapt into the tram suddenly, did you think he was a robber?'

(silence)

'He could very well have been one.'

'But you didn't really think he was one. Because all of you were laughing.'

'The man was by himself, and quite old... None of us thought he was a robber.'

'You were laughing too, Sharbari Debi?'

'We were all laughing.'

'Shiuli Debi, you were saying the man was...'

'Yes, he muttered something, then turned round and...'

'Couldn't you hear what he was muttering?'

'No.'

'Is that why someone...'

'Pushed him off the tram?'

'Of course not.'

'Don't talk rubbish.'

'Did he collide with something?'

'Impossible.'

'Collide with something? With nothing, possibly. With the wind, perhaps.'

'We all saw him jump off. That's why we thought he might be mad.'

'I even grabbed his arm.'

'You grabbbed his arm? Did you really touch him then?'

'Yes, as soon as he turned around... But I couldn't hold on to him.'

'Were you still laughing when you grabbed his arm, Sharbari Debi?'

'No, why should I have been laughing?'

'Are you sure, Sharbari Debi?'

'Of course I'm sure. Still the man...the gentleman...jumped out, it was an accident.'

'Did you see him fall on the road?'

'The road was dark. The sky was dark that evening. The tram was going past the maidan, it's dark over there.'

'Yes, dark.'

'Why did you say he was pushed off the tram?'

'All of you were laughing.'

'Yes, we were. But it was an accident. He deliberately jumped off the moving tram... It was travelling very fast.'

'All of you were laughing from the moment he leapt into the tram.'

'Yes, we were, so what? Someone had said something funny...'

'It happens all the time... Is it a crime to laugh?'

'Who was it that said something funny? Does anyone remember the joke?'

(silence)

'You were saying you remember everything, Shiuli Debi...'

'Does that mean I have to remember which joke each of us had told?'

'Only one of you did, remember?'

'Yes, only one of us did. I was just saying.'

'Everyone else was laughing. It was drizzling. The sky was

overcast… Did the tram halt at once?'

'No, all of us screamed, but still the tram travelled some distance before coming to a stop…'

'Where was the conductor?'

'He was right at the front.'

'Didn't he say anything?'

'He's a complete idiot… This same idiot's on duty most of the days.'

'Didn't any of you ring the bell?'

'No, we didn't remember to, the driver heard us screaming and…'

'Did any of you get off for a look when the tram stopped?'

'The conductor did…'

'None of you?'

'Who wants to see a macabre sight like that? How would it have helped?'

'It wasn't exactly a macabre sight, anyhow.'

'The tram was stalled for almost half an hour, there was a big crowd. Then the tram continued on its way, each of you got off at your respective stops, everyone at home must have been very worried that evening because you were late. Meanwhile the rain had intensified, forcing the crowds to disperse, the man lay on his back, he hadn't bled at all. The ambulance came, we saw it, then the tram moved. We hadn't imagined though that he would actually…'

'None of you had imagined he would actually die. You had expected him to have fractured his limbs at most, bleed through his mouth, or maybe even roll over a couple of times and get to his feet.'

'We didn't expect that either. We expected nothing.'

'You were laughing.'

'Why do you keep harping on that? Aren't we supposed to laugh if someone says something funny?'

'Did someone say, "Don't you have eyes?"'

'Yes, I did, it's not a crime.'

'Your lives have been the same since then, nothing has changed for any of you.'

'Why are you asking so many questions? Did you know him?'
'What if I tell you he was my father?'
(silence)
(silence)
(silence)

 'No, he wasn't my father, I didn't know him at all. I don't want
to impose a burden of guilt on any of you. I'll tell you whatever
I've come to know. His neck must have snapped as soon as he
hit the ground, killing him instantly. For he didn't make a sound,
didn't call out to anyone, he looked for all the world as though he
was sleeping. He was taken to Shambhunath Pandit Hospital. The
doctors declared him dead on arrival. He could not be identified.
He had five rupees and seventy paise in his pocket. And some useless
scraps of paper. A handkerchief, a pocket Gita. A slim gold ring on
his left ring finger. None of his belongings yielded an address or
information about his family. His corpse was sent to the morgue at
Mominpore. Even after news of the accident was published in the
next day's papers, no one turned up to inquire about him. Eleven
days later the police department advertised with this photograph,
for his clothes, the gold ring, the pocket Gita and expression had
suggested he was an educated gentleman. But no one turned up with
enquiries. No one came forward to claim the gold ring and the five
rupees and seventy paise. After a month, the corpse was cremated.

 Maybe he was redundant on earth. The kind of person whose
existence was irrelevant, whose death would not be a loss to anyone.
Perhaps he had no one in this world to weep or mourn for him.
Or even feel his absence. Maybe, he was completely alone. No one
knows where he might have been going with five rupees and seventy
paise in his pocket! Or, maybe wandering around the roads was
his only occupation. It was probably his fate to drop dead on the
streets some day. If he had just died in his sleep on the pavement
there wouldn't have been a stir over his death. Isn't this what would
have happened? Isn't it surprising that not a single person inquired
about him? Are there so many lonely people in this city? If he really

had been so lonely, then the sound of so many women laughing in unison...he must have been wandering around the roads as he did every day—when it started raining he leapt into the wrong tram... then he heard the sound of laughter, so many women laughing at the sight of him... Who knows whether he had ever married, whether he had ever even come into contact with a woman, he might have had a relationship of some kind if he had, with at least one person... No, no one wept over his death, no one felt his absence, he was an unnecessary man... Still, it is a matter of good fortune for him that you, Sharbari Debi, grabbed his arm at the last minute to save him, that you, Chandra Debi, dreamt of him thrice. Perhaps this death was the most memorable incident of his life. I believe he had seen a dream a moment before his death. A dream of several laughing faces. Maybe even this had not been given to him earlier in his entire life.'

nineteen

THE MARBLE TABLE

SANJIB CHATTOPADHYAY

The marble table stood on the first floor, by the window looking out onto the road to the south. Neither perfectly square nor round, it had a scalloped edge. A lot like those ritual patterns drawn on the floor. It was set lightly on a rather baroque frame. Its own weight kept it in place. The table top was a marble slab that weighed about seventy kilos. A wooden lattice was attached to the frame, which was also surrounded by numerous small, wooden balls. Like circular dumb-bells with tapered ends. A lot like well-polished pieces of patol, the vegetable. They whirled furiously when spun. The four legs were like embellished pillars. A broad footrest lay at the bottom.

Around the time my father was in the prime of his life, with a head full of curly hair parted with a razor-sharp gash, sporting a butterfly moustache above his upper lip, when he was at the age at which he used to put on his highly burnished shoes every evening to take the greyhound gifted to him by Mr Young for a walk by the river, the table was also in the prime of its life. Baba had bought it at an auction. The table had entered our house at the same time as a swing was to be hung from the beams.

When I grew tall enough to rest my chin on the cold marble, I saw my father squatting on a chair every morning, shaving before an egg-shaped mirror with a contorted face. Baba used to get very angry if anyone stood by his side when he shaved. In any case, he ruled with an iron fist. It was the age of the redoubtable Bengali. He was bad-tempered too. When he came home every evening, he would thrash each of the two young menservants with his shoes on alternate days before sitting down at the table to drink his tea with an infuriated expression.

My docile, sociable uncle—the younger of my father's elder brothers, whom I addressed as Mejo Jetha Moshai—would occupy the chair without armrests to his left. His hair was partly black and partly copper, with a few streaks of silver. He would dye it, as he sat wrapped in a bristly towel. Anger was bad, Jetha Moshai would explain. This shoe business, in particular, first thing in the evening after getting home from office, sucked extra energy out of the body. Servants always tended to be slightly callous. Baba didn't pay much attention to the mild-mannered Jetha Moshai. It was difficult to say which of them was the elder brother. 'Mustn't poke your nose in here,' Baba would say, setting his cup down with a clatter on the table. 'Discipline, first and foremost. Have to think of the boy. They have been using foul language all afternoon. Referred to the offspring of a horse and a donkey.' Baba was a Puritan. He would not utter the word 'khachhor', literally a mule, but actually a choice Bengali term of abuse. I was the one who had presented the report the moment he came home. And the action was instant. Baba chased Niranjan down the long veranda, beginning the flogging at the eastern end and throwing his shoe away after reaching the turn of the staircase at the western corner.

Jetha Moshai was fond of Niranjan, who lovingly prepared his fishing bait every Sunday with rotten bread, bits of paneer and ant eggs. That was probably why he had tried to make excuses for Niranjan. But he couldn't say a word now, and departed slowly for the bathroom. Baba could never tolerate obscenities. I remember one morning, during the holidays, when my maternal grandfather, whom I addressed as Dadu, and Baba were sitting at the table eating muri and telebhaja, rice puffs and deep-fried vegetable fritters. The father-in-law and son-in-law were in animated discussion. Dadu had used the mild invective 'shala' several times. This word was permitted. Suddenly, Dadu uttered the Bengali word for rectum—paachha! Baba stood up in silence and fetched a paper packet from another room. Transferring Dadu's share of the puffs and fritters into the packet, he handed it to his father-in-law, saying, 'Eat this in your own home or outside on the stoop where loafers congregate. You're not civilized enough to eat at the table. Your sphere is distinct from ours.' Dadu was a senior citizen. His complexion was ruddy, and he was built like a wrestler. His face became redder still at what Baba had said. 'What's the matter?' he blurted out childishly. 'Why are you so upset all of a sudden?' Dadu had not yet realized his crime. 'Your language is improper,' Baba told him. 'Oh, you mean the paachha,' said Dadu, looking guilty. 'Don't repeat it,' Baba broke in, raising his hand. 'What should I say, then?' asked Dadu, flustered now. 'Can you not refer to it as the behind or the cheeks!' Baba responded. Dadu still didn't give up, attempting a weak self-defence. 'I'm an old-fashioned man, you see, Parameshwar,' he said. 'These were the words we used in our time.' Without giving him the opportunity to further argue, Baba abandoned the marble table for his own room. Dadu sat where he was, the packet in his hand. He didn't know what to do next. Finally, he said with a sheepish smile, 'Parameshwar really is very angry.'

My mother was oppressed by my father's tyrannical rule over the household. On holidays, she did not appear to be a living being, going about her chores almost like a shadow. She used to make tea for my father about two dozen times during the day. Serving Baba his tea was a complicated ritual. Spilling even a single drop from the cup into the saucer would ruin the whole thing. The cup had to be filled to the brim and then brought to him, carefully balanced on the saucer.

I believe one of Ma's legs was shorter than the other. Every doorway in our classical era house had a raised doorstep, which made things difficult for her. When she brought the tea she appeared to be carrying a liquid bomb which would explode at the slightest tremor.

Soon after Baba had departed in a rage, my mother brought the tea in. Dadu was still sitting at the table, clutching the packet. The oil had seeped through the paper. 'I'm not staying for tea, Tulsi, your husband is very angry.' Ma knew what had happened, since I had reported the events to her already in the kitchen. 'Have your tea and leave,' she whispered to him.' 'I would have left by now,' he said, 'but I'm stuck.' 'Stuck to what?' Ma asked in surprise.' 'Deep trouble!' Dadu replied. Ma was worried. Dadu was reckless when it came to food, he would do astounding things like knock back the juice of an entire jackfruit with two litres of milk, or down half a bottle of raw ghee with dal. Ma thought Dadu might have done it in his clothes. This had happened a couple of times in the past. 'Have you gone and done it!' 'Oh no, nothing awful like that,' Dadu asserted boldly. He seemed quite proud of not having done it. 'What have you done, then?' Ma was baffled. Dadu began to resemble a naughty boy. Shifting in his chair, he said, 'My finger's stuck to the table.' 'Let me see,' said Ma, bending over. The index finger of Dadu's right hand was wedged into one of the holes amongst the hearts and clubs and spades patterned into the wooden frame of the table. 'Why don't you pull it out?' Ma asked. 'It won't come out,' said Dadu helplessly. 'How did it go in?' Dadu described the events that had taken place. 'Parameshwar had left in a huff, leaving me here. I was running my fingers across the holes in distraction when a finger suddenly slipped into one. I had oil on my finger. And now I just can't get it out. He put the muri and telebhaja into the packet with such care. There are still a couple of fritters to go. And now my right hand's stuck.'

Ma paled in fear. 'What do we do now?'

'I could break the frame and pull my finger out, but what if Parameshwar gets angry,' Dadu said childishly.

'Oh no, the frame can't possibly be broken. It'll lead to Armageddon. You'd better try again.'

'Afraid I can't, Tulsi. I have been turning my finger round and round for so long that the skin's come off.' Putting the teacup down on the marble table, Ma went off to the veranda on the north side of the house. Next to it was Baba's kitchen garden on a handkerchief-sized plot. It didn't get enough sunlight. Still, Baba's efforts were unflagging. All kinds of trees were to be found on that small plot of land. All of them grew tall in spite of the lack of sunlight. A few papaya trees were about to reach the second floor parapet. Baba was in the garden. With Niranjan as his assistant. In the mornings, Niranjan had no equal. Evenings, well, the same Niranjan was thrashed. The roots of the trees were being watered from a rotting husk. The slightest mis-step would make Niranjan tread on seedlings. Baba kept howling frequently, 'Damn, there goes the daffodil.' 'Not at all, Chhoto Babu.' Niranjan was unperturbed. 'Bloody bugger, you're standing on it, you crystallized idiot,' Baba said through clenched teeth. 'That's why they say everyone needs a minimum education.' 'Plants everywhere,' Niranjan said, 'how do I avoid stamping on them?' 'Why, is your big toe paralysed, this is how you should walk, don't you know how to move around on tiptoe?' Baba attempted a demonstration, 'Oh dear, now I've trod on it myself, there goes the fuchsia, blast it.' Niranjan tried to be reassuring. 'One or two are bound to die, sir. Not every child you give birth to survives, does it? One or two are bound to die.' 'Right you are,' Baba said. 'Keep planting, keep planting them. Six inches apart, don't forget.' Ma knew this would go on until noon. Baba would endure mosquito bites as well as several cups of tea without budging from his garden. Then, trying to prune the branches, he would nick his hand and rush upstairs with shrieks of imminent doom. Iodine and bandages were always on hand for such emergencies.

Ma came back from the north veranda to Dadu, who was stuck to the table. Sanatan's tiny picture-framing shop was just across the road. Tall, dark and wrinkled, he hammered away all day with a small implement. When he took breaks to take a bidi out of a small aluminium tin, he would gaze at our house; his eyes looked a murky yellow. 'Can you quietly ask Sanatan to come over?' Ma instructed me.

'What do you want, Ma?' he asked when he arrived. He may have been thin, but he had a stentorian bellow.

'Softly,' whispered Ma. Lowering his voice as much as possible, he asked, 'What is it, Ma?' Ma showed Sanatan what had happened. Kneeling next to Dadu's chair, Sanatan said, after examining the table carefully, 'The wooden border is attached with a couple of screws. If I remove the screws it will be detached automatically.'

'Then detach it,' said Ma. 'Quick. Without a sound.' Sanatan clomped down the staircase in his clogs. On Ma's embarrassed request he took them off and went off barefoot to fetch his tools from his shop.

The screws were ancient and their heads had rusted. Sanatan had to struggle quite a bit. The table couldn't be moved, since Dadu was stuck to it. Sanatan was engaged in performing the impossible in a dark and narrow hole. Dadu looked rather amused. Ma's expression betrayed suppressed anxiety. Her ears were cocked for sounds from the garden. Whenever she didn't hear Baba's voice she tiptoed away for a look.

Suddenly, a heap of wooden balls cascaded to the floor like a stream of patol.

'Oh dear, what's happened now?' Ma asked.

Sanatan looked up with a smile. 'I've removed the frame on this side.'

'Why did you have to loosen these?' Ma asked.

'They come away with the frame, Ma. These balls were held in place by the pressure from the frame above.'

Sanatan concentrated on removing the rest of the frame. Dadu realized it wasn't right to remain silent. 'You're good at your work, I see,' he applauded Sanatan. 'You've got it to come away.'

Ma gathered the balls and hid them in the end of her sari so that they weren't caught red-handed.

Eventually the frame forsook its relationship with the table and came away, with Dadu's plump index finger still stuck within it. But at least Dadu wasn't still attached to the table; his joy was a sight to behold. He seemed to have been released from prison. Spinning the frame around his finger a couple of times, he said, 'It fits rather well, Tulsi.' Ma couldn't quite participate in Dadu's celebrations. I knew what was playing on her mind. Baba would soon come upstairs all sweaty from his efforts in his kitchen garden; he would be emitting all sorts of strange noises, a consequence of working hard. Hiss…s. Hiss…s. A lot like today's pressure cookers.

His work in the garden finished, Baba's second major task that Sunday was to scrub the marble table clean. He had deliberately skipped it the previous Sunday. That was quite an episode too. My friend Bipul had written his name on the table with a pencil: Bipul Roy. In a large, clear hand. Baba spotted it the day after he had written it. Drawing an arrow pointing at it, Baba wrote in even larger letters: bloody bugger. Baba always got agitated whenever he saw something written or drawn in chalk on the door, or the owner's name on the first page of a book, or doodles in exercise books, or the display of one's name on the marble table. A psychological campaign against the writer would be launched.

A graffiti battle had been waged on the wall by our front door for quite some time. Anyone about to enter our house was sure to be surprised if he were to notice the writing scrawled on the wall. The first words were 'Tiger's Den'. The writer had probably expressed his honest view of our house when he had dubbed it 'Tiger's Den'. 'Scoundrel,' wrote Baba. 'Theatre of Lunatics,' the invisible writer countered. 'Swine,' Baba responded. 'Butterfly', came the response. Possibly the writer had commented on my father's moustache. 'Stupid,' riposted my father. There was no lack of space by our enormous front door for writing. The weekly game of accusations and counter accusations had warmed up nicely.

However, Bipul's writing hadn't made any progress on the marble table. For he had personally seen the epithet 'bloody bugger' and was unlikely to set foot in this house again. Can you tell me what 'bloody bugger' means, he had asked. I didn't know. Bipul had left with a miserable expression on his face.

Ma quickly made Dadu leave the table. It was decided that he would shift to Sanatan's shop. Sanatan would make one last attempt to free his finger while keeping the frame intact. 'Just a minute, Tulsi, I'll just eat these two fritters in a second with my left hand.' Ma was aghast. 'Oh no, it's time for him to come upstairs, you'd better run.' Dadu went down the stairs in his black canvas shoes, his packet in one hand, the other with the finger stuck in a hole in the wooden frame, followed by Sanatan with his tools. Meanwhile, Baba came up the back stairs, making pressure cooker sounds, followed by Niranjan with a shovel and a pitcher of manure.

It wasn't possible to tell at a glance that the embellishments beneath the marble slab had been shed. Ma was hoping that the accident would not be spotted immediately. Perhaps it could be kept under wraps for some time. You never knew, maybe Sanatan's amazing dexterity would ensure that the wooden frame came loose smoothly from Dadu's finger, as thick as a ripe plantain, and be reinstated in its rightful place on a weekday in Baba's absence. Baba demanded a glass of water as soon as he came upstairs. He had a large tumbler of thick glass, which could hold about a litre of water. He squatted on the floor with the glass in his hand at a little distance from the table. This was his special way of drinking his water. He sipped the water and glanced at the sun-dazzled blue afternoon sky, occasionally emitting a peculiar 'ah' sort of sound. Ma stood anxiously at a distance. The table stood in front of the window, its marble as pristine and white as a tombstone's. The Sunday peace seemed to be interred beneath the table at that moment. Draining his glass, Baba emitted a final sound. A sparrow flew out of the ventilator at the top of the wall. Baba glanced at the small opening and said, 'I'd been hearing for several Sundays now that it would be blocked with a sheet of tin.' Pouring the last drops of water into his throat, Baba rose. Thank goodness he hadn't spotted the missing frame. He could easily have. The lower part of the table and its sides were visible from his position.

Baba clomped off to the bathroom. His speciality was doing everything at top speed. The only activity he had not succeeded in injecting speed into was evacuation. Constipation. If only there was a way to get rid of the intestines, he'd say angrily sometimes. Niranjan would pump his stomach from time to time according to instructions he received from Baba. Only when the marmelo, with its laxative property, was in season would he fuss a little less.

This meant we had half an hour at least or even forty-five minutes. There was no possibility of his emerging from the bathroom earlier. Ma and I ran to the window overlooking on the road. Efforts to separate Dadu's finger from the wooden frame were underway in Sanatan's shop. Sanatan was alone in his shop, but Dadu wasn't visible. At other times Sanatan looked up at our window frequently. But now he was rapt—in what? After a long time Sanatan raised his yellowish eyes. Ma signalled a question with her hands. Dadu had inserted his finger into a club. Chuckling, Sanatan lifted two pieces of wood to show us. His freedom had been obtained by splitting the frame. Ma's faint smile was replaced by an ominous expression.

Baba issued his bulletin as soon as he emerged from the bathroom—absolutely no evacuation. Niranjan was standing before him. Even without knowing English, he knew the phrase. 'A little pumping,' he said at once. 'Not now,' answered Baba. 'Let me try some tea.' Ma made him a cup of tea with great compassion. Not only had he not cleared his bowels, but the table had also been broken. And that too, by her father. Maybe a well-made cup of tea would soften him slightly.

At one thirty, the scrubbing of the marble began. Ma took shelter in Mejo Jetha Moshai's room. Swathed in a bristly towel, Jetha Moshai was dyeing the hair at the back of his neck with an old toothbrush. He was the protector of all the sinners in this household. Liberal, ever-smiling. He didn't give a fig for morals; he was ruled by emotion.

I had turned to Jetha Moshai for protection several times, but without much success. It was hard to say what lay in store for Ma. As soon as he came home from office, Baba would sit me down every evening at the marble table with my books. Everyone at home would be tense. Anything could happen. It started with homework. On which I tripped at once. One mistake, two mistakes. Baba's temper rose like a barometer. Weather forecast. Incipient thunderstorm. The clouds rumbled—'What have we been up to all day? Marbles? Kites?

Storybooks?' Sins can never be kept under wraps. Baba rose. The first item of sacrifice at the wide-mouthed family oven was a copy of the adventure novel borrowed from the local library. It had been hidden in the footrest of the marble table. Baba possessed the incredible ability to unearth hidden objects and hidden thoughts. Next into the oven were the spool and kite string concealed next to the safe. The string had just been given a cutting edge. Then came the crack of the kite frames being snapped. I felt as though my ribs were being broken, to the accompaniment of Baba's ferocious war cries and roars—'Devil, Devil, Satan, Satan!' Ma would say to me from a distance, as though speaking to a convict sentenced to death from the other side of the bars, 'Why couldn't you have got the sums right?' Having destroyed everything, having turned the place into a cemetery, Baba would return to the table. A jungle of salt and pepper hair on his chest. Flowing drops of perspiration. Despite all this drama, my eyes would grow heavy with sleep. Baba would lie in wait. As soon as my head approached the surface of the table, he would slap me hard on the back of my neck. The impact with the marble would dispel all sleep immediately. The white marble before my eyes, the agony of the lump on my forehead, a hirsute parent carved in stone, black letters dancing across the pages of the open book. A macabre pursuit of light on the darkest day of life. Jetha Moshai's desperate plea—'Let the boy go now.' As though a tiger had me in its jaws. 'Don't poke your fine nose in here,' the tiger roared briefly. 'How many times do I have to tell you, you condensed idiot, that when the subject is singular the verb is also singular! Write it down. In large letters.'

On this fateful Sunday, as the storm gathered, outside the house a few pedestrians went about their business. Numerous dogs fought pitched battles. Ma had taken shelter with Mejo Jetha Moshai. It was hard to say what was coming. The hair-dyeing had been halted. From behind a door, I watched with one eye, like a spy. 'Don't be afraid,' Mejo Jetha Moshai assured Ma, 'I will face him. I am ready to lay my life down for you today.' The scrub hit the surface of the table. Baba scrubbed, walking around the table. When he reached the section near the window, he suddenly jumped in the air with a loud yell. Stooping, he picked something up from the floor. A screw. 'What's this?' he asked himself. 'Where did this come from? Which devil's work is this?' Ma's face was shorn of colour. Mejo Jetha Moshai was prepared. He looked as woebegone as the prisoners of war whose photographs appeared in the magazine named *The War in Pictures* during World War II.

Holding the screw in his fingertips, Baba bent to examine the side of the table, where the screw had fallen from. That was it. He had found out. He looked once. He looked twice. Then he stood upright. 'What the...?' he muttered to himself. 'Niranjan!' He called out twice. 'Disappeared! Vanished into thin air!' Moving away from the window, he faced the door and bellowed, 'Is Niranjan dead?'

Jetha Moshai emerged. The hair at the back of his neck was partly black, partly copper. Putting his hand on Baba's shoulder, Jetha Moshai said softly and gently, 'Come, let's sit down, let's not get worked up.' Baba looked at him in utter surprise. 'Come, let's sit down. Let's sit.' Jetha Moshai repeated the refrain of sitting several times like a thumri. 'Stop singing, nightingale, stop singing now, stop singing.' 'But I have no time to sit down.' Baba conveyed his lack of time to Jetha Moshai with a contorted face and clearly articulated words. The communication held a hint of contempt. For Jetha Moshai was dyeing his hair, while Baba was cleaning the table. One of the tasks was useful; the other, useless. 'I have something to tell you,' Jetha Moshai said with a touch of embarrassment. 'It won't take more than five minutes of your time.'

They took a chair each. Baba just about managed contact between his behind and the edge of the chair, resting his weight on his legs. His arms were taut on his knees, his teeth were clenched, his jaws were set, his eyes looked up towards the sky. It needed strength to confront such body language, such an expression. Jetha Moshai described the events that had taken place. Baba listened with a faint sneer, without looking at Jetha Moshai for a moment. His brow would furrow slightly above his nose every now and then. Finishing his account, Jetha Moshai touched Baba's hands. 'Don't throw a fit over all this now. Bouma is terrified.'

A few seconds of silence. Followed by action. Slapping his knee loudly, Baba said, 'Why Sanatan, why Sanatan? Am I dead?'

'Oh no, there's no question of your being dead. You're misunderstanding the whole thing. It wouldn't be proper for you to detach Mr Mukherjee's finger, which is why...'

'Because it isn't proper, some upstart has to be summoned to ruin the table! I might have been able to free him without damaging the frame. I was not even given a chance. Why wasn't I? Can you tell me why not? Explain.'

'Such a trifle, why bother you, that's why. Sanatan is an old hand at all this. Has all his tools. Took it off in a flash.'

'Where are the frame and the balls?'

Jetha Moshai was unaware of the second half of the story. He looked helplessly at the door. 'Bouma.'

'I see, you do not know either. Did you call Sanatan?'

'I... I was in my room. Sanatan is always here, isn't he? There he is. He turned up as soon as I caught his eye. Didn't even have to call. A signal was all that was needed.'

'A signal from whom?'

Jetha Moshai was in trouble. Baba had pushed him into a corner.

'Do you see how household discipline has degenerated? Without telling anyone, the housewife signals through the window to summon a loafer posing as a workman. The table isn't the point, Mejda, discipline is the point. Even in the next room, you're in the dark. Even in the garden, I'm in the dark. Hide-and-seek. Nip it in the bud.'

Baba rose. Jetha Moshai made a last attempt. 'Look, this is a request, I'm your elder brother, I'm requesting you not to make a fuss about this. It's very delicate, you see. I understand your point.'

'No compromise,' responded Baba with an odd flourish of his hand.

Jetha Moshai seemed to be on the verge of tears. He had assured my mother of protection but my father had checkmated him with his chess moves. Jetha Moshai rose too. He was taller than Baba and thinner, with a slight stoop.

Far too weak to contend with Baba's out-thrust chest.

We had all expected Baba to march towards his room. Instead, he went to the window overlooking the road, suspending half his torso in mid-air through the unbarred French windows. It wasn't clear what he was trying to do. Bewildered, Jetha Moshai stood at a distance. I thought Baba might be trying to cool his head with fresh air. Or perhaps he would call out to Sanatan. Suddenly he thrust his hands out of the window and clapped several times. Who was he calling? Shouting out anyone's name was 'out of English etiquette'. The claps didn't work. He called out, as softly as possible, 'Sarat, Sarat. O, Sarat.' What could Sarat do? He was probably passing by. He looked up on hearing his name.

'Bring the car round at once.' Sarat's reply floated up from the road. 'Just closed the garage, I'm going for lunch.'

'The world won't come to an end if you have your lunch half an hour later.'

'Can't I eat first, Chhoto Babu?'

'You'll get ten rupees, you'll get twenty, get the car at once.'

Sarat owned an ancient car with a tarpaulin hood attached to hooks. Open on all sides, with half-doors. All the locks were broken. The doors had to be tethered with rope when passengers got in. There were pillows instead of seats at the back. This was the car that we hired on family trips and for celebrations.

Baba moved away from the window. It was obvious that Sarat had been compelled to return to his garage. Baba went into his room, his heels thudding loudly on the floor as he was wont to do. Jetha Moshai followed him. Observing Baba gathering his dhoti, he asked apprehensively, 'What do you need the car for at this hour?' Instead of replying, Baba shot off like a projectile in a different direction. We saw him put on his dhoti in workman-like fashion, followed by a white tennis shirt. He hadn't shaved because it was a holiday, his cheeks were covered in black and white stubble. 'Where are you going?' Jetha Moshai got no reply to this question either. Everything was taking place at spectacular speed.

A car was heard stopping. 'Niranjan,' Baba yelled. Niranjan materialized in a flash. 'Put this in the car,' he commanded, pointing to Ma's chocolate-brown trunk in the corner. He spoke as though Ma's corpse had been rotting for days inside the trunk. Baba advanced towards Jetha Moshai's room. Ma was seated on the bed with a wretched expression, her legs hanging over the side. She was unbelievably fair. Drained of blood, her complexion looked more pale. Ma had been in bad health ever since I was born.

Apparently, I had not been particularly keen on being born. I had been lurking in the northwest corner of the womb, possibly out of fear of Baba. Then, seeing no alternative, I had finally slithered out, much as people slide down a diagonally laid plank of wood. At the critical moment, I had made sure to wrap a vital part of my mother's anatomy around my neck like a ceremonial thread. This was possibly how a chip off the old block was born. They don't need to poke their head out to size up the situation first. Still, Ma was so elated! She wanted to be the mother of innumerable children. Like guinea pigs they would swarm all over the room. Baba was just the opposite. One is enough. A second is acceptable, with a stricture.

Spreading her palm flat on the bed, Ma was quietly counting her fingers. Long, tapering digits. A white topaz gleamed on her ring finger. Baba went all the way up to her. 'Get up.' Ma stood up apprehensively. 'Come.' Baba started walking. He knew no one had the courage to ignore this command. Ma was dressed in a blue polka-dotted sari. This was Jetha Moshai's last chance. He had got the opponent on his own turf. He blocked the door. 'Where do you think you're taking Bouma at this hour?'

'Have you read the *Panchatantra*?' Baba asked, coming to an abrupt halt a short distance away. Jetha Moshai was perplexed. 'I see you haven't. When would you read it, after all? There are just two things in your life.' Raising two fingers, he gestured with his hand. 'Your hair and fish. Know this, you should be ready to sacrifice an organ for the sake of your body. A locality for the sake of the village, a village for the sake of the city, a city for the sake of the country. Let them be removed for the sanctity of the family.' As he uttered the 'moo' of 'removed', Baba advanced to break through the cordon at the door. But Jetha Moshai stood his ground like a true hero. Back then, during the freedom movement, a particular phrase used to be heard often—'Do or die'. Jetha Moshai's valour made it seem that his mission on this day of crisis was also do or die. 'Your tyranny knows no bounds. You've become a dictator like Hitler. You cannot take Bouma anywhere. I won't allow it.' When Jetha Moshai spoke in English it was an indication that he was angry. As a gust of wind was about to blow the dry towel off his shoulder, he grabbed at it with both hands, and Baba slipped through the door like a kabaddi player. Ma kept standing, not knowing what she should do. 'I'd better go,' she said finally.

'Where will you go, Bouma? You shall stay put here. Who is he? A tyrant. I shall deal with him.'

'Niranjan!' Jetha Moshai bellowed.

'Coming, Mejo Babu,' came the response from the street.

'Bring it back.'

'The trunk?'

'Yes, the trunk.'

Niranjan went off to retrieve the trunk.

'Don't you dare take it back,' Baba issued counter-instructions. Niranjan flopped down at the turn of the stairs. Sitting on the chair beside the table, Jetha Moshai announced, 'No one is allowed to set foot outside the house. This is a joint family. This household does not run on one person's authority.'

'Is it possible to live with an untrustworthy, conspiring wife?'

'Bouma is none of these. You always make a mountain out of a molehill. I don't agree with you.'

'My family must run according to my rules. No lenience.'

'What's going on?' Sarat screamed from the road.

'Get the trunk, Niranjan, you rascal, and give Sarat ten rupees and get rid of him,' Jetha Moshai shouted.

'Chhoto Babu will whip me.'

'I will beat you up, you rascal. What do you mean your family? We arranged your wedding. Bouma doesn't belong to you alone. She's the housewife of this household.'

Niranjan carried the trunk upstairs. Sarat started his car and drove off.

'Are you getting out of those clothes or not?'

'Your indulgence will send this family to the dogs, Mejda.'

'Let it. Don't forget, the household is not your office. You cannot charge-sheet or discharge anyone at the drop of a hat.'

'Let her admit her fault. I will pardon her.'

'Bouma.'

Ma approached hesitantly. She had been standing stock-still near the door. Her face was drained of colour.

'Say it was your fault.'

Baba stood with his chest thrust out, chin raised in the air. Draping the end of her sari around her neck, Ma said softly, 'It was my fault.'

Baba continued with his nose in the air. 'Don't do it again. This is very bad. Punishable offence. Never take decisions yourself. Born a woman, stay a woman.'

As she turned and retreated, Ma listened to this final piece of advice on the rights of women.

That was the slab of marble. The slab that now leans against the wall. The intricately patterned frame has been consumed by termites. The white of the marble has turned grey with disuse. Having discharged forty sizzling years like steam from his life, it is my father who now has hair as white as snow. Ma is an indistinct memory on an oil painting. Jetha Moshai, a dusty picture. Spider saliva on a withered garland. Dadu's tambura hangs from the hook with a rope around its neck. Baba can still stand erect with his chin up, but there's no one left in the family to kneel at his feet.

twenty

~

FLAPPEROOS

NABARUN BHATTACHARYA

Never enter the yellow halogen zone if you prefer to drink black market liquor. At Erfan's or Mandal's, whoever the black market liquor dive belonged to, sometimes things did go out of control. Maybe a wasted plainclothes policeman would suddenly start hissing, 'Lih, lih'. At once the obscene cry would be taken up by all the drunkards present. The man who was asleep, leaning against a post, would wake up abruptly and riddle the dude who was making chasers with well-aimed sprays of chewing tobacco. That was it. Crapfest.

That's why the best policy was the one followed by D. S. or Director's Special. His initials were resplendent on either side of his briefcase. D. S. Black as sin. Looked like a bullfrog. Dressed in a Terylene shirt. A locket with an image of Chaitanya peeping out between the buttons. Briefcase stuffed with share forms. A ballpoint pen with the name of a foreign brand of booze. A dirty comb whose teeth were fossilized with grit from the hair of hundreds of people. A photograph of an old woman. Sleeping pills. A metro rail ticket. A diary that he had actually bought. This year's.

It was a sweaty night. Crowded and noisy. D. S.'s policy was to charge himself at top speed with a pint and then leave. But that night he fell into the clutches of a man in a thin kurta, fair-skinned and lean, with shoulder-length hair dyed black, a hooked nose and not a single tooth.

His name was Madan. Madan gave him a gummy smile. Then, poking D. S.'s belly with an emaciated finger, he said:

'See all these drunks? Dirty foxes, all. Ready to be kicked by their wives when they get home. You know what it's called? The Bengal

Bad Company. That's why I hate Bengalis. Henpecked bastards. And the wives? First chance they get, they'll run away.'

D. S. was flustered by this. Because his wife had actually run away. With a successful insurance agent. She was from the suburbs. D. S. asked Madan:

'Are you a detective?'

'What do you think? The main thing is—if not today, you'll definitely be in the same boat tomorrow, D. S.'

Reaching into his pocket, Madan pulled out a set of dentures. Tilting the pint in his hand, he rinsed them in a little liquor and then fitted them into his mouth. Smiling, he said:

'Don't worry about it. We always get smarter when our wives run away. I did too. It was bullshit, all that I told you. Just giving you a sob story to make your heart bleed. All for a pint. I have no money, will you buy one?'

D. S. bought one. Madan consumed most of it.

'What's the use of dying over money. This fucking Mandal, spent seven years in jail before opening this liquor joint, do you think he's poor? His daughter goes to a convent school. But every time you look at him, he's moping.'

'Why?'

'Suspicion. Very suspicious of his wife. Don't go telling him.'

'Of course not.'

'Did you watch the English movie on TV last Saturday?'

'No, I didn't.'

'Obviously. Why should you care for good cinema? Bloody scary, the film. A bunch of flying fish. Flying up in the air and biting people's throats till they die.'

'Vampires.'

'No, no, vampires are bats. These are fish. They live in the hull of a sunken ship. Come out at times in a group to kill people.'

'Flying fish!'

'Must be some sort of shark or alligator. Whatever, the film was terrifying. Let's go. Time to get some air. My name's Madan, you know.'

'I do.'

'How did you know?'

'That's how Mandal addressed you.'

D. S. and Madan crossed the dark and uneven patch of land in front of the drinking dive. There was a row of garages next door. In one of them some people were playing cards by the light of a candle inside a car. A bald man appeared on a cycle, a sack stuffed with bottles in his hand. A scooter was parked nearby.

D. S. stumbled. Madan said:

'Watch your step. Elections next year. Congress will go to hell. There'll be a mixed chowmein government at the centre. Good days ahead for you.'

'What do you mean?'

'I've been studying your forehead. You'll find the markets booming.'

'What markets?'

'Share prices. Buy some cheap shares now. Janak, Turbo, Reliance, Petro, Vrindavan, Aqua—you'll see.'

'Last I bought was a hundred of DCM Toyota.'

'It's at seventy, seventy-two now. But it'll gain. Don't sell.'

'You know the share market quite well. Do you trade?'

'Are you crazy? Who's got the cash? And I don't need any either. I'll live out the few days I have as a Flapperoo.'

'As a what?'

'A Flapperoo.'

'What the hell is a Flapperoo?'

'Very interesting creatures. Here I was, studying your forehead, but you won't be able to study mine even if you try.'

'Not even if I know how to? Suppose I read Cheiro's book?'

'Not even then. No planet can influence Flapperoos.'

'What are Flapperoos, then?'

'I can't exactly tell. But they are very special. You understand? History teaches how all these great men try to think of ways to remake human beings. Personally, I think we Flapperoos have been hand-picked after a lot of search.'

D. S. and Madan tottered off towards the main road. The head of the lane was awash in yellow halogen light. It was deserted, silent. Buses were asleep in the darkness across the road. A ramshackle police van passed by. First, they had drunk on the black market. Then there was the yellow halogen zone all over. Calmed by the gentle breeze, D. S. leaned against the metal lamp post with the yellow halogen light, gripping his briefcase between his legs, and closed his eyes. Not even half a minute had passed when it began to...

Flap flap, swish swish...

D. S. heard someone whispering in his ear, flap flap, swish swish, flap flap, swish swish, flap flap... When he opened his eyes he discovered yellow halogen lights whirling around, no Madan by his side, the indiscreet pleasure of insects sprouting wings all over his body, the ardent kisses of his vanished wife in every pore of his skin, and elsewhere, Gagarin's innocent boyish smile from space. Looking up, D. S. saw that...

...Next to the square yellow halogen light, a flying Madan was hovering in the air. Flapping his arms slowly so that he could stay in the same place. The halogen lights had cast a golden hue on his dentures.

'Madan!'

'Didn't I tell you the usual shit doesn't stick on Flapperoos? Come on. Come up here.'

'How?'

Holding his briefcase, D. S. tried to flap his arms and fly. He began to sweat.

'Not that way. Move your arms up and down.'

'Like this?'

'Yes. And say...'

'Say what?'

'Flap flap, swish swish, flap flap, swish, swish...'

Madan's fine kurta seemed well-ironed. D. S. began to chant:

'Flap flap, swish swish, flap flap, swish swish...'

D. S. didn't realize at first that he had begun flying. Looking down, he found himself floating a yard or so above the pavement. Distracted, he fell down with a thump. Madan scolded him from the heights:

'You stopped chanting as soon as your feet left the ground. Prick. I wish you'd fallen from a greater fucking height. Come on, chant.'

'Flap flap, swish swish, flap flap, swish swish...flap flap, swish swish, flap flap, swish swish...'

This time D. S. rose effortlessly into the air. Flying all the way up to Madan, he beat his arms rhythmically. A mangy bat circled them twice, glaring. Perched at a distance from the yellow halogen lights, owls hooted.

'You won't have to chant any more once you're used to it. Just say it in your head whenever you find yourself being pulled downwards.'

'That's all very well, but how do I descend?'

'Fuck you! How do I descend! Now that you're a permanent member of the Flapperoos, there's no question of ascending or descending. When you need to, your corpse will lower itself on its own.'

'Corpse?'

'You know what I mean. Body. Come, there's a breeze over the Ganga. Let's do the new bridge.'

D. S. and Madan rose higher. Suddenly, the moon pierced the clouds.

'There's the light from the new bridge. Not any old light, Philips lighting. Come on.'

Beneath them, the houses and roads slid away. Patches of darkness now and then—fields, trees. D. S. was enjoying the flight.

'Thank goodness I met you. I couldn't have become a Flapperoo otherwise.'

'That's true. See that three-storeyed house? We'll land on its roof.'

'Why?'

'For a smoke. See that dish antenna? We'll rip out its wires.

Smash it into pieces.'

'What harm has the antenna done?'

'Why so many questions? Why do you need to know so much? Just do as I say.'

For some unknown reason, all the TV sets in the neighbourhood went blank. Calls began to be made to the local cable TV operator. Climbing to the roof, the cable TV men saw by torchlight that the wires had been cut, the antenna damaged from being hammered by a brick, cigarette stubs inside the dish antenna and the horrible stench of piss smelling of hooch. They realized that thieves had scaled the rainwater pipe. But the antenna was too heavy and too firmly set in the cement to be stolen.

'This was your baptism. Got it?'

'Got it.'

'Got what?'

'Baptism for Flapperoos means smashing things, tearing things up, pissing.'

'Now we're talking. I'll say this, you chose an auspicious night to become a Flapperoo.'

'Why?'

'Just come with me, you'll see for yourself. The Flapperoos have a major programme tonight.'

'You mean there are more Flapperoos? Besides us?'

'More? There are hordes of Flapperoos. They have a programme every night. Tonight's, for instance, is at the Floatel.'

'The Floatel?'

'Yes, don't you know about the Floatel on the Ganga? Foreign bitches dance, rich men fool around, everyone eats and drinks— haven't you heard of it?'

'You bet I have. I heard the NRI owner was going to float some shares.'

'Back to shares? Tonight is the night of Operation Floatel—when we attack the floating hotel.'

'Like the vampire fish?'

'Oh no, no murders or injuries. Only scare them. Spoil everything. That's where the fun is.'

'Those ghostly attacks with bricks and stones on the pleasure resorts on Diamond Harbour Road that they wrote about in the papers, were those also...'

'Yes, that was the Flapperoos' doing too. You're an excellent Flapperoo. You'll do well. You really get us.'

'But I don't understand how I became one.'

'You need the right qualifications, of course. You visit these large companies, they refuse to meet you, keep you waiting, but you don't take it lying down, you swear at them in your head, you dig your nose and put the snot on the chairs, you tear up the cushions with your nails—tell me you haven't done all of these things.'

'Yes, I have.'

'Damage. You must cause damage wherever you can. Mustn't forget. We recruit those who do these things. Handpicked from the hopeless cases, the half-dead, bullied all the time...'

'You know, I've cracked mirrors in office lavatories, broken sinks, written dirty words on the walls...'

'You think we don't know already?'

'And yet, I was such a good child. On Netaji Subhas Bose's birthday they'd give us a couple of extra fries at the telebhaja stand. Then all of would shout together, "Come back, Netaji".'

'We know.'

'My father would beat me up. Randomly. I grew up. Learnt the tricks of the trade. Got married. And then, like always, my wife ran away with someone I considered my friend...'

'That's right...'

'Waste of a life.'

D. S. began to sob.

'Shame on you, D. S. If you weep you'll just get depressed and so will I. No time today, else I'd have shown you some fun things.'

'What fun things?'

'Bedroom scenes. A little voyeurism. Peeping Tom.'

'What, really?'

'Hot games. In high-rises. Sometimes on the terrace. In swimming pools.'

'Don't say any more. Getting a hard-on.'

'So easily?'

'Obviously. Been so long.'

'Never mind, get these dirty thoughts out of your head and look below.'

An amazing garland of lights dangled around the neck of darkness. D. S. was astonished.

'We'll land exactly in the middle of the bridge, all right?'

'I believe standing is not allowed.'

'Flapperoos don't care for the law.'

Panting, Madan and D. S. alighted on the bridge. The moon was again obscured by seashell-shaped clouds. There was a murky glow. A strong wind had flattened everything.

'Madan, my friend, now that I'm a Flapperoo, will I ever go back to a normal life? You know, things like voting, going to the shops, meeting my sister…'

'Why not? You can keep doing whatever you used to. But you must always remember you're a Flapperoo. No one else will find out.'

'Are Flapperoos also split between the Congress and the CPM?'

'Of course. All the time. But Flapperoos' programmes always involve joint action.'

'I'm sleepy.'

'So am I. Pretend to sleep for a while, you'll be fine.'

Trouble with the Cops

Their reverie was interrupted by the sound of a motorcycle. Astride it a gigantic police sergeant, who looked even more bizarre because he had goggles on at night. Keeping his engine rumbling, the man asked:

'Oye, where have you parked your car? Don't you know you're

not allowed to stand on the bridge? And lying down is out of the question. Let's go, not another minute here...'

'But we didn't drive here.'

'What do you mean? Walking is forbidden.'

'We didn't walk. We flew.'

'Very clever. What's in that briefcase. Unlock it.'

'Don't open it, D. S.'

'What do you mean, don't open it? I have ways to make him unlock it. I'm arresting both of you.'

The sergeant reached for his revolver. But his hand froze, because Madan and D. S. were flapping their arms and rising up in the air, continuing to climb. The sergeant's bluster had vanished by now. Pulling his goggles off, he began to mutter feverish prayers. Up in the sky, Madan and D. S. could be seen flying in circles around the lights on the first pillar of the bridge, holding hands. Just like intrepid skydivers.

'Let's go, we've scared him shitless.'

'Where to now?'

'What do you mean? The Floatel, of course.'

Swim in Formation

In the darkness there were cries of 'Ole Ole' from the Howrah side of the river.

'There they are.'

'Who?'

'The hicks from Howrah. They live in lanes and by-lanes like snails and oysters, they open their mouths whenever they get into open spaces—they sound different from everyone else.'

Amidst the sound of arms slicing the air, war cries of 'Layla O Layla' were heard.

'Kidderpore, Ekbalpore, Kantapukur—they're all here. You can identify them from the way they talk—bloody freaks.'

Soon the air was filled with sounds of flap flap, swish swish.

'See that gang there? With rings on their fingers, dressed in dhotis and shirts? All cheats. From north Calcutta. Of course, there are four or five shopkeepers too.'

A flock of giggling women in nylon saris flew past D. S. with brooms, shards of clay ovens, rotting potato curry in earthen pots, and goat-head ghugni. There were some plump old hags among them too. One of the flying women tickled D. S. under his arm, going off into peals of laughter. When they had moved ahead Madan whispered to D. S.: 'All whores from Sonagachhi, Garanhata, Bhallukpara. Don't instigate them. See that group there on the right, beating drums and singing? All eunuch Flapperoos. The more you see, the more dumbstruck you'll be. See that man there, the one with three upper teeth, trembling and beating his arms? He's a writer—writes novels and poetry and shit. Actually a dipso clerk—you'll see Flapperoos like these too.'

'This my friend is practically an Air Force.'

'Get ready to dive, D. S.'

'What?'

'The Floatel's up ahead.'

The brightly lit up Floatel was a sight to behold. On every level, there were mirrors from Hong Kong, music from Singapore, folk tunes as well as rap, modern Bengali pop and Tagore songs. Tonight was a special Tandoori Night. All the NRIs, cabaret dancers, smugglers, money-launderers, fashion designers, models, politicians, beauticians, mistresses, mafiosi, senior police officers, pimps and their MOU drafters, MPs, MLAs, life coaches, gigolos, editors, court poets, kings, queens—all of them were sinking their teeth into tandoori drumsticks, tandoori breasts, tandoori chops, tandoori liver, tandoori trotters, tandoori noses, tandoori eyes, tandoori hair with rice noodles, tandoori bleeding hearts, tandoori pulses, tandoori lips, and tandoori armpits on their plates. Suddenly, like a bolt from the blue, several turds, a cascade of urine, an entire briefcase with the letters D and S on it, shards of clay ovens, fish-heads, brooms, mud, rotting curried potatoes, stinking goat-head ghugni, rejected toothbrushes, examination scripts, bound uncorrected proofs, hair gathered from saloons, bedpans and such like began to fall from the sky.

'Well, D. S.? How does it feel?'

'Incredible.'

'Did you enjoy yourself?'

'Oh Madan, today I seem to have found...fulfilment.'

'Can't use Western concepts everywhere. Nirvana, you mean.'

'Yes, yes, that's it. Flap flap, swish swish.'

The Fat Lady hasn't Sung

Ten eyewitness accounts of levitation were not enough for the story of Madan and D. S. or of the enormous fleet of Flapperoos to be accepted.

Investigating the attack on the Floatel, the Calcutta police discovered D. S.'s briefcase, complete with his name and address.

A special squad, including the Rapid Action Force, arrested a sleeping D. S. from his home. He burst into tears. It didn't help. He was sent to the police lock-up. While D. S. was sunk in slumber, the man who was ushered in with a clanging of the iron gates took his dentures off, put them in his pocket, and whispered gumlessly to D. S.:

'The slightest of harassments and you forget you're a Flapperoo?'

'You, Madan!'

'Remember the chant?'

'Yes, flap flap, swish swish.'

The lock-up cell had a window.

~

twenty-one

AIR AND WATER

AMAR MITRA

I

Talapatra Babu may not have belonged to Pasandpur, but fourteen months of living in this market town had turned him into a local. A food department inspector who accepted bribes energetically and lacked the benevolence to spare anyone from kickbacks, Ramshankar Talapatra was transferred from Sonarpur in 24 Parganas to our Pasandpur on the border between Bankura and Purulia after falling foul of the authorities. No story about Pasandpur can be complete without him, because it seems that Pasandpur, with its rough terrain and rocks and hillocks and vanishing jungles and red soil, had charmed Talapatra Babu. It had captured his heart. He used to assert with conviction that he had never been posted to such a wonderful place in his career of thirty-five years—where he could breathe deeply and easily, and accept both official and unofficial payments with equal ease, without anyone asking questions or sending anonymous applications to the higher authorities; a place where one could work happily for a hundred years.

Let me tell you about Pasandpur. Call it a market town or even a city, but the fact remains that outsiders have never cared for Pasandpur despite the pasand in its name. No local ever gets a job here—outsiders work at the offices and courts in this town. And from the moment they arrive, they count the days to freedom from this sentence of exile. Tarapada Babu, the high school teacher, openly says that once the remaining five years of his working life are done, he'll move to Durgapur or Burnpur, buy some land, and live his life out there. 'What attractions does Pasandpur hold for me?'

We don't exactly know what attractions Pasandpur holds for people, but what we have seen is that because of the offices and courts and the narrow gauge railway line, we are never deprived of new faces. Clerks or vagabonds, those who arrive never stay on. We don't see why they should. What does Pasandpur have to offer besides the unpolluted air here? The tiny toy train loses its novelty quickly. We cannot persuade the people who come here to stay, even if we want to. They leave. If they can't, they grow old criticizing Pasandpur. Inspector of Food Talapatra Babu, and a few vagabonds are the only exceptions. Their faces are wreathed in smiles as they try to pronounce the name of the town. As Talapatra Babu himself acknowledged, even those with whom he played cards in the evening paid him his bribes during the day, saying softly, 'Here you are, sir, five hundred it is.' The Food Babu had never seen anything like this in his life.

When he heard this, Rabilochan Babu, the headmaster of the high school, said, 'But this is your legitimate due, how can my nephew expect to run a business without paying you off?'

Examining his cards, Talapatra Babu said, 'Not everyone understands, you know, they think all that is needed is a smile to get things done. For heaven's sake, if the doctor or priest or teacher aren't paid...'

Talapatra Babu paused halfway, seeking his fellow players' support. The headmaster was the first to nod in assent, 'Of course, of course...'

The headmaster's nephew had a kerosene oil dealership. He had been entreating the inspector to increase his quota of oil—could he not make a recommendation to headquarters? And, yes, he did sell the oil on the black market at inflated prices instead of giving it to ration card holders, but then how was he to expand his business? Talapatra Babu had found him out, and had promptly held out his palm under the table. He had haggled intensely with the nephew, making off for the card session as soon as he had pocketed the payment. The headmaster's nephew's wife served tea and chanachur.

Sipping his tea, Talapatra said, 'There can be no relationship between work and leisure, you know, the other thing is a matter of the day job...'

'Of course, of course.' The innocent headmaster smiled at the inspector. 'Thank goodness you take bribes, that's how things get done. The previous inspector had got my nephew into all kinds of trouble. He was almost arrested, saved himself only by paying off the police.'

Talapatra Babu didn't spend a single night outside Pasandpur during his fourteen months here. The place had offered him sanctuary, he would say, given him relief during his last days at work, so he would not leave.

'Why should you go, you must help my nephew establish himself first, sir,' the headmaster had told the inspector deferentially, 'you're not exactly without friends here.'

Pasandpur offers sanctuary to people. Vagrants take shelter here. Besides those who are transferred on work, the rest of the visitors are all wanderers. Some on their way in, others on their way out. Some of them are empty-headed, while others are brimming with intelligence, holding on to their ponderous heads and grey matter and brain cells carefully as they climb out of the palanquin-like bogies on the narrow gauge railway. It's this train with two bogeys that brings people with jobs as well as drifters to Pasandpur from time to time. It had brought Ramshankar Talapatra too.

A befuddled Talapatra Babu, halfway to old age, had got off the evening train one day with his suitcase and bedding. His skin blackened by the smoke from the coal engine, his drooping white moustache, blackened too, a faded, ancient pair of Terylene trousers hanging loosely around his waist, dressed in a khaki, full-sleeved sweater, his feet shod in an old, patched pair of strapped sandals, his greying hair untouched by oil for months. People had mistaken him for a vagrant, eyeing him suspiciously, trying to size him up—was he half-mad or entirely mad, cunning or simple, a stayer or a traveller? But when the man had said, looking around him as he got off the train, 'What a nice place,' their suspicion had ebbed. He had not got off at Pasandpur only to declare it napasand.

No one knows when Pasandpur became a pilgrimage site for eccentric vagabonds. Probably it was from the time the narrow gauge railway was set up. The toylike train would frequently deposit an empty-headed or brainy drifter on the platform in the afternoon or evening and whistle its way along to the next station. There is a station here, it's true, but that's just an empty field, with neither an office nor any railway employees. There is no stationmaster, no pointsman, no tickets. There's no fixed schedule for the train either. It might not show up for two days before arriving unexpectedly one evening, whistling. It might then stay here all night, periodically snorting and emitting smoke. The headmaster cannot sleep on those nights because of the sound made by the engine's exhalations. He isn't married, lives with his nephew and nephew's wife instead. One of his nephews is established, but not the other one. One of his nieces isn't married yet. Worry has made him a light sleeper. Rabilochan Babu, the headmaster, doesn't care for the train or the engine or its bogies. Once, a rather manly drifter had got off the train and had almost torn asunder one of his nieces after dragging her into the jungle. Such a commotion! Pasandpur's people had decided to beat him to death. But, fearing charges of murder, the headmaster had said, 'Never mind, put him back on the train, are the people of Pasandpur really capable of killing a fellow human being?'

It had certainly caused a furore. The people of Pasandpur still talk about it whenever the subject comes up. What else do we have here, after all, besides the train and the outsiders? Even the hailstorms are not as severe as they used to be. There was a hailstorm once, a long time ago. A twenty-kilo block of ice fell into the jungle from the sky. The cowherds saw it and told everyone. Apparently, the ice took seventy-two hours to melt. Just that one time. And the other time was what the terribly beautiful and rather manly vagabond had gone and done. Forcing him onto the train had not proved easy, either. The guard and driver had refused to take charge of the man, asking, 'Where should we take him?'

'Wherever you like, he's a criminal.'

'No,' the guard had flared up, 'I won't do anything ugly like that.'

'Then hand him over to the police,' the railway people had said.

Word would get out in that case, with his niece becoming involved, scandal would follow, which was why the headmaster had not taken that route. He had said, 'The man came by your train, we're returning him.'

But the drifter hadn't wanted to leave, saying with a strange smile, 'I shall be back, no one can love the way the women here do, oh how exquisite her eyes, how bewitching her smile, how silken her breasts. There's meaning to this town.'

The headmaster had turned red. 'What meaning?' he had muttered.

'There's a meaning to all this—why the sun here is so hot, where the winds swirl in from, why the girls here are so lovely inside.'

The headmaster had felt overcome. He was told that the drifter had not forced his niece into the jungle—on the contrary, it was she who had ensnared him. She was not particularly beautiful, but her eyes held the magic of water. It was the height of summer. Their joy had made flowers blossom on the palash trees in the forest. They had touched each other the way the breeze touches the flowers and the leaves. When a cowherd saw them, everyone came to know, and then the trouble started. People had raced to the spot to find the young woman with her arms around the vagabond's unclothed, rock-solid body, covering his rough chest with kisses. The sound of kisses spread through the jungle like the splashing of rain in Pasandpur. The smell of damp earth rose from the scorched clay of summer. Much more would have taken place had the cowherd not seen them. The headmaster would have had to tackle everything. The girl is now a mother of two children, living in Burnpur. She has not been to Pasandpur in a long time. Because, when she visits, she has no inclination to return, forgetting her husband and family and home.

Now the headmaster became Talapatra Babu's companion. No one except that drifter and this Food Babu had ever loved Pasandpur.

Sometimes, the headmaster mentioned the vagabond in passing, 'He had said this spirited sunshine, balmy breeze, a woman with a beautiful heart, her eyes like a limpid pool—none of this has ever happened before, and I don't even know why they have now. Can you tell me, where is the real home of the wind that swirls about in Pasandpur?'

Talapatra said, 'I've come here from Sonarpur, but that's not where my home is. My home is in Midnapore, it's been such a long time since I've been there.'

'Won't you go home?'

'I'll stay here as long as I'm happy—after all, no one's filed a petition accusing me of taking bribes or stealing, so I'm not likely to be transferred again.'

II

One evening, the headmaster, Rabilochan Babu, turned to Talapatra, 'Will you do me a favour?'

The food inspector's experienced eye had discerned that the headmaster was in trouble, that he really needed help. 'Come to my office tomorrow afternoon,' he said sternly.

'No, this isn't for my nephew.'

Dropping the cards in his hand, Talapatra said, 'I know, I have my eye on your nephew. I know he's selling kerosene at six rupees in the open market instead of two-and-a-half as he should.'

Looking troubled, the headmaster responded, 'What can I do, he's so obsessed with money that he simply won't listen.'

'If he listened he would be a kerosene dealer all his life. Did you know he's selling cement too?'

The headmaster said, 'He has no choice—he didn't even finish school. Do you think I enjoy listening to people saying that my nephew hasn't even passed his higher secondary exams? The other teachers taunt me.'

Talapatra chuckled, 'It's all out of envy—do they have any idea that out of the twenty-six dealers in this area your nephew pays me the largest amount?'

The headmaster summoned his nephew's wife, 'Can you make us another cup of tea, Lalita, my dear, Inspector Babu will be here for a while.'

'No tea,' said Talapatra, 'I'm off now, Rabi Babu, we'll talk tomorrow afternoon.'

The headmaster wouldn't relent. He followed Talapatra, catching up with him. 'That's not it, I just wanted to talk about my niece's wedding.'

'Tomorrow afternoon, then.'

They did talk the next afternoon. Not that Talapatra Babu charged a fee for listening. But he said, 'Pay me for matchmaking, it won't amount to a bribe.' The headmaster would have to pay, for he had made a match with one of the dealers. The groom lived in Rangamati, close to Pasandpur, young, of marriageable age. Could Talapatra finalize the match, on condition that the dowry would have to be reduced?

'Is that all? It'll be done. I have him under my thumb,' Talapatra Babu had said with a smile. 'He sells the entire quota of rice and wheat meant for the ration shop in the open market. Just watch what I do to him.'

The headmaster had told his intimate associates everything afterwards. The match would not have been finalized if Talapatra Babu hadn't intervened. The groom could not ignore the inspector. The headmaster was relieved after the marriage. Like her sister, this girl too had started frequenting the station and the jungle of palash trees. He wouldn't have been able to take it if something untoward were to happen.

Talapatra Babu was a double beneficiary, extracting a fat fee for matchmaking and remaining in the headmaster's good books. He would claim he needed money desperately, that there was no way to survive without money. And yet, he cooked for himself, slept on a khatia, put on a freshly washed shirt just once a week, and freshly laundered trousers just once in two months. Someone used to visit him from Midnapore at the beginning of every month—his son, possibly. He would leave by the evening train with money. In addition, Talapatra also sent a money order around the middle of every month. He had no bank account here. He would be anxious at the beginning of the month, looking relieved only after his son had arrived and he had handed over the money. He would keep track through the month of the ways in which his twenty-six dealers were breaking the law. Using this information, he would corner them, 'Two hundred won't do this month, Parimal, add another hundred, I can't bear to look at what you've done with the sugar.'

He had got hold of a ramshackle cycle from the headmaster, promising to return it when he left. He would patrol Pasandpur, Rangamati, Shaltora, Naw Pahari and all the other areas on this cycle. When one of the tyres was punctured, he got the headmaster's nephew to pay for a new one. 'The people of Pasandpur are the finest of all,' he would say.

One day he observed, 'It's amazing—when I got off the train last winter, my hair was so grey, and my skin sagged, but just look at the change in me over this past one year, Headmaster Moshai.'

'Really!' The headmaster was astonished.

'Oh yes. Check for yourself.'

He was right. The inspector had indeed arrived with a head full of grey hair and a stoop. Looked like a vagrant. But you wouldn't know that now when you looked at him.

'What hair oil do you use?' asked the headmaster.

'I don't use hair oil.'

'Then how?'

'It's the air and the water here, I've never encountered such fresh air anywhere, not even such water, all the grime in my inner machinery has been washed away.'

The headmaster was pleased. As a long-time inhabitant of Pasandpur, he couldn't stand criticism of his town. Something happened to him in his happiness, and he asked, 'What was that you were saying about the air?'

'Not just the air, the sunshine too, one is warm all the time, very useful.'

The sunshine too! The headmaster began to mutter, 'Do you know what this air and sunshine mean?'

Talapatra Babu guffawed. Meaning, 'What do you mean, how can they mean anything?'

'Where do they come from?'

Talapatra Babu laughed uproariously again. 'Where on earth will it come from? What are you talking about? By the way, my days here are drawing to an end, a month and a half to go.'

'A month and a half! And then?'

'I'm retiring, got my letter already. Tell your nephew to increase my payment this month, all right?'

The headmaster asked, 'And after retirement?'

'I'll go home.' A note of mourning entered Talapatra Babu's voice.

'You'll get a pension, won't you?'

'It's a pittance. The salary's a joke, you know, my real earnings come from the dealers. The salary is just evidence of having a job. What I earn is from bribes. Can you imagine how much I have to cycle around for it? No one lets go of money easily—neither your nephew, nor anyone else. But, yes, extracting bribes in Pasandpur is easy. Let's say I buy a packet of cigarettes and tell the shopkeeper that so-and-so dealer will pay, he doesn't object. My son takes away toiletries too every month, besides the money.'

The headmaster said, 'It's all thanks to the air here, don't you think?'

As he left, the inspector said, 'Remind your nephew to double the payment this month...'

'I will,' nodded the headmaster.

III

Talapatra Babu arrived panting a fortnight later, 'Didn't you tell him, Master Moshai?'

'Of course I did.'

The inspector had become thinner in a mere fortnight. He seemed to be combing the area on his cycle all day, returning home late at night, and becoming irregular at the card sessions. The nephew had said, 'Inspector Babu is desperate for money, but now that he's about to retire, why should people pay him more?'

'But he's been here so long.'

The nephew had chided his uncle, the headmaster, 'Don't you speak up for him now.'

The headmaster gave up his seat to the inspector. 'Let it go, it's only a matter of a few days more.'

Talapatra muttered, 'I wrote home saying I'm retiring next month—so my wife wrote back, "Bring money".'

'You have your provident fund, gratuity...'

Talapatra Babu shook his head. 'I've already withdrawn my provident fund, only the last few months' money is in there now, a couple of thousand at best.'

'And the gratuity?'

'No knowing when I'll get it, and they'll deduct most of it anyway. I embezzled government money once for my eldest son to start his own business. The business failed, I've been ruined too—no increments for four years, they'll take away most of the gratuity, and my salary isn't high enough for a fat pension.'

Talapatra's hair suddenly appeared greyer to the headmaster. For the first time he realized that the inspector used dentures, for in his agitation Talapatra had forgotten to put them on. So he was looking very old, his cheeks sunken, eyes clouded over. He had aged a great deal in a fortnight. He stuttered when he tried to speak.

The headmaster couldn't make any promises. The inspector disappeared for the next few days. One evening the nephew said, 'The man is sniffing around like a dog, he's even harassing dealers at home in the middle of the night.'

The headmaster said, 'He's in trouble, before he leaves you'd better...'

The nephew said, 'We'll give him a farewell.'

But what farewell? With ten days to go before his retirement, the inspector said, 'I'm getting an extension.'

'Wonderful, six months more in that case, right?' The headmaster inspected Talapatra closely. The man had acquired a stoop, his shoulders seemed bent. He had not shaved for at least a week, and even his eyebrows seemed to have greyed suddenly. He looked like the man who had got off the train on a winter evening. His hands shook as he picked up a cup of tea.

Sipping his tea, Talapatra said, 'I don't need cordiality—my rates have increased, I need my payment at once.'

'Why are you telling me all this?' The headmaster seemed irked.

'No, not you, but please tell your nephew.' The man suddenly fell silent. Then he said in a low voice, 'There's no place like Pasandpur, Master Moshai. Nor people like the ones here. Moreover, you're my friend.'

'Yes,' said the headmaster inaudibly.

'Then let me tell you that my wife has written that she will only let me enter the house if I hand over whatever money I have to her and my two sons. How much money do you suppose that is? I informed them, but they don't believe me.'

IV

'But the house is yours, what do they mean they won't let you in?'

'No, sir, my wife is the official owner. My sons have written, "If you're retiring, you won't have any money to give us—so better look for work". What do I do?'

The headmaster was silent, experiencing a significant lack of ability to offer advice.

The next day the headmaster was told by his nephew, 'All lies, how can he get an extension—his corruption is legendary, the dealers in Sonarpur even beat him up, they know everything at headquarters.'

'Never mind, he's leaving.'

'That's why we aren't saying anything, but he's making unfair demands. If we'd known he would do this we'd also have beaten him up and thrown him out. But then how could we have done that—the previous inspector got us into deep trouble, that's why this one was spared.'

The headmaster said, 'Give him a proper farewell at least, find out what he wants, a TV set if possible, he probably doesn't have one at home.'

'He doesn't want any of that, he wants cash—we had thought of using the last month's payments for a grand farewell. Pasandpur would have earned a name for itself.'

The inspector arrived again on the day before his retirement. Floppy trousers, khaki sweater, uncombed hair, sunken cheeks, trembling on his feet, 'Yes, I admit I lied, everyone knows there was no chance of an extension, I had tried to collect three months' extra payment in advance, but everyone's come to know, I'm a thief after all, how can I get an extension?'

He was raving, thought the headmaster.

'When I saw how rich some of my relations were I began to take bribes in Ranaghat, then it got to be a habit. I even smuggled rice myself when I was in Murshidabad, it's all a matter of habit, during the food movement I took government-supplied rice home, all out of habit, terrible. And not just me, my family has become used to it too. When I wrote that I would go home penniless after retirement, they replied, fend for yourself in that case, you can't get away with lies...'

'Forget it, forget the whole thing, would you like some coffee?'

Talapatra Babu shook his head. 'I took money from you too, although it was put to good use, but what do I do now, I'm in such a hole, let me see how much I can take with me, Pasandpur's air and sunshine are lovely...'

Talapatra Babu didn't budge even after retiring on the thirty-first of the month. Never mind the farewell, he hadn't even received his allowance for the final month. His successor had warned all the dealers to stop bribing Talapatra Babu. 'He's a thief, don't any of you give him any money. Why should you have to pay if you're running a clean business? And if you must pay, give it to me, I'm the Inspector of Food at Pasandpur now.'

The headmaster asked, 'Why did you have to lie?'

Talapatra Babu grimaced at the headmaster's question. 'I was forced to lie so that I could make a little extra money.'

Talapatra couldn't extract any money. Nothing at all. He spent his final days wandering from one shop to another, from one godown to the next, from one house to another, returning despondently each time. Everyone promised to pay the next day, or the day after. Eventually they didn't even invite him in anymore. Even when they invited him in they didn't talk to him. Even when they talked to him it was just small talk, 'When are you going home?'and so on. No one offered him a cup of tea. No farewell. People who used to genuflect before him twice a day averted their eyes now.

He kept saying,'Make the payment, I need the money desperately, I'm retiring.'

No one paid any attention. Eventually, he spent his days alone at a tea shop, sitting on a bench, facing the road. Winter had left, but its last bite was still to come. A bitterly cold north wind blew every morning. It raised each of the grey hairs on his head. His head drooped, his body trembled. He looked exactly like a sick, infirm tiger, its teeth fallen out, but its greed for flesh intact. He kept hailing passers-by, 'Just a minute, Saha Babu; here, Netai; I believe you're planning to increase your wheat quota, Mandal Babu…'

The ration shop owner strode past without heeding him. Only the headmaster noticed him on his way back from school. Stopping, he said, 'Not here, Talapatra Babu, come home with me for a cup of tea.'

The inspector got to his feet with a wan smile, 'Not today, Gobindo Saha is about to return, the dealer from Shaltora, owes me three months' payment, I'm lying in wait for him.'

'How can you, just send word, he'll send your money to you.'

'He won't, the treacherous miser that he is. I have no choice, I can't go back empty-handed, can I?'

The headmaster said, 'The people of Pasandpur aren't traitors—all right, I shall send for him, his son goes to my school.'

'Yes, I had always thought the people of Pasandpur wouldn't turn out this way. I'll be leaving soon, Master Moshai, I'll just sit here till then to feel the sunshine and the air, why don't you go home? Ah—even breathing is such a joy here. There's meaning to this town, don't you think?'

The headmaster was reminded of the drifter. He had said something similar when he was being hustled out of Pasandpur. The inspector had been caught in the same web.

That evening the headmaster told his nephew, 'All of you should give Talapatra Babu something, it doesn't feel good to see him sitting there all day.'

The nephew shook his head. 'He doesn't want a TV, he wants money, the dealers aren't interested anymore, they're all chasing the new inspector.'

'Ask them once more.'

'Everyone's avoiding him. They think there's no point throwing money at him now that he's retired—he took quite a lot during these twelve months, after all.'

The headmaster couldn't accept this. He realized that his nephew was also avoiding Talapatra. But there were other people in Pasandpur. When they heard, they said, 'This can't go on, the man just sits there breathing in the dirt and grime, he's aged visibly, we can't bear to see this. No one in Pasandpur can be allowed to be unhappy. Those of us who are long-time residents of Pasandpur said, how much does he want, we'll take up a collection, let him go back home.'

Talapatra shook his head at this, 'No, the dealers must pay, why should you, I didn't do anything for you.'

'That doesn't matter, you've lived in Pasandpur for over a year, we shall give you a farewell so that you can go back home.'

Talapatra Babu kept shaking his head, mumbling, 'Who will I

go back to? They know money, but they don't know me. I made a big mistake—if I had come to Pasandpur earlier, thirty-five years ago, I wouldn't have developed this habit of taking bribes. The air and sunlight here mean something, don't you think, that's why I cut down on the bribes here, I used to earn a lot more at Sonarpur...'

Talapatra Babu kept repeating the same thing for several days, there on the roadside. The man began to change visibly. If he had come here thirty-five years earlier, he might have never taken bribes, he rued. The bribes had done him no good. He had just become a slave to his wife, sons, and money. 'Ah! What a lovely place Pasandpur is, even my grey hair had turned black.'

Then Inspector Talapatra disappeared suddenly. That is to say, he boarded the train without being observed by anyone. The next day we confronted the guard and the driver, 'Have you taken the inspector back?'

The aged driver, covered in coal-dust, and the aged guard both began to chortle, 'Yes, we took him back, the last time all of you had forced a vagabond on us, this time we took him back of our own volition, 'Get in, Talapatra, we told him, why spend any more time here?'

'He got in?'

'He did, but he has promised to return, he won't abandon this place—just as it is easy to take bribes here, it's also possible to live here happily without taking bribes, here grey hair turns black, teeth stop wobbling and set themselves firmly back in the gums, sagging skin turns taut, eyesight improves, apparently there's meaning to living here, there's...' The guard and the driver, two aged men, chattered on.

The headmaster's eyes misted over. Talapatra won't return.

A month and a half later, Ramshankar Talapatra's sons came instead, two demons in search of their ungrateful father. They began to scream, 'The swine has escaped. Where does he think he can hide, we'll find him and get our money.'

The people of Pasandpur beat them up and forced them back onto the train. Boarding, they said they would take revenge on their father, or on Pasandpur. Sonarpur was much better, even though their father had been beaten up there he had made lots more money, Pasandpur had corrupted him.

Now the headmaster of Pasandpur gazes at the railway lines all day long. He has retired, after all. The lines are clearly visible from his veranda. I wonder what he stares at. Even though he cannot recognize people a couple of feet away, now and then he calls out to his nephew's wife, 'Isn't that a drifter there, bent over and covered in coal dust? Could it be Talapatra Babu? Or is it the beautiful man who had come earlier... Inspector Babu...he-e-e-e-re...'

The dust blows across the empty road. The summer winds are encroaching on Pasandpur, a little at a time. The nephew's wife's eyes mist over too. She covers her mouth with the end of her sari.

NOTES ON THE AUTHORS

Rabindranath Tagore (1861-1941) was the fourteenth son of Debendranath Tagore and Sarada Devi, and started writing early in his life. He joined the Swadeshi Movement against the British in the 1900s. He won the Nobel Prize for Literature in 1913, and used his earnings to partly fund his school and university Visva-Bharati in Santiniketan. His influence on Bengali culture extends far beyond his highly regarded poetry and prose, into music, visual art and theatre.

Pramatha Chaudhuri (1868-1946) was born in Jessore (now in Bangladesh), and educated in Calcutta. He was the founder and editor of the literary journal *Sabujpatra*, and influenced many young Bengali intellectuals. He wrote essays and short stories under the pseudonym Birbal, and was also a poet, critic, and satirist. He is celebrated for his championing of a colloquial style over more formal forms of writing.

Sarat Chandra Chattopadhyay (1876-1938) was a novelist and short story writer. He was born into poverty in Debanandapur, and received very little formal education. He began to write in his teens, and went on to become an extremely prolific writer producing many novels, novellas, short stories, essays, and plays, including *Parineeta* (1914), *Palli Samaj* (1916), *Charitraheen* (1917), *Devdas* (1917), and *Griha Daha* (1920). His works have been adapted into numerous films in many Indian languages.

Bibhutibhushan Bandyopadhyay (1894-1950) was born in the village of Muratipur to an impoverished family. His father was an itinerant storyteller. He took up a string of jobs before he wrote his first novel, *Pather Panchali*, for which he became very well known. He led a peripatetic life, and was fond of taking long walks in the woods, where he would write. *Aparajito*, *Aranyak*, *Ichchamoti* and *Chander Pahar* are among his most well-known works. His novels, *Pather Panchali* and *Aparajito*, were famously adapted by Satyajit Ray into the Apu Trilogy.

Tarashankar Bandyopadhyay (1898–1971) was born in Labhpur. While he was a student, he joined the Non-cooperation Movement against the colonial regime, and was imprisoned for a year. After his release, he became a writer and a social worker. He published novels, short story collections, plays, books of essays, memoirs, and travelogues. He was received the Rabindra Puraskar in 1955 and the Sahitya Akademi Award in 1956 for his novel *Arogyaniketan*.

Banaphool (1899–1979) is the pen name of Balai Chand Mukhopadhyay, novelist, short story writer, poet, playwright, and physician. He began writing as a teenager and adopted his pen name (meaning 'wild flower') to hide that fact from his tutors. Over a career spanning sixty-five years, he wrote over five hundred short stories, sixty novels, thousands of poems, five plays, many essays, a number of plays, and an autobiography, but he is most renowned for his short vignettes.

Premendra Mitra (1904–1988) was a novelist, short story writer, poet, scriptwriter and film director of the 'Kallol' era in Bengali literature. He also wrote thrillers, fairy tales, ghost stories, and science fiction, and was associated with the journal *Kalikalam*. Born in Varanasi and brought up in Uttar Pradesh, he later lived in Dhaka and Calcutta. He created the beloved children's book character, Ghanada. He was awarded the Sahitya Akademi Award, the Rabindra Puraskar, and the Padma Shri, among many other honours.

Buddhadeva Bose (1908–1974) published his first book of poetry at the age of seventeen, and his first novel a year later. He was a versatile and prolific writer, and published 160 titles during his lifetime, including the classic novel, *Tithidore* (1949). He was also a teacher, editor and translator. He received the Sahitya Akademi Award in 1967, the Padma Bhushan in 1970, and was posthumously awarded the Rabindra Puraskar in 1974.

Ashapurna Debi (1909-1995) was a novelist and poet. She was born into a conservative family, and learned how to read by eavesdropping on her brothers' lessons. Despite never having had access to formal education, she wrote over two hundred novels, over two thousand short stories, and sixty-two books for children. Her trilogy of novels—*Pratham Pratisruti, Subarnalata* and *Bakulkatha*—depicts the struggle of middle-class women in a patriarchal society. She received the Jnanpith Award, the Rabindra Puraskar, and was elected a fellow of the Sahitya Akademi, among other awards and honours.

Narendranath Mitra (1916-1975) was a writer, journalist, editor, and poet. He was one of the most prolific writers of short stories in Bengali, with over five hundred published stories. His story *Abataranika* was adapted into *Mahanagar* by Satyajit Ray in 1964. The films *Saudagar* (1973) and *Phera* (1988) are also based on his stories.

Satyajit Ray (1921-1992) was born in Calcutta, and educated in the city and later at Visva-Bharati in Santiniketan. He then joined an advertising firm, and started illustrating books and designing their covers. He made his first film, *Pather Panchali*, in 1955, and it won several international prizes, including at the Cannes Festival. It is the first part of Ray's famed Apu trilogy. He was also a well-known writer, and created the popular characters Feluda and Professor Shonku. He revived *Sandesh*, a magazine that had been founded by his grandfather. In 1992, he won an honorary Oscar, and was awarded the Bharat Ratna.

Ramapada Chowdhury (b 1922) was born in Kharagpur in West Bengal. He has an MA in English Literature from Presidency College. He is a prolific writer of novels and short stories, and has received many awards, among them the Rabindra Puraskar and the Sahitya Akademi Award. He was awarded the Rabindranath Tagore International Award for his lifelong contribution to Bengali Literature

Ritwik Ghatak (1925-1976) was a filmmaker, scenarist, critic, author, director of theatre, and actor. He was born in Dhaka and spent his adolescence in the part of Bengal that is now Bangladesh. After he moved to Calcutta, he joined the pathbreaking Indian People's Theatre Association (IPTA) and the Communist Party of India. In 1952, he made his first feature film, *Nagarik*. He made a total of eight feature films, and ten documentaries, including *Meghe Dhaka Tara* and *Titash Ekti Nadir Naam*.

Mahasweta Devi (b 1926) was born in Dhaka into a literary family (to which Ritwik Ghatak also belonged). She was educated at Vishva-Bharati and Calcutta University. She then became a writer, journalist, and professor. Her first book, *Jhansir Rani*, was published in 1956. She retired from her professorship in 1984 and became a full-time writer of fiction, and a champion of Adivasi rights. For her achievements as a writer and human rights worker, she has been given several awards and honours, among them the Ramon Magsaysay Award and the Jnanpith Award. Her works *Rudaali* and *Hajar Churashir Maa,* have been adapted into films.

Moti Nandy (1931-2010) was born in Calcutta, studied at Calcutta University, and worked as a sports editor for *Anandabazar Patrika*. As a novelist, he created an entire body of work on different kinds of sports, in over fifty books written for adults and children. The film *Koni* is adapted from his work. He was awarded the Ananda Puraskar and the Sahitya Akademi Award.

Sandipan Chattopadhyay (1933-2005) was a writer of novels and short stories. He was part of the avant garde and anti-establishment Hungryalist Movement, which he left in 1963. He published many novels and short story collections, among them *Kritadas Kritadasi* (1961) and *Ami O Banabihari* (2000), for which he was given a Sahitya Akademi Award.

Udayan Ghosh (1934-2007) was an important figure in the little magazine movement in Bengali literature. His first book, *Abani Bonam*

Santanu, was published in 1971. His short stories include *Kanaklata*, and *Bonduker Nol Theke Ekoda*.

Sunil Gangopadhyay (1934-2012) was born in Faridpur, which is in modern-day Bangladesh, but moved to Calcutta as a child. He was the founding editor of *Krittibas*, a magazine of poetry. He was the author of over two hundred works of fiction, poetry, and nonfiction. He was the creator of popular fictional character Kakababu, who features in his writing for children. He was awarded the Ananda Puraskar and the Sahitya Akademi Award.

Sanjib Chattopadhyay (b 1936) is a novelist and short story writer. He also writes for children, and contributes to newspapers and magazines. His fiction concerns families in the city of Calcutta, and many of his protagonists are elderly men. Some of his novels are *Duti Chair*, *Eke eke*, *Sheuli*, and *Tanki Saaf*. He received the Ananda Puraskar in 1981.

Nabarun Bhattacharya (1948-2014), the radical writer of poetry, short stories, and novels, was born to Mahasweta Devi and playwright Bijon Bhattacharya in Behrampur. He won several awards for his first novel, *Herbert*, including the Bankim Puraskar, which he returned in protest against the then government's land-grab in Singur and Nandigram. He is known for his magic realist writings, in which he created the radical, anarchic creatures he called fyataru.

Amar Mitra (b 1951) lives in Kolkata, and has thirty novels, four books for children, and ten collections of short stories to his credit. He was awarded the Sahitya Akademi Award in 2006 for his novel *Dhrubaputra*, and the Bankim Puraskar from the West Bengal government for his novel *Aswacharit* in 2001.

ACKNOWLEDGEMENTS

Grateful acknowledgement is made to the following copyright holders for permission to reprint copyrighted material in this volume.

'The Music Room' by Tarashankar Bandyopadhyay. Reprinted by permission of Amalsankar Banerjee.

'The Homecoming' by Banaphool. Reprinted by permission of Penguin India.

'The Discovery of Telenapota' by Premendra Mitra. Reprinted by permission of Mrinmoy Mitra.

'And How Are You?' by Buddhadeva Bose. Reprinted by permission of Damayanti Basu Singh.

'Thunder and Lightning' by Ashapurna Debi. Reprinted by permission of Nupur Gupta.

'Ras' by Narendranath Mitra. Reprinted by permission of Abhijit Mitra.

'Two Magicians' by Satyajit Ray. Reprinted by permission of Sandip Ray.

'India' by Ramapada Chowdhury. Reprinted by permission of Ananda Publishers.

'Raja' by Ritwik Ghatak. Reprinted by permission of Samhita Ghatak.

'Urvashi and Johnny' by Mahasweta Devi. Reprinted by permission of Seagull Books.

'News of a Murder' by Moti Nandy. Reprinted by permission of Niti Nandy.

'Ten Days of the Strike' by Sandipan Chattopadhyay. Reprinted by permission of Trina Basu.

'Swapan is Dead, Long Live Swapan' by Udayan Ghosh. Reprinted by permission of Nandin Sen.

'Post Mortem' by Sunil Gangopadhyay. Reprinted by permission of Shouvik Gangopadhyay and Supernova Publishers.

'The Marble Table' by Sanjib Chattopadhyay. Reprinted by

permission of Ananda Publishers.

'Flapperoos' by Nabarun Bhattacharya. Reprinted by permission of Tathagata Bhattacharya.

'Air and Water' by Amar Mitra. Reprinted by permission of Amar Mitra.

We regret any errors or omissions in the above list of acknowledgements and would like to be notified of any corrections that should be incorporated in future editions of this book.